"THEN, WEBB, IF WE HAVE ONLY THIS NIGHT LEFT, I SUGGEST WE USE OUR TIME WISELY."

She stepped back from him and pushed first his jacket and then the narrow silk bands of her gown off her shoulders. The silk fell in a soft heap at her feet.

Webb's mind reeled. Lily stood naked before him. Not Lily, but a goddess . . . He shook his head, trying to make sense of this, all the while his body reacting with hot, coursing desire.

Take her, his body screamed. *Take what she is offering, you fool.*

"No," he said. "We can't do this."

Her soft, green eyes, so full of need, haunted his very soul. "I think we can."

"Lily, this is foolhardy. I can't—"

"—make any promises? Offer your heart?" She reached up and plucked off her tiara, the diamonds winking at him. She tossed the heirloom onto the bed. Tipping her head, she shook out her hair and let it fall about her head and shoulders in a wild tumble. She smiled, moving closer to him, and stood up on her toes so she could whisper in his ear. "I wouldn't want them if you did. I want only you. Now. Tonight."

DELL BOOKS BY ELIZABETH BOYLE

Brazen Angel
Brazen Heiress

Elizabeth Boyle

Brazen Heiress

A DELL BOOK

Published by
Dell Publishing
a division of
Bantam Doubleday Dell Publishing Group, Inc.
1540 Broadway
New York, New York 10036

ISBN: 0-440-22638-4

Printed in the United States of America

Published simultaneously in Canada

January 1999

10 9 8 7 6 5 4 3 2 1

OPM

This book is dedicated most lovingly to my mother, Tess Herlan. A daughter couldn't ask for a more wonderful mother and mentor. Thank you, Mom, for taking us to the library every week and instilling in us a love of learning and reading, for always encouraging us to follow our dreams, and for teaching us the rewards of hard work and dedication. And thank you most of all for being my best friend.

Prologue

Byrnewood Manor
England, 1795

"I'll never find my way out of here with my virtue intact."
Amelia, the Countess of Marston cast a sly glance over her
shoulder at her companion, Webb Dryden, who lounged
nearby.

Seated on a marble bench in the secluded inner garden of
Byrnewood's old-fashioned boxwood maze, Amelia held no
doubts as to why she'd been invited to explore the twisting
paths. Within the dense, tall hedges, a quiet fragrant garden
lay hidden, providing a welcome hideaway far from their
host's frantic household.

The late afternoon sunlight glinted off the tawny hints of
gold that touched her lover's brown hair and Amelia smiled
at the handsome rogue. "What devious intentions do you
have in mind?" she asked him. "Perhaps to hold me for
ransom?"

Webb grinned slowly, his look promising the price of her
release would hardly be monetary.

She adored the wicked way his mouth curved when she
teased him. Though only three and twenty, Webb was well
aware of his assets and how to use them to open doors—

doors to powerful men's secrets, and the doors to their wives' boudoirs.

"A ransom, you say? Now that's an idea." He strolled toward her, looking her up and down with the assessing gaze of a rogue. "What might you have to offer that I haven't already seen or sampled?"

Wretched beast, she thought, acknowledging that it was his self-assured arrogance that had attracted her in the first place. Resisting the urge to poke him in the side with the sharp tip of her parasol, she peeked out from beneath its fringed edge instead. "I wouldn't be so sure, sir. A lady of my experience always holds back a wealth of secrets. Why, I don't think I've shared with you any of the truly delicious tidbits I acquired while on assignment last year in Egypt." She glanced up to see if she'd caught his attention. "Priceless information I gained from personal visits with the Pasha. Morsels that certainly did not go in my report to the Foreign Office."

He was feigning disinterest, studying one of the tumbling rosebushes growing near the small fountain. But she knew she had him by the way he shifted uncomfortably in his tight breeches.

"A pasha, you say," he murmured. "Aren't they rather old and fat?"

"Hardly." Amelia smiled. "In fact I would guess you to be about the same age." She continued watching Webb's reactions as she spoke, all the while knowing that beneath his military-style, double-breasted jacket and starched white shirt lay hard, muscled limbs and a youthful ardor, not unlike the Pasha's. "And about the same . . . height." She sighed, mostly for the effect, but also in remembrance of what she definitely had not put in her report to Webb's father, her superior at the Foreign Office.

"In the East," she continued, laying aside her parasol,

"men take lovemaking very seriously. They are introduced to sensual pursuits from the time they are young, so really any comparison to Englishmen would hardly seem fair."

She nearly laughed as this Englishman's brows rose.

Webb was a great lover, but she wondered if an angry Webb would be even better. And how she loved a man pushed to the point of savagery.

"So why did you bring me here?" she prompted again.

" 'Tis the only privacy to be found," he grumbled, snapping a white rose from the bush and handing it to her. "Between my family and your relatives, we haven't had a moment's peace."

As true as that was, Amelia knew the real reason for their hidden rendezvous—their hostess's fifteen-year-old sister, Lily D'Artiers.

The girl was in the throes of first love, and Webb, the object of her affections was making a frightful blunder of it, in Amelia's opinion. "What you really mean is that Lily won't find us here. Or rather more to the point, *you*."

He paled and shuddered, just like Amelia thought he might. "Don't even say her name. If I'd known the little imp was visiting I would never have agreed to join my father here. She's followed us riding, placed herself at my elbow at every meal, and tagged along while we tried to 'tour' the west wing." He sent her a knowing look, as if she should have been just as annoyed at the young girl's interference.

But she couldn't help tweaking him a little bit further about his *ingénue*. "I think you will miss Lily when we leave Byrnewood. She is quite spoiling you with all her attentions. She'll ruin you for every woman you'll ever meet."

"Come now, Amelia," Webb began, leaning over her shoulder so his lips were just a whisper away from her ear. "Forget Lily, forget our hosts, forget everything but us—

hidden away, trapped if you prefer, within this verdant prison."

"We're hardly hidden," she replied, ignoring the picture her lascivious imagination began to create. "Why, anyone could stumble upon us."

"That's what makes it so exciting," he offered, his fingers plying the neckline of her gown, edging the blue satin slowly off her shoulders.

Amelia leaned back and let him begin his seduction. It was just as he said, the danger of being caught added to the excitement.

The same dangerous thrill of disclosure they shared in their mutual profession, spying.

It had been Webb's father, Lord Dryden who'd recruited her into the ranks of the Foreign Office at two and twenty, when she'd gained her freedom as a widow. In the nine years since, she'd become one of England's top agents—deception and amorous pursuits her most valuable contributions to King and country.

Webb's lips teased a sensitive spot at the nape of her neck. "If my father wants us to pose as lovers in Vienna, shouldn't we start practicing our roles?"

Oh, she wanted him. But she wanted him demanding her favors. Pulling away, she rose from the bench and straightened her gown.

"I really can't do this. As a woman of honor, that is." She ignored his snort of disbelief. "I can hardly allow myself to be the instrument of your ruination. I have it on good authority you are saving yourself for your young fiancée."

"My whaaat?" Webb choked out, as he backed away.

"Lily, of course. She confided to me last night that once she turns sixteen, the two of you are to be wed."

"The hell if I . . ." He paced a few steps away, tromping the grass beneath his feet. When he whirled back around, he sputtered, "How could you believe her? She's a lying, con-niving little . . ."

"*Tsk. Tsk.* That's hardly the way to talk about one's be-trothed," she teased. "I'll certainly cry at your wedding. But then I always cry at weddings."

His frantic steps came to an abrupt halt. "Wedding? I'll not wed her or anyone for that matter."

"Anyone?" Amelia retrieved her parasol and twirled it back and forth. It wasn't that she had any intention of mar-rying a man like Webb Dryden, who possessed neither title nor wealth, but still she found his declaration insulting. She tipped her chin up and looked away from him.

"Dammit, Amelia. You know what I mean." He began pacing again. "I am heartily sick of everyone teasing me about that child. She's followed me around like a stray mon-grel since the first day we met—much to my misfortune."

"Oh, you are too cruel," she cooed back. "Besides, that *child,* as you so dismissively call her, is growing up—or haven't you noticed?"

"Noticed what? She's a skinny, gangly creature. She is so awkward, I'm surprised they take her out in public. Why, she nearly destroyed half of her sister's salon last night, what with her tripping and bumping into everything. And that gown she wore, why it was indecent on someone that young. I can't see how her parents allow her to parade about clad like that."

"I thought you said you hadn't paid that much attention to her." As much as Amelia disliked his eyes being anywhere other than on her, their conversation was having the desired effect. "That child has all the markings of a beauty," she said quite honestly. "Look at her sister and mother. Give your little fiancée another year, perhaps two, and she'll fill out and grow into those awkward limbs you so heartily dis-avow."

Webb shook his head. "Lily D'Artiers grow into a beauty? Preposterous! They should consider locking her away in a convent as a mercy to society."

"She wants only to impress you, and you ignore her."

Webb's mouth fell open in dismay. "I don't dare encourage her! Why, I'll never be rid of her as long as she thinks I harbor some slight *tendre* for her. And rid of her I mean to be or else I'll have her tagging after me until I am in my grave."

"Sir, I think thou protest too much," she quipped. "Why it sounds to me as if you do harbor some feelings for her, whether you care to admit it or not."

At this, he launched into an angry tirade on Lily D'Artiers and her numerous shortcomings. Amelia almost felt sorry for the girl. But any pity was quickly set aside. She would have bet the sapphire necklace the Pasha had given her that the fair Lily would grow into a sensational beauty. One day Webb Dryden would find himself standing in line for the chance to gaze upon the girl's heart-stopping golden hair and pale green eyes. Then Lily would have him dancing to her tune.

By that time, Amelia would be . . . well, she didn't want to count the years today. Though she still passed for twenty and five, even that, she knew, wouldn't last much longer. She needed to start seriously looking for a titled, and more importantly, wealthy husband.

However, she thought, as she watched Webb's dark blue eyes flash while he continued his litany of Lily's endless faults, her search for another husband could begin after their mission in Vienna. Webb's eyes promised too much passion, too much excitement, something too dangerous and compelling to rush hastily into a convenient marriage.

Besides he'd nearly reached his boiling point. For that matter, so had she.

Amelia glanced up and listened to his final objections.

"You would have me encourage her, Amelia?" he said, his tone as amazed as outraged. "Knowing that Ramsey blood-line of hers, I'd very likely find her sneaking into my bed in the middle of the night, declaring her undying passion for me. T'would be a bit crowded with the three of us, now wouldn't it?" He caught her hand, his tight grip evidence he had no intention of releasing her as he hauled her into his embrace. "There is barely enough room in my bed these days for me, given how you chase me around."

"I do not chase. . . ." She leaned against him, her lips coming within inches of his. "I prefer the word *pursue.*"

"Then start pursuing, my lady."

His lips caught hers in a bruising kiss. She nearly cried out in triumph as his pent-up frustrations poured forth in his ravenous exploration of her mouth. They sank to the ground, pulling off each other's clothing in heedless abandon.

It took Amelia but a moment in her lover's fevered embrace to set aside her concerns about his amusing little "betrothed."

But she may not have forgotten so easily if she'd looked to the entrance of the secret garden and seen the tall, gangly figure poised in horrified silence at the opening in the hedges. Nor did she hear the tear-choked vow as the broken-hearted maiden stumbled away.

"I hate you, Webb Dryden. I'll hate you 'til the day I die."

Chapter 1

"**Y**our reasons for tearing me away from London had better be important, sir," Webb Dryden said to his father, seated at the imposing desk of his long-time friend Giles Corliss, the Marquess of Trahern. Byrnewood Manor, Giles's ancestral home, was situated a few miles outside of Bath, and though it was a delightful town, London was where Webb wanted to be, not rusticating in the countryside in the frosty depths of late autumn.

As far as he was concerned, other than an imminent French invasion, there couldn't be reason enough to drag him away from the delights of town. He'd spent the last two years mucking through the wars and courts on the Continent and had been recalled only after he'd been injured and needed the safety of home to recuperate.

And that had only been a month ago.

Damnation, he was bone weary of traveling and wanted only to yield to the comforts of a soft bed and an even softer woman. Not that he'd found that in London.

He'd made the mistake of mentioning in passing to his worried mother that he was considering settling down.

He'd only said it to appease her fears about his missions, but she'd taken his words to heart and had been dragging him through the Marriage Mart ever since.

"Why are you still limping?" his father asked, ignoring his rude inquiry. "I thought McTaggart patched you up in Paris."

"He did," Webb said. "He also said I needed rest, and I should avoid bruising carriage rides across the countryside."

"*Harrumph*," his father replied, not looking up from the papers before him. He'd arrived from their family estate, Webb knew, minutes earlier, for the Dryden coach with its plain trappings and small, tasteful crest still stood in front of Brynewood's ivy-fronted entrance, the lathered horses prancing in their traces. The elder Dryden had used his extra time to appropriate the room's most commanding seat, a leather-bound monstrosity behind Giles's large oak desk.

"Your note only said to meet you here," Webb stated, bowing briefly to their hosts—Giles and his wife, Sophia, the Marchioness of Trahern—both seated on a sofa to one side of the desk.

As bad as all that, he thought, noting the worried frown marring Sophia's normally unruffled features. Even in the toughest of spots, the lady rarely looked anything but enchantingly amused.

Surely the news of his little nighttime excursion into the Tuileries right past Boney's guards hadn't reached his father's ears yet. They'd only winged him as he'd escaped, and the fact that he'd survived the fall from that first-story window was a testament both to his resiliency and to the gardener's laziness at not having cleared away an enormous pile of autumn leaves. And even if the entire venture hadn't received his father's blessing beforehand, Webb had obtained the documents they'd sought.

For the life of him, other than that minor issue of insubordination, he couldn't think of any other reason why he would be summoned into the country for an interview with this grim-faced tribunal led by his father.

Still, Webb had the distinct feeling he'd been summoned for a funeral.

His, to be precise, gauging from Sophia's sympathetic expression. More than likely another demotion. Or worse, a desk assignment in the catacombed basement of the Foreign Office.

Lord Dryden waved Webb toward an open seat. "I was just telling Lord and Lady Trahern the news, my boy. News far too delicate to discuss in my office."

Too delicate for the formidable stone walls of the Foreign Office? His prospective desk in the damp basement took on the proportions of a looming coffin.

His father cleared his throat and announced, "Henri de Chevenoy is dead."

"Henri dead?" he repeated quietly, startled out of his own selfish musings. But even then, an impish part of him drew a sigh of relief. That meant his escapade hadn't been bandied about as yet.

Webb watched his father slowly take off his gold-rimmed spectacles and wipe them with a white linen cloth. The measured movements told Webb that de Chevenoy's death, a disastrous event in itself, wasn't the only piece of bad news his sire wished to impart, merely the beginning.

But what could be worse than the death of Henri de Chevenoy? Webb wondered.

For nearly twenty-five years, de Chevenoy had been England's primary agent across the Channel—and not just for the operations in France. De Chevenoy had been trusted to oversee most of England's activities on the Continent. Once a high-ranking nobleman in Louis XVI's court, he had disappeared into the nominal safety of the countryside during the first deadly tides of revolution. Though not one to call attention to himself, de Chevenoy had never been far from the administration *du jour*. With the ever shifting political forces, the man had developed an uncanny knack for disconnecting himself from one regime and latching onto the ascending fortunes of the next, all behind the scenes. Lately, his friendship with the upstart Corsican, Napoleon Bonaparte, had been a great service to England's war efforts.

And now de Chevenoy was dead, just when England needed him most. Webb's earlier fears seemed foolish in the face of this calamity.

"When?" Sophia asked quietly, breaking the stunned silence.

"Well, now, 'when' you ask," Lord Dryden blustered as he sorted through his papers. "A month ago. His valet, Costard, found him face down in his dressing room. The man stepped out to retrieve something, and when he returned, de Chevenoy was dead. Apparently a heart ailment. Sad business it is, my lady, but I wanted you to hear it from me, because I knew you were fond of the Count."

Sophia nodded her appreciation.

"Now, the real muddle to all this is . . ." he paused, looking vaguely uncomfortable at having to continue in the presence of a lady, even one with Sophia's nefarious background.

"You know I'll not leave, my lord," Sophia said, smiling politely and settling deeper into the sofa. "You can't drop such havey-cavey business within my earshot and then expect me to bow out like some insipid miss when you finally get to the gist of the matter, now can you?"

Webb knew his father had never quite approved of her involvement in these operations, but not even his father's stiff-lipped mien could argue with her natural skill for spying or her ability to plan strategy. While Giles had long been considered one of the Foreign Office's best operatives, Sophia was her husband's partner and equal in every sense, and had been since the first day they'd met.

And even now, when she was obviously far gone with another child and clearly unfit for whatever mission his father had in mind, Webb saw her glancing at her husband in that secret, unspoken language they shared. Webb swore the Traherns could stand across a room from one another and have an entire conversation without uttering a word.

You'll not go without me, her expression seemed to say.

Giles's foreboding glower answered his wife's stubborn determination.

"Well, since you seem intent on staying," Lord Dryden huffed, "you may as well hear it all." His father returned his spectacles to the bridge of his nose and continued. "De Chevenoy's death, however untimely, has left our entire operation on the Continent in exceedingly dire straits.

"Surely, sir, the situation isn't as grim as all that," Giles commented, drawing a frown of disapproval from Dryden for the interruption.

"As grim as all that?" Lord Dryden exploded. "The fool man may be dead, but he forgot to take his journals with him."

"Journals?" Sophia was no longer settled back on the sofa, but was perched at the edge of the cushion, her blue eyes glittering.

"Aye. I suppose I shouldn't be surprised that you understand the problem we're facing," Lord Dryden said to her. "Yes. A damned chronicle of his activities and all his contacts. From what I've gathered, there are volumes of them. The man was worse than Johnson and his blasted dictionary." Dryden sat back and groaned. "His retirement, the damned fool liked to call them."

"So he would have leverage if he was ever discovered." Webb shook his head. "Am I correct?"

"Exactly," Dryden said. "Now you see why I've never liked that damnable frog you thought so affable. He taunted me about their existence, all the while promising me they'd never end up in the wrong hands, as long as his accounts were kept full. But I never suspected he would just die like this and leave them unguarded."

"So you want me to retrieve them?" Webb mentally made his departure plans even as he spoke. This wasn't a job for any but the best of his father's agents—which meant him or the Traherns—and with Sophia's imminent confinement, that could only mean this briefing was for him.

"Go get them, you say?" His father's outburst held the startling timbre of the first note of a dirge. "If I knew where the blasted things were, I'd have sent for you the moment I heard of his death."

Webb nodded. De Chevenoy had been no fool and would hardly have been expected to keep such damning evidence in the top drawer of his desk.

Giles stood up and began to pace. "If these journals pose a danger to all our agents on the Continent, then they also pose a danger to those agents' families." He stopped and turned to his wife. "Especially yours, my dear. If any of this comes to light, Lucien can forget any hopes of reclaiming your family's lost titles and lands," he said, referring to her elder brother.

"I was coming to the same conclusion," she said, her features lined with concern.

"Is your entire family back in France?" Webb asked.

"Just Lucien," Sophia replied, glancing quickly at her husband and then at Lord Dryden. "With my brother Julien at sea, Lucien thought it best to leave his wife and children in Virginia, to look after my mother and father."

Webb noticed while she mentioned her younger brother, she made no mention of her sister, Lily. While he'd heard from his mother that Sophia's sister was safely married away, even the mere mention of her name sent a shiver of fear down his spine.

It had been on his last visit to Byrnewood that Lily's unrelenting schoolgirl attentions had nearly driven him mad. Even worse, her romantic infatuation with Webb had become something of a Dryden family joke—one Webb found neither amusing nor worth repeating, though his sisters delighted in teasing him about Lily and their impending "betrothal."

Webb shuddered. The last thing he wanted was an opportunity for Lily, married or not, to add fuel to his family's pyre of humiliation.

No, he'd not risk asking for any more information about Sophia's family. Better to think of Lily as married to her Virginia farmer with a passel of children clinging to her skirts than to consider she might be as close as upstairs.

He glanced over at Giles, the man's brow furrowed with concentration. Here was where his thoughts should be, Webb realized, for it appeared his friend was caught amidst a seething dilemma—loathe to leave his wife in her condition, yet at the same time bound by duty to see her family safe.

Webb knew Sophia's pregnancies were not easy for her, and Giles would never forgive himself if he wasn't with her when her time arrived.

Webb rose from his seat and clapped Giles hard on the shoulder. "You must stay here, my friend. Besides, if you were to go now, your lady wife would only follow. Stay here and use all your wits to see that she doesn't slip away to Paris, and I'll go over and fetch de Chevenoy's journals and be back in time for the christening."

Sophia opened her mouth, obviously to lodge her protest.

Webb shook his head at her. "Though I bow to your superior skill in burglary, my lady, I have no doubts I can enter either of de Chevenoy's houses without detection and retrieve his journals."

"Bah!" Lord Dryden tossed aside the paper he'd been perusing. "If it were that simple, do you think I would have summoned you all the way to Bath to discuss it? There is more to this than I've said. Sit down, both of you, and listen." His sharp tone sent Webb and Giles scurrying back to their respective seats, like two schoolboys caught in some mischief.

Lord Dryden opened a leather-bound portfolio and began sorting though the jumbled dispatches "De Chevenoy's estate has been placed under seal by order of the First Consul, Bonaparte."

"Bonaparte?" Webb said, more to himself than aloud.

His father nodded. "Aye. De Chevenoy had been cultivating a fast friendship with the First Consul. Since Bonaparte is anxious to cement his position with all the opposing factions, he saw de Chevenoy with his vast contacts from the old regime as a means for bringing the nobles back to France. So it should come as no surprise that our wily Corsican has posted guards at each house to "protect" the property and that he has ordered de Chevenoy's solicitor to guard the estate with his life."

"More likely to give that upstart and his henchman, Fouché, time to ransack the estate," Webb muttered.

His father shook his head. "While I would never underestimate Fouché, it appears that the First Consul is adamant that the de Chevenoy estates be protected."

"But why and from what?" Webb asked.

"Not 'from what,' but for whom. No one is allowed in, other than the servants, until the heiress is brought home."

"The heiress? What heiress?" As far as Webb knew, de

Chevenoy had lived like a monk, secreting himself away on his estates or in his Paris home, granting hardly anyone access into his clandestine and dangerous life.

Dryden handed Webb a single sheet of paper, a devious gleam in his otherwise imperturbable features. "See for yourself, my boy. De Chevenoy willed everything to his daughter."

Webb scanned the document, an apparent copy of de Chevenoy's last will and testament. He needn't ask how his father obtained this so quickly, for his father's connections never ceased to amaze him. "A daughter? Why, I didn't know he had a daughter."

"Yes, Adelaide," Sophia commented. She turned to Lord Dryden. "If I may, m'lord?"

"Yes, go right ahead," he said, granting her a nod of approval and a small smile of pride. "You obviously know more about it than these two wastrels."

Webb and Giles exchanged looks of condolence at once again being shown up by Sophia in front of their superior.

"De Chevenoy's family," she began, "like mine, intermarried with their English connections. De Chevenoy's mother was English, as was his wife, the Lady Mary Haynes, until she became the Comtesse de Chevenoy. I met her only once, when I was young. Since her ladyship and my mother had been friends as girls, we visited the Comtesse in her apartments at Versailles just after Adelaide's birth. The Comtesse died of a fever a few years later."

Entranced at this unbelievable revelation, Webb leaned forward to listen to Sophia's tale. De Chevenoy married? And had a child? In all their years of working together, the man had never let slip one word of a wife, let alone a daughter. "But what happened to this Adelaide?"

Sophia looked up, obviously caught in her own private reveries of the past. "From what my mother told me, the

Comte sent his daughter to a convent in Martinique when the first pamphlets began littering Paris with ideas of revolution. If there was to be violence, de Chevenoy couldn't bear the thought of his only child being anywhere near it. Many thought him a fool to retreat from Versailles so early, but those who heeded his dire warnings now live."

Lord Dryden reached into his packet again and drew out a small, palm-sized portrait. He handed it to Webb.

Webb gazed down at the young girl, probably no more than ten maybe twelve years old. Her smile glowed brightly back at him, her green eyes dancing with innocent mischief, and her fair, blonde hair curled about her shoulders in the promise of one day being a glorious crown of gold. "But he never mentioned having a daughter," Webb said, more to himself than anyone else. He looked up at his father. "She's probably quite enchanting now."

So this, he realized was why his father wanted him for this mission—perhaps his talent for being *too full of charm and manly vigor,* as his sister once described him, was about to come in handy.

"So you want me appeal to de Chevenoy's daughter. Find a way past the guards and into her home." Webb grinned at Giles. "Ah, the joys of the unmarried state. Now I see why you aren't being slated for this one, old boy."

Sophia laughed. She leaned toward the desk and told Lord Dryden in a conspiratorial whisper, "I think your son believes, my lord, that you want him to woo the heiress to secure your journals."

His father let out a bemused chuckle, much to Webb's annoyance.

"What is so funny?" he demanded.

Sophia stilled her laughter long enough to reveal the joke. "I don't think even the King could command you to do that, since Adelaide died before her boat even docked in Martinique."

"Dead?" Webb and Giles said in unison.

Webb shook his head. The lively portrait felt suddenly cold in his hand. Hastily, he set it back on the edge of the desk. "De Chevenoy left his estates to a dead daughter?"

Lord Dryden nodded. "Yes. The man refused to believe her lost, so he continued to act as if she were alive. Even insisted I pay her board at the convent, so the good sisters would be inclined to send letters home from Adelaide. Keep up appearances, as they say."

"You must be quite popular with the Mother Superior," Webb commented.

His father let out an exasperated breath. "She is quite in my debt with all the gold I've sent her. I don't know how and I'm not sure why, but de Chevenoy went to great lengths to ensure that, as far as his solicitor and everyone else was concerned, his daughter spent the last nine years sheltered in a West Indies convent awaiting her father's summons to return home."

"And when Napoleon finds out . . ." Webb didn't have to finish his statement.

Everyone knew exactly what the greedy little Corsican would do—keep everything of value for himself and bestow the lesser holdings onto his family or his current favorite.

"De Chevenoy's solicitor wrote to the convent and directed the abbess to have the girl sent home." Lord Dryden smiled, a rare event in itself, as he held up a tattered dispatch. "We were able to intercept the note, and I have composed a response, for which I could, Lady Trahern, use your elegant hand and command of the language to translate and write." He rose and crossed the room to hand her his reply.

While Sophia scanned the lines Lord Dryden had composed, she glanced first at the note and then at the portrait still sitting cock-eyed on the desk. Webb knew by the wicked grin finding its way to Sophia's lips and the sparkle of mischief in her eyes that she'd quickly unraveled his father's devious plans.

She winked at his father. "I see now why you need our help—if I take your reply to mean what I think it does."

"It does," his father answered mysteriously.

Sophia nodded in agreement. "I'm not sure what the necessary party might say, but I think once the gravity of the situation is explained, said party will see that it is not only a duty, but a way to repay the debt our family owes you."

She handed the sheet and the portrait to her husband, who read the text quickly, ending his perusal with a hearty chuckle. Husband and wife shared a brief glance at each other and then looked at Webb as both of them started to laugh again.

Before Webb could find out what amusing plans his father had devised, Giles handed both items back to Lord Dryden.

Sophia reached behind the sofa and gave the bellpull a firm tug. Within minutes a young maid entered the study, bobbing her head at her mistress, while casting speculative glances with her large brown eyes at the stranger at the master's desk. Sophia whispered her instructions to the girl, who then left as she entered, staring fearfully at Lord Dryden.

I know how you feel, lass, Webb thought as he shifted uncomfortably in his seat and all eyes in the room gazing thoughtfully in his direction. The uneasy sense that he was attending his own funeral returned. "Well, since everyone else seems to know the plan, would you mind enlightening me?"

Sophia nodded to Lord Dryden. "He'd better hear it from you."

"We intend to send our own 'Adelaide' home to claim the de Chevenoy inheritance."

Webb didn't see anything amusing in this idea, though where his father would find a qualified agent on such short notice was a wonder. "Am I to assume you have someone in mind?"

"Yes."

Webb knew enough to be cautious when his father responded in one-word answers. "How old would this chit be? Nineteen, maybe twenty?"

"Twenty-one," Sophia said. "Adelaide was twelve when she was sent away."

Webb considered all the agents in the office and came up with a blank as to whom his father intended to send. "A substitute who speaks French without any trace of an English accent."

"Precisely." Lord Dryden began cleaning his spectacles for a second time.

Webb's intuition told him his father had more bad news. Something akin to hearing one's last rites.

"This can't be some *émigré* guttersnipe you've discovered," he said, fishing for information. "She'd have to be of noble birth, with knowledge of the old Regime, Versailles, the King and Queen."

"Exactly."

Webb blanched at his father's one-word reply. "How is someone to learn intimate facts about the de Chevenoy family, like the names of servants or the lay of the rooms, in the time you propose?"

Giles stood up and walked over to behind Webb's chair, his hand resting on Webb's shoulder. "I suppose you, old man, of all three of us, would be able to instruct her in the de Chevenoy estates, since you claimed just moments ago to know them so intimately."

Webb didn't bother to look over his shoulder; the amusement in Giles's voice rattled at his pride, and he didn't want the added humiliation of looking at the man's grin. Sure, he'd been boasting before, yet his friend needn't fling it in his face. Webb turned his attention to his father. "You have a new agent in mind, don't you, sir?"

"Yes."

"And you want me to train her?"

"Yes."

He took a deep breath. "Am I to travel with her and make sure she doesn't meet with any difficulties?"

"You could say you were made for the job." Giles slapped him on the back. "Ah, the joys of being a bachelor and all."

Out of the corner of his eye, Webb spied the miniature of Adelaide, and even she seemed to be laughing at him. He looked again and realized there was something familiar about her features, something he didn't want to see.

It was too impossible to believe, but all he could do was hope his suspicions were for naught.

"You have a girl of noble French birth, approximately one and twenty years, fair in coloring, and willing to go along with such a wild scheme?"

His father didn't even bother with the expected one-word answer; he just nodded.

Webb looked over at Sophia—her glittering gaze danced with mischief and fire. For the first time in years, his usually steady nerves failed him. "Where are we going to find such a woman? If I didn't know better I'd think my father was describing that hoyden sister of yours, Sophia." He laughed nervously.

"He is," she told him.

Lily.

How on earth did he deserve such a fate?

Then he realized he'd been correct from the start. His father had heard about the Paris incident and obviously decided a desk assignment wasn't punishment enough for his youngest son.

Chapter 2

Lily D'Artiers Copeland walked up the wide stone steps to the main entrance of Byrnewood, her afternoon stroll in the rare bit of November sunshine having revived her spirits.

As she entered the house, a maid immediately approached her.

"Mrs. Copeland, Lady Trahern would like to see you in the study." The girl eyed her disheveled appearance with a critical gaze as she held out her hand for Lily's wrap. "There's company as well."

Mercy and Mary, she thought. She'd hoped to arrive back from her walk before Adam and his mother arrived. They'd escorted her to England and promised to visit her at her sister's home after Adam had finished his first round of business in London.

Lily glanced down at the borrowed gown she wore. Since her trunks had been delayed in reaching Byrnewood, she'd borrowed several of her aunt's gowns since nothing her petite sister wore would ever fit Lily's tall frame. Luckily, their aunt, Lady Larkhall, lived on the adjoining property and she and Lily were of the same height and roughly the same weight, a testament to their shared Ramsey heritage. However, all her aunt had been able to offer were gowns cut in the severest fashion for mourning, which she had worn ever since her beloved husband's passing.

Though it was almost a year since her own husband's death, Lily had hoped to arrive in England well out of mourning. Now it seemed her mourning was destined to follow her, a mockery of the lack of grief she'd felt over Thomas's untimely death.

She peeked in the mirror and sighed.

The black gown enveloped her like a shroud, paling her already fair features. Her hair, blown from the wind and adorned with bits of twigs and leaves left over from her climb through a thicket to find her way back to the main path, looked as if birds had taken to building a nest in it. Even her face hadn't been spared, for there was a good-sized smudge of dirt along her cheek down to her chin.

Holding out the skirt, she realized the hem and a fair portion of the petticoats beneath were muddied from her cross-country jaunt as well.

Unwilling to face her always flawless sister and her company in this state of *déshabillé*, she started for her room to change into another of her aunt's proffered gowns.

"Oh, no, miss," the maid said, "you were wanted in the study as soon as you came in. Her ladyship was most insistent."

I've made a mull of it this time, Lily thought as she ventured over to the imposing dark oak door that guarded Giles's study from interruption. At least Adam will have brought my trunks, she thought.

Lightly she tapped on the door until her sister bade her enter.

Lily walked into the room slowly, unsure why Sophia had sequestered their company in the relative discomfort of

Giles's study. But the moment she set foot in the room, she realized she'd been mistaken about Adam's arrival.

Sophia and her husband sat on the horrible horsehair couch Giles kept for his less-favored guests. Wondering at this strange arrangement, Lily then noticed the elderly man rising from her brother-in-law's usual place behind the desk.

Though it had been five years since she'd last seen him, Lily recognized him instantly. And he was the last man in England she wanted to find staring at her with his perceptive and piercing gaze.

"Lord Dryden, how pleasant to see you again," she said, her voice coming out scratchy, still chilled from her stroll.

"Been walking, eh, Lily?" Lord Dryden commented, his gaze falling to the muddied hem of her gown. "Good girl. Makes for a hearty constitution. My wife takes a stroll every day, and she's more fit and fine than most women half her age."

"Yes, well, it seemed like such a nice day, I didn't want to miss the opportunity." Lily hoped her words sounded light and airy, belaying the anxiety that now sent her heart racing.

Lord Dryden? The head of England's Foreign Office?

This summons wasn't the result of some passing fancy of Lord Dryden's to call on his best agents; rather, it meant business.

Could it be that . . . She mentally shrugged off the wild thoughts which followed her speculations. Glancing shyly at the other occupants, she couldn't see any indication she was about to be hauled away for treason.

Giles, Sophia, and even the normally cantankerous Lord Dryden wore such false smiles plastered on their faces, she felt sure that if she announced she'd just set fire to the west wing, they'd offer her a cheerful round of "huzzahs."

"Have a seat, my girl," Lord Dryden said, waving his hand toward the unoccupied chair before the desk.

Slowly, she settled into the large chair and glanced about the room. The door to the garden stood propped open. A chilly notion for November, but not unlike Giles or Sophia, who were both enthusiasts for fresh air.

Really, nothing appeared amiss about Giles's orderly study, other than the odd demeanor of the threesome around her.

Lord Dryden turned to Sophia. "Perhaps you should do the honors, my lady. She may have an easier time of it coming from you."

Lily's breath stilled in her throat. She'd known this might happen, been duly warned this was one of the risks she would take if she chose to . . .

"Don't look so worried, Lily." Sophia's instant smile and first statement eased her runaway imagination. "Everyone is fine. No one has died."

"Then what is it?" she managed to ask, hoping her calm words belied her thundering heart.

"It's Lucien," her sister said.

Lucien? Lily thought. What does he have to do with my being in England? Perhaps nothing, but she'd never know until she asked. "Have you word from Paris?"

"Well in a way, yes." Sophia sighed. "I suppose I will just come out and say it. I'm afraid my work for Lord Dryden has placed our family in grave danger. In fact, it may jeopardize all our lives if we ever choose to return to France."

Whatever was Sophia getting at? "Well, you can rest assured I have no plans of going back there anytime soon." Lily started to rise from her seat.

"We need you to go to Paris, my lady." Lord Dryden's abrupt announcement stopped Lily in her tracks.

"Sir, I hardly think that would be prudent," Lily replied. "My sister just said—"

"Your sister didn't tell you all of it," he said. "Sit back down and listen."

As much as she wanted to refuse, Lord Dryden's tone commanded respect and brooked no resistance. She returned to the entombing depths of the wingback chair.

Over the next twenty minutes, as he made his unbelievable case for her to go to Paris and impersonate Adelaide de Chevenoy, Lily could only stare at the man. Her sister and brother-in-law remained mute, other than to add an occasional nod to underline the importance of Lord Dryden's plan.

Even as he drew to his concluding argument about the "delicate balance by which so many lives hang," Lily knew there was a missing element in his scheme.

Something he was deliberately leaving out.

"So as you can see, we need you, Lily. Make no bones about it, I am loathe to send someone of your innocent nature and tender age into such a dangerous situation, but I have no other choice."

She sat for a moment in the stillness of the study and considered how to craft her reply.

"Lily, you will be in no immediate danger," Sophia assured her.

Lily didn't deign to give a response to her sister's words. Who was Sophia kidding? If caught, she'd be shot, or worse. But it wasn't the fear of being arrested that made her give the only reply she could to Lord Dryden.

She didn't have the time. Not right now.

"I'm sorry to disappoint you, my lord, but I cannot go to Paris," she said. "I came to visit my sister under the tightest of constraints. I am set to sail home in three months time and cannot miss my sailing."

"We'll have you back to England before anyone misses you, my dear," he promised her.

She shook her head. "I came here to go shopping in London, and Sophia has already scheduled appointments for me with all the best dressmakers. I've been wearing mourning for so long, and when I return home, I would like to be done with my widow's weeds."

"You'll be allowed to do all that before you go to Paris," he told her. "You'll need a completely new wardrobe if you are to appear as the de Chevenoy heiress. I've sent for Madame Volnay, who is the best modiste in London. She and her assistants will attend to all your needs from here."

Oh, how thoughtful, she wanted to say. Racking her brain for more excuses, Lily cast out a hodgepodge of them, hoping one would work.

"It's been years since I've seen my sister and brother-in-law and I've promised each of my aunts a good visit," she said. "I just don't see how I can do what you ask and get in my other family obligations. And what will I say to Mr. Saint-Jean? He and his mother were so kind to chaperone me on the crossing. I'm expecting them to arrive any minute and they were so looking forward to spending a fortnight with us here. What would I tell them if I were to so blithely disappear right after their arrival?"

"We can tell the Saint-Jeans our aunt in York is ill, and since I am in no condition to travel, you have been called to her bedside," Sophia suggested.

Damn you, Sophia, Lily thought. Her sister had a convenient lie for every occasion.

"I truly have my heart set on spending time with all of you, as well as the children. Perhaps in the spring I could return and then we could discuss this matter." She smiled hopefully at her sister.

"Aren't you listening, Lily?" Sophia began, in that know-it-all tone that Lily detested. Her very pregnant sister struggled to her feet. "Lucien is in France this very minute. His life is at stake. You can't turn your back on our family because you might be inconvenienced. Do you think you would be alive if I hadn't taken the very same risks?"

At this, Lily's temper flared. How like Sophia to throw it in her face as if the entire situation were her fault.

She rose from her chair and faced her sister with equal tenacity. "You should have realized by choosing to ally yourself with England, your actions would eventually place our family in danger. *Your* misdeeds, sister, are jeopardizing Lucien's life, not my unwillingness to die fixing them for you."

For a moment, a rigid, inflexible silence held the room in an uneasy thrall as the two sisters, more alike than either cared to admit, stared at each like warring barn cats.

Giles broke the tension by coming to his wife's side and guiding her back to her place on the couch. "Sophia, Lily has every right to refuse this request. We have lived too long with danger at our backs, not to remember that others do not find it a natural way of things." He smiled up at Lily. "Lord Dryden only makes this request because you favor Adelaide so closely. In both age and beauty."

He picked up a gilt-framed miniature from his desk and pressed it into her hand. "See for yourself, Lily-bee," he said, using his old nickname for her. "The two of you could be twins. And if things had been different, you might even have been friends." He nodded for her to examine the likeness.

Lily's anger cooled some at Giles's words. But then he always had that effect on her, though she hated the way he so easily smoothed her ruffled emotions. She resisted looking at the portrait for as long as she could, but her curiosity soon won out and she gazed down at the girl staring up at her from her timeless cage of gilt and oil paint.

In those seconds, she felt herself transported back in time, to her childhood, before the revolution in France had ripped her world apart.

She saw herself then—the pampered and spoiled daughter of a respected comte, growing up in a fairy-tale château, staying in the family apartments at Versailles.

Adelaide would have been a friend, just as Giles said. They might have gone to the same convent school near Paris, shared secret hopes of marriage, and eventually been presented to the King and Queen in all the glory and honor generations before them had been granted.

She shook her head. No, she wouldn't fall prey to Giles's planted sentiment. Everything from that life was gone, as lost as Adelaide's own brief existence.

Lily had her own life to live, and that meant being in London not Paris.

And no one would convince her otherwise.

"I don't think I'm the right woman to send," she demurred. And though it galled her to say it, she continued. "I haven't your cleverness or courage, Sophia. I am sure I would fail or make some other mistake. Sending me would be a disaster."

"Not to worry, my girl," Lord Dryden interjected, "I'd not send you into that nefarious city without someone to keep you from harm."

Lily watched as her brother-in-law nodded in agreement. Was Giles going to leave Sophia right before her confinement? The situation was grave indeed and for a moment she wondered if she could possibly spare the time and venture to Paris. If only to see that Lucien remained safe.

"Do you think it wise for you to leave Sophia, Giles?" she asked.

"I'm not going, Lily," he said. "Lord Dryden has assigned his best agent to assist you. I'm sure you, of all people, will be quite pleased with the arrangement."

She didn't like the way he almost smirked as he said it. If not Giles, then who else could Lord Dryden consider sending to Paris?

Clearing his throat, Lord Dryden continued with his fatherly assurances. "Lily, I will make every arrangement possible to see you are sent home in time for whatever obligations you feel you cannot miss. And as for being clever or brave, you look a sturdy enough girl to me, and capable as well. You'll be just fine. Consider this your great adventure." He continued outlining her qualifications and the steps he was taking to ensure her safety.

Lily only half listened, absently twisting the small garnet ring on her finger while she considered her options. She had to be in London by the first week in January, but to tell Lord Dryden why was impossible.

She needed a reason that even he would consider important enough to call off his entire scheme.

She glanced down at the ring, an odd piece her father-in-law had given her just before his death. The gold band fit her finger precisely, and for some reason she'd continued to wear the whimsical piece, even before she'd known its true significance or why Thomas's father had asked her to wear it. Something about the bumblebee insignia and the eyes made of deep claret stones—which even now twinkled in the sharp sunlight streaming through the windows—had attracted her to the strange piece. Looking up and outside, she spied the dense, green foliage of the maze, a harsh reminder of her last visit to Byrnewood.

The visit in which her foolish, girlish fancies of love and matrimony had died.

And you thought by now you would be wed to that heartless wretch.

Married and blissfully happy.

In an instant, as she momentarily mourned the future she'd envisioned as a girl, she found her excuse.

A reason so good, so compelling, not even Lord Dryden could continue his plaguing arguments.

Taking a deep breath, she announced, "I couldn't possibly go to France. I've been loathe to reveal this, as it was to be a surprise, but I have no other choice but to tell you. I must be in London by the first week in January, as I am to be married."

Webb Dryden had stood outside listening through the open garden door long enough. Lily's early protests seemed likely enough, but this blatant lie about her alleged nuptials, . . . well, it was time to call an end to her charade.

Once she realized who her partner would be, he thought, she would forget this imaginary bridegroom and be more than willing to go to Paris. While the notion sounded vain, everyone knew Lily D'Artiers held a deep *tendresse* for him, and if he must use her feelings for the safekeeping of his country so be it.

He'd just have to remember to find a way to double-lock his bedroom and bar the windows while they were on assignment together. She was, after all, a more experienced woman than she had been at fifteen, and a widow to boot, he'd learned in the last hour.

"Married again? Who are you following around now?" Webb said as he stepped from the garden into the study. He looked at Lily for the first time in five years and couldn't imagine how his father thought to pass her off as the gentle convent-reared young lady Napoleon expected.

If she'd grown up, it was hard to tell, for the gown she wore seemed too big for her, the black cloth leaving little hint of anything other than the thin, gangly child he remembered. He smiled to himself as out of nowhere he remembered Lady Marston's persistence that some day she would grow into a great beauty.

The next time he saw Amelia, he'd have to collect the crown he'd bet her that that miracle would never happen.

As it was, the somber black color of Lily's gown only further paled her already fair features, leaving her lifeless next to her always vibrant sister.

Life in the Americas obviously hadn't tamed her boisterous manners, he thought, looking at bits of leaves and a small branch stuck in her hair, as if she'd been out climbing trees.

While her face might be fair enough, it was hard to tell for all her wild hair and the dirt marring her features.

In truth, he thought, dismissing Amelia's predictions without another thought, the little hoyden looked pretty much like she had five years earlier, and he didn't give her appearance another thought.

Even now, she just stared at him, her mouth open at his sudden arrival.

Probably shock at his unexpected return back into her dull and otherwise colorless widow's existence.

He crossed the room, grinning at her, turning up his charm. "Marriage? Really now, Lily, can't you come up with a more believable excuse than that? Toss aside this fiancé and come to Paris with me." He held out his hand to her, expecting her to take it up with greedy delight, but to his consternation, she stared down at his fingers as if they were covered in some horrific plague-infested lesions.

What was this? Webb thought, suddenly seeing the differences between the gawky fifteen-year-old and the woman before him. Where were her soft, come-hither glances? Fluttering lashes? Shy flirtations?

No, her steely green gaze bore into him hard and sharp,

cutting him into pieces, as if she'd measured the changes in him and found him lacking.

No, Lily hardly looked amused, or in awe, or like a woman reunited with her one and only true love, as she'd called him in her written devotions five years before. Actually, if Webb was going to be honest and admit it, she looked spitting mad.

Probably just angry that he'd taken so long to come back into her life, he told himself as she spun around and faced his father.

"This," she said, jerking her thumb under Webb's nose, "is the highly regarded agent you would send with me? I won't have my reputation sullied by traveling with the likes of this indiscreet Lothario."

"Lothario?" Webb's ears burned at the contempt literally dripping from her words.

"Yes, womanizer, rake, deceiver, cad," she added. "Need I go on, or are there other sins you would like me to add to the list?"

Webb smiled as it struck him. Lily was jealous. Sophia had probably mentioned the names of one or another of his mistresses in the hope of turning her little sister's affections away from him, but it had only made Lily all that more possessive.

He glanced at her again. Well, hadn't it?

Both Sophia and Giles looked a little too amused by this turn of events to convince him his assessment was correct.

"I'll not be sent to my death with this incompetent wretch," Lily continued.

"Incompetent?" he said. Now it was Webb's turn to get a little annoyed. He was many things, a little too daring at times, perhaps, but incompetent, never!

"Lord Dryden, while I understand that your request must to be taken care of immediately, I really must decline. Your son and I are completely unsuited for any kind of partnership. And if my fiancé ever discovered that I had been traveling in the company of such a man, my future happiness would be compromised, as would my reputation. I beg you to find someone else. I can't go to Paris. And certainly not with the likes of *him*."

Him? She made him sound like a leper.

Webb looked down at Lily's fair features and saw no evidence of her playing hard to get.

No, she detested him and she meant every word.

Lothario. Rake. Incompetent.

Her utter disdain irritated him, when rationally he knew he should be relieved. However, the idea of Lily detesting him just didn't fit his view of the world.

Somewhere in all the danger, in all the escapades, in all the times he thought he might lose his life, there had always been a little whisper in the back of his mind, calling him back to the green, untouched hills of England.

A place where innocent girls like Lily waited for their heart's desire to come home.

And while it had never meant too much to him except in those desperate, dark moments, it did now. For no other reason than he wanted his topsy-turvy world righted.

Besides, *he* was supposed to be protesting. Not her. Everyone knew that Lily loved him.

"Lily, we didn't know you intended to get married," Sophia was saying. "Mama never mentioned a word of an impending wedding in her letter."

"I haven't told them as yet," Lily replied. "It happened . . . aboard the ship. Yes, during the crossing. He proposed one stormy night when I was convinced all was lost. Quite romantic, isn't it?"

Webb turned a critical eye on Lily.

For years he'd staked his life on being able to judge people's credibility and right now Lily's came up short. Her story, one moment rushed and the next hesitant, remained too full of holes. Even now she stood twisting her odd little ring with nervous motions that belayed her steady, false smile.

No, Lily was lying. He'd suspected as much when he'd been out in the garden listening to the conversation, and now as he stood here and watched her features, he was convinced.

But why?

"Do tell," Webb said, stepping around her and retaking his place in the wingback. Lily shot him a vexed look at being left out in the middle of the room. He only grinned back, leaving her stranded and on display for everyone to monitor her every move.

All the better to catch her lying, he thought, as he stuck his legs out in front of him and crossed his arms over his chest. "I love tales of romance. Is it some common sailor or did you hook the affections of some toplofty captain?"

Her brows furrowed and Webb thought she looked ready to dash the first available object over his head.

"Neither," she shot back. "He . . . he . . . he is . . ."

"Alive and breathing?" he offered.

"Is it your Mr. Saint-Jean?" Sophia asked. "Is that why you asked them to visit us here at Byrnewood?"

Webb sat up and watched Lily's features intently. She seemed caught for a moment, as if she didn't know which way to turn—which thread to cast out and which one to cling to in her entanglement.

"Yes," she said, "I'm engaged to Mr. Saint-Jean."

Sophia smiled at her sister. "Well, that must have been some crossing. I know Mama was well pleased that he and his mother were so willing to escort you here, but imagine her surprise when she discovers they are now to be family.

Oh, dear, no wonder you've been anxious to get up and change, with them scheduled to arrive before supper."

Webb perked up at this news. "Your Mr. Saint-Jean coming here? Imagine that. I can't wait to meet the bridegroom-to-be." Even as he spoke, he chanced to see movement on the driveway. "As providence would have it, here comes the lucky man now."

The little minx had the decency to pale, though whether it was from the idea of being caught by her fiancé looking such a fright or whether she was afraid her day of reckoning had arrived sooner than she expected, he didn't know.

Lily glanced out the window as well and watched with horror as the gilt Trahern carriage rounded the last bend.

"Mercy and Mary," she said aloud, before she could stop herself.

Sophia rose from the couch. "Go on and change. Giles and I can make our introductions without you."

Without her? Lily thought. Not likely. Not with Webb Dryden standing on the sideline waiting like a cat to pounce on her credibility.

His grin said it only too plainly. He didn't believe her lies. Why the great oaf probably thought she still harbored feelings for him.

He was right about the engagement, but she'd die before she'd ever allow herself to fall in love with Webb again. Even if he was still the most handsome man she'd ever met. The subtle changes time had brought to him—the cynical cast of his gaze, the small wrinkles about his eyes, and the wariness that had never been there before—did little to dispel the heart-wrenching appeal of his rakish smile and the lean, solid lines of his body.

"Go on, Lily, they are almost here," Sophia said, shooing her toward the door. "You don't want them to catch you on the stairs."

"Oh, Mr. Saint-Jean doesn't care about those things," Lily said, quite truthfully. No, Adam quite forgave her hoyden manners and dress, for he admired the way she could ride and handle her estates as well as any man. In truth, he'd find her stunning announcement a great lark and would jump right into the deception wholeheartedly.

He'd even asked her several times to marry him, but he'd made such light of the subject and always done it so cavalierly that she'd never taken his youthful advances seriously.

"He will be most anxious to see me. If you'll excuse me, I'll greet them and bring them right in."

With every ounce of reserve she possessed, she walked slowly from the study, that is until she cleared the door. Then she raced across the foyer and down the front steps, even as the carriage pulled to a halt.

She glanced over her shoulder and found all four occupants of the study shamelessly watching the proceedings from the window.

If anything, she had some measure of satisfaction as Adam Saint-Jean stepped out of the carriage. She hadn't missed Webb's dismissing glance in her direction. He still thought her nothing better than a troublesome child.

Well, take a good look, Mr. Dryden, she thought, *at the kind of man who does find me attractive.*

Adam Saint-Jean raked a lazy hand through his jet-black hair. At three and twenty, he was just growing into his tall, elegant frame, which he now stretched out of the confines of the carriage. He stepped toward Lily immediately, a wide, sensual smile at his mouth, his bearing testament that, despite his mother's questionable heritage, the gallant blood and breeding of his French forebears, courtiers and noblemen every one, coursed through his veins.

"Adam, listen quickly, I haven't much time," she said,

leaning close to his ear as he bent to kiss her outstretched hand. "There has been a mishap in our plans."

At this Adam looked her straight in the eye. "Problems? Lily, you worry too much. And besides, if there are any, that is why I am here and at your most willing service."

She nodded at his usual gallantries. "I can't explain it right now, there isn't time. But to avoid a . . . a family matter that would take me away for several months, I told my sister and brother-in-law a small lie."

Lily had been able to pull him away from the carriage a few steps and hopefully out of earshot of his mother, who was taking her time alighting.

"A lie? I like this better and better," he said grinning.

"This isn't a laughing matter, Adam. You need to play along with my deception. Seriously. Our lives depend upon it."

While Adam's father traced his family lineage back to the time of Charlemagne, his mother's was an entirely different story. It was told that the elder Saint-Jean, while serving in the Americas with Lafayette, had found the unpretentious Imogene Evermont a captivating change from the coquettes of the French court. Though it was easy to see why the third and unlanded son of a French baron would stay on in the new country, given all the opportunities it offered, it was hard to understand why he'd chosen to marry his serving-wench mistress. Yet, the couple had three sons and four daughters as proof of the lusty nature of their relationship, and they had lived, for all intents and purposes, quite happily in Virginia since the end of the American Revolution.

"What is this, Adam, what is this?" Mrs. Saint-Jean interjected. "What are you two saying? I need help out of this wretched contraption. My bones are weary and I've the most aggravating case of vapors from being jostled about for the last eight hours." She glanced up at the impressive walls of Byrnewood, her nearsighted eyes squinting as they took in the width and breadth of the large stone house. "A regular Sodom and Gomorrah, isn't it? Well, the rich do like to flaunt their gold before the hard-working of the world." She sniffed and glanced back at the elegantly appointed Trahern carriage Giles had graciously dispatched to convey them to Byrnewood. "Well, I can see now we've been sorely treated. Sorely treated, Mrs. Copeland. Why we've spent hours of extreme discomfort in this . . . this . . . horse cart, when it is obvious your relations could have sent something much finer for us to travel in."

Lily gritted her teeth against Mrs. Saint-Jean's familiar complaints and glanced up at the study windows to gauge her timing. To her distress she found the panes deserted. She flinched again, this time because she wagered her sister and brother-in-law had just heard Mrs. Saint-Jean's crass statements and were more than likely no more than a stone's throw away from this disastrous scene.

She'd forewarned Sophia and Giles about Mrs. Saint-Jean's forthright manners, but she hadn't intended to introduce the offensive woman as her future mother-in-law.

Not that she wanted to now.

She closed her eyes and turned her head toward the front door. As she opened her eyes, she found everyone lined up awaiting an introduction to her betrothed and his mother.

"There is no time to explain," she whispered to Adam, as his mother turned to harry the footmen about their mishandling of her trunks. "We're engaged. If my family says anything we are planning on getting married in London the first week in January."

"Engaged?" Adam glanced up toward the house, and Lily could see him weighing his audience. His mouth broke out in a wide grin. "Engaged it is." With that he lowered his head and took advantage of the situation by claiming his betrothal kiss.

"Engaged? Who's engaged?" Mrs. Saint-Jean asked, her voice loud enough to carry not only to the porch but probably to the next property. "Adam! Stop kissing Mrs. Copeland immediately."

Adam did so, but not after a few more seconds of taking his liberties. When he finally deigned to lift his mouth from hers, he grinned, like the last time he had stolen a kiss from her.

Though this time she couldn't very well box his ears, as she'd done then.

And dammit if he didn't know it. "Smile, my love. You look anything but convincing right now."

With her back to her family, she shot a glare at her newfound fiancé and then turned a radiant smile on her approaching relatives.

As much as she wanted to think it was for Sophia's and Gile's benefit, an annoying tug at her heart told her this performance was for one man and one man only.

Webb Dryden.

Sophia and Giles, with Webb trailing behind, had left their place on the porch and were now crossing the gravel yard.

"Who is getting married?" Mrs. Saint-Jean repeated, her shrill voice growing louder.

"Why, your son and Lady Lily," Webb told her, his gaze locked with Lily's. "We just heard the happy news."

Mrs. Saint-Jean's mouth fell open and then the woman wavered, looking as if she were going to faint. A quick glance told Lily that Adam looked more likely to try another swipe at her lips than to save his mother.

Lily dodged Adam's errant embrace and rushed to the lady's side. "Yes, Mrs. Saint-Jean, I'm sorry to have it so rudely thrust upon you like this," she said, "but aboard ship I consented to be your dear son's wife."

The woman's stubby eyelashes fluttered, as her mouth gaped for air like a freshly caught mackerel. "First, I agree to come to this royal Sodom and Gomorrah—placing my very soul at risk, I do say, with the temptations of nobility and all. But this! My dear boy, marrying some highborn miss," she huffed. "Lady Lily, indeed! I expect, Mrs. Copeland, you'll be badgering my Adam for a grand new house back in Virginia. Well, you are in for quite a come-uppance. If Waterton," she said, referring to the stately Saint-Jean plantation, "was good enough for me, it will have to be good enough for you." She turned her piercing gaze onto her grinning offspring. "How can you do this to your mother, Adam?" She clasped her son to her great frame, nearly crushing him in a hug. "Oh, my heavens. How proud your father would be." The lady turned her watery gaze to Webb. "I never dreamed of my Adam marrying royalty. Why I can hardly believe it!"

"And neither can I," Webb whispered into Lily's ear.

Chapter 3

"Ah, port and cigars," Webb said as the gentlemen entered the male-only sanctuary of the Trophy Room later that evening, "the true blessings of a civilized society, eh, Mr. Saint-Jean?" He clapped the man across his wide shoulder blades with a hearty thump.

Mr. Saint-Jean smiled broadly. "Oh, yes. I have a terrible weakness for good liquor. Especially someone else's!" He brushed past Webb, his features appreciative of the obviously male decor surrounding them.

Byrnewood's Trophy Room, the pride of Giles's hunt-crazy grandfather, boasted a terrifying and unusual collection of stuffed beasts and glittering weapons.

"I've never seen anything like this," Adam said, the awe and admiration in his voice tangible. "Did you kill all of them?"

Giles shook his head. "This was my grandsire's work. He loved to hunt and hated it when no one would believe his tales. So he convinced the local upholsterer to stuff his prizes."

"I'd say he was quite a marksman," Adam said, nodding at the collection. "How lucky you are to have them."

"Don't let my lady wife hear you," he told the younger man. "She despises this room. Claims it's a bother to keep clean since none of the maids are brave enough to venture in here to dust."

They all laughed.

"I fear my addition to the room is only the billiards table," Giles said, reaching for a cue that hung on the wall next to a collection of pikes.

"Before you start, I propose a toast to the luckiest man amongst us," Webb said, crossing the room to the tray of spirits the butler had just left next to a stuffed fox atop an armory chest. The upholsterer had posed the poor animal in a state of perpetual flight, its spindly legs racing from the hounds, its narrow nose twisted in fear.

Mr. Saint-Jean, Webb hoped, would soon resemble the fox.

He poured four glasses of port, whistling a hunting song he remembered from his school days.

"Why, thank you, Mr. Dryden," Adam said. "Stop me after four or five, as I tend to make an ass out of myself if I drink too much."

Webb, well pleased at his adversary's admission, made a note to keep Adam's glass topped off.

"Mr. Dryden? That is too formal for such an occasion," Webb told him. "Call me Webb. I have a feeling that before this night is over," he said, pouring another measure into the man's glass, "we will be the best of friends."

Mr. Saint-Jean smiled in a vague sort of way. "Then you, sir, may call me Adam." He tipped his glass and drank deeply.

"Adam it is!" Webb told him with a hearty laugh. "And if we are to be friends, my first obligation is to drink to your good fortune on finding such a bride." He raised his glass to his father and Giles.

His father and Giles reached for their own glasses.

"To Adam and his expedient marriage," Webb said.

"To Adam."

The three of them downed the port, and after they were finished, Adam finished off his glass as well, which Webb quickly refilled. Adam strolled through the room, admiring the trophies and other hunting pieces.

Out of the corner of his eye, Webb studied the man, much as he had for most of the evening. If there was one thing he'd learned in all his years of working for the Foreign Office, it was to wait and watch, for opportunity arrived eventually, and patience always rewarded those who respected her rules.

At dinner Lily had appeared cleaned up and dressed in another oversized gown of black. Hardly the appropriate dress for a newly engaged woman, he thought, though he hadn't said anything.

Mrs. Saint-Jean had dominated the conversation, decrying the gluttonous amount of food at the table while eating plentiful portions from each dish.

Webb had sat mutely through the unbearable meal, knowing full well after the last course was served, he'd be able to get Mr. Saint-Jean away from his mother, and more importantly, Lily, when the gentlemen retreated for their port.

"Do you play, Mr. Saint-Jean?" Giles asked, holding out a cue.

The man nodded. "I've been known to play from time to time. But I think I will defer tonight. I would rather admire your family's fine collection of guns." His fingers ran over an old musket. "May I?" he asked, his fingers poised over the butt.

"Certainly," Giles told him. He glanced over at Webb and

shrugged, before handing the stick to Lord Dryden. The two of them commenced their game in silence, but Webb knew their real attention was fixed on his planned interrogation of the unwary bridegroom.

"I take it you like hunting," Webb asked.

"Immensely," Adam said quite enthusiastically. He held the gun up to his shoulder, pointing it toward the fireplace and siting one of the boars. "Though I haven't had much time of late."

"Ah, with the betrothal?"

Adam paused for a moment. "Yes. That's it. The betrothal. My Lily keeps me very busy." He replaced the musket on its pegs and turned his attention to a jeweled blade.

"Hmm," Webb said, reaching for the decanter again, "I would have sworn she said you hadn't become engaged until you were aboard the ship."

Adam stilled for a moment.

Webb sensed the other man's tension. Caught in a tiny lie, but a lie just as well.

But the man's features immediately spread wide with his affable smile. "Ah, yes, that we did. But the courting—now that took all my time and wits, if you know my Lily." He tipped his nearly empty glass at him.

The challenge had been laid down and Webb admired the way the man had covered his tracks. That is, almost. And with that he refilled the man's glass.

"Certainly you'll need all your wits about you once you take our Lily as a wife," he told Adam. "She's a cunning little minx. I know it only too well. It took all my wits just to avoid that fate. That is, marriage to Lily."

If Adam took any notice of his admission, that Lily had once been interested in him, he gave no indication, nor did he seem to mind the implied insult.

"Fate, you say? I call it fortune," Adam said, his soft

American drawl never losing a bit of its languid tones, as he strutted back and forth in front of a collection of dueling pistols. "I have much to gain by taking Lily to wife. The land she inherited adjoins mine, and together we will have one of the largest plantations in the county. Not bad, eh. Just for letting her marry my best friend and waiting."

His casual, laughing manners stopped Webb.

Could it be true—did Lily intend to marry this self-absorbed popinjay? Webb shook off the unlikely thought. No, Lily didn't want to marry this man, of that he was sure. He'd watched throughout dinner and she'd shown no indication that she returned this man's obvious passion.

So why had she claimed this engagement to keep from going to Paris?

"Besides," Adam said, running his hand over the hilt of a Seville blade. "There is a certain air about her, a grace, you might say, that is so elusive, that to ever possess it would be a life's accomplishment." His tone suggested he'd possessed that grace and found it to his liking.

"Grace?" Webb asked, not too sure they were discussing the same woman. If Lily had obvious charms, surely grace couldn't be one of them. "Why the last time I was at Byrnewood, she nearly ruined that collection of Oriental vases in the salon. Do you remember, Giles?"

Giles smiled. "She kept the potter in town busy for months repairing everything she broke."

"Well, she's certainly outgrown those tendencies," Adam said, in a knowing tone that niggled at Webb's sensibilities. It was almost too glib, too full of bravado, as if he were posturing, pushing Webb to challenge what he said.

Like a rooster strutting about the yard. A rooster working on his third glass of Giles's best port.

"Glad to hear it. The family can ill afford the breakage," Webb said, nonchalantly. He stretched his legs out in front of him and tipped his head to examine the shot his father was lining up on the table.

There was a flash of rakish honor in the man's eyes. "I would always make amends, sir," Adam said, "for protecting Lily will be my life's vow."

Webb acknowledged this overblown gallantry by refilling the boy's glass. "And you'll start your work very soon indeed. And Lily still in her mourning. Yet she consents to marry another. How odd." Swirling the deep claret liquid in his own glass, he watched it hypnotically dance within its crystal enclosure.

Adam had enough remaining sense to look almost embarrassed. "I think it is to her credit that she still mourns Copeland, and not just her husband, but her father-in-law as well. She's a credit to their name. Lily would hardly be so scandalous as to be seen in anything else, not until the proper time." The man crossed his arms over his chest. "That's why we chose to keep our agreement private . . . until now, it seems," he said, stumbling over his own pretensions.

Webb bit back his remark. Proper and Lily in the same breath hardly seemed correct. Lily and scandal, now there was a pair to draw to.

"Now the cat's out of the bag. But I'd say you're a cagey one, my friend." Webb raised his glass to the man and took another drink. "Catching the widow before she sheds her weeds and the rest of us have a chance to see her. Rather risky, wouldn't you say?"

"Not really sporting, I will admit, but it is the early bird that gets the worm," Adam said quite defensively. He straightened to his full, lanky height and looked Webb square in the eye. "But if you are implying that I took advantage of my position, I must demand satisfaction."

"I suppose you would." Webb held back asking any more

questions, allowing the silence to build build between them. "But save the pistols at dawn, I truly meant no offense."

For a time, the cracking of the billiard balls and the ticking of the timepiece on the mantel were the only sounds in the room.

"Is this your first trip abroad, Adam?" Webb asked.

"Yes," he replied. "My father used to come every year with Mr. Copeland, for they both had business interests here. That was before he died a few years back. He liked to call it his sabbatical. Well, behind Mother's back he called it that." He grinned almost apologetically at this small confession.

Webb smiled back. "And now you are following in your father's footsteps. Coming to England with a Copeland. A noble endeavor."

Warming up to his story, Adam continued. "Yes, I suppose it is. In a sense. Once Lily decided to come to England to see to some of her business matters personally, I offered to assist her. Then, naturally, Mother thought it best if she came along as well."

Webb got up and poured himself another measure of port, holding the decanter out to Adam, who tossed back what remained in his glass and allowed Webb to fill it yet again. "What business matters could a young widow like Mrs. Copeland have here in England that a capable man like yourself couldn't handle in her place? Especially a man she is marrying?"

Adam stared down at his glass, looking as if he could wish the words back into the silence from which they'd come. His lips narrowed into a tight line and it appeared anything further the man said would be carefully weighed and measured before it was given a public airing.

Damn, Webb cursed silently. He'd overstepped himself. He glanced over at the billiard table.

His father shot him a look of exasperation.

Webb raised his glass and tipped it in offering, as if to say, *be my guest*.

His father only smiled and continued soundly trouncing Giles.

Webb paced in front of the sofa. "Adam, I respect your silence. You are a prudent man. Even among friends, and you are among friends I assure you, a man must practice reserve," he said, trying to think of the right approach for regaining Adam's confidence.

The man gave him a speculative glance before he rose from the sofa and meandered over toward the windows. But not one word would he say.

The man was a good match.

But Webb hadn't met a man yet that he couldn't outwit.

Strolling toward Adam, he spied through the window a cloaked figure stalking across the lawn toward the faux Grecian temple the fifth Marquess had built.

Even at this distance and in the limited light cast from the illuminated windows of Byrnewood, he had no doubt who the person was, though he could only guess at her intent.

And whatever that was, Webb wanted to make sure he wasn't too far away from Lily's as yet unknown plans.

Adam yawned and stretched before he edged past Webb to stand beside the billiard table. "I suppose I should excuse myself and call it a night. The long drive today and that excellent meal, Lord Trahern, have left me quite ready for a good night's sleep." He paused for a moment. "But before I venture upstairs, would you mind if I took a stroll around your magnificent garden?"

Giles looked over at Webb who, behind Adam's back nodded.

"Certainly," Giles told him. "That door over there leads directly into the wilderness."

"Wilderness?" Adam said with a laugh. "I have yet to see anything in this ordered land that verges on wilderness."

Giles laughed. "It is what my great-grandfather, in his 'ordered' way thought a wilderness would look like. Actually, by Virginia standards, you will find it quite tame."

"It sounds perfect," the man said, bowing to his host and nodding to the other gentlemen in the room. "If you will excuse me." He opened the door next to the ferocious-looking bear and stepped out into the darkness.

As the door closed, Webb poured himself another drink. "That went fine, I think," he said, turning back into the room.

Giles laughed. "If you weren't looking for any information." He eyed his next shot. "Gads, where does Lily find these self-important fools."

Webb stared at his friend. "You don't think for a minute that she means to marry that . . . that witless boy?"

"Her previous choice wasn't much better."

"What do you mean?" Webb asked.

"From what Sophia and I have learned, Thomas Copeland was no prize." Taking his shot, Giles continued his explanation. "Wealthy enough, good plantation, but he kept with a rough lot, drank heavily, and was known all over the county as a womanizer. The family thought he saw Lily as a way up in the Virginia social circles."

"Then why on earth did she marry the cad?" Webb knew he shouldn't care, but he didn't like the idea of the small, innocent girl he'd once known being introduced to the world by such a loutish man. Then he thought again about why Lily D'Artiers might have chosen Copeland—Sophia and Lily shared a fiery bloodline inherited from their mother's Ramsey side.

Ramsey women, even by another name, were independent, passionate, and always stubborn.

Webb would bet that more than a fair share of those Ramsey traits had found their way under Lily's skin. "Never mind. We are discussing your sister-in-law, after all."

"Exactly." Giles poured himself a drink, while Lord Dryden studied the table. "All in all, I think everyone was relieved when he stuck his spoon in the wall, though the bastard died just as he lived, embroiled in scandal. He fell off his horse dead drunk, while leaving the establishment of the local madame not two weeks after his marriage to Lily. Broke his neck and left Lily a widow. And when his father died three months later, she inherited everything, for he was the last of his line."

Webb shuddered. "This Copeland took the easy route out—for sure enough Lily would have snapped his neck if she'd found out where he'd been."

Giles tipped his drink in agreement.

Having won the game with his last shot, Lord Dryden coughed and called their attention back to the matter at hand. "Well, now that you've let Mr. Saint-Jean go, what is your next plan?"

"To do what any good spy does," Webb replied, heading for the door, "follow him."

"What took you so long?" Lily whispered as Adam made it up the temple's steps.

He paused halfway up. "You look as if you belong here, in this setting, a goddess of old sent down to tempt my earthly heart—"

Lily nearly groaned aloud. Adam only resorted to the classics when he'd been drinking too much. "Oh, bother! This is no time for your poetry and gallantries. Where have you been?"

"With your good friend, Webb Dryden. We've been sharing a few glasses and he's been trying to elicit information out of me."

Lily groaned. "I warned you not to talk to Webb Dryden. And no drinking. Do you hear me? Not with him. The man is dangerous."

He laughed. "I can handle Webb Dryden. Or anyone else. Why I would defend you from a fierce tribe of—"

"Enough!" She cast a glance in the direction of the house, fighting the urge to go in and ring Webb's neck for his interference.

"So tell me," Adam was saying, finishing his progress up the steps and swaying back and forth on his unsteady feet, "why have you suddenly consented to be my wife?"

"I haven't. It's just that I needed an excuse, they wanted me to leave, to, uh, . . ." she stumbled now for another lie. A lie to tell to the one man who'd always been her friend. So this sorry state was what Webb was bringing her to.

Webb was more like Thomas than she cared to admit.

"To what, my love?"

"To go north, to York. I wouldn't have been back for weeks, and I couldn't allow that, now could I?"

"You could go on. I would be more than willing to—"

"Adam, no more of that," she told him. "You came along with me on the condition that you would follow my orders. Well, my order is that you pose as my betrothed. At least until we return to London."

"Why not just tell them you had business matters to attend to and that you couldn't leave. I mentioned it and everyone seemed surprised that you would have any business here in England. Webb especially. You should have just told them the truth, for the man is quite astute."

She gulped back any barbs as to Webb's astute observations. He'd already found one chink in her precarious stronghold of lies. She couldn't afford to let him find another. Not as long as he was still dismissing her as he had when she was fifteen. She'd seen it in his eyes, and she knew it was the only way to keep him from prying too deeply.

"Adam, it is best if we just continue to pretend—" Lily stopped herself, suddenly sensing they weren't alone.

Deep in her gut, a nagging choir of caution warned her the peaceful gardens surrounding them were not as empty as they appeared.

Catching Adam by the elbow, she dragged him to the middle of the temple floor, and whispered, "Quietly tell me where Webb was when you left."

"In the Trophy Room, pouring himself another drink," he replied. "His father and Lord Trahern were playing billiards." Adam looked left and right. "I take your question to mean you don't think we are alone."

Lily nodded and considered her choices. She knew what she would be doing if she were Webb Dryden—and it wouldn't have anything to do with another glass of port.

"Put your arms around me," she told Adam.

He grinned. "Do you think that would be honorable or—"

"Do it!" Lily ordered as firmly and loudly as she dared.

Only too willingly, Adam put his arms around Lily, one arm around her shoulder and the other intimately around her waist. His dark eyes deepened with amusement.

As if to emphasize his role as the besotted lover, he tugged her closer, waggling his eyebrows at her.

"Adam, is this necessary?"

"Depends on your point of view. And I hope our friend's vantage point lets him see exactly what he's missing. Though why he would be out here spying on us, I can only guess. Care to enlighten me?"

"He doesn't believe me. Believe us." She sighed and looked directly at him. "Believe that we are engaged."

Adam's eyes sparkled with challenge. "Let me wipe his doubt away."

He was about to lower his mouth to hers, but she wasn't about to let him kiss her again. It only complicated matters. Instead, she laid her head on his chest and hoped they appeared to anyone watching them like a young couple in love.

"Now this isn't very convincing," he whispered into her ear.

"Adam, I apologize for the engagement, but it is absolutely necessary. Suffice it to say, we must fool my family, and especially Webb Dryden, or else I will be . . . well, I'd be sent away on other family obligations that would keep me from our meeting in London."

She felt him nod his head in understanding.

"When I asked you to come to England with me, I knew there might be complications. This is just one of them."

"But I could vanquish the devil in a flash. Just let me call him out, why I'll—"

"You'll do no such thing. Promise me you won't do anything to provoke Webb Dryden. Just steer clear of him." Out of the corner of her eye, she saw the vaguest shadow moving in the twilight. As she looked closer, she thought it might have been a hint of winter wind moving through the long row of trees lining the path to the temple, for their empty branches swayed ever so softly.

The wind, perhaps, but more than likely, Webb.

Though she couldn't see him, she'd wager last year's crop of tobacco that he was somewhere nearby.

"He's there, just beyond the tree line," Adam muttered. "What the devil is he doing spying on us?"

She took a deep breath. "Because that is what he does. Adam, Webb is a spy. His father, Lord Dryden, is the head of a special division of the British Foreign Office."

Adam took a deep breath, his chest rising and then slowly falling, the gravity of the situation washing over him, cooling some of his reckless bravado. "We could leave for London tomorrow. Make your excuses and we'll be gone in the morning. We can't stay *here*."

Lily drew back and laughed as if he'd just made the most amazing jest. Laying her head back down on his chest, she whispered to him. "That would only make the situation worse. No, we need only convince them that we are engaged, happily engaged and nothing more." She gazed up into his features and said aloud, "Oh, darling, you are so amusing, so droll. But of course you may kiss me. Though just once. You know your passion makes me senseless, makes me consider such unthinkable notions."

Adam's alarm faded in the light of this invitation and he obliged her request only too willingly, covering her mouth with his.

As his lips continued to caress hers, she wished that Adam's kisses evoked in her something akin to the elusive fire that haunted her dreams.

A passion that would consume her.

Unwanted and unbidden, the image of Webb rose up in her mind, and for a moment she wondered what it would be like to be kissed by him. To have his arms entwined around her body, his lips pressing down on hers, his . . .

As if he suddenly sensed the change in her, a momentary melting in her resolve, Adam pressed his case further, trying to deepen his kiss, but his actions only brought her out of her own foolish musings.

She pulled back from him. "Go back to the house," she whispered. "Leave me and I'll take care of this."

"Do you think that's wise? Truly I could call him out. I'd only wing him a bit, but that ought to keep him off our trail."

She shook her head at him. If anything, she needed to keep as much distance as she could between Adam and Webb.

"No. Remember, you promised—no duels. Please, Adam, go inside," she said, her hands folded across her heart. Raising her voice, she said loudly enough for anyone else to hear, "If you dared such liberties again, I know for a fact I would swoon."

He stood poised at the edge of the steps, his gaze pleading with her to allow him to handle the situation. She shook her head slightly at his silent request.

His features masked, hiding what she was sure was hurt, and he turned on one heel and strode toward the house, his footsteps grinding on the stones beneath his feet, their unspoken disagreement punctuated by the sound of a heavy oak door slamming shut as her fiancé sought his own peace behind Byrnewood's stone walls.

Humming to herself, she leisurely strolled down the path back toward the house.

The stillness of the night was broken suddenly by solitary applause and then a man's hearty laughter.

"Bravo, my lady," Webb Dryden said, stepping out from behind a tree, blocking her path. "Such a beautiful display of passion and so well performed."

Lily sidestepped him and continued on. "I don't know what you are talking about."

He fell in step beside her. "I mean that kiss. Why, for a moment one would almost believe it to be real."

She came to a dead halt. "Aren't you a little old for such puerile antics? I mean, really, spying at your age?"

He folded his arms across his chest. "You seem to have forgotten. That is what I do."

Cocking her head to one side, Lily sniffed. "Spying on couples engaged in a private moment? The French have a word for men who prefer such one-sided pursuits. Would you care to hear it?"

He looked both scandalized and affronted. "No, I would not. What I want to know is what you think you were doing up there."

Lily reached out and patted his arm. "I can see tonight must have been a great challenge for your skills in spying, *Mr. Dryden*. As you have already so expertly pointed out, I was kissing my fiancé."

Smiling at him, she started down the path again, but he caught her by the elbow, holding her in place.

Lily took a deep breath and said nothing.

"I know you are up to something, *Mrs. Copeland*. You are no more engaged to that man than you are to me."

He still hadn't released her arm, his grip steady and sure. She laughed at his assessment. "You can rest assured I'd rather be engaged to a baboon than to you. Why is it so difficult to believe I want to marry someone like Adam?"

It was Webb's turn to laugh. "Oh, Adam, your passion leaves me senseless," he mocked. "Did you really think anyone would believe such a pile of nonsensical rubbish?"

At this, Lily's pride ruffled. She jerked her arm free of his grasp and took a step back from him. "Just because most of your romantic interludes begin with a vulgar exchange of coins, don't blame me if you can't recognize true love," she said, her finger prodding the hard wall of his chest, sending him back two steps.

"True love? Not likely," he scoffed, closing the space between them. "You might recall, *Mrs. Copeland,* I have seen you in love. I know how your adoring gaze follows a man. How your only thoughts are to be with him. If you truly loved that walking fashion plate, he wouldn't be shivering in his solitary bed right now, with his feet tucked up to a warming pan and the covers pulled up to his chin." He pressed closer. "*I* know what it means for you to be in love with a man. And to what lengths you'll go to be with him."

You detestable, arrogant beast, she wanted to say, but she didn't trust her mouth to open and not say a whole lot more.

Towering over her, his eyes glittered with wolfish glee as his words implied what he obviously thought.

Five years, ten years, twenty years, it won't matter, Lily. No matter the time, I'll always be the one man you truly love.

Worst of all, she suspected her errant thoughts might be right.

She shook her head and pushed away the unthinkable idea. Loving Webb Dryden was akin to courting the plague, insidious and fatal, and the best way to deal with it was to wall up her heart and fortify her resolve. "You really are quite insufferable," she said. "I don't have the vaguest notion what you mean."

"Oh yes you do, Lily. You can't expect me to believe that kiss up there—" he jerked his thumb toward the temple, "—was anything but your miserable attempt to hide whatever it is you don't want me or your family to find out."

He was getting dangerously close to the truth—the truth about the past and the present—neither of which Lily had any intention of discussing.

"I love Adam and I intend to marry him."

His eyebrows rose in an arrogant response.

"I'm not fifteen anymore, Webb. I am a woman grown, and I won't squander my affections on rakes and bounders anymore. I want a steady, reliable man. A husband I can trust." Oh, there was a ring of truth to her words, for unlike anything else she'd said to him, these words were from her heart.

Yes, she'd fallen in love with Webb long ago, and when he'd broken her heart, she'd allowed Thomas Copeland, so like Webb in his charm and masculine confidence, to step into that shattered place, only to pile on his own measure of grief.

"I want a man like Adam in my life," she whispered, hoping he didn't hear the bitter pain in her words.

"I don't believe you, Lily."

"Please, Webb. Leave me alone. This is no longer a game."

He held her at arm's length. She wondered what he saw as his gaze traveled up and down her. The awkward girl of fifteen he'd scorned, or a woman grown? Unwilling to allow him to hurt her again with his mockery, she glanced away.

But when she looked up she saw the real reason Webb Dryden was so dangerous to her plans.

For in his dark blue eyes smoldered a passionate appreciation. He was seeing her anew under the stars and in the crisp cool night air. And Lily knew enough about men to know that he liked what he'd found.

His hands moved under her heavy cloak, and his warm fingers stroked her bare arms.

"Your Adam might dare to hold you like this," he said, drawing her into his embrace, one arm wrapped indecently around her waist and tugging her hips up against his. His other hand twined beneath her lace cap and into her hair, gently drawing her head back. His lips moved to within a whisper of hers. "But does he know that you like to be kissed right here." With that his lips brushed against the sensitive spot behind her ear.

How could he have known? "Let go of me," she said weakly, as his lips continued their teasing exploration of her neck, trailing down the bare column of her throat.

Even as she said it, she didn't want him to release her. Her body seemed to be melding to the heat of his legs, while his touch scorched through the fabric of her gown and teased her senses with the promise of even hotter passion.

Suddenly her childhood dream of Webb sweeping her into his arms and demanding a kiss was coming true.

"Lily," he whispered, "a fiancé should make you feel like this."

Her mouth parted as she started to protest, but then Lily discovered it was difficult to let go of dreams so long held. They overpowered her common sense in their need to be answered.

Webb's lips captured hers and not only answered her fantasies, but gave them a grounding in reality that even she could never have imagined.

Fierce and hard, his mouth descended upon hers. She couldn't stop herself from opening up to him, answering him with her own strangled need, which had been bottled up and sealed away for so long.

And even as her secret passion clamored at this unthinkable awakening, Lily realized she knew exactly how to stop Webb Dryden from undermining her plans.

He was, after all, still only a man.

Chapter 4

Webb suspected there was witchery afoot in Byrnewood's gardens, or perhaps the full moon rising in the distance cast a different light on Lily. Suddenly she was no longer a sallow-faced, dreary widow.

When she'd tilted her head and looked up at him with her soulful green eyes, he'd forgotten how to breathe. To further still his heart, a stray lock of blonde hair had fallen out from beneath her black lace cap, the tendril curling around her cheek, the soft, enticing color glowing in the meager light.

He told himself later he'd only meant to brush back the wayward strand, but then it had become more. That wary, innocent gaze of hers had asked for him to kiss her, to teach her a lesson about what went on between a man and woman, not that nonsense she'd been playacting with her gallant blade of a fiancé.

But before he knew it, Lily's soft lips, innocent and reticent at first, enticed him, then trapped him into a sensuous melting kiss.

Her body, no longer narrow, as he had remembered, suddenly seemed to blossom beneath his hands into a curving bounty of feminine charms—hips that swayed, brushing up against him and teasing him into believing that the two of them weren't standing in a garden but were lying naked atop a fabulous bed.

Before he realized what was happening or could pull together the wherewithal to break away from this enchanting armful, he found his senses not only being taught a trick or two, but trussed up and trounced as she left him considering unspeakable notions.

Ideas that all involved undressing and seducing Lily.

What the hell was he thinking?

Seduce Lily?

Even as he tried to comprehend the unbelievable notion and to reconcile his imagination to what he knew to be true, she released him from her erotic spell and drew back from his grasp.

A movement akin to being dashed with a bucket of cold, hard reality.

For there before him stood the same, plain little widow whom he'd first met on the path, her rigid stance having replaced that of the supple courtesan who'd wielded her spell on him just moments before.

Then it hit him, as much as it unnerved him—Lily had moved away first. And from the conquering gleam dancing in her bright green eyes and her delicate shrug of disinterest, he knew he'd been found wanting.

"You have a lot to learn about women, Mr. Dryden," she said, her head held high. "I would have thought a man of your *experience* would have mastered a thing or two in his travels." She sighed, the sound echoing a sense of unspeakable disappointment across the lawn.

The lady turned and started down the path. A couple of steps away, she paused and thrust her final and most humiliating parry over her shoulder. "You might consider asking

Adam his secret if you think to sway me with just your kiss.''
With a smug toss of her head, she continued toward the
house.

He swallowed his pride and started after her, limping
slightly on his injured leg.

She'd gotten to him in more ways than one. But he'd be
damned if he'd let some slip of a girl get the best of him, he
thought, glancing again at the mocking sway of her hips as
she tromped up the path.

He might well have to admit that he'd blundered this so
far, but he knew his patience would reward him if only he
could find the right tack.

The right inroad. A way to make this haughty little miss
falter in place.

He fell in step beside her. "So are you enjoying your visit
to England?" he asked, as if they were enjoying nothing
more than a simple, companionable stroll in the gardens.

She glanced over at him, her gaze rolling skyward in
feigned exasperation, as if he were no more than an insistent
child pleading for a new toy.

Webb intended to see that she learned the true meaning of
the word *persistence*.

"I'm so glad to hear it," he said with great enthusiasm.
"And I too am finding Byrnewood as intriguing as the last
time I was here," he commented, answering as if she had
politely inquired as to his own health and welfare.

Suddenly she halted her double-time march. "Why are
you limping?"

"I was hurt recently."

She swallowed, a frown on her lips. "Was there anyone to
take care of you?"

"I got by."

Her mouth pursed, as if she wanted to ask the details but
knew better. "You should take better care of yourself."

"I'll remember that," he told her, as she started back to toward the house, her pace now more matched to his.

Her concern knocked him off his course for a moment, but he quickly regained his bearings and laid his trap.

"My dear *Mrs. Copeland,*" he began. "I know you are up to something. Something I intend to uncover."

"Go play your games elsewhere, Mr. Dryden," she said. "You're wasting your time chasing after me. That is what you are doing, isn't it? Chasing after me? Oh, how the mighty have fallen. Whatever did you do to get yourself such a dangerous assignment?"

Webb was starting to wonder the same thing. "My father wants you for this mission, and I intend to see that you agree to it."

Not that he agreed with his father's decision. He personally thought Lily a poor choice, but as his father said, there was no time to start culling the streets of Southwark looking for a likely *émigré* to take her place. So if his father wanted this unlikely chit for the mission, then Webb would do his damndest to see that she went.

"And he's sent you as his emissary?" At this she laughed. "Here I'd always thought of Lord Dryden as an intelligent man." She paused for a moment, coming to a halt. "And just how do you propose to entice me to travel with you to Paris? Your kiss failed, and beyond that all you seem to have is your infamous charm, to which I find I am also immune. What do you have left in your arsenal of wile?"

He hated the way she sounded so smug, so confident. But he still had one thing left.

Persistence.

It was obvious Lily didn't want him around her colonial Corinthian. And why was she so determined to remain in England?

Well, if he stayed with her long enough, he'd find out.

Webb grinned. "What have I got? Let me see." He tapped his finger to his chin. "Ah, yes, what say you to my companionship. My tenacious, never-ending presence in your life."

She eyed him suspiciously.

"Listen well, little hoyden," he said, leaning closer to her, "for I vow right here and now that I will follow you, hound you, and watch your every move until I discover the truth behind your reluctant answers and half-truths. You see, whether or not your family believes this nonsense about your marriage, I don't. I think you are up to something, *Mrs. Copeland,* and I intend to find out exactly what it is."

Her brows furrowed. "Stop calling me hoyden."

He grinned.

"And don't even think of following me about. It would be unseemly. I am betrothed. Having you, of all people, hanging about my every move would lead to gossip, possibly the ruination of my engagement."

"Now that would be a terrible shame, wouldn't it."

For a moment she glanced away, considering, he guessed, her choices—if the way she nervously twisted her ring back and forth were any indication. "If I agree to participate in your father's plan," she asked, her words slow and deliberate, "will I have his word that I will be back by the first week in January?"

"You have *my* word."

She shook her head. "I want your father's."

"Fine, you will have my father's word first thing in the morning that you will be back in London by your *wedding* date."

"And you will leave me alone from here on out, not interfere in my engagement until we leave for Paris?"

"As little as possible," he told her, not quite sure he could believe that she was acquiescing so easily. "We'll need to start your background training immediately, so you'll play a convincing Adelaide."

She pursed her lips before nodding her assent.

"I'll go to Paris with you. But afterward I never want to see you again."

"You'll get no disagreement from me on that point, Mrs. Copeland. We'll start tomorrow." But as Webb watched her walk away, her steps once again meting out a confident and sure beat, he wondered again why she'd agreed so readily after her earlier vehement protests.

And when she reached the door and turned, smiling ever so sweetly in his direction, he knew for sure Lily had no intention of keeping her word and tomorrow morning would see not only the rising dawn, but the unfurling of Lily's next scheme.

Lily closed the door to her bedchamber behind her and, for a moment, stood in the shadows of the room trying to compose herself.

Embers glowed in the fireplace, casting a warm radiance. She moved toward the light, her hands reaching out to catch some of the heat and ward off the chill of the autumn night.

"And what were you doing out so late?"

Lily jumped at her maid's question.

"Celeste," she said. Lost in her own thoughts, she hadn't seen the tall, mulatto slave woman bundled in the counterpane and sitting next to the fireplace. "What are you still doing up?"

Along with the Copeland lands, Lily had also inherited a plantation of slaves, one of them being Celeste. Though born in Martinique, Celeste had arrived at the Copeland plantation at the worldly age of seven, having been raised for the most part by her grandmother, a fortune-teller of some renown around the French held island. Celeste had been purchased as a companion to Thomas's sister, and had grown up in the main house and been educated alongside the only Copeland daughter. In the ensuing years, Celeste had grown to be a regal, intelligent woman.

When Thomas's sister had died of a fever, Celeste had assumed a wide range of the household management duties, that is, until Thomas married Lily. Instead of consigning the headstrong and beautiful slave back to the kitchens, or worse, to the fields, as another mistress might have done, Lily welcomed Celeste's experience and friendship amidst the loneliness of the Copeland house.

Lily repeated her question. "What are you doing up? I would have thought you'd have gone to bed hours ago."

"I despise the cold, and I was worried for you." Celeste rose and pulled another chair closer to the fire. Her coffee-colored complexion, golden eyes, and brightly colored skirts and kerchief made her an exotic standout amongst the fair-skinned and plain-dressed servants of Byrnewood. "Something is wrong, I saw it in my tea leaves tonight."

Celeste held tightly to her grandmother's long ago lessons in divination. Lily smiled as she took the offered seat, holding her chilled hands out to the fire.

And though Lily gave little credence to Celeste's soothsaying, she considered her one of the wisest women she'd ever met and, more to the truth, her dearest friend.

But where she had been able to share her feelings and thoughts with the talkative maid before, she suddenly felt shy about what had just happened in the garden.

"What is it?" Celeste asked. "A man, I think."

Lily nodded. She ran her fingertips across her still-burning lips.

I can't go to Paris with him. Not now. Not after . . .

Celeste laughed. "Tell me it isn't Master Saint-Jean. I

heard that nonsense about you and him in the servants' hall. Whatever kind of lies have you been telling?"

"I had to tell my family I was engaged to Adam. Otherwise they would have sent me to Paris."

The maid's eyes grew wide with alarm. "Paris? You can't go to Paris."

"I know," Lily said. "But it was the only excuse I could think of at the moment."

"So if it isn't Master Saint-Jean, then is that young buck I spied leaving the master's study?" Celeste grinned. "I knew it. The one from the past. Just like I foretold."

"You know I don't believe in that folly," Lily said. Though Celeste was famous around the plantation and even their county for her accurate predictions, Lily didn't like the idea that her future was already laid out before her, all in the palm of her hand.

She turned her palms from the fire and stared at the lines Celeste claimed held her destiny.

A man from her past. Her one true love, Celeste had foretold during their long voyage across the Atlantic. A gray, rainy day, when Lily had been so bored she'd welcomed the diversion—until Celeste's words had come too close to the secrets she held in her heart.

Now she'd all but run straight into a future she didn't want.

"You kissed him." Celeste, a romantic at heart, sighed.

"How did you know?" Lily asked. "Surely you can't see that in a palm."

Celeste shrugged. "How can you be so certain?"

Lily shot her a suspicious glance.

The woman had the decency to blush. "No, I didn't see that in your palm. But I do have two good eyes." She grinned. "I saw you from the window. A fine-looking man, that one. And some kiss, from the look of it."

"What would you know of kissing?"

Celeste's dark brows rose. "I know plenty about kissing."

"Well a kiss isn't supposed to be like that," Lily said. It just wasn't. How could a single kiss make her feel as if the world around her ceased?

It was the passion that she'd dreamed of, but could fate be so cruel that she'd only find it with Webb Dryden? She glanced back down at her hands. "A kiss just shouldn't be like that."

"If you have to say such nonsense, then you've never kissed a man before," Celeste said.

"I was married to Thomas Copeland for goodness sakes. And you are well aware of *his* reputation."

Celeste huffed, sticking her bare feet out in front of her. Her black toes wiggled at the warmth. "Thomas Copeland was no man. Not a good one, that is."

"Well neither is Webb Dryden. He's the worst sort of rake."

"But he can kiss?"

It was Lily's turn to blush. She hadn't wanted to stop. Not for a moment. Not until they'd . . .

At this thought, her cheeks grew even warmer, and telling herself she was just too close to the fireplace, she turned her face away from the soft glow of light and warmth and toward the chill of the distant reaches of the room.

Into the shadows, where she could hide her blushes and her secrets.

"You'll marry him, you know. Not once, but twice. He is your heart, your fate." Celeste fingered the wooden beads she always wore.

"Nonsense, Celeste. I won't marry that devil once, let alone twice. You should find yourself new tea leaves. The man you call my 'heart' is blackmailing me into going to Paris with him. He said if I didn't agree to go, he'd follow me until he learned the truth behind why I lied about Adam." Lily paused. "And we can't have that, now can we? Not if we want to live the rest of our lives anywhere other than in an English prison."

Celeste nodded. "So what did you say to him?"

"What could I do, I agreed to go. At least for now."

Celeste grinned. "I think you should go. Then you will see he is the man I told you about."

"I have no intention of going to Paris with him. You know I cannot go gallivanting off to the Continent, when I am expected in London."

"You wouldn't have promised that man, unless you wanted to go." Celeste leaned back in her chair, smiling to herself. "You will go to Paris and he will fall in love with you."

"*If* I go," Lily told her.

Celeste's brown eyes narrowed. "What are you saying?"

"Leave that to me." Lily hadn't really been lying when she'd told him she'd go. If there was one thing Lily prided herself on, it was keeping her word.

She'd kept her vows when she'd found out what a wretched beast Thomas Copeland was, and she'd sworn to keep his family's secrets when her father-in-law died three months after his only son. And while a small part of her wanted to keep her word and go to Paris with Webb, she knew that would only mean disaster.

Still, she'd given her word.

She'd just have to convince Webb to break it for her.

Webb arrived at breakfast the next morning only to find Lily had beaten him to the table. She and his father were thick as thieves at one end, their heads bent together, and as he approached the open chair beside his father, their combined laughter filled the room.

"He didn't really?" Lily was saying. "Not on his first mission?"

His father nodded, and the little hoyden grinned from ear to ear.

Webb winced. He knew exactly what they were talking about. His first mission. It was still a Foreign Office legend and one field officers used as an example to their trainees of what *not* to do.

"We're lucky he's still with us," his father laughed back. "Ah, Webb, there you are. Have a seat. We were just talking about you."

"So I gathered, sir." He sat stiffly in his seat. A servant stepped forward and Webb told him what he wanted. Another poured him a cup of thick coffee.

Across the table, Lily nodded to him, as if acknowledging their agreement last night, but nothing more.

If there was any sign of the passionate armful he'd held and tousled with, she gave no evidence of it. Though she still wore her widow's black, she'd trimmed it today with a white lace shawl, a feminine and delicate contrast to her bleak gown.

She held a cup of tea up to her soft pink lips and blew lightly on the steaming liquid. Looking over the rim of the gold-edged china, she said, "Your father was telling me you were in France recently and how you acquired your injuries." Amusement danced in her eyes. "Perhaps you would prefer this chair here," she offered, patting the overstuffed seat beside her. "Sophia keeps it for my Aunt Dearsley."

Webb clamped down on the biting remark he wanted to issue at being compared to an elderly and infirm lady. "Despite what my father has told you, I am quite well and comfortable."

"Now, now. Where's your sense of humor?" His father leaned back in his chair, a cup cradled in his hands. "I was just trying to calm Lily's fears about her role in this endeavor. I told her the worst you've ever suffered is being shot in the—"

"—Father!" Webb said, cutting off any further explanation. Before his father could butt in again, their host and hostess arrived.

"Ah, good morning all," Sophia said, as she glided into the room despite the advanced state of her pregnancy. Giles escorted his wife to her seat before sitting down beside her.

"Lily has had a change of heart," Lord Dryden announced. "We'll need to start her training immediately and I want each of you to take a turn sharing your advice and insight with her." With a warm and fatherly gesture, he reached over and patted Lily's hand. "Girl seems to think she'll make a muck of it. And you all know I won't tolerate that!"

For once Webb was willing to agree with Lily. He had no doubts she'd be the worst type of hazard in the field.

Untrained, undisciplined, unwilling to take orders, and worst of all, unpredictable.

If she knew his thoughts, she gave no indication in her pasted smile. "Lord Dryden has been telling me of your mistakes, Webb. So much to learn and so many dangers." She shuddered delicately. "I don't see how I will be of any assistance to you with so little time to prepare."

Before the conversation could continue, Mrs. Saint-Jean and Adam arrived. The large lady seemed genuinely perturbed that the morning repast had already commenced. She passed by the long low table against the wall where the breakfast dishes were laid out, inspecting each one before taking the well-cushioned seat next to Lily.

Adam followed her, dressed in a resplendent jacket and buff breeches more suitable for Bond Street than an early country breakfast. He grinned rakishly at Lily before taking the seat beside Webb.

Mrs. Saint-Jean let out a great wheezy sigh. "Oh, I see I have taken already to your leisurely hours. I thought for sure I would be the first up and dressed. We Saint-Jeans pride ourselves as early risers."

No one seemed to know how to reply to this, and the lady appeared well pleased to have stopped the general conversation.

"Did you sleep well, ma'am?" Sophia inquired politely.

"*Harrumph,* I would say not! That room you placed me in is terribly drafty. But I suppose they don't think about a body's general comfort when they build these stone monstrosities. Well if one's going to flaunt their wealth, they ought to make sure the practicalities are taken care of first, I do say. At Waterton, we boast five chimneys. And none of them smoke or lead to drafts, mind you."

After a few moments of silence, Mrs. Saint-Jean spoke again. "Now I know you are plump in the pockets," she said, with a wave of her toast in Giles's general direction. "And with your fancy title, you must be as well," she added, with a second imperial wave toward Webb's father. "But you," she said, waggling the butter knife in her other hand at Webb, "what do you do to keep out of mischief? I hear you young bucks do nothing but cause trouble wherever you go."

Webb wasn't too sure how to answer such a rude question. No one had ever come straight out and asked him what it was he did with himself.

As he struggled to find the most innocuous explanation possible, Lily blithely did it for him.

"Didn't I tell you, Mrs. Saint-Jean?" she said, passing the silver butter dish to the lady. "Mr. Dryden is a spy."

Chapter 5

After breakfast, like a prisoner to the gallows, Lily had been led into the study by Lord Dryden, Webb, Sophia, and Giles. That is, after Sophia had bundled Adam and his mother off on a day-long shopping trip to nearby Bath.

Adam had gone only too willingly when Giles offered his prize stallion as his mount. And Mrs. Saint-Jean had found herself happily ensconced in the Trahern's gilded barouche.

"I've said it once, Father, and I will say it again, she is a liability." Webb turned an accusing glare on Lily before he turned back to his father. "There are thousands of *émigrés* in London and at least a hundred girls who could play your heiress. You can't tell me that scouring St. George's Fields or the tenements in and around St. Pancras wouldn't yield a better Adelaide than . . ."

Again his scathing wrath turned in Lily's direction.

She had the good sense to bow her head and try not to smile.

Lily remained stoically perched on the couch, listening not only to Webb voicing his disapproval of continuing the mission with her, but also to Giles and Sophia adding their own, albeit measured, words of caution. It wasn't easy listening to oneself being described as incompetent, but Lily knew it was her best chance at being removed from the task ahead.

She'd explained her plan to Celeste the night before: if she showed herself to be a complete bufflehead at the spy business, Webb would insist to his father that she be removed. Though she hadn't expected him to start arguing for her dismissal after just one incident.

And while she was sick of this bombazine mourning and had been since a week after Thomas's death, it veiled her from closer scrutiny. As long as she appeared the perfect dowd, the better her plan would work.

The de Chevenoy heiress expected in Paris would have to be a lithesome, pretty creature, and Lily was going to do her damndest to make sure no one would ever think to describe her with any of those qualities.

Peeking out from beneath her downcast lashes, she studied Webb. He sat straight in his chair, his stony mien revealing nothing.

With a measure of pique, she wondered if Webb had ever felt anything for her other than contempt. Or if he'd even thought about the kiss they'd shared last night. Not that she cared what he thought of her, she told herself.

The problem was, she did. Once again she found herself feeling fifteen and caught in this hopeless one-sided love affair.

Closing her eyes, she shook off her wayward thoughts.

"A spy! She told that fishwife I was a spy!" Webb complained.

At this, Lily bit her lips to keep from smiling. It had been rather amusing to watch Mrs. Saint-Jean's reaction to her startling announcement at the breakfast table.

Lily had done an excellent job of timing her statement,

just when the lady had taken a rather large mouthful of herring. If it hadn't been for Giles's hasty assistance, pounding the choking lady on her back, Lily might have done Adam a real service and made him an orphan.

As for the rest of the breakfast party, they had stared at her as if she'd lost her head somewhere between her pillows and forgotten to put it on in the morning. Lord Dryden, Sophia, and Giles recovered their composure quickly, masking their shock behind strained expressions, while Webb's anger and outrage had been as clear as the sunlight streaming through the long windows.

Of course, between Sophia's smooth manners and Lord Dryden's quick thinking, they were able to convince the indignant lady that Lily was something of a family card and her outspoken declaration was her way of being humorous.

Eventually even Mrs. Saint-Jean had laughed, although after lecturing Lily about the abhorrent sin of lying.

And Lily had played along, convincing her future "mother-in-law" that she really hadn't meant a word of it.

"I won't be held accountable for her safety if she blurts out whatever happens to be on her mind at any given moment." Webb paced in front of Giles's desk before depositing his agitated form into the wingback chair, his arms crossed over his chest and his legs stuck out like two exclamation points.

Smoothing her skirt, Lily tried her best to appear confused by all the fuss and rumpus around her.

"I have to agree with Webb, my lord," Sophia added. "Lily is my sister, after all, and I would hate for anything to happen to her."

Lily wondered how much truth there was in that. If anything, from Sophia's sharply drawn eyebrows and tight smile, her elder sister was most likely mortified at her earlier performance, especially one displayed in front of near strangers.

"Well, I have to say, I was surprised myself at your imprudence, Lily," Lord Dryden said to her. "This puts a different light on my confidence in you for this mission. I had thought you would be more like . . ."

He didn't finish his sentence, but Lily knew what he wanted to say.

More like your sister.

Sophia. The always brilliant, the exceptionally daring and mostly perfect Sophia.

All she'd heard since she was old enough to toddle about was, "Why can't you be more like Sophia?" Even when her sister had brought disgrace to the family, she had still been revered for her charm and manners.

Gads, how Lily hated always living in her sister's overwhelming shadow.

Well, she wouldn't be stuck in that unfavorable light much longer.

"I didn't think it would be a problem, my lord," Lily told him serenely. "Mrs. Saint-Jean is practically family. I truly find her the model of discretion."

"Discretion?" Webb bounded up from the wingback chair. "The fact that this girl believes that long-winded harridan is anything close to discreet should be evidence enough that your plan won't work. Taking Lily to Paris is like signing my death warrant. She'll kill us both within a week, if we live that long." He let out a loud, frustrated sigh before settling back down in the chair. He frowned at her, his hand absently rubbing his injured shoulder.

Lily had the good sense to look downcast, while at the same time holding her tongue against the biting desire to tell Webb Dryden a thing or two about discretion.

Lord Dryden leaned back in Giles's chair, having once again commandeered the best seat in the room. He shook his head. "I don't see what else we can do."

Lily held her breath, for she hadn't thought it would be this easy to convince everyone that she was utterly incompetent to be a spy. But her momentary thrill of success faded, as the very astute Lord Dryden continued.

"The reports I received early this morning are not good. The situation on the Continent grows more dire each day. This will mean doubling up her training and putting in extra time." He paused for a moment and smiled at her. "You made a small mistake, but if you listen to Webb and your sister, you should come through this without any more of these mishaps."

As all eyes turned on her with skeptical regard, Lily had the distinctly embarrassed feeling of being a new puppy who'd left an accident in the front hall.

Lord Dryden folded his hands on top of the desk. "The dressmaker arrives tomorrow. Sophia, I want you to choose her clothes," the intractable Lord Dryden instructed. "Webb, you worked with de Chevenoy the closest and know his households and staff best. Work with Lily so she can walk through that house as if she'd grown up there. Then move on to the current situation in France." He turned to Lily. "You attended a convent school, didn't you?"

Lily shook her head. "I was enrolled to start at the one Sophia attended near Paris, but then . . ." She faltered, for she never really like discussing what had happened in her childhood, a childhood cut short by the Terror and relived more often than she cared to admit in the nightmares that plagued her sleep.

"Yes, well, of course, that was rather inconvenient," he muttered. "We'll only have to reconstruct the particulars of the classes at *Les Dames du Providence* where Adelaide would have spent her years." He pulled a sheet of paper from the leather packet on the desk. "Yes, I have the curriculum here.

You'll need to be able to show competency in dancing, embroidery, and conversation." He paused for a moment on the last one, frowning at the document in front of him. "Yes, we'll definitely work on the conversation part. How is your dancing?"

"I'm not a very good dancer," she admitted quite honestly, hopeful at last to have found something that would leave Lord Dryden no choice but to replace her.

"Dancing," Lord Dryden informed her, "is all the rage in Paris. This just won't do." He glanced over his papers, until he found a rather tattered one. "Yes, here it is. It seems the celebrated master of the St. Pierre Theater, Monsieur Francois, spent much of the Revolution teaching at *Les Dames du Providence,* therefore it will be expected that Adelaide excel at this entertainment." He sighed. "You'll just have to learn."

Now back in his usual position of delegating and ordering, Lord Dryden seemed perfectly at east with the entire situation. "Giles, I have a number of dispatches that must be in London immediately; and we need to fetch someone from town who will be of great assistance to us. Order your fastest carriage sent around. We have only a fortnight to get this mission prepared. But I have every confidence each of you will put forth your best effort."

Looking around the room from one glum face to another, Lily knew Lord Dryden was the only person in the study who held that optimistic conviction.

"No! No! *No!*" The last word came out with a painful cry of anguish. Monsieur Beauvoir, London's finest dancing master, pounded his heavy cane down on the ballroom floor a fourth time. *The* dancing master to ladies of quality, the pinched face little man regarded his students as being only the luckiest disciples on the face of the earth to receive the blessed gift of his tutelage. "No, Mrs. Copeland, that is not where your feet should be. Don't you remember? I explained this yesterday and—"

—and the day before that, and the day before that, Lily mimicked silently, as the poor, beleaguered Frenchman turned his protests heavenward, lamenting his wretched fate in his native tongue.

Dancing master, bah! Torture master, Lily thought grimly, flexing her tired and battered toes encased once again in her despised dancing slippers.

"Now watch your *chère tante et moi,*" he instructed, holding out his hand to her aunt, Lady Larkhall, and signaling with a brief nod of his head to his ever-silent wife, stationed at the pianoforte, to begin to play.

Because of Sophia's advanced pregnancy, Lady Larkhall had been mustered to come over to Byrnewood from her adjoining estate to act as the master's partner. A more graceful and lovely dancer the halls of Byrnewood hadn't seen for some time.

Meanwhile, Mme. Beauvoir's fingers flew over the keys, the music issuing forth from the delicate pianoforte with military precision.

Now, as M. Beauvoir bowed to Lady Larkhall and then swept her into his arms, Lily could only marvel as the pair floated across the room, each step and movement perfect in both grace and harmony.

Every day since M. Beauvoir's arrival, Lily had spent her mornings in the ballroom undergoing his exacting tutelage. A series of unfortunate partners had been drafted to aid in her lessons, including Giles, Lord Dryden, and eventually even several footmen, for each day her previous partner and his predecessors seemed to disappear as the clock neared the fateful hour.

This morning, when M. Beauvoir announced lessons

were to begin, there had been a dearth of able male bodies in Byrnewood—the entire house seemed empty, every man and boy having scattered to the four corners of the vast estate to escape the painful possibility awaiting them in the ballroom.

She glanced down at her aching toes and then looked up apologetically at Webb, her dancing partner *du jour,* whose pained expression barely hid his frustration at her failure once again in another important layer of her successful transformation into the elegant Adelaide de Chevenoy.

With single-minded determination, Lily had muddled her lessons on de Chevenoy history and proved a disaster at embroidery. Her practiced recollections of the vistas and virtues of Adelaide's convent home on Martinique made the flowered paradise sound like a visit to St. Petersburg in the middle of January.

Each day's progress, or lack thereof, was reported to Lord Dryden with a shake of the head and the urging that he reconsider using her.

But Lord Dryden wouldn't listen and only instructed his top agents to try harder. The reports from France were grim indeed. They were in danger of losing too many agents if Henri's journals were discovered before the British could retrieve them.

"Please, try harder to watch and listen to Monsieur Beauvoir," Webb told her, echoing his father's exasperated and oft-used phrase.

"I am," Lily said quite honestly. She'd love nothing more than to glide about the room as elegantly as her aunt. But somewhere between the instructions and the music and the master's pounding cane keeping the beat, she lost the rhythm, forgot left and right, and missed the timing of the steps.

Not waiting for the master to stop, Webb caught her in his

arms and started moving her through the steps, slowly and surely, as if he were ordering a regiment into battle.

She didn't dare as much as look at him. Between keeping up the pretense of her false engagement with Adam and staying one step ahead of Webb, who seemed to always be watching her, she wondered how she'd ever make it through the next twelve hours, at the end of which Lord Dryden would make his decision about the fate of the mission.

So far, Webb had been able to beg off from the dancing lessons, claiming that his other studies with Lily were enough. But this morning, he'd returned from his morning ride early and been caught.

He was the last partner Lily wanted.

Dancing meant contact. So far they'd been able to avoid any further physical contact, neither of them raising the subject of the kiss in the garden.

But the memory of his kiss still haunted her, and when Adam placed his lips on hers, to continue their charade, he claimed, she found herself wishing it was Webb enfolding her in his arms.

She was foolish, she told herself. A man like Adam, loyal, steady, though a bit arrogant, was a good man. So why didn't his kisses ignite her blood like Webb's had.

M. Beauvoir, a martinet of precision and excellence, tromped back and forth across the floor in front of them. "Can you not count, milady? It is one, two, three, and then turn to your left. Your left, not your right!" His silver-tipped cane pounded on the floor, and the music came to an abrupt halt. "Tonight is your sister's party, and I will not have you parading about like a wooden ox, ruining my reputation." He turned his martyr's wrath on Webb. "Monsieur, *s'il vous plaît*, Mistress Copeland is not made of porcelain. She is a lady, a *desirable* lady," though the way he said the word left little doubt in anyone's mind that he found Lily's ungainly trotting about anything but that. "You must hold her close, dance with her." The man leaned closer to Webb and whispered loudly, "Dance with her as you would make love to a beautiful woman." He turned to his patient wife and snapped his fingers.

"Bah, the English," the man muttered. He held out his hand to Lady Larkhall. "Surely, milady, you must be French, for you move as if the music were born in your soul."

Lily held her tongue, wishing she could pitch the insulting little man out the window. A dancing ox? That one stung. If only she could shed her widow's weeds and tell the world she wasn't the ugly dowd she'd worked so hard to become in the last fortnight.

Webb smiled gamely, and holding her close, they began to move to the music.

The last thing she wanted was *his* pity. Poor, unsightly Lily. Unfit for society.

Concentrating, she clung to his hand, which squeezed back with a reassuring and gentle grip. His body swayed with hers, pulling her along in time to the music. She glanced down at her skirts, matching her movements to his legs—masculine legs encased in riding breeches and black, polished Hessians, his muscles moving with steady grace. His arm wrapped around her waist, his hand cradling her. His fingers seemed to burn through her bombazine, the heat of his touch once again igniting her imagination.

She stumbled and his hand slipped upward, cupping her breast as he caught and steadied her.

The heat of his touch and the intimacy of it, kept her moving, kept her dancing, kept her looking forward to the next time they touched.

She tipped her head and glanced at him, forgetting herself in the witchery of the moment.

Like you are making love.

The master's words teased her. With the romance of the music pouring out of the pianoforte and the powerful temptation of Webb's body, Lily found she could almost dance.

One, two, three, she counted, *and move to the left.* Webb grinned at her and immediately the memories of their kiss and the dreams that had haunted her for a fortnight assailed her. Try as she might to remember her next steps, she forgot they'd turned, and she frantically struggled to discern her right from her left.

Oh, Mercy and Mary, she thought as she twisted her body to what she thought was her left, only to find that it was the wrong way. As she spun around, she slammed into Webb, their feet tangled, and this time, because of Lily's momentum, they fell in a heap onto the floor.

Lucky for Lily, she landed atop Webb, his arms wrapped around her to keep her from falling any further.

When she opened her eyes, she found herself face-to-face with him. At first she thought he was going to explode, his body shaking with what she assumed was anger, but suddenly he burst out laughing.

"I think you took his suggestion about making love a little too literally, hoyden."

She looked at herself and found that she was straddling him, their legs wrapped around each other, her hips brushing against his, her breasts pressed to his chest. All that was missing was the deep feather mattress and soft sheets of her dreams.

"Don't call me that," she exclaimed as she struggled to get up, only to find her skirt pinned beneath him.

It seemed they were trapped.

"Monsieur, Madame!! This is unsightly, unseemly. I do not allow such frolics in my lessons," the master lamented over their prostrate forms.

Webb laughed again, and this time, Lily found herself joining in.

"This is not amusing," Monsieur admonished them. "It is an affront to my sensibilities. If anyone were to see you, I would be ruined, utterly ruined."

"I think it's too late to avoid that. It appears we've been caught," Webb said, a grin on his face.

Lily followed his gaze only to find a frowning Adam standing at the doorway.

"Now this is an interesting surprise," her fiancé said, striding across the room until he stood over them. "What are you doing with my betrothed, Mr. Dryden?"

There was no mistaking the challenge in the young man's words. Lily cringed. She'd have a devil of a time keeping Adam from doing anything foolish now.

Webb grinned at her. If she wasn't mistaken, he'd probably spotted Adam the moment he'd stepped into the room. She continued to struggle to get free but his hip still held her skirt to the floor.

The lout, she thought, as she yanked the bombazine free. Then with Adam's quick assistance, his hands wrapping possessively around her, she found her way to her feet.

"Adam, what are you doing here?" she asked. "I thought you and Giles were going shooting this morning."

"So it seems," he said, his gaze flicking toward Webb, who had also gotten up off the floor and was standing behind Lily.

"Couldn't you tell?" Webb asked, a touch of amusement and something else Lily couldn't quite identify in his words. "We were dancing."

Adam turned to her. "Dancing? You?"

He needn't sound so surprised. Though it was no secret in their Virginia circle that Lily D'Artiers Copeland never danced, and only a handful, like Adam, knew the real reason why.

She couldn't.

"I wanted to surprise you," she said, casting a glance over her shoulder at Webb.

Adam nodded. "Your sister is so set on announcing our engagement this evening at her party, and it will be expected that we lead the first set out."

Lily shook her head. "Adam, we agreed. There wouldn't be any announcement of our engagement until after the holidays. Not until I've finished my mourning for Thomas."

"Yes, dear departed Thomas. Wasn't he a friend of yours?" Webb chimed in, but he was ignored by both parties.

"We'll discuss the announcement later," Adam said. "The real question is why you felt compelled to keep this such a secret and why you would want to practice with him? You should have told me, and we could have done this together."

The tension in the room rose, and at the pianoforte, Mme. Beauvoir nervously tapped at the keys, the delicate instrument sending out notes of protest.

Later he wasn't sure why he did it, perhaps he was tired of the younger man's constant posturing, but Webb put his hand on Lily's shoulder and stared into the other man's eyes. "Don't be so hard on her, my good man. We were just learning some new steps." He grinned his most lascivious smile at Lily. "It's like she said, she just wanted to surprise you. No harm in that."

"She never stops surprising me. And neither do you," Adam said, taking Lily's hand and pulling her out of Webb's reach. "But if anyone's going to teach her new steps, she'll learn them from me."

"Oh, but I think I have more experience with these steps

and with the lady," Webb said, reaching out and hauling Lily back into his reach.

Both men stared at each other, and Webb wasn't about to back down. In watching Lily with her fiancé over the last two weeks, he was more convinced than ever that her engagement to this arrogant fool was either the second biggest mistake of her life or, just as he'd suspected all along, a farce.

Though why Lily would go to such lengths to avoid the mission to Paris, he still hadn't been able to determine.

At this point, Lord Dryden wandered in, having deliberately waited until he was assured he would not be drafted into dancing with Lily. If he noticed the tug-of-war going on between Adam and Webb, he gave it no notice. Instead he inquired of Monsieur as to how the lessons were progressing.

"Bah, it is no use!" M. Beauvoir declared. He pounded the silver-tipped cane on the floor, its hard staccato beat punctuating each word. "She is unworthy of my talents, she is unworthy of dance." The man motioned to his wife, who started to gather up her sheets of music.

"It would utterly ruin my reputation as a master to have anyone think I was possibly associated with this, this, leaden-footed baggage. Your money, my lord, would have been better spent teaching an ox to do a Scotch Reel," he told an open-mouthed Lord Dryden, and with that, demanded his hefty fee. All Lord Dryden's carefully worded protests fell on deaf ears, until Monsieur was able to extract and collect his fee, at which time, he made a courtly bow to Lady Larkhall and promptly left, his little wife scurrying along in his affronted wake.

"Why is Lord Dryden paying for your dancing lessons, my dear?" Adam asked.

Before Lily could answer, Webb's father stepped in. "A wedding gift. She confided in me her desire to learn to dance, and I asked Monsieur Beauvoir to come here to assist her."

Adam seemed somewhat satisfied with that answer. "Lily, if you please," he said, holding out his arm and escorting her from the ballroom.

While his father and Lady Larkhall exchanged pleasantries, Webb followed the betrothed pair.

At the door he heard part of what was obviously a heated exchange as they descended the main staircase.

"I won't stand still and allow him to manhandle you. I wouldn't be a gentleman if I did," Adam was saying. "And I won't stand by and allow that man to impugn your honor with his ugly insinuations."

"Calm down, Adam. You know why we are engaged and it matters not what Webb Dryden says or does. I'm doing all this to protect you, to protect both of us."

Protect them, from what? Or better, from whom?

At that moment M. Beauvoir and his wife arrived in the grand foyer, bags in hand, the little Frenchman still lamenting his first failure in twenty years of instructing ladies to dance.

As Lily and Adam paused, Webb couldn't hear Adam's next response, but he did see Lily's features.

A wide self-satisfied smile tugged at the corners of her mouth. Webb could only wonder if it was at the sight of having finally driven the dancing master out of Byrnewood with her hapless tromping, or something else.

Something akin to satisfaction. As if she'd planned to fail all along.

Chapter 6

Lily halted on the landing and looked down the staircase at the milling group of arrivals.

"A coming out," Sophia had explained a few days earlier. "A small yuletide party to test your new skills."

A little party, Lily thought with chagrin. It appeared every member of the *Ton* in Bath and the surrounding countryside had ventured out to sample the Marchioness of Trahern's legendary hospitality. Festooned in garlands and yuletide decorations, the house appeared ready for Christmas, though it was still well over a fortnight away.

None of the guests appeared to mind, and from the wide smiles and cheerful greetings, all seemed more than delighted to get an early start on their holiday merrymaking.

Lily groaned. It was bad enough she'd spent the last two weeks making everyone in Byrnewood think her a complete idiot, now she would have to continue her charade in front of half of the *Ton*.

At least she had convinced Sophia and Giles not to announce her engagement as yet. She still had a month of mourning left and she'd argued quite convincingly that it would tarnish her reputation to announce this second marriage.

Downstairs the musicians were tuning up their instruments.

A group quite popular for their lively sets, Sophia promised. They would play all night if requested.

But not even the master's expert instructions had left her with any sense of timing and rhythm for dancing. One note always sounded like another to her and timing her steps to the beat was more a matter of luck than of a good ear.

Well, she sighed, tonight would be her final test, a test she was out to fail so miserably, Lord Dryden would have no choice other than to find another Adelaide.

While in the back of her mind, she worried about her elder brother's safety in the mercurial world of Napoleon's court, especially if Sophia's role in the English Foreign Office were revealed, Lily knew Sophia had sent him a warning note.

Lucien was no fool and would see to it he had an escape route out of Paris, if necessary.

"There you are, my dear," Adam said, quite smoothly. When he got to her side, he whispered softly to her, "And I see that you have decided to continue your charade to the bitter end."

She smiled, looking down at her dress. She and Celeste had worked all afternoon to alter one of her bombazine dresses. Sophia had specifically instructed her to wear one of her new dresses, and thus she had.

Well, they'd given the old dress a new life. So it could be called a new dress, Lily reasoned. They'd added black lace to the neckline so it covered her up to her neck. Then they'd capped the long sleeves and added a band of black lace around the hemline. She'd pulled her hair back as severely as she'd dared without pulling it out from the roots. It made her face look pinched and pained. Atop her head went her black lace cap. Their final touch was the rice powder Celeste had been mixing with a dash of saffron to give her complexion a sallow, yellow color that made her appear ill.

"Well, there, my dear, don't you look just . . . perfect," he said, his eyebrows raised in mock horror.

Lily smiled at his feigned gallantry. "Thank you, Adam. You're turning into quite the Corinthian."

And he was. Giles had taken him to the best tailor in Bath and the wealthy young Virginian had spared no expense in remaking himself into a youthful and dashing country gentleman.

"And you would too if you would only avail yourself of your trunks, which I brought out here so I would never be forced to see you dressed in those wretched weeds ever again."

"I won't be wearing them for much longer, I promise."

"Good," he said. "Then will you trust me enough to tell me what is going on?"

She twisted the ring on her finger, the garnet on the bumblebee winking at her. It wasn't that she didn't trust him, she just didn't want him to know anything more than necessary.

"After tonight, there will be no more of these secrets between us, understood," he said, before placing a gallant kiss on her fingertips.

"Ah, the happy couple," Webb said, joining them on the landing, his languid voice startling her.

She flinched. If she was celebrating her near victory over Lord Dryden and his unwanted plans, it was this Dryden who left her feeling like anything but celebrating.

With each of her failures, she could feel Webb's cool censure on her back. She didn't have to know what he said each night to his father behind the closed door of Giles's study, she could see it in his face when he rejoined the ladies in the salon.

And rid of her I mean to be.

Those words, spoken so long ago, still brought a wave of embarrassment over her, chilling her heart with their cold cruelty.

That Webb still saw her as that gangly creature he'd so heartily disavowed to Lady Marston, had given her pause more than once during the fortnight.

She'd locked Webb Dryden out of her heart that day so long ago, but his kiss in the garden, like a long-lost key newly found, had opened her tightly closed memories of first love, treasured dreams, and adolescent self-doubt.

And like Pandora, it had unleashed all those unwanted emotions.

Well, after tonight, she wouldn't have either problem— not her unwanted daydreams nor Webb's constant vigilance.

As if on cue, Webb clapped Adam heartily on the back. "There's the lucky bridegroom. Where is your dear mother, Adam?"

Adam cocked one eyebrow and looked at the unwanted hand perched on his shoulder with all the cool disdain of his noble French ancestors. "She is just finishing dressing. I know she is most anxious to dance a set with you, Webb."

Webb flinched before he turned a critical eye on Lily. "You've really outdone yourself tonight, Lily. Can that be one of your new dresses?"

She ignored his smug expression. "How kind of you to say so, Webb. But I'm afraid this is just the same old dress I've been wearing for most of my visit. My maid and I were able to make some lovely alterations to it, more appropriate for a party." She didn't need him to tell her she looked ridiculous, she already knew that, but in a few hours, once his father declared her unfit and they'd left Byrnewood, she'd leave this disguise behind forever.

Judging from Webb's frown, she'd obviously succeeded, not that it didn't dent her feminine heart to have him looking at her as if he found the experience distasteful. It was bad enough the room was already filling with the neighborhood's prettiest young misses, each of them dewy and fresh in their fashionable muslins and pastel silks.

Once down the stairs, she'd look like an old crow settled among a flock of sweet singing canaries.

But it was only for one more night, she told herself. One more night, then she'd be once again free to live her own life.

He leaned back, studying her anew. "If you say so. For a moment there I thought you looked almost festive. It is after all a celebration to announce your *engagement*. At least that was what I thought I overheard your sister telling Lady Larkhall not two minutes ago."

Adam nodded at this, his cool assurance taking Lily aback. Announce their engagement? They'd agreed not to! Once announced it would be a terrible scandal to back out. She looked back at Adam, a sly smile pulling the corners of his mouth.

He meant to trap her with her lie. He meant to announce this false engagement and force her hand.

"I would have thought," Webb continued, "that mourning and such a happy event would be rather a contradiction."

"There isn't going to be any announcement," she said through clenched teeth.

Both men looked askance at her, as if she'd just become a recalcitrant child. Each with their own motives.

Before Lily could put a stop to either of them, Sophia and Giles arrived at the bottom of the stairs. Her sister smiled up at her, though Lily could see the disapproval crinkling the corners of her eyes. After all, there were half a dozen new dresses upstairs, which the frantic dressmaker and her assistants had been sewing since their arrival, that were more appropriate for a party.

Far be it, though, for Sophia to make a scene in public and instruct her to go change.

Besides, it was too late. Sophia and Webb weren't the only ones staring up at Lily and her outlandish costume.

As if sensing the need to overshadow Lily's latest *faux pas*, Sophia smiled brightly. "Lily, Adam, there you are. Come along. Giles wants to make the announcement so we can start the dancing."

With Webb leading the way, Lily started to back away. She was willing to do many things to make herself look the complete fool, but announcing an engagement was akin to sealing her fate.

Adam took her hand and placed it on his arm, pulling her down the stairs.

"We decided not to announce our engagement," she whispered to him, a smile plastered on her face.

"I changed my mind." He paused for a moment. "Someone needs to watch over you and keep you out of whatever mischief you've found yourself in with these Drydens. Hardly sporting of them to use you like this. Once you're my wife, there'll be no more of this blackmail. You can put aside these ridiculous clothes and blundering manners and act like the lady I know you are."

Lily ground her teeth. "No one is blackmailing me, except you."

Webb turned around.

Lily could only guess as to how much he had heard.

"What is this?" he asked. "Dissention from the bride-to-be?"

Lily smiled sweetly. "Of course not. Whatever makes you think so?"

He shrugged. "Oh, nothing in particular." He continued down the stairs.

Lily focused on the steely grace of Webb's shoulders as he strolled forward, moving like a great regal cat.

She hadn't missed how *he* looked in his evening clothes. His coat of black encased his shoulders and back in form-fitting elegance.

Since that night she couldn't forget the sensation of running her hands over his body. Try as she might, and she had, she didn't want the traitorous memories of being held by Webb to steal away her resolve. Or the memories of how his lips claimed hers, the breathless rush of passion and desire as his hand had moved beneath her cloak and . . .

Lost in her own wayward thoughts, she ran straight into those shoulders, and even as she tried to right herself, she went stumbling headlong into an arriving duchess.

Much to her chagrin, it was Webb's strong hands that righted her and his sensual mouth that whispered into her ear, "Careful, little hoyden. It may look to the rest of the guests like you are trying to get away from your beloved betrothed."

Before she could give him the heated response that sprung to her lips, he turned and flashed the scowling Duchess one of his most charming smiles.

The dimpled lady immediately blushed, to which he bowed low, and when he rose he held out his arm to her. Without another look in Lily's direction, Webb paraded into the ballroom.

As the crowd cut a path for the venerable society maven and her handsome escort, Lily watched two misses, no doubt just out of the schoolroom and entering society, sigh with delight as he glanced in their direction.

"Well, that worked out well," Sophia said. "Lily, please be more careful." Her sister took her husband's arm, while Giles shot Lily an apologetic smile before leading his wife into the ballroom.

"Sophia, I'd prefer not to announce my engagement tonight," Lily told her sister.

Her sister patted her arm and looked up at Adam. "Bridal nerves. You were so right, Adam." Sophia smiled at her. "Once Giles makes the announcement you'll settle right down."

They continued for about two more steps before Lily panicked, scooting and skittering backward on the marble floor like it had suddenly turned to ice. "I don't like this," she said. "I'll not be forced into a marriage—"

Giles stood in front of them, blocking them from the view of most of the guests crowding Byrnewood's grand ballroom, though Lily spied Webb standing solicitously behind the chair where the Duchess had planted her imperious backside.

His quizzical glance landed first on Adam and then on her.

She couldn't let him see her panic, her reluctance. But how could she let Giles announce an engagement she didn't want?

Her betrothal to the wrong man. She shook her head. She was starting to wonder if there was a right man for her.

Giles's booming voice held everyone's attention and Lily could feel the anticipation in the room building as he continued. "And it is with the greatest pleasure that the Marchioness and I wish to introduce all of you to . . ."

"Adam," Lily whispered furiously into his ear. "I'll never forgive you for this!"

"Yes, you will. Once we're married. You'll see. Everything will be fine then."

She thought about his reasons for forcing her hand.

Blackmail . . . her charade . . . her outlandish behavior . . . blundering manners.

She turned and gave her betrothed a fine smile. She just hoped he'd forgive her for what she was about to do.

"Oh, Lord Dryden, how will you ever forgive us? It pains me to think this is my sister," Sophia said as she and Giles approached Lord Dryden and Webb, who stood off to the side of the dancing. Her hostess smile glowed as if nothing were amiss.

But beside Webb, Lord Dryden flinched as Lily once again trod on her dancing partner and sent the entire set of dancers scrambling out of their places to escape her blundering path.

While Sophia's face continued to hold a sunny expression, her words were anything but elated. "I'm just as shocked as you are that Lily hasn't lived up to your expectations, my lord."

Webb knew it must be killing his sire to see one of his plans go awry, for they so rarely did. But the evening had turned out to be a rather enlightening one for Webb and he wasn't about to give in to pessimism just yet. "Your sister has truly outdone even my expectations this evening." He glanced over at Sophia. "No offense meant, my lady."

"None taken," Sophia said with a sigh of resignation. "I didn't know what we were getting ourselves into. I never thought of Lily as that much different from me. Perhaps it is just this engagement that is making her edgy."

"Edgy?" Giles laughed. "I'm starting to think your sister is working for the French."

"Lily, a double agent?" Lord Dryden laughed. "Lord help the French."

Giles tipped his head and stared across the ballroom. "Speaking of Mr. Saint-Jean, who is that woman he's been spending so much time with this evening? She looks vaguely familiar."

Lord Dryden huffed. "She should. That is the Countess Allen. She's rumored to be an agent for the Americans, though I haven't been able to find any proof. She was born in Boston and married Lord Allen during the Colonial War."

"Don't look at me," Sophia said. "I didn't invite the woman. But I haven't got time to worry about that now, Lily just toppled Lord and Lady Lewis. How anyone can be so graceless on the dance floor is beyond me. I must make our apologies immediately."

As she hurried off to make amends, Webb took a deep breath. Lily's plaintiff words rang in his ears.

I've done all this to protect you, to protect both of us.

He glanced again at the Countess and Adam, and the final piece fell into place.

"Well, this does put a new light on our plans," his father muttered. "Lily will never do."

"Oh, I wouldn't say that," Webb told him.

For a fortnight he'd waited for her scheme to unfold.

And nothing had added up. Until today.

The Lily he'd held in his arms that night in the garden had hardly been the clumsy, socially inept chit he'd spent the past fortnight watching.

That woman had been like a shooting star, a woman of fire, fallen from the sky and into his embrace. And just as quickly, she'd extinguished, in a blinding flash of passion leaving nothing more than a fleeting memory of something incredibly tantalizing.

Yet, the evidence against her seemed insurmountable.

As close as he could tally it, Lily had made more than twenty social gaffes, insulting the Duchess as to her choice of gowns, trampling each of her dancing partners, scandalizing the local vicar with her accounts of the proper manner in which to encourage pigs to breed, and then if the night couldn't have been any worse, she'd taken it upon herself to consume large quantities of wine and then flirt quite inappropriately with half the married men in the room.

Even her fiancé had deserted her, and his mother was loudly demanding an immediate retraction of their betrothal.

Instead of practicing her cover as a sheltered, convent-reared innocent, she'd performed like a Covent Garden doxy who'd stumbled into the wrong party.

Performed. That was the key to it all.

I've done all this to protect you, to protect both of us.

All this, he thought, adding it up—the clothes, the dancing, the poor lessons, the manners.

To protect her traitorous fiancé.

"I suppose we should tell her as soon as possible," Lord Dryden was saying. "I hope she isn't hurt by this, because she has really made such a tremendous effort."

Webb glanced across the ballroom at her. In that ugly black dress, she was easy to spot—that and the confusion surrounding her on the dance floor.

As last notes of music faded away, her relieved and limping partner led her from the floor.

Since he'd moved to one side of his father, she couldn't see him studying her, and to his surprise she was intently watching his father's discussion with Giles, the sly grin on her face evidence of her awareness that she was the subject of their conversation.

Before she spotted him, he saw something else in her expression that finally confirmed all his suspicions.

Triumph glowing in her jade green eyes. As if she'd just won.

"I still find it hard to believe," Webb's father was saying to Giles, "that anyone could be as bad as all this."

Hard to believe, indeed, Webb thought. More like impossible.

He glanced back at her, looking beyond the black gown, the misplaced manners, and the hundred or so other mistakes she'd put forth to hide her skills.

She'd played the incompetent to perfection. And if she could do half as well playing Adelaide, she'd have Paris at her feet.

And the woman of fire? The woman who'd haunted his dreams for the last fortnight . . . well, he couldn't help but wonder how deep he'd have to scratch Lily's veneer to find her.

When he looked for her again, he found she'd slipped into the crowd and disappeared from sight.

Webb turned to his father. "Sir, I think we should reconsider, at least until the morning. I'd like to give her one more chance."

A chance to save herself from being throttled, he thought, as he marched across the floor in search of the conniving little baggage.

Chapter 7

The evening, in Lily's humble estimation, turned out to be a social nightmare and a smashing success.

Wait until she got upstairs and told Celeste that all her predictions of disaster had come to naught.

Palm reading, indeed, Lily thought, as she ducked into the gallery that adjoined the ballroom and then collapsed into a chair in one of the three curtained alcoves at one end of the long room.

Sophia, true to her promise to make sure Lily got in her dance practice, had enticed, more likely bribed, half the young bucks in the county to dance with her. And she'd proceeded to mash everyone one of their toes.

Tomorrow there wouldn't be a man left in Bath, or the surrounding countryside, who would walk upright, Lily thought with some measure of pride. At least not any who had danced with her.

With Webb, Lord Dryden, and Giles conferring in the corner, their expressions a mixture of dismal failure and utter exasperation, she knew her plan had worked.

Even Adam had left her alone, having sought the company

of a countess. She'd embarrassed him completely with her performance tonight.

Served him right, she thought, forcing her hand about the engagement.

False it was, and false it would remain.

Exhausted not only with all the dancing, but with the playacting as well, she reached over and pulled the curtain closed, secluding her from any prying eyes.

In fact she'd chosen this spot because it was hidden away, and for the moment, she could remove her dancing slippers, rub her aching toes, and wish she didn't have two left feet.

Just as she wished she'd never returned to Byrnewood and Webb Dryden.

"Lily?" a voice inquired, breaking into the solitude of her hideaway.

Adam.

Probably come to berate her for her outrageous behavior.

Well, she realized, he had every right.

"I'm here, Adam," she said, parting the curtains.

He crossed the room and stuck his head into the alcove, while Lily fumbled for her discarded slippers and at the same time tried to get to her feet. She failed in both, catching her toe on the hem of her gown and stumbling halfway up.

He laughed, then pushed the curtain aside, so he could enter into her private hideaway. "Don't get up. I'm certainly not about to ask you to dance."

The curtains closed in around them and they were alone.

"Thank you for that favor," she said, tossing her slippers back to the floor.

"Truce?" he asked.

"Certainly."

"We're partners, you know," he said. "I don't want you to regret bringing me along on this adventure. It sure is grand."

A grand adventure, she thought wryly, twisting the ring on her finger and thinking about the day she'd received it. Thomas's father had pulled it from his pinkie and slipped it onto her finger before he'd died. She'd thought it no more than the sentimental gift of a dying man.

But he'd given her more than that when he asked her to wear it. He'd asked her to continue the Copeland legacy.

Several months after her father-in-law's death, Adam had told a stunned Lily that once a year a Copeland supplied a British customs agent with a lion's share of gold. Throughout the year, the man then provided lists of ships going in and out of the London pool, as well as other ports.

More importantly, he also provided naval movements.

The ability to track British naval movements had aided American ships in avoiding the increasingly unpleasant encounters with their English counterparts. Ships stopped. Cargoes seized. American sailors and passengers pressed into the Royal Navy.

Confrontations the Americans were as yet unable to stop.

This arrangement had been going on for over twenty years, and after the death of Lily's father-in-law, the British agent had refused the overtures of a new American contact. "I'll only do business with a Copeland," the man had stubbornly declared. He wanted to see the bearer of the ring. A bumblebee ring. Her bumblebee ring.

And so the American government, led by the wily Vice President, Thomas Jefferson, and his neighbor and her friend Adam had enlisted the last of the Copelands, Lily D'Artiers Copeland, to carry on the family legacy of espionage for the Americans.

And though she wasn't a Copeland by birth, Lily informed her adopted government, she thought she had the right blood to be an excellent spy.

Adam had begged to be allowed to come along, for he'd

been looking for just such an adventure in which to serve his country. Besides, he argued, Lily needed someone to watch her back. He'd vowed to guard the last of the Copelands with his very life.

"Lily, I think you should tell me what's going on." He reached out and took her hand, holding it almost reverently between his. "I can help you. I can take you away from here. Marry me, and we'll finish your work here in England without any further delays. Then I'll take you home. To Virginia. Think of it, us married. Why we'll be tremendously happy, and think of the tales we can tell all our grandchildren."

For all his playfulness, all his teasing, all his jokes, Lily now saw it, now knew the awful truth of the matter.

Adam was in love with her. His playacting during the last two weeks as the dutiful fiancé, the outraged betrothed had been so real she'd marveled at his skill in deception.

A deception which fooled even her. For he'd meant every word, every kiss.

If anyone knew the feeling of unrequited love, it was Lily, and his honest admission wrenched at her heart.

"Come with me, Lily. We'll be married before we sail, and we'll live a long and happy life together."

She closed her eyes. She should be in love with Adam. He was so handsome and dashing and charming, and so much like Webb, and yet . . .

So much like Webb?

She was doing it again—comparing every man she met to Webb.

She should never have kissed him, never have come to Byrnewood, never have come to England.

Never have fallen in love with him again.

"But I'm not in love with him," she whispered.

"With whom?" Adam squeezed her hands. "Thomas? Of

course you're not in love with him anymore. He was a cad and a fool. I would never do anything to hurt you, Lily, and I'll spend the rest of my life proving it."

The right words from the wrong man. She shook her head at him, hating herself for letting him see the truth. "No, it isn't Thomas. It's . . ."

For all Adam's outward foolery, he was a very intelligent man.

"Webb." He said the name quietly, without any malice, rather with the resignation of a man who knows there is nothing he can do.

She nodded.

He looked away for a moment. "Does he know?"

Lily bit her lip, then shook her head. It would be forever before she ever heard Webb utter the words Adam so freely offered.

"Is that why you feigned this engagement? To hurt him?"

"No. Not that it would have worked anyway. He still thinks of me as the gawky little girl he met so many years ago."

Adam laughed. "Well, if you'd stop wearing those awful weeds and doing whatever it is you've been doing to your face, I doubt any man would look at you and not see what I've seen, a beautiful woman."

Lily looked away, unsure of how to react to Adam's praise now that she knew his true feelings. "I've treated you terribly."

"No, you haven't," he said. "No more than I've allowed myself to be taken in. Though tonight's performance, for whatever your reasons, truly was your finest. I think everyone in that room considers me a complete fool for not having called off this engagement. But I doubt you want me to do that, at least not yet. Tell me one thing: why, Lily? Why have you gone to such great lengths to deceive . . ."

Before he could finish his question, the curtain whisked open and Lily found them faced by a furious Webb Dryden.

How much had he heard? Too much, she gathered, judging by the way every muscle in his neck and arms appeared tense with rage. And then he confirmed her suspicions as he finished Adam's question.

"Yes, Lily, do tell. Why have you attempted to deceive everyone with your nearly flawless performance?"

Deceive.

All Webb needed to hear was the one damning word that told the truth about Lily.

She'd deceived them all, including her beloved betrothed.

He wondered how many lies, like a juggler, she had tossed up in the air. Well, she'd thrown up one too many of them, and now they were all about to crash around her feet.

"Come, now, Lily," he said to her. "No witty response, no quick falsehood to save your hide?"

At this, Adam rose to his feet. "I don't think your presence is welcome here, sir." His rich Virginia accent rolled over the words, adding to the threat behind them.

Webb gave Adam credit for standing his ground. When her young hero filled out his lanky limbs in a few years, Webb knew he would have to think twice before manhandling the fellow, but for now he used what advantage he had over his opponent.

Webb turned an icy stare on Lily's fiancé before grabbing him by the collar and dragging him upward until he stood on his tiptoes. "One more word from you and I'll have you and your friend the Countess hauled in for treason."

Lily bounded to her feet, her hands pulling at his sleeve. "What the devil are you talking about? Treason? Have you gone mad?"

Webb glanced over at her and, for the first time since he'd

arrived at Byrnewood, saw what might be honesty in her stormy features.

"Your beloved here has spent most of the evening with a suspected American spy, the Countess Allen." He turned to Adam. "Isn't that right, my friend."

The man didn't even flinch. "I haven't the vaguest notion what you are talking about."

But Lily's performance wasn't as convincing. She visibly paled and looked first from Webb then to Adam, her face awash with disbelief and, if he wasn't mistaken, anger.

Still, if she was mad at her betrothed for risking such outright treachery in her sister's house, she wasn't going to let Webb denounce him. "Unhand him, Webb, or so help me I'll cause a scene that you'll never forget."

Webb let go of the man only because he knew she would.

"This is none of your business," Adam said, straightening his cravat, and brushing off the last creases Webb's grip had left in his otherwise immaculate coat. "You have no right to meddle in her affairs."

"Her *affairs* are my business." Webb jerked his head in the direction of the door. "And if anyone is leaving it will be you. Leave now and I might forget what I've seen, but if I catch even a glimpse of your face in this house in an hour's time, it will be the last hour you spend in freedom."

Lily pushed between them and faced her too-eager champion. "Adam, this is unnecessary," she said, her voice conciliatory and whisper-soft. "I'll be all right." She held out her hand to the man. "Do as he says and go. You know you must."

He looked ready to protest, but she shook her head at him and smiled, holding out her hand for him.

Adam Saint-Jean, every ounce the gentleman of his aristocratic French ancestors, bowed over her outstretched hand as if this were nothing more than the end of a courtly dance.

Then with a curt nod to Webb, he shouldered past him and stalked through the gallery toward the crush of the ballroom.

Lily's gaze followed him until he disappeared into the crowd; then she turned a blazing glare on Webb.

He couldn't resist asking, "What, no tears for your betrothed?"

"What do you care?" Following Adam's example, Lily started to make her escape toward the crowd.

Webb caught her by the elbow. "Not so fast. If you thought your little plan was going to work, you're wrong."

He hauled her back into the alcove and yanked the curtain shut. When she started to pull it back open, he caught her hand.

"I have a few things to discuss with you."

"How interesting," she told him, "as I have nothing to say to you after that embarrassing scene. Why you manhandled poor Adam like some peevish, jealous lover. It is hardly your place to tell me—"

Tired of listening to her lies, furious that she'd jeopardized the lives of so many agents on the Continent with her selfish deceptions and delays, Webb reached around her and opened the door. Before she could protest, he shoved her onto the narrow balcony, where rain was falling in heavy sheets.

As Lily whirled around to escape the inclement weather, Webb slammed the door in her face. With a quick snap of the latch, he locked her outside.

Now let her see what it is like to have one's life hang in the balance.

For a moment she stared at him through the square panels of glass, her face a mask of disbelief, then outrage. Especially when the gutter above her let loose an extra measure of water.

The overflow drenched her from head to toe.

"Let me back in!" Holding up the edge of her skirt, she displayed her stocking clad toes wiggling in a puddle. "I don't have my shoes on."

He looked around the small alcove, and picked up not only her discarded slippers, but also a black lace shawl she'd left lying across the back of her chair.

"I doubt this would help much now, would it?" He dangled the shawl before her.

Her face turned stormier than the clouds overhead. Given the choice, she'd probably use the narrow cloth as a noose for his neck rather than as protection from the elements.

"Let me in," she railed, beating on the door frame with her fists.

"A well-brought-up girl would hardly leave her clothing lying about during a ball, now would she?" he teased, hoping to fan the flames that burned through her disguise.

"I'm getting soaked," came her unrepentant cry.

Setting aside her discarded shoes in a spot where she could still see them, Webb settled into the chair she'd vacated and propped his feet onto the other one. He flipped the shawl over his legs like a small blanket. "Pretend you have an umbrella. You seem quite adept at make-believe."

She muttered a colorful oath in French, followed by a rather disparaging remark about his parentage.

Finally, he thought, with some satisfaction, *the Lily I remember*.

Leaning back, he crossed his arms over his chest and closed his eyes. For a time he relaxed in silence, with only the patter of rain against the panes.

"Webb, please?"

He knew what that pitiful request had cost her, but still he wasn't quite ready to relent. She'd wasted two weeks of valuable training time with her calculated scheme.

A scheme for which he'd nearly fallen.

She crossed her arms over her shivering chest. "I won't make a very good Adelaide if I am dead from a chill."

Damn her, he thought, realizing she was correct. And he wouldn't put it past her to contract something fatal just to get out of going to Paris.

Reluctantly he flipped the latch.

Lily bolted inside in a hailstorm of droplets. She shook most of them on him.

"Why you bas—" she sputtered.

"*Tsk, tsk*," he told her, opening the door again. "Hardly the language of a gently reared innocent. Do you need another lesson?" He nodded toward the balcony, his fingers wrapping around the curve of her elbow.

"It won't be so easy for you this time," she shot back. "I'll scream until I bring down the house. The scandal alone will ruin whatever plans you have of finding yourself a suitable bride."

"What do you know about that?" he asked, astonished that she knew of his plans to settle down.

"Your father told me. Good luck once you are seen taking advantage of a poor defenseless widow. And one engaged to another man. There won't be a mother in England who will allow her daughter to marry you. At least not the decent, well-brought-up one that I'm sure you want."

"As if you know anything about decent," he said, letting go of her elbow and the doorknob.

Though wet from head to toe, Webb had to admit the drenched look was hardly an improvement on her wretched widow's weeds.

The bombazine looked like a funeral crepe that had been left out in the weather for a couple of weeks. Her hair hung in wet clumps, the wind having whipped it free from its confining pins.

Yet the rain had done one thing. It had washed away most of her deceptions.

Her hair now lay in soft, enticing curls. The powder on her face was running down her cheeks in yellowish streams. He reached out and ran his fingers over her skin and looked down to find the painted layer of her deception coloring his fingers. When he looked back up he saw that the skin beneath her makeup glowed with a rosy, healthy sheen.

Nothing, however could hide the outrage and fire glowing in her eyes. Yet, he had to wonder, how much else had she been hiding behind her pretenses of paint and bombazine?

He had been so quick to dismiss the ardent look in Adam's eyes when he'd spied the young man gazing at her with such obvious admiration.

The mystery enticed him to uncover what he'd let his memories of Lily and his emotions blind himself to.

Then the thought of their kiss sprang to mind. Her passionate touch, her enticing wiles. If he dared to close his eyes, he would be able to imagine the seductress capable of such intoxication, but before him stood only the outraged and wet little kitten he'd always seen.

Yet Adam had been privy to Lily's secrets all along—with an easy familiarity and closeness that left Webb fighting back an unwanted jealousy that demanded he find those answers as well.

Webb caught her by the shoulders. "What game have you been playing, Lily? Did you think you could protect your lover from his own stupidity by claiming an engagement?"

Lily shook herself free from his grasp. "My lover? The only one who suffers from stupidity is you." She shook out her skirt, the water puddling around her stocking feet.

"Perhaps I should have Adam followed and then we'll see what secrets you've been attempting to hide," Webb offered.

Her gaze shot up, and for the merest flicker, a flash of alarm illuminated her eyes. Then she blinked and shrugged. "You said he could go free. You gave your word."

"I lied."

Her jaw set in a stony line. "I don't know why I should be shocked. Lying must come quite easily to someone of your *ilk*."

There it was again, that word. *Ilk.*

The way she said it made him sound like some loathsome creature. He wasn't the one harboring a possible spy.

He turned toward the ballroom. "Well, if I can't get the truth out of you, then I think I will call that young fool out, just to see if I can knock some facts out of him. I'm sure he knows why you've gone to such great lengths to avoid going on this mission with me."

She caught his arm and held him fast. "You will leave him out of this." There was no mistaking the intent to her words.

"Too late," Webb said, turning to leave.

Lily spun him around. "Leave him alone, Webb."

"Tell me why you've put on this great charade to avoid going to Paris."

"I've done no such—"

"Stow it, Lily. I told you before I would follow you. I can just as easily add your betrothed to my list and have him followed as well."

Her eyes narrowed. "I told you to leave him alone."

"Mark my words, I will follow Adam and shake the truth out of him, and if that doesn't work, I'll toss his hide in Newgate until you both come to your senses."

She ungrit her teeth, her words level and terse. "If you leave him be, I'll go to Paris with you. There'll be no more trouble, no more charades, but only if you vow to leave Adam alone."

Webb looked down at her hand where it held his arm.

Her fingers were chilled and the cold cut through the cloth of his coat to the skin beneath.

But the ice in her hands couldn't match the passion of her words. There was no denying Adam was important to Lily and to whatever secrets she held.

Again, a niggle of jealousy poked at Webb's sensibilities. Why should he be concerned if Lily cared for this man? Her importance to him was her resemblance to Adelaide de Chevenoy and her obvious skills in subterfuge.

Wasn't it?

Her green eyes, luminous and vibrant against her pale skin, for a moment didn't glare at him with their usual hostility. But rather they regarded him with a mixture of trepidation and something else, like an unfilled longing.

Later he realized he should have stopped himself, but there were too many questions that could be answered by just one kiss. It seemed so simple.

But he should have known better. Nothing about Lily D'Artiers Copeland was ever simple.

He pulled her close and sought out his answers.

A fortnight of watching her with another man had burned his blood with jealousy. And the memory of their kiss in the garden, which the next morning seemed more phantom than real, still left him breathless.

Her hands pushed at his shoulders. She tried to turn away from his lips.

If he let go, she'd make the scene she promised. Then again, Webb had no intention of letting Lily go until he found out the truth.

His lips closed over hers, taking what he wanted. Her struggles faded away, and soon her arms wound around his neck, her mouth opening quite willingly to his.

And, for a time, he kissed her, let his lips seek the truth, uncover the woman he suspected was hidden beneath her paint and mysteries.

She melded against him, her wet dress soaking his coat, his breeches.

True passion, hot desire coursed through him. Lily's kiss drove him beyond his questions and past all sanity.

Deceit, his reason screamed. *This is Lily, a woman of deceit.* The staggering thought pulled him back from her.

She let go of him instantly and turned, shivering anew. Without thinking, he snatched up her shawl and drew it around her. Wielding it like a fisherman's net, he pulled her back into his easy reach.

"You'll go to Paris, and there will be no more of these antics or delays?" Webb's hands rubbed her wet arms.

She glanced over her shoulder, toward the ballroom. "Yes." She turned her gaze back to him. "And you will keep your word?"

He tried to look away from her lips, not think about the way they tasted or how they felt pressed against his own.

She was his. Well, at least for this mission.

"Yes," he finally answered, though he wouldn't be breaking his promise if he just happened to run into Adam again tonight. Like on the road out of Byrnewood.

"Why did you break your vow, Lily?" he asked, his earlier anger changed now to something else. "You said that night you would go to Paris with me."

"I didn't break my promise," she said. "But I never said I would make it easy for you. Besides, you're the one who's been clamoring for another partner. Not me." Her hand went to her kiss-swollen lips. It hid a small, satisfied smile.

He conceded her point. "Yes, but you helped."

They stared at each other, and Webb couldn't help but feel a grudging respect for her nearly successful deception.

The little hoyden had grown up.

She wrapped her shawl around her a little tighter and shivered again. "I should go change. I'll catch my death if I don't get warmed up."

It was on the tip of his tongue to offer his services, but he shook the errant thought aside.

The devil take him, he was losing his mind. This was Lily. Little Lily. Annoying, troublesome Lily. Hadn't she proved that again with all her theatrics to avoid going to Paris?

She started to leave the alcove, pushing the curtain aside, then stopped and glanced over her shoulder. "What gave me away?"

"Pardon?"

"What gave me away? I mean how did you figure out that I wasn't really as bad as I made myself out to be?"

He didn't know if he should tell her, but decided to anyway now that she was caught. "Your dancing. It was a little too cowhanded."

She looked vexed. "My dancing? Some agent you are." Her mouth set in a stony line.

"What do you mean? You deliberately went out of your way to look terrible. Monsieur Beauvoir wasn't far off—for he isn't the only one tonight comparing you to a dancing ox." He laughed. "Really, Lily, no one is that bad."

Lily didn't share in his jest. Instead she reacted.

How she did it, Webb never quite figured out, but she moved so quickly, and with the strength of one of Egypt's famous Mameluke warriors, that he didn't have time to stop her.

Lily whipped open the balcony door and suddenly Webb found himself outside in the rain, the door latched in his face.

An angry Lily glared at him from the warm comfort of the house.

"The dancing, Mr. Spy," she said in a tight voice, "was

the only thing I did not fake." And with that she whirled out of the alcove and left him to the elements.

"*Auchew*," Webb sneezed.

"Bless you," Lily called out from behind the dressing screen where she was undergoing the last of her fittings with the modiste.

If his father, Sophia, and Giles hadn't been in the room, the only blessing necessary would have been one over Lily's dead body. As it was, the four of them sat in Sophia's morning room, which for the past fortnight had been transformed into their war room of preparation.

"What ever possessed you to go out on that balcony last night?" Sophia clucked in her most motherly tones. "You're lucky you aren't dead from a chill."

When no one had responded to his banging on the door, he'd been forced to climb down the ivy-covered facade of Byrnewood. In the last ten feet, his freezing-cold fingers had lost their grip and he'd fallen nearly into the arms of the departing Duchess.

"Really, Mr. Dryden, you should be more careful," Lily chimed in from behind the screen.

The delighted giggle in the shameless little chit's voice nearly drove him to his feet. He ought to give her the throttling she deserved.

"An error in judgment on my part," he said, ignoring the amused looks on his father's and Giles's faces. By the time he'd escaped her trap, he'd been unable to find Adam, Adam's mother, or the Countess. Cautious inquiries to the other guests and staff revealed the threesome had been seen hightailing it away from Byrnewood.

If Sophia and Giles had any comment on their houseguests' hasty departure, they hadn't said anything in front of him.

Another mystery added to Lily's arsenal of secrets.

One he vowed to uncover and unlock.

From her post behind the screen, a suddenly brilliant Lily continued her recitation of the de Chevenoy lineage, a room-by-room description of both houses, and an almost tearful story of the wreath of native flowers she'd prepared for the funeral of one of her most beloved teachers, Sister Marie-Rufina Helena.

The uncanny girl put the best agents in the Foreign Office to shame, Webb thought.

As if seconding his conclusion, his father chimed in his approval. "Well done, Lily, well done. I should have recruited you into the business years ago. Whatever was I thinking allowing your family to take you off to the wilds of America? Your talents have been wasted."

As for her previous ill behavior, she'd very convincingly explained that away as a case of nerves and fears about returning to Paris. Especially after her traumatic childhood experiences in the Terror. Her luminous eyes glistening with well-timed tears had gained her a full pardon from his father.

Webb conceded she'd done well on all those points, but there was still one obstacle for her to overcome.

Adelaide's portrait hinted of a girl about to bloom into startling beauty.

While he knew Lily had the inner passion of her Ramsey forebears, she still needed to show the outward beauty expected in Paris.

This, then, was to be the final trial. When Mme. Pontius, one of London's most favored modistes, unveiled her work of art, either Lily would be accepted for the mission or she would gain her freedom.

After his initial anger last night at being duped by her, he'd thought long and hard, stuck as he was on the balcony two stories above the ground, why was he fighting so adamantly to drag her unwilling carcass to Paris?

Alone in Paris with Lily? What was he thinking?

If she thought nothing of leaving him locked out in the rain, what might she say or do in front of Paris society?

And then there were those strange feelings she'd evoked in him last night. Protectiveness, jealousy, longing.

As for the kisses they'd shared, he didn't like even considering those emotions and Lily in the same thought.

Mme. Pontius stepped back from her work and clucked her tongue. "I think you will be pleased, my lord," she said to his father. "This is my best work to date. You will see, I have created your heiress. An angel to behold."

Webb smiled as politely as he could at the lady, for he knew his father held her in high regard.

And if Madame wanted to crow about her latest work of art, so be it, but Webb didn't believe for a minute that even the highly talented Madame could transform Lily into an angel.

For beauty was something not even Lily could fake.

Yet even as he came to this silent conclusion, Lily stepped out from behind the screen.

Though held together mostly with pins and blue basting threads, the dress she wore molded to her body like the marble drapings on the Grecian statues in Brynewood's grotto. The sheer silk, held at her shoulders with gold clasps, cascaded to the floor in a waterfall of white foam. The *V* front fell deeply into the cleft of her breasts, so their rounded fullness threatened to spill out.

Webb took a deep breath and another look. He suddenly found he couldn't trust his eyes, though the rest of his body reacted with a jolt of awareness and seething memories.

Until now, she'd been hidden beneath the black depths of that hideous bombazine. Released from her widow's weeds, she looked like a dove in flight, free to fly, free to show her fine bright feathers to the world. Her face, which had been framed by her black cap and had seemed pale and lifeless under the layers of powder, came to life.

Though his hands had caressed her form while they'd kissed, now he could see that what he had imagined was indeed very real—the slim rounded lines of her hips, her wisp of a waist, the perfection of her small, upraised breasts.

She'd tied her hair up with a pale green ribbon, and the shimmering tresses fell down from their simple binding in a cascade of spun gold. It was as if Diana had stepped from her prison of marble and now stood before him, a living and breathing woman.

As if an angel had dropped from her heavenly perch.

He knew he was staring, but he couldn't believe the transformation.

This fair goddess before him was little Lily? Where was the hoyden? The little pest who tagged after him, the bothersome little girl with her gawky ways? Where was the pale widow with her bleak dresses and washed-out features?

Somewhere in the back of his mind he remembered Lady Marston's long forgotten prediction.

That child has all the markings of a beauty.

She now stood before him, her elegant grace mocking all his illusions. Lost forever was his image of the hoyden menace, lost to this enticing creature before him.

And he wasn't the only one transfixed by her sudden metamorphosis. Everyone else sat gaping in open-mouthed amazement.

"What's the matter now?" Lily asked. She turned left and right, twisting and looking around herself as if trying to find the problem.

Madame laughed. "No, *ma chérie.* I think you are too perfect."

Webb suddenly saw his life swim before his eyes.

Their mission suddenly took on a new and extremely dangerous turn.

Looking like that, Lily would take Paris in a riot it hadn't seen since the fall of the Bastille.

And that would leave them open to every possible danger.

Oh, they'd found their heiress, Webb thought. But somewhere along the way, they'd unearthed a temptress.

Chapter 8

M. Bernard Troussebois arrived at the back door of the de Chevenoy house as had been his custom since the first day he'd been retained as Henri de Chevenoy's solicitor. The quaint stone house, with its three stories of pale stone and crenellated roofline sat on the quiet *Rue du Renard*.

The solicitor preferred to arrive at the back door of his clients' homes as it gave him an opportunity to visit for a moment with their servants and learn the latest about his clients' welfare and business.

Bits of information a client may be reluctant or too embarrassed to share.

He'd always liked coming to the de Chevenoy residence for it meant a chance to sample a bite or two of Mme. Costard's latest baking before he continued on to his business with the Comte. How the woman constantly secured food for the household, he wasn't sure, but it probably helped that Henri de Chevenoy always managed to have more than enough gold to pay the inflated prices.

And Troussebois didn't count out the formidable Mme. Costard herself.

He doubted there was a butcher or grocer in Paris who would refuse the giant lady service, though he knew her to be soft-hearted and kind despite her size and ferocious looks.

After his second rap on the door, M. Costard answered. Wherein his wife looked about the size of a draft horse and just as strong, M. Costard was a narrow, angular man who looked as though he hadn't seen a good meal in months.

This, Troussebois knew, wasn't true, for Mme. Costard was an excellent cook. Still, he found them an odd pairing at best.

"Come in, Monsieur Troussebois," Costard said. "Come in out of the cold." The man's pinched face held a worried frown and his gray bushy brows jutted out in anxious lines. Despite his obvious anxieties, the good valet never forgot his duties, taking Troussebois's rain-splattered coat and hanging it by the fire.

"So the heiress has arrived." Troussebois took his usual seat at the kitchen table. Before him sat a plate of almond studded cakes. They smelled heavenly, but good manners dictated he wait until offered.

To his disappointment, the normally generous Mme. Costard didn't immediately begin filling a plate for him.

"Oh, yes. Our heiress is home," Costard replied, before sitting down at the head of the table. De Chevenoy's faithful valet and his wife were the only servants in the house, and had been, for as long as Troussebois had worked for the Comte.

He'd thought it was because the reclusive de Chevenoy preferred his privacy, but since Henri's death, the solicitor had learned the true reason for his employer's limited household staff.

One he shuddered to think of, and for the thousandth

time since his employer's death, asked himself the same question.

How had he ever gotten involved in this mess?

Well, he thought, it was too late to consider any other course than the one he and the Costards had agreed upon.

"She arrived not an hour ago and is settling right in," Costard explained. "Trunks, a servant, and . . ." the valet leaned forward, his narrow elbows propped up on the wooden table, ". . . a fiancé."

A fiancé? Troussebois gulped, speechless at this notion. A fiancé could only mean trouble, or worse yet, needless questions and inquiries.

Calming the panicked butterflies ratcheting through his stomach, Troussebois lamented his fate at ever accepting Henri de Chevenoy as a client. Never mind the fact that the de Chevenoy account had kept bread on his table for the last seven years when many of his profession had starved or, worse, lost their heads.

No, Troussebois, he said to himself as he often did when faced with a challenging legal dilemma, *you must have courage*.

Their lives depended upon the de Chevenoy heiress—the Costards' for their living and the roof over their heads, and his for the fees he charged for handling her vast estate.

But a fiancé.

He didn't like the notion one bit. It wedged an entirely new set of problems into their carefully laid plans, but he didn't have time to consider that now, when the most important question remained unanswered.

He looked from husband to wife, his concern growing. "Is there any chance of us passing off this imposter as Adelaide de Chevenoy?"

★ ★ ★

Lily paced across the Oriental carpet in the de Chevenoy salon and stopped in front of a tall secretary in the corner. Without a second thought she began pulling open drawers and pawing through the contents.

"What do you think you're doing?" Webb said, bounding off the couch and spinning her away from her task. His hand closed over hers, and for a moment he held her, both of them staring at each other, the heat of their bodies once again joined.

In the instant she raised her gaze to his, he dropped her hand as if it burned and glanced away.

"I'm looking for the journals, what does it look like I'm doing?" she snapped, tired and cranky from their travels and the wariness of being in Webb's constant company. While an unspoken truce had risen since the ball at Byrnewood, that didn't mean there still wasn't an undercurrent of tension rippling between them.

As she turned to renew her search, he pulled her away from the tall cherry-wood cabinet, and with his free hand pushed all the open cabinets closed. Before she could utter a word of protest, she found herself being dragged toward a brocade-covered sofa. Pointing to a spot on the cushion where she was supposed to sit and stay put, he released her.

She sat down, slowly though, if only to annoy him.

"You search when I tell you to search," Webb said, resuming his seat on a wide chair next to the sofa. "What would you say to the Costards if they walked in and found you rifling through the house like a common thief?"

Lily bit her lip to hold back her retort.

The only difference she saw between herself and a common thief was that a thief had the good sense to come and go in the dead of night and be done with his dirty business.

"I just don't like all this waiting around." She crossed her arms over her chest and stared at the closed salon doors. The entire house stood beyond those doors, and Henri's journals could be anywhere.

No matter how soon they found them and got back to England, it wouldn't be soon enough for Lily.

Some spy she made, she realized. Here they'd arrived at the de Chevenoy house only an hour ago and she was already itching to leave.

She should be coursing with excitement, for she'd passed the first test of their mission—deceiving Henri's long-time servants, M. and Mme. Costard.

The first tense moment, when M. Costard opened the door and frowned through his bushy eyebrows at her, had quickly turned into a happy reunion. The Costards welcomed her with open arms, a series of great hugs and many tears, holding her at arm's length and claiming her the very image of her dear, departed mother.

Napoleon's guards, still posted at the door, had paid her little heed once Costard told them who she was. One of them had even been cajoled into assisting the driver with carrying her trunks into the house.

The de Chevenoy servants had taken Celeste's arrival into their midst, in her red silk skirts and colorful kerchief knotted around her head, with nary a bat of an eye, welcoming the stately mulatto to their home and apportioning the small room next to her mistress for her use.

Webb they'd given a more thoughtful and careful scrutiny, especially after Lily gave her rushed introduction that he was her fiancé and had seen her safely to Paris.

She and Webb had then been settled in the salon, while Mme. Costard went to prepare a tray for them and Costard directed the driver and guard in carting her trunks up to Adelaide's room for Celeste to unpack.

"How long do you think it will take Mme. Costard to

bring in the food? Perhaps I should go see what is taking her so long," Lily offered, half rising from the sofa.

Webb shot her a reproachful glare that sent her back to her seat before he returned to perusing the thick book he'd plucked from a shelf.

If only, she thought, Adam hadn't been so foolish as to be seen with the Countess at the ball, she may have been able to bluff her way out of this assignment. But once Webb had laid his steely gaze on her friend with a fellow spy, she knew Adam's life wouldn't be worth a farthing if she didn't offer Webb what he wanted most—her agreement to play Adelaide.

A bargain with the devil, she thought, glancing over at him, her foot tapping on the carpet.

He lounged like a young lion in the oversized chair. His tawny-brown hair lay brushed back in a very American-style queue, tied as it was with a black leather strip. One lock strayed free and curled over his forehead giving him an almost boyish look. He wore a somber black coat and buff breeches, with a white shirt and cravat completing his plain dress. Only his boots, glistening to a fine sheen, added any polish to his otherwise boring disguise.

He looked for all accounts the cover he and his father had devised, Mr. Milne, Yankee shipowner, and Adelaide's fiancé.

Fiancé! Gads, she hated this ruse. It was bad enough having to spend the last few days jolting along in a carriage with him, but now they had to feign an affection for each other that neither of them felt.

At least Webb didn't. She sighed softly and glanced away from him. Of that much she was sure.

Since her unveiling at Byrnewood in Adelaide's new clothes, he'd said nothing more to her than was necessary and he'd rarely looked her in the face.

If only she could be so similarly afflicted.

But, like now, she found herself watching him, peeking out beneath her lashes and studying his hard features, the curve of his jaw, the cleft in his chin, the startling blue of his eyes.

Adam was just as handsome, she argued to herself. Some might say better looking, for unlike Webb, her Virginian neighbor knew how to smile. Yet it was Webb not Adam who made her heart quicken when he walked in a room.

Worse yet, every time he touched her, bumped into her in the carriage, the heat of his body, the touch of his fingers sent ripples of desire twining through her limbs.

Like moments ago, when he'd pulled her away from the secretary. A traitorous part of her wanted to get up and start overturning the furniture so as to have him haul her bodily into his arms.

She took a deep breath and let it out before she glanced back over at him. She tried to recall her hatred for him, issuing up images of him with Lady Marston, his hateful words that day in the maze, but the comfort they used to offer was lost. Instead it only brought another round of niggling questions.

Did he have another mistress now? Who was she? Did he miss her?

Lily knew he spent most of his time in France, so was the woman here in Paris or in some cozy country house just outside the city?

Mercy and Mary, she would drive herself crazy with this sudden return of every adolescent insecurity she'd ever possessed when it came to Webb Dryden.

If only there were a cure for this plaguing affection she'd contracted for the wrong man.

"When do you propose we start searching?" she asked, tired of the silence.

Webb closed his book with an annoyed snap. "When we can find an excuse to get the Costards out of the house. Thankfully Henri's profession meant he kept a limited household staff, so it shouldn't be much trouble to invent enough errands to get the pair out of the way for a good part of the day. Besides the most logical place to find the journals is in Henri's study behind some hidden panel or strongbox, and the door to that room is locked."

"How do you know?"

"I checked it when we came in. His study is the first door to the left. When no one was looking, I tried to open it. That's why we'll need the Costards out of the house—it may take me some time to pick the lock. Henri was a rather particular man about his study, and I am sure the lock on that door is the best money can buy."

She got up, ignoring the scolding arch of his brows and paced across the room to stand by the mantel, feigning interest in the line of porcelain figurines displayed in a tidy row. Frolicking maids and lovesick shepherds. Lily turned from their bright happy faces. "What do we do until then?"

"You do what a young lady who's spent the last few years cloistered in a convent would do, mind your betters."

Lily sniffed. "When I meet someone who qualifies, I will."

Webb laughed. "Just settle in. Besides the solicitor will be here soon and you'll find out how wealthy you are."

"Wonderful. A fortune at my disposal, and all I'm allowed to do is sit in this room." Lily started prowling around the salon again eyeing the small tables, the portraits on the walls, and the gilt fixtures around the door and windows. "Maybe I'll go upstairs and help Celeste unpack. At least then I'll be doing something." She started for the door again, but Webb was in front of her before she could take more than a few steps.

His hands went to her shoulders and he held her fast. "How would that look? The heiress unpacking her own trunks?"

She glanced over at his hand, where his fingers curled around her shoulder. His thumb rubbed against the bare skin where the gauzy lawn of her gown ended.

Unable to stop herself, she moved closer to him. She wondered again about his mistress and what kind of woman she was. Bold? Biddable? As hungry for his touch as she?

Lily didn't want to know.

She only wanted to kiss him anew, to discover if her memories of their kisses were real. To taste once again the intoxicating ether of his lips which still burned through her veins and infected her senses.

"Hoyden," he whispered, "don't make this more difficult." His hand now caressed her bare arm, his warm fingers sliding over her skin.

"You shouldn't call me that." She glanced up from beneath her lashes.

"Hoyden," he said, softly, as if daring her to correct him.

She moved even closer, rising on her toes, her gaze never leaving his deep blue eyes, caught by the flickering emotion she found there, an emotion so unsettling, it almost set Lily back on her heels.

For there, reflected in Webb's eyes, was the same raw need that coursed through her veins.

He wanted her.

She didn't care that later she might regret it, that her eyes might only be seeing what she desired, she knew if she didn't kiss him now, she'd never answer the questions that plagued her thoughts, both awake and asleep.

Bringing her lips to his, she let her experiment go forth.

To clear her conscience.

To appease her thundering desire.

The kiss started slowly, as if they were both tentative and unsure. The other two times they'd kissed had been born out of passion and anger, but now there seemed to be something else.

Longing.

As her mouth opened and welcomed his exploration, she knew her desire for him was only going to get worse.

Webb's kiss was something worth dying for.

His tongue curved and danced with hers, teasing her to follow his enticing motions.

She sighed softly, stretching her body against his. Her arms wound around his neck, entwining her fingers in his hair.

He pulled her closer, his hands running along the small of her back and working their way up, stroking her and moving her just that much closer to him.

Webb wondered at his own sanity, as he deepened his kiss. He still couldn't believe the seductive woman in his arms was the same annoying little hoyden he'd spent so many years avoiding.

How he wished for her damned bombazine again. At least wrapped in her hideous black gown, she didn't stop his heart every time he looked at her.

His senses reeled as her hands roamed over his shoulders, caressing him, while her hips rocked expectantly against his.

His body responded with a hardening awareness of her every touch. His fingers toyed with the slim sleeve of her gown, teasing to push it aside.

For a second, Lily pulled away, her breath rapid and hot in his ear. "Webb, I . . ."

He didn't want to hear anything other than her acquiescence, and so he covered her mouth again, kissing her deeper until the only sounds he heard were those of her soft moans of longing.

"Aahem." The polite cough at the door drove them apart.

Webb whirled around to find Costard and a blinking rabbit of a man standing in the doorway.

So lost in kissing Lily, he hadn't even heard their approach or that of the door opening.

Webb Dryden, the pride of the Foreign Office caught unawares because he'd been too preoccupied kissing?

He could hear the howls of laughter from his peers and the underlings in the hallways of the Thames-side government building.

"Ah, young love," Costard said, nudging his elbow into the other man's side. "Isn't it a sight to make you long for your youth, eh, Troussebois?"

"Well, I . . . I . . ." the man said, blushing about four shades of red.

Behind him, Webb gauged from the sound of her frantic movements, Lily was doing her best to repair the damage and straighten her gown, for when she stepped around him, her serene appearance belied the passion that had been boiling between them not moments earlier. For himself, he could only tug his jacket down and hope he didn't look as disheveled as he felt.

"Mistress," Costard said, inclining his head to her. "My apologies at this interruption, but this is Monsieur Troussebois, your father's solicitor."

"How kind of you to come by on such short notice, Monsieur," Lily said, crossing the room, and allowing the solicitor to take her hand and bring it to his lips. Her brilliant smile seemed to fluster the man further, for he spilled the contents of his portfolio all over the carpet.

The man blushed scarlet and knelt to hastily pick up his papers, mumbling his hasty apologies and greetings in a jumbled mess.

When he'd composed himself and gathered his papers,

stuffing them rather haphazardly into the black leather folder he carried, he stood and stared at her.

"I told you," Costard said. "The very image of her mother, isn't she?"

Troussebois gulped. "You forget, Costard. I never met the Comtesse de Chevenoy."

At this point, Mme. Costard arrived bearing a heavy silver service, the tray laden with cakes and breads, along with a fragrant pot of coffee.

"Husband," the lady said, "go find our dear lady's portrait. It is in the attic, I think. The old master put it away after her death, for it grieved him to see what a treasure he had lost." Mme. Costard smiled at Lily, her whiskery chin wobbling as she held back another bout of tears. "Would you like that, mistress? To have your mother's portrait hung in this room?"

She inclined her head politely. "That would be lovely."

With that the Costards left. Following Lily's cool lead, Webb sat down next to her on the sofa, deliberately placing himself where they wouldn't touch.

He hadn't really given much thought to the type of man Henri de Chevenoy would hire—after meeting the kindly Costards, he certainly hadn't expected this nervous man.

Bernard Troussebois stood no higher than Lily, his little pinched nose twitching like a rabbit's as she introduced Webb as her dear fiancé.

Troussebois tipped up his spectacles and eyed Lily carefully, as if he didn't quite believe this was indeed his new client.

Webb glanced at her and watched her cool demeanor. It was as if they'd never kissed, for he couldn't see a trace of the fiery woman he'd held. She'd disappeared behind this professional mask.

He didn't know whether to marvel at her skill or wonder

if her entire performance, from the moment she'd stepped into his arms and driven his senses wild with her erotic touch until they'd been interrupted, had been an act.

Her punishment to him for forcing her to come to Paris.

Sweet torture indeed, he thought, considering the possible weeks ahead they would be in each other's company until they found Henri's journals.

He didn't know whether he wanted to throw the little solicitor out right now and start searching the house immediately or delay finding the journals for as long as he could.

Beside him, Lily poured M. Troussebois a cup of coffee.

Webb took a deep breath and struggled to concentrate on the matters at hand.

Lily heard Webb's deep sigh and, glancing over at him, offered him a small smile. "Coffee, my love?"

He didn't speak, only nodded at her in that tense sort of way of his.

Mercy and Mary, she thought as she poured him his cup, adding the heavy dose of sugar and cream she knew he preferred, did the man have any heart to him?

Instead of an encouraging glance or any sign that their kiss had touched him in any way other than lust, he sat there poker straight, as if the entire meeting bored him.

Meanwhile, M. Troussebois shifted his tiny frame this way and that, until he seemed to find a comfortable spot in the chair. He'd tasted his coffee, then set it aside to open the leather folder he'd brought with him, sorting through his papers, absentmindedly dropping some, reviewing others, and for all Lily could tell, he had forgotten his client altogether.

Lily glanced over at Webb.

He shrugged his shoulders as if he too were at a loss as to what to make of the de Chevenoy solicitor.

Feeling ill at ease with the lack of conversation, Lily said,

"Would you like some cake with your coffee, Monsieur Troussebois?"

Startled, the man looked up at them, his pinkish eyes blinking rapidly as if trying to figure out where they had come from. "Oh, my. Oh, yes. If it is no trouble," he said in a rush.

She placed several tasty-looking morsels on a plate and handed it to him. "I suppose this is difficult for both of us. But I hope we can have the same working relationship you had with my father. I know he held you in high esteem," she lied, wondering what had ever possessed a smart man like Henri de Chevenoy to hire such an obvious ninny.

"Oh, yes, your father," he said, with an odd smile. "A good man, though not without his own idiosyncrasies, shall we say. Like why he left his dear daughter in Martinique for so long? Or kept your existence such a secret from so many, including myself, I am afraid to admit. Imagine my surprise when I found his last will and testament left everything to you, a daughter few knew he had."

Lily smiled. This was ground she felt comfortable with, as Webb had drilled the responses into her.

"My father thought it best that few knew of my existence so as to better protect his family," she offered in quiet even tones, trying to sound like a girl who'd been closeted away for the last eight years and unused to such attentions. "France has been through some turbulent times since I've been away. From my father's letters and the news that reached the good sisters, I am sure the secret of my existence, while a shock to most, is easily understood as the extraordinary steps taken by a protective, loving parent."

Her smooth words seemed to put the man at ease. As he continued to ask questions about her life in Martinique, her memories of her home, and how she found Paris changed, his nervous demeanor softened subtly. By the end of his

quizzing, he appeared almost pleased as she answered his
inquiries with a practiced recitation of her fictitious life.

M. Troussebois sighed as she finished a quaint story about
her admitted inability to learn to dance.

"Why Monsieur Francois was nearly driven to distraction
with my two left feet."

"Oh, Mademoiselle de Chevenoy, I can't see how such an
enchanting young lady as yourself could be anything but
graceful as a bird on wing," he told her. "Now that we are
thoroughly acquainted, I must address the more necessary
business part of our relationship. As you know, your father,
the former Comte de Chevenoy, known most recently as
Citizen de Chevenoy, left you a rather handsome inheritance. In fact, from my preliminary estimation, you could be
worth close to . . ." the man paused, shuffled through his
papers and then named the amount.

While Webb remained outwardly cool, not showing any
surprise at the astronomical amount, Lily didn't miss his
slight intake of breath. It had taken all her self-control not to
let her jaw drop upon hearing the amount of de Chevenoy's
accumulated wealth, which, as Adelaide, was now at her
disposal.

"I can see," Troussebois said, "that you didn't realize the
extent of your father's estate. As it is, you are easily one of
the wealthiest women in Paris."

While Lily guessed that Henri's work for the British government paid well, she could not understand how he could
have made this tremendous fortune.

And more importantly, held on to it during the Terror and
the recent Directory regime without drawing undue attention to himself.

No wonder the little solicitor looked so nervous.

She wondered just how much Troussebois knew about de
Chevenoy's business with the British and what other illegal

ventures the wily agent had dealt in. Lily knew Webb would ring a peal over her for departing from their practiced scripts, but she took a calculated risk to see if she could ferret out the truth.

She took the approach she thought the flowery, oblique little solicitor would find the most unnerving, the direct one.

"How could that be possible, Monsieur Troussebois?" she said, trying to look as confused and innocently demure as possible. "There must be some mistake. The Tribunal seized my father's estates just after I left. I hadn't thought there was anything more than this house and perhaps a small trust from my mother's dowry. Surely not such a tremendous fortune."

Webb edged closer to her, taking her hand in his, squeezing it. *Leave off, don't pursue this.*

She ignored his subtle warning and continued anyway.

Troussebois, hiding behind his cup of coffee, smiled over the rim of the china cup as if he hadn't quite heard her question.

For most of their meeting, she'd felt the solicitor had been grilling her as if testing her veracity, and now it was time to see how much he knew.

"How could that much money be possible?" Lily asked again, lowering her voice and hoping she sounded nothing more than truly concerned. Setting Webb's hand aside, she leaned forward and waited until Troussebois had taken a large swallow from his coffee. "I hope there is nothing illegal in any of this."

The solicitor sputtered. "Mademoiselle! How can you think of such a thing? Your father was a model citizen, a true patriot."

Lily nodded. "You misunderstand me. I am just a little overwhelmed to find out I have inherited such a vast fortune, and at the same time, I am trying to be cautious, Monsieur. I may have been in Martinique, but I am not so innocent as to not understand that my inheritance will lend itself to some serious questions regarding how my father, during the most tumultuous period of history, amassed such a fortune! I only fear for myself and for what people might say as to your dealings with my father."

There, she'd laid it out, and if there were more brains than wool between his ears, as she now suspected, he would understand her meaning fully.

Betray me, and as surely as I breathe, you will go down with me.

His nose twitched. "Well, I can assure you there is nothing untoward about this money. Your father was just an extraordinarily fortunate man and a shrewd investor. While the de Chevenoy *château* and lands were forfeited, the Comte was able to keep this house and your mother's dower house in the countryside."

"That still doesn't explain how my father retained two properties and continued to prosper. My eyes were wide open as I entered the city. I have seen the condition of the houses and the streets and the businesses, while this house appears to have remained untouched. It just seems unusual."

"Count your blessings, my dear girl, and think nothing further of this. It is better for all concerned." He scratched his chin. "A house in the country can be quite a nice respite in the summer. Perhaps you recall it? It is about an hour's drive from here."

"Ah, yes. It is near *Château Malmaison*," she said. "I remember it quite well."

"Good. So you will understand that your wealth puts you in a rather enviable position. There are many other *émigrés* returning to France who are coming back to much less, if anything."

Lily lowered her gaze. "How good you are to point out

my happy fate, Monsieur, in light of the misfortune of so many others. I will do well to remember that."

"I have tried my best to conceal the amount of your inheritance. This type of money tends to bring out the worst sort of rapscallions, especially when the holder is as gentle and kind as you."

Lily demurred to his praise by attempting to blush.

"At least," M. Troussebois said, "you have the protection of a fiancé to ensure that you are not abducted or compromised." He turned his gaze on Webb. "I can count on you to protect our heiress?"

"You can be assured of it, sir."

"Mr. Milne," Lily said, "is quite protective of my good interests. He was so kind as to provide one of his ships for my crossing and made every effort to see that I arrived in Paris without any delays." She paused and beamed up at Webb, hoping she looked as lovesick as she sounded. "I am sure my father would have more than approved of such a husband for me."

"Ah, yes, this marriage," Troussebois said, clearing his throat. "That is a . . . difficulty. While I can see you have chosen well for yourself, it was not your place to do so."

Lily felt a strange foreboding even as the man continued. "What do you mean? I am of a legal age and with my father gone there isn't anyone to object to this marriage."

"That may have been true in the past, but because of the size of your inheritance, the court was ordered to appoint a guardian for you. Your guardian will have to give his approval before you can consider undertaking this marriage."

"My guardian?" Lily asked. "And who might that be?"

"The First Consul." Again Troussebois swallowed. "General Bonaparte. He has taken an immense interest in your welfare, for which we should all be most grateful."

Lily thought the man sounded anything but grateful.

Troussebois took another sip of his coffee before he continued. "In fact, I have here a standing order from our illustrious leader that you are to present yourself at the Tuileries Palace on the first reception night after your arrival." The man paused for a moment. "Which, as it turns out, is tonight."

Chapter 9

"What ever possessed you tell that man we would be delighted to attend the reception tonight?" Webb said as he watched Troussebois scurry up the street, his great flapping black coat twisting and turning in the blustery afternoon wind.

He turned and glanced over his shoulder at Lily, who sat primly on the settee, in the process of selecting another roll. Her lashes fluttered with an innocent air, as if she hadn't the vaguest notion as to what he was talking about.

How many times did he have to remind her *she* was the inexperienced agent, which meant she followed *his* orders precisely?

Obviously once more.

"You are not in charge of this mission," he told her, "and from here on out you will do as I say, and not take any more of these untrained, undisciplined forays on your own."

She buttered the bread, and just before she popped it into her mouth, she said, "I think Monsieur Troussebois suspects I'm not Adelaide."

Webb stared at her, unsure of what to make of her preposterous notion. "And you came to this conclusion after thirty minutes with the man."

She nodded, her mouth full of roll, stray crumbs clinging to her chin.

Oh, this was perfect. Now she was directing their mission with probably nothing more than some female intuition. The day he started living his life based on the assessment of this overweening chit was the day he'd hand in his resignation. Crossing his arms over his chest, he asked, "What makes *you* think that?"

From the stormy look on her face and the flash of green fury in her eyes, his gibe hit the spot.

She swallowed and rose to her feet. "He was testing me. You were here. Didn't you think he asked an inordinate number of questions about my family and my life? Why would he ask these things unless he didn't believe who I was? When Thomas died, I'd never met his solicitor, but when the man arrived at our home, he never questioned my identity. He just expressed his heartfelt condolences and then proceeded to tell me how his bill was paid and how much he received."

Webb opened his mouth to make some glib remark about her quick, inexperienced appraisal, but then he realized she might be correct.

"If I didn't know better," she said, "I would think that Monsieur Troussebois is well aware of Henri's, shall we say, duplicity, and was testing me to see how much I knew of my 'father's' business." Her brows slanted upward, as if challenging him to come up with a better assessment.

He'd been so busy trying to keep her from carrying her deception too far, that he hadn't paid as much attention to Troussebois's seemly inane chatter.

Now it almost killed him to admit she was right. Troussebois had asked her a lot of questions, even asked some of them twice. At the time, he'd been willing to chalk that up to just being part of the nervous solicitor's bumbling ineptitude.

But wasn't that exactly what a good agent did? Ask a lot of questions—always on the lookout for a momentary lapse in the facts, something to prove this person wasn't who they claimed to be.

And what other reason was there for a rabbit of a man like Troussebois to do that, unless he . . .

Unless he was as atrociously bad as Webb had first surmised or Troussebois knew of de Chevenoy's duplicity and was now working for Napoleon, or worse, his Minister of Police, Joseph Fouché.

Possibilities more credible than he cared to admit.

Especially given the amount of money de Chevenoy had left to his heiress—a fortune in gold a cash starved ruler like Napoleon would stop at nothing to get his hands on. Either by seizing the estate outright, or by controlling her future through marriage.

Napoleon might need the de Chevenoy connections in Paris right now to cement his alliances, but if he decided to brand the family as traitors and seize everything, who would dare stop him? Given that the General had all but left two thousand of his troops to die of fever in the East after his Egyptian campaign, what was the life of one heiress?

He glanced over at Lily, a little in awe of her astute handling of what could have been a disastrous situation.

She sat happily munching a piece of cake.

Had it been pure luck or was there more to her than any of them, his father included, had suspected?

"Not bad for someone so, . . . how did you put it?" she said. "Ah, yes, so untrained." She sat back down on the settee, a self-satisfied smile on her lips. "Now you see why I had to accept the invitation? If I refused to attend it would have appeared as if I had something to hide. After all, what woman in her right mind would turn down a chance to meet the hero of Italy? To see the inside of the Tuileries? Meet Madame Bonaparte?" Lily's gaze rolled skyward. "I had no choice. And I am going, with or without you."

Webb turned his back, afraid she might see in his eyes the grudging admission that she'd made the right choice.

What the hell was wrong with him? He'd been doing this for twelve years. He should have spotted Troussebois's nervous manner and blatant inquiries as the fishing expedition it was.

He knew exactly what was wrong with him, and she was sitting across the room, grinning over her cup of cream-laced coffee like a cat. With her kiss she'd turned him into the worst kind of green agent and then left him floundering to catch up with her.

If he hadn't known better he would suspect she was the professional spy sent to outwit him.

He glanced over at her again and shook his head.

Crumb covered, hair out of place, smudge of jam on her cheek. One moment the siren of his dreams, the next his frustratingly familiar hoyden.

Professional spy? Hardly. Sent by his enemies to drive him crazy? In all likelihood.

"Really, Webb. It is one night." She licked the jam from her fingers. "Tomorrow we'll find the journals and be gone. What possibly could go wrong in one evening?"

With her in his life, he didn't want to consider the possibilities. But perhaps if he could keep from kissing her, could keep bottled up that temptress who seemed to well up from out of nowhere, he'd live long enough to return to England.

And hand in his resignation.

★ ★ ★

Not long after Troussebois left, Webb announced he had business in town and left as well. At first glad to see his glowering presence gone, Lily suddenly found herself alone in the house that was supposed to have been her girlhood home.

Alone as Adelaide, when she hadn't the slightest idea what Adelaide should be doing. Mme. Costard solved her dilemma by asking her if she would like a tour of the house to "reacquaint" herself with everything.

"It must feel strange to be back here," the woman said as they climbed the stairs to the upper stories. "You were such a small mite when you left, I'm surprised you even remember where your room is."

Lily nodded. The house wasn't so unlike many other houses in Paris, and not that much different from the house her parents had kept in the *Fauberg St. Germain*. The brocade covered furniture, ornately carved molding around the doorways and staircase, the smell of lemon oil and beeswax.

In many ways it did remind her of home.

A home she'd been forced to leave at about the same age as Adelaide.

She and Henri's daughter had more in common than Lily cared to admit.

A beaming Mme. Costard guided her every step, proudly opening the doors to the carefully preserved rooms. Lily spent her time cataloguing places where Henri might have stashed his journals.

Yet what struck her most was how the de Chevenoy house appeared to have been passed over by the sweeping tides of the Revolution.

Caught in a magic spell, the little house and its occupants had ridden out the storm with nary a picture out of place.

This, she knew, had been due to Henri's wily maneuvers and his cache of gold.

How much, she wondered, had the man spent to keep himself and the Costards from coming under suspicion? From being turned in? From being arrested in the middle of the night?

Plenty, Lily guessed, as they toured from the attic back down to the ground floor.

"We haven't gone in Father's study, Madame," Lily said, recalling what Webb had said about the locked door. Her hand went to the handle, but she found it was still locked. "Where is the key?"

Madame ignored her, spending the moment polishing an imaginary spot on the gleaming walnut hall clock. "Oh, your father always kept it locked and I guess I just forget he is no longer here." Madame turned as if to head back to the kitchen. "You must be thirsty after all that climbing about. How about a nice cup of tea?"

"What I would really like to do is finish our tour." Lily held fast to her position at the door. "Do you have the key?"

She hadn't been born a D'Artiers for nothing, and she made her statement in the same no-nonsense tones she'd heard her mother use to issue orders to servants when she'd been the chatelaine of a great house.

Mme. Costard responded by reluctantly fishing in the pocket of her apron and drawing out a large ring of keys.

"Your father spent much time in here," Mme. Costard said as she unlocked the heavy oak door and pushed it open. "I'm sorry, mistress. It's just that I don't want you to blame me for the mess. Your father had the strictest orders that I was never to clean this room."

The smell of dust and something else, a faint hint of roses, assailed her senses as the door opened.

No wonder Madame was reluctant, Lily thought, as she entered the cluttered room. Where the rest of the house was in a state of tidy order, Henri's private study seemed at direct odds with Mme. Costard's proud, shipshape custody.

Mme. Costard *harrumphed* from the doorway as dust billowed about Lily's hemline. The lady's prominent nose and rather obvious mustache wrinkled as she followed Lily into the dark room. The windows were shuttered over, and what light did stream into the room from the cracks between the boards showed a maelstrom of dust motes at their entry.

The woman *tsked* several more times at the unsightly mess. "I never could convince him to let me tidy up. And even after he died, Troussebois refused to let me clean, saying that it was better if he organized your father's papers lest I throw out something that had better be burned."

Lily glanced up from the bookshelf she'd been studying. "Burn my father's papers? Whatever for?"

She had no doubts about why Troussebois didn't want the room disturbed, but she wondered why the formidable Mme. Costard had followed the rather timid solicitor's directions.

"Well, uh," Mme. Costard said, waving her apron over a particularly battered old chair, "it's just that your father, he was a bit worried that others might find out about his . . . well, his studies." At this the woman brightened. "Yes, with all these books. He studied in here—that's what he did. He loved his books and wrote many papers on his studies. He corresponded with very important men on a number of subjects. He was quite fearful of losing anything. Troussebois says your father wanted his papers left just like this until someone trustworthy could be found to carry on his work."

"Why would Troussebois go to so much bother?" Lily asked, distractedly running her finger first through the dust on the bookshelf, then across the spines of the books.

"Oh, attorneys. Busybodies all of them. 'Tis a wonder any of them are left, times being what they were."

Lily smiled. "Kill all the lawyers," she muttered under her breath. "It seems you have kept your word, but what say you and I spend the afternoon straightening up this room?"

Mme. Costard's features turned to horror, and on the rather homely woman's face, it was a sight indeed. "Oh, no, mistress. You cannot do that."

Lily only smiled, moving away from the bookshelf toward a small writing desk shoved into one corner. A guttered out candle sat in its holder beside a bottle of ink and a well-used pen.

It gave Lily a moment of pause to realize whatever was on the desk might be a clue as to what he had been working on.

A true spy, she thought, never missed such a golden opportunity. She moved toward the desk entranced, her curiosity outweighing her caution.

Mme. Costard was instantly at her shoulder. "Oh, mistress, I don't think you want to start nosing around here. You'll be a mess in no time, and then where will you be? Late for your party tonight." This time her tone brooked no resistance, and her firm grip at Lily's elbow only added to the finality of their time in the study.

Lily wondered how many spies had to come up against the likes of Mme. Costard?

Her newly appointed duenna clucked away, even as she towed Lily out of the room. "Now a lady should be resting during the afternoon and thinking of all the bright, witty things she will be saying that night. That was your mother's secret."

Frantically Lily drank in every detail of the room, trying to discern some place, a clue as to where Henri had hidden his journals, but only clutter beset her vision. That is, until something bright, something shiny sparkled before her.

At that moment, Mme. Costard released her grip and began fishing again in her oversized pocket for the key ring.

Lily took a step back and looked again.

Tucked beside the door frame, hung a brass key on a small hook.

A spare key to the library? To a strongbox? To a hideaway?

Lily hadn't the time to consider it, only the mere seconds it took to snatch the key from its spot and hide it in her fist.

Wouldn't Webb be proud of her? she thought, ashamed to realize it did matter to her what Webb thought of her capabilities as a fellow spy.

As a partner.

No, she told herself, as she climbed the stairs to Adelaide's room to lie down and rest as Mme. Costard had "ordered." She didn't care what he thought of her.

Oh, yes you do, a small, waiflike voice whispered. *You care. You always have.*

She hurried into Adelaide's room and closed the door behind her.

"Have not," she muttered to herself, flouncing down on the narrow bed with its pink silk coverlet and white lacy trim.

Then forget Webb. Forget his kiss. Forget . . . the voice taunted her.

But Webb's kiss and ardent touch, and the tension flowing between them, hinted of something far more passionate.

Lily studied the key.

If this was to be her one chance at adventure before she returned to the Copeland plantation and settled for another husband, as her parents and neighbors had been hinting for her to do once she completed her period of mourning, she wanted to make sure the secret tale of this mission, which she'd have to carry hidden in her heart, would sustain her for the long years ahead.

Next to the dressing table across the room, Celeste had

laid out her clothes for the evening. The white silk gown was one of Mme. Pontius's more daring creations.

Daring enough to capture Webb's attention, she thought as she rose from the bed, before, like Cinderella, she returned to her life of ashes and memories.

That evening, Webb discovered keeping Lily's siren charms out of sight and in control was easier said than done.

He'd left the de Chevenoy house in a foul mood, his pride sorely pricked by Lily's astute handling and assessment of the solicitor.

His afternoon investigation into Troussebois and his connections hadn't produced any further information about the man other than that he lived in a bachelor flat behind his office. He rented the upstairs portion to several tenants. Troussebois had no debts, no secrets, no mistresses that Webb could find and, more important, no connections to Napoleon.

In fact most of Troussebois's neighbors considered him a sad little man, with no real future. To a one, they urged Webb to find legal counsel elsewhere, rather than seek the aid of Bernard Troussebois.

Now he stood pacing in the foyer of Henri's house, waiting for Lily to finish dressing for their evening at the Tuileries Palace. Part of Webb wanted to grin.

He'd been to the Tuileries on numerous occasions, but never as an invited guest.

He glanced at the clock and realized they were going to be late if she didn't hurry up. Troussebois had kindly lent them his carriage for the short drive to the Tuileries and the driver was awaiting them.

That would never do, he thought. He'd laid out a strict plan to Lily before he'd left—they would slip in with the crowd of guests and be as nondescript as possible, make their presence known and get out of there as quickly as possible.

He still had his misgivings about the evening. Today had proven that Lily could hardly be trusted to stay to their script or keep a civil tongue in her mouth. Though she'd been rather astute about Troussebois, this was Napoleon they were dealing with, and it was better if they stuck to Webb's plan of attack.

Above him Lily cleared her throat.

"You're late," he grumbled before he raised his gaze to her. His mouth went dry at the vision before him.

Ravishing.

The word came to his mind unbidden. Even as he tried to fix his gaze on her, he was distracted by the winking and glittering of diamonds.

Diamonds everywhere.

Around her neck a thick string of diamonds glittered in their gold settings.

Not one to be impressed with jewels, having always thought of the cold stones as merely a woman's security for her old age, he realized he'd never seen a necklace look so alive.

The faceted stones winked and sparkled as if they had just been formed within the fires of the earth.

She literally sparkled with diamonds, winking from her ears in low-hanging earrings, in thick bands around her wrists, and even in her hair, where the white jewels and warm gold of a small tiara seemed to be an extension of the silken and glossy strands.

She started down the stairs, his vision finally discerning the woman illuminating the jewels.

The diaphanous fabric glowed in the candlelight. Her lithe, willowy body moved with the gown as if the fabric were a second skin. The low-cut neckline and the girdle of silk bound beneath her breasts created the illusion of great bounty.

Further down, the gown hung in a straight willowy line revealing the long, coltish length of her legs. Legs a man could imagine wrapped around his waist, legs entwined with his.

Any man that saw her tonight, he thought.

She appeared to float down the steps with all the grace and elegance of a woman born to the manners of Versailles. With a regal, delicate movement, she inclined her head to acknowledge him.

Her hair twinkled with the lights of hundreds of tiny gems.

This is Lily, he tried to tell himself. Troublesome, bothersome, hoyden Lily.

His little Lily.

Not for the first time did he stop for a moment and wonder where that girl had gone—and who this incredible creature was standing in her place.

"Do you think the diamonds are too much?" she asked, twisting her wrist back and forth in a sparkle of brilliance as the stones caught the light of the candles. "Madame Costard insisted I wear my mother's jewelry. They are rather pretty and it is a shame to think of them languishing in a jewel case when they look so perfect with this dress. A fashionable entrance is so very important for making the right impression. I think this dress will make quite an impression, don't you?" She smiled and swept past him.

Before Webb could interrupt and explain to Lily that the jewels she wore weren't her mother's, that she wasn't going anywhere with half the de Chevenoy fortune hanging around her neck, and she certainly wasn't going out half dressed in what should be called a shift, and barely one at that, Costard and his wife came up from the kitchen.

"Oh, don't you look—" Mme. Costard started, before giving way to motherly tears of pride.

"*Harrumph,*" her husband muttered. "Why that dress isn't decent!" He snatched up her shawl, which Celeste had left for Lily on the chair in the entryway, and wrapped it around her shoulders. "Don't you have anything less, less . . ."

"Transparent?" Webb finished for him. "Why, I can see your . . . your . . ." He stopped himself as Lily's eyebrows rose in a mischievous twist.

"Then perhaps, sir, you shouldn't look." She rose up on her tiptoes and kissed Mme. Costard on the cheek. "Thank you, Madame, for your help and thoughtfulness."

"You are not going out dressed in that manner," Webb said. A nodding Costard moved to his elbow in a show of masculine sensibilities. "Why . . . you'll . . . you'll freeze to death."

Hadn't she heard a word he'd said this afternoon about blending into the crowd? Being nondescript? Why a blind man wouldn't miss Lily the way she illuminated the room with those blasted diamonds.

Not to mention her scandalous dress.

"Both of you sound like old fools," Mme. Costard said, wrapping the shawl a little tighter around Lily's shoulders. "*Oui,* the dress is a bit daring, but this is what they are wearing and I won't have a daughter of the Comtesse de Chevenoy appearing in anything but the latest fashion."

Troussebois's driver poked his head in the open door. "Monsieur, if you want to be there on time, we've got to leave now." His blinking gaze caught sight of Lily, and Webb thought the man was going to choke.

"See, I told you," Mme. Costard declared. "Our dear girl looks *magnifique.* So, there it is." With that Mme. Costard started shooing them out of the house and down the steps.

One of Napoleon's guards let out a low whistle.

As Lily swirled past Webb, a triumphant smile on her face, he whispered in her ear, "Just make sure you keep that shawl on."

"You really don't want me to, do you, Webb?" Her voice purred over him in soft, sultry tones.

Webb closed his eyes, wondering if he'd suddenly lost all his skills as a detached, cool agent. Had his thoughts been that transparent?

As transparent, he realized as he followed her sashaying form into the carriage, as her damnable dress.

Chapter 10

During their ride to the Tuileries Palace, Lily found Webb's strained silence a relief. She'd expected him to lecture her the entire route about her deliberate dereliction from his instructions.

Blend in. Be nondescript. Lily couldn't think of anything more foolish. If she wanted to gain control of the de Chevenoy house and get rid of the guards and strictures, she needed to prove she was in control.

And that meant charming Bonaparte.

As her mother had always told her and Sophia, the best defense in the world of men was a fast and underhanded offense. This gown, embellished with the de Chevenoy diamonds, was the best kind of subterfuge she could muster. Though it was freezing, she thought, tugging the lap blanket higher.

Besides, after Troussebois had left, Webb had fled out of the de Chevenoy house. She couldn't help but wonder whether his excuse about seeing to his own lodgings wasn't just that, an excuse for him to get away from her.

The carriage ride to the Tuileries Palace, where Napoleon

Bonaparte, the First Consul and his wife Josephine, resided, turned out to be a short distance away, but in that time, Lily once again saw the tremendous price Paris had paid during ten years of revolution.

Their carriage passed one tumbledown house after another in a neighborhood that had once been the glory of Paris. For blocks she had yet to see a window without broken frames or boards to cover the gaping scars. Remnants and tatters of once-fine draperies flapped softly in the wind. Ornately carved facades and decorated doorways bore the ugly pockmarks of chisels where the thieves had come after . . .

After the owners had lost their heads, she realized.

Gone were the tree-lined boulevards she'd often recalled when she'd thought of her homeland. Heaped amongst the chopped stumps of the once-proud poplars and birch lay piles of garbage, the odor of sewage and rotting remains, filling the air with their ripe and stagnant perfume.

As the carriage took a terrible bounce over a gaping hole in the pavement, the driver tossed down an apology.

Gone was the bright and beautiful Paris of her childhood. Left in its place, she found a broken and aged crone.

"Is the entire city like this?" she asked.

Webb nodded. "Like you saw when we drove in. Though the First Consul has promised change."

She shook her head and drew back from the window. Could anyone return Paris to the jeweled city she remembered and loved?

But all of this made the little house on the *Rue du Renard* just that much more remarkable.

How had Henri saved his home and his head?

Slowly the driver picked his way through the city and finally stopped the carriage before the entranceway to the palace. A footman opened the door and assisted her down. As Webb alighted, he paused, glancing around the yard.

"Is something wrong?" she whispered, shivering in the cold and wrapping her cashmere shawl tighter around her shoulders.

He shook his head. "There's been quite a few changes since I was here last."

"Was that long ago?"

He patted his injured shoulder. "Not really."

This was where Webb had been shot during his last assignment. Lily swallowed, her lighthearted take on the evening and her overblown self-confidence suddenly deflating.

The danger before them suddenly became too real. When she'd agreed to Jefferson's proposal to spy for the Americans, she'd been well counseled that her life would be forfeit if she were caught. Except for a few moments, when she'd first found Lord Dryden in Giles's study, she hadn't really given much thought to what that notion meant. Now, as she looked up at the doorway looming before them, she noticed the guards standing at attention.

Guards at the doors. Guards at the gates. Guards lining the walkways. All carrying rifles fitted with shining bayonets.

A ready and waiting firing squad at a moment's notice, she thought wryly.

And as her frantic gaze danced from guest to guest, she realized further that most of the men alighting from the other carriages or strolling in wore uniforms of one kind or another.

And most of them were looking at her. Not just glancing, staring.

Oh, what had she done? She'd made herself a target for every man in the room. In her naïveté, she'd ignored Webb's good advice, thinking she knew what was best.

She tried to breathe, but the air around her seemed to have disappeared.

Webb patted her gently on the back. "Now do you see what I meant about blending in?"

She nodded, still unable to find the air to speak.

"Just smile," he told her, patting her hand and placing it on his arm as he guided her up the steps.

Smiling brightly, as if the panic forming in her belly were nothing but excitement for the party ahead, she clung to Webb's arm. "Talk to me," she managed to whisper. "Tell me what changes you see."

Tell me we'll live through this night, she wanted to say.

Webb pointed over toward a grassy section in front of the entrance. "The 'Liberty' trees planted during the Revolution are all gone. And the walls," he said, nodding over to the newly whitewashed stonework, "were covered with slogans and symbols from the Revolution. Had been for years."

The warmth of his hand renewed her confidence as they continued their slow progression up the crowded steps.

"During the Revolution, the palace housed the Committee of Public Safety, the men responsible for the worst of the Terror."

"Robespierre." The name still gave Lily nightmares. He'd been responsible for the price on her sister's head, and the near destruction of their entire family.

"Yes, your sister's good friend. It seems Napoleon is removing all visible signs of the previous tenants and distancing himself from their heinous part in France's history."

"Good riddance," Lily whispered, mustering back some of her confidence.

Webb's brows quirked. "That would be a sentiment shared by many, but voiced by few. Stay away from discussions of the past, the future, and anyone currently in power."

"And that leaves what?" she asked back.

"The weather."

She laughed. "A subject you would be well versed on, given your recent experience in the inclement nature of it."

He laughed as well. "You little hoyden. I don't know how you got me into that predicament, but let me tell you it won't happen again."

"I think I may have put us in a worse one."

Down the ornate hall they walked. The robin's egg blue color, white trim, and liberal use of gilt gave the palace an airy, yet regal feel.

"All this is new," Webb commented with a nod toward the paintings and the newly refurbished furniture. "Someone has been very busy indeed."

They passed a group of men, some in uniforms and others clearly taking the dandified fashions of the *Incroyables* to new heights with their ill-fitting trousers and high collars. Their conversations stopped the moment they spied her. Their open-mouthed gaping only confirmed the worst of her fears.

Lust burned in their gazes, but whether it was from the revealing nature of her gown or the wealth in gems she wore, she couldn't tell.

However it didn't take but a few moments for them to recover and fall in step behind her and Webb like a pack of hounds who'd caught the scent of the fox.

Webb noticed the unwanted attention they were garnering and made a point of repositioning Lily's hand and placing it on his forearm with a great show of manners.

It was a possessive move. Motivated, he told himself, to demonstrate to every man in sight that she was off limits.

But whether it was for the betterment of their mission or for something else, he was in no mood to explore his reasons.

Lily's grip on his arm tightened and he glanced down at

her. Part of him wanted to tell her how well she looked, but glancing over his shoulder and seeing the growing trail of admirers she was gathering in her wake, he could only grumble, "What were you thinking, accepting those diamonds?"

Her gaze flicked ahead, her mouth pursed in disapproval. "They were my mother's."

"Need I remind you the Comtesse de Chevenoy was not your mother?" he whispered into her ear, an intimate gesture, again meant for the men who watched her.

"Do you think me that foolish?"

He didn't answer.

She smiled and nodded at the next group of lingering guests they encountered.

This group was no subtler in their overt curiosity than the last.

"Madame Costard insisted," she whispered back. "What was I supposed to do? No, Madame, I cannot wear my mother's jewels because the woman was not my mother?"

"Did you have to wear all of them?"

She muttered something under her breath about men, a disparaging comment he chose to ignore.

"Really Webb, no woman would refuse—"

He held up his hand. "—refuse to wear her mother's jewels?"

"Precisely." She smiled at him.

This time they passed a group of ladies who immediately set to whispering behind their fans.

"Don't you find these people excessively rude?" Lily commented. "They stare as if they have no manners. I'll be glad to be away from here tomorrow."

"That is, if we find the journals tonight. We can't leave Paris until we find Henri's journals."

"We'll do that tonight when we return."

"I doubt it," he confided. "I checked the door to Henri's office while I was waiting for you, and it's still locked. I even tried to pick the fool thing, but no luck. The man was meticulous about having only the best locks."

"Then it helps to have the key," Lily commented, sliding back the edge of her glove. She tipped her arm and revealed a green ribbon tied around her wrist, and attached to the ribbon, a brass key.

"Where did you get that?"

She grinned, readjusting her glove. "From Henri's office, when I was in there this afternoon with Madame Costard. She didn't give me much time to look around, but as we were leaving I spotted this on a hook by the door. I assumed it might be important so, you could say, I borrowed it." Her eyes sparkled like the gems in her hair.

It was sheer luck, he told himself that she'd found the key. Sheer luck. But he knew it wasn't just that.

She was his match and partner in every sense of the word, but before he could tell her, a commotion to the right of them erupted.

"Oh, my gracious!" a large woman exclaimed, stepping in their path. "The de Chevenoy diamonds. I would recognize them anywhere."

The woman's voice carried down the hall, stopping most of the conversations, as the other guests tipped their heads to get a better look at the developing scene.

"And if these are the diamonds, then you must be my dear, lost Adelaide." The woman hustled Lily into a hearty hug, drawing her into a motherly embrace, great rolling tears springing to the woman's dark brown eyes.

After several moments of wailing and carrying on, the woman thrust Lily out at arm's length. "You are the image of your dear mother, my girl. Why the very image. You nearly gave me apoplexy when I saw you coming down the hall, for I thought it was my dear Comtesse de Chevenoy come back from the dead." The woman glanced over at Webb, but only for a second as she turned her watery gaze back to Lily. "You don't know who I am? You don't remember me, do you?"

Lily shook her head. "I am sorry, Madame. I have been away so long."

"Oh, your father was criminal to send you away from me. I told him I would raise you as my own dear daughter after Marie's death, but he was a stubborn fool and insisted on sending you to that infernal convent. But now you are back, and I will be able to see you take your rightful place in society, just as your mother would have wanted."

"And you are?" Lily prompted.

"Why your dearly beloved godmother, Roselie-Jeanne Paville. Well, not your real godmother, but it's what your mother would have wanted if she hadn't died. Your father never honored her wishes, but that is such ancient history now. You must call me *Tante* Roselie, as you did when you were a child."

Lily's performance even took Webb aback.

Where she found it, he didn't know, but his little hoyden had more daring than he'd ever suspected.

Her mouth fell open at the woman's introduction, and very prettily, she brought her hand up and touched the woman's face. "*Tante* Roselie? *Vraiment*?" Tears sprang to Lily's eyes. "*Ma chère Tante* Roselie! How kind you are to still remember me."

Webb spied several women in the crowd drawing out lacy bits of handkerchief to wipe their own tears. The little scamp was charming the room with her pretty display.

"This is all my fault," Roselie said, "that you do not know me. But your father insisted on sending you away, and then with all the . . . problems in the last few years, I have been a terrible godmother to you. Why, you are a young woman, and I have been deficient in seeing you brought up. But all that is forgotten now, and I shall make up for all our lost time."

Now with the introductions well in hand, *Tante* Roselie threw her arm around Lily and began towing her down the hall. Lily glanced back at him.

Webb shrugged at her, trying to tell her this was all part of the deception—the unexpected.

He caught up, and fell in step with Lily and her new champion.

The woman turned to him. "And who might you presume to be?"

"*Tante* Roselie," Lily said, "this is my betrothed, Monsieur Milne."

Roselie shook her head. "A betrothed? Oh, my dear child, what have you done?"

"Is something wrong?" Lily asked.

The woman waved her hand. "No, it is nothing. Tonight I want to introduce you to everyone and show Paris what your wicked father has kept from us these many years."

"An introduction, Madame Paville," one of the men from behind them called out. "To your sister, is she not?"

The others laughed at Madame's blush, but were quick to lean forward for the lady's proud introduction of Mademoiselle Adelaide de Chevenoy, newly arrived from Martinique.

He had felt them circling like Russian wolves since they'd entered the palace. Now they grew bold . . . and hungry as they pressed forward throwing out a flurry of offers.

Webb noted that Mme. Paville ignored him, nor did anyone seem to care whom the man at Adelaide de Chevenoy's side might be.

"Mademoiselle, a dance later, if I may," said an older man wearing a stylish coat and bowing low over Lily's hand.

This would-be suitor was hastily elbowed aside by a younger man, his ridiculously high collar rising nearly to the top of his head. "Leave off, Letourneau, she is too young for you," the man announced, a wicked grin flashing across his face. "I offer you a personal tour of Paris, Mademoiselle. All you must do is but ask, and I am your most grateful and willing servant."

The sudden swell of attention sent Lily slightly off balance, and she clung a little tighter to Webb's arm, glad for the steady support he offered.

"Gentlemen," Webb said, the strength of his voice enough to quiet even the most attentive of her newfound admirers. "I would ask that you give my fiancée some air. She is newly arrived in Paris and not used to so much attention. I would hate for her to take ill and miss tonight's entertainment. *N'est pas?*"

Lily fluttered her hand in front of her face and added to the drama of Webb's announcement by wavering slightly, as if she were about to faint.

His warning worked, though not without some grumbling from the crowd.

"Thank you," she whispered. "Whatever is the matter with them?"

"You are what is the matter. Given the impression you've made already, we'll be lucky if we get out of Paris alive."

"Don't you think I look like the de Chevenoy heiress?"

"Only too well," he said, his voice lowered for only her to hear. "The jewels and the gown are bait enough to attract some, if not all, of Paris's finest fortune hunters. If you looked like an ox rather than just danced like one, at least we'd be able to winnow out all but the most unscrupulous. As it is, Mademoiselle, you are too enchanting, too enticing, and all together too much of a temptation." He brought her fingertips to his lips and kissed them, sending grumbles of displeasure throughout the male half of the crowd.

Lily thought Webb was teasing her at first.

Enchanting? Enticing? A temptation?

Then the heat of his lips seared through her gloves, teasing her fingers. She glanced into his hooded gaze, where desire and admiration blazed to life.

Webb found her tempting! Dizzy with the very notion, she barely heard *Tante* Roselie, as the woman stepped back to where they were standing.

"Oh, dear, you are the talk of the evening and you haven't even entered the rooms yet! And once everyone finds out you went to the same school as our dear Josephine, you will be the toast of the city. Why you have the same regal bearing and refinement, though I think that is more a matter of your breeding than any gentle education the wife of the First Consul claims. I noticed it the moment you approached." She fluttered her fan, her face a study of rapture. "You'll be copied and aped before the evening is out."

Lily half-smiled at the woman's rush of words.

"Oh," she said, "how successful it will make me to have such a connection to Josephine. My dear little goddaughter practically schoolmates with the most important woman in France."

Schoolmates? The word snapped Lily's attention back to the danger at hand. Webb's grip on her hand increased, and she felt as if he were willing her to be cautious. "Why would you think that, *Tante* Roselie? I've never met the First Consul's wife."

"Of course not," Roselie said, "Our Josephine grew up in Martinique, but came to France several years before you arrived there. Surely you know of her family there? Oh, what was her name before she married that Beauharnais rascal?" The woman tapped her chin with her fan. "Oh, yes, I recall. De Tascher de la Pagerie. Her family called her Rose." The lady leaned forward. "That is why I am so close to dear Josephine. We share the same name, as well as the time we spent together in the Carmelites Prison just before that wretched Robespierre lost his head. I must say, prison has such a way of binding people together."

Lily hardly knew what to say, but Roselie didn't seem to notice her loss of words, continuing on in her uniquely oblivious way.

"Well, what I have been trying to tell you is that Josephine attended the same convent school as you did in Fort Royal. *Les Dames du Providence*." The woman laughed. "Oh that is quite amusing, *Les Dames du Providence*. And now it is providence that brings you two together."

The tension Lily felt in Webb's hold on her hand spread through her limbs like fire.

Why hadn't anyone told her?

Surely of all the information Lord Dryden held in his packet of papers, the fact that she and Bonaparte's wife had attended the same convent school might have merited mentioning.

Roselie turned back to the room before them as she announced, "I suppose you two will have much to talk about."

"Oh, yes," Lily said, forcing a smile to her lips, as she realized they were the next in line for announcement. "It should be a rather enlightening evening."

Chapter 11

Roselie Paville clearly meant to take center stage with Lily's presentation. And she proceeded with all the determination of a field marshall, using the growing curiosity about the newcomer at her side to part the crowds.

Much to Lily's relief, the crush of guests prevented her from making Mme. Bonaparte's acquaintance for almost an hour.

Not that Roselie seemed to mind, having made good use of the delay by dragging Lily from one clustered knot to another, introducing the de Chevenoy heiress as if she were newly arrived royalty.

Lily saw immediately the error in her decision to wear so much jewelry. As she remembered, her mother had worn an inordinate amount of gems while at court, so she hadn't thought her own modest choices overly much.

In Napoleon's nouveau clutch of friends and hangers-on, such obvious wealth was something to notice and something that inspired whispered speculation, and worse yet, envy.

"Oh, about time," Roselie huffed. "Josephine is finally

free. Come along, my dear, now is your moment of triumph."

Or my complete and utter ruin, Lily thought, as Roselie once again caught her by the arm and dragged her across the room.

Lily had caught glimpses of the first lady of France throughout the evening, and was struck by her ethereal grace, her calm, pleasant mannerisms, and the way she held herself with noble ease—attributes her guests would be well advised to copy, Lily decided.

Looking around wildly, Lily hoped to spy where Webb had shied himself off to, but the man was nowhere to be seen.

So much for that thread of fate Celeste was always jabbering on about. If she and Webb were bound, as the woman liked to predict, then why couldn't Lily pull him to her side right this moment.

"Madame Bonaparte," Roselie began, "you will have to excuse my terrible lapse in not presenting this dear girl earlier, but you have been so popular this evening that we have had to beat a pathway to your side. I hope you will find this young lady as enchanting as everyone else has, for she has been touched by the grace and serenity of your Martinique origins. I would like to introduce . . ."

Lily took one more frantic glance around the room.

It was no use, she realized. She'd have to brazen this out all on her own.

While Roselie continued on with her long-winded introduction about Adelaide's time in the West Indies, Lily kept her gaze demurely focused on the floor, all the while taking one calming breath after another to still her beating heart.

At the appropriate moment, she dropped into a deep curtsy, one Sophia had taught her, and rose to take the outstretched hand of Josephine Bonaparte.

She glanced only a moment into the bright eyes of Napoleon's wife and then found herself staring at the man at her side.

"*Enchanté,* Mademoiselle," Mme. Bonaparte said. "May I introduce Monsieur D'Artiers, another newly arrived *émigré* to Paris."

Lucien's startled expression told Lily her brother hadn't received Sophia's note.

She had the presence of mind to hold out her hand to him. "How nice to meet you, Monsieur. Have we met? Your name and face are terribly familiar."

He took a step back and stared at her outstretched hand, at the diamonds, and finally at her face.

"Lily—" he began.

"Lily?" Roselie repeated, stepping back for a moment. "Why Monsieur D'Artiers, how droll of you to give our Mademoiselle such an enchanting nickname." She slapped his shoulder with her closed fan. "Why she does look like a pale spring lily, and soon to be the fairest lily of Paris, if I don't miss my mark."

She shook her head at her brother so slightly she wondered if he even noticed through his confusion and outrage.

Lucien, don't say another word.

Lily tried to breathe again, the stifling air of the room closing in around her. What the devil was she going to do?

"Oh, dear," Josephine said, gazing over Lily's shoulder. "It appears my husband is insulting more of my guests, and he's stormed out before offering the appropriate apologies. I must make amends before the damage is too great. Madame Paville, I may require your assistance. I am sure Monsieur D'Artiers will act as an escort to your lovely friend while we smooth over the ruffled feelings across the room." She turned to Lucien. "Do you mind, Monsieur?"

"Not at all," he said, wrapping Lily's hand firmly into the curve of his arm.

As the two ladies left, Lucien immediately steered her into a corner out of earshot and as removed from the gathering as was possible without drawing too much untoward attention. She took the seat he offered and fluttered her lashes in feigned innocence, hoping to defuse the obvious questions about to explode from her eldest brother.

"Don't even try to be coy with me," he said. "Lily, what the devil are you doing here?"

"Don't call me that," she whispered back. "As far as you and everyone else in this room is concerned, I am Adelaide de Chevenoy."

"Adelaide de Chevenoy? You're stark raving mad is what you are." He stood up and paced a few steps around her. "And I'm going to take you home immediately and put an end to this nonsense right here and now."

Joseph Fouché, Napoleon's Minister of Police, excused himself from the party the moment the note reached him, entering Bonaparte's office a few minutes later.

"Did you see her?" the First Consul demanded. "Did you see how every man in the room fawned after her attentions?"

For a moment Fouché was at a loss as to which woman Bonaparte referred—his foolish, flirtatious wife or the de Chevenoy heiress. Instead of replying, he nodded his head knowing full well it was only a matter of time before the man's explosive temper would lash out and reveal the true object of his displeasure.

"A fiancé! Who said she could become engaged? I will not have it. De Chevenoy was a valuable servant of the Republic and I will not have his daughter taken advantage of." Bonaparte rose from his desk and began pacing about in front of the fireplace, his boots tromping across the carpet in precise measured steps.

Fouché nodded, placing his most placid and thoughtful expression on his face, as if he agreed with his master's displeasure.

De Chevenoy a valuable servant of the Republic! Bah! Fouché had his own thoughts about the man, but not ones he was going to voice in front of Napoleon Bonaparte. Not until he had proof. When his leader turned and shot him a questioning look, he knew he needed to answer. "It does seem rather inconvenient. But I am sure with her so close to your Majesty's affections, you will be able to redirect her future most advantageously."

The perfect response, the Minister of Police thought, just the right amount of adulation. Many in the court surrounding Bonaparte had started using the title "Majesty" when addressing him, if only to curry favor or gain his goodwill.

And in this case, the flattery worked.

"Hmm. I think you are right. Without a father or husband to look over her, she's lost. A woman needs the right man to direct her future, not some fortune hunter. And that fellow has the look of one, don't you think?"

Fouché nodded again.

Napoleon continued. "The de Chevenoy heiress can't be lost to some upstart American. She should have a French husband. A loyal one."

"And one to manage her fortune as well."

Napoleon returned to his seat, his blue eyes narrowing. "The fortune, yes. Such a lot of money. How is it that Henri de Chevenoy was able to amass so much?"

At this Fouché smiled. This was his element. And it was the right time. He spoke softly at first, forcing Napoleon to lean forward, his growing greed evident with each word Fouché spoke. "The de Chevenoy name is one that has been

tossed around in the wrong circles for as long as I can remember. And now suddenly he has a daughter. I've verified
his wife did bear a child—but there has been no record of
the girl since the Revolution. At least none that I can find—
as yet. Perhaps his daughter will be able to enlighten us as to
her father's source of income. And how she has spent her
last few years.''

"You suspect she is an imposter?''

Fouché watched the First Consul mentally tallying the
heiress's fortune, his eyes lit with greed. "To prove her an
imposter would leave us with no course but to seize all the
de Chevenoy holdings.''

Few in Paris did not know that Josephine's creditors were
once again clamoring for payment. Foolishly Bonaparte had
handed over the remodeling of the Tuileries to Josephine,
and while her taste was impeccable, the woman paid whatever price the merchant named, no matter how exorbitant.

The idiot woman hadn't any more sense than the last lady
who'd presided over the palace—Marie Antoinette. Greedy,
grasping harpies both of them, Fouché thought, though
hardly a point worth sharing with the lady's husband.

Not if he wanted to live.

"We cannot just seize her money,'' Napoleon said, his
voice a mixture of reluctant justice and regret. "De Chevenoy had too many friends—from the Royalists to the
Jacobins to the Directory. He was too well connected. Taking her money and arresting her would anger the wrong
people. People whose support we need. It would also dis-
courage many of the *émigrés* from returning. And I need
their support.''

Fouché realized what Bonaparte wanted of him was to
give him the hope that the girl was a fraud. Find a way to
"legally'' steal the fortune now held by this mere slip of a
woman. He had some evidence, but not anything he was

about to share with Bonaparte. Not, that is, until he had his case completely prepared, for he didn't want anything to ruin his opportunity to bring such a great prize to the First Consul's feet and cash-strapped coffers.

"Might I suggest," Fouché began, "a citizenship hearing. Apply some legal pressure to the situation. If anything, it would give us a good cover with which to do some, how should I put it, some untidy investigations. You know, make her prove she is who she says she is."

"Yes, yes, that is an excellent idea, Fouché. Set it as soon as possible."

The Minister of Police knew a note of caution would be best, thereby covering his own neck in case the girl could truly prove her case. "And if she is de Chevenoy's legitimate heir? Her fiancé will more than likely do everything in his power to ensure his future bride retains all the money due her."

"What betrothal?" Bonaparte said, his voice rising in anger. "I gave no permission for this *mésalliance*. An American shipowner, bah." He waived his hand in dismissal. "I don't like the look of this Monsieur Milne. An opportunist if ever there was one."

It takes one to know . . .

Fouché cut off his errant thought as Bonaparte started to spill out his plans for Henri de Chevenoy's daughter and her impressive fortune.

"You are right, my friend, if she truly is de Chevenoy's legitimate heir, then we have to make plans for her future, if you understand what I mean."

Fouché nodded, his mind now awhirl with plans. "How unfortunate for the dear girl if she and her betrothed were tied to smuggling, or perhaps Royalist connections. Treason can be so disastrous for young love."

"As long as it is all legal. I will not have anyone say my rule in France is not fair and just." At this, Bonaparte smiled, the two men in perfect agreement.

If Adelaide de Chevenoy and her fiancé proved to be difficult, then Bonaparte wanted the problems removed.

Permanently.

Webb put on his most bored expression as he eased back into the party and past the knotted groups of guests, like he hadn't a care in the world.

No one looking at him would have guessed he'd just heard the First Consul and his Minister of Police discussing the murder of the crowd's new favorite, the de Chevenoy heiress.

When he'd noticed Bonaparte's abrupt departure, and overheard Fouché hastily summoned to attend the First Consul's private office, his natural curiosity had gotten the better of him.

If there was one place Webb was familiar with, it was the Tuileries. His first visit, some eight years earlier, was when he'd been arrested by the Committee of Public Safety. He'd been interrogated in the very room that was now Mme. Bonaparte's bedchamber.

Since the fall of the Committee and then during the Directory, he'd slipped in and out of the palace on missions for his father, to the point where he probably knew the hallways and passageways, secret and not so secret, better than its current occupants.

Moving silently in the shadows of the doorways, he'd managed to slip into the office of Bourrienne, Bonaparte's harried secretary. He'd seen him earlier at the party and only hoped the quaint mademoiselle the man had been chatting with was still holding the man's rapt attention. Once he gained access to the office, he quickly found exactly what he was looking for—a stairway that led from

Bourrienne's ground floor office to Bonaparte's first floor suite.

He knew that stairwell only too well—for it had been after his sentencing by the Committee that he'd been led down the same steps on his way to *Abbaye* prison.

It had only been a matter of positioning himself behind the door that opened into Bonaparte's office and listening.

Not that he'd liked what he'd heard, but hopefully the key Lily held was to Henri's study, and they would find his journals tonight and be gone before first light.

Back to England, back to safety, back to their separate lives.

It was a thought that should have filled him with joy. But instead it filled him with questions. With each kiss, he found himself drawn closer and closer to the little hoyden. She was weaving a spell around his heart, entrapping him with her siren ways.

What could he do? Make her his mistress?

He certainly didn't want to face Giles or either of Lily's brothers at the end of pistols at dawn over that insult, but he certainly wasn't about to marry her just to satisfy the longings she brought out in him.

Marry Lily? He almost laughed.

He had always envisioned himself retiring to some country manor, taking his place in society, finding a suitable miss to marry and raising a respectable brood of well-behaved children.

The little hoyden had too much of the Ramsey lineage in her blood to ever be called respectable.

He glanced casually around the room, looking for her. She was nowhere in sight.

Taking a deep breath, he continued on through the crowds, trying to catch a glimpse of her.

Not that she should be that hard to find, with all those diamonds, she glowed like a walking candelabra.

So where the hell had she gone?

He tried to ignore the fact that he hadn't heard all of Fouché and Bonaparte's conversation. What if they'd made plans for Lily before he'd been able to position himself in the stairwell?

He felt his composure slipping as his heart thrummed against his chest and his hands knotted into hard fists. For the first time in his life, Webb found himself fighting a growing wellspring of panic.

That's what happens when one is forced to work with a partner, he thought, as he edged his way along the dance floor. You spend more time worrying about your partner's safety than the mission itself.

He should never have left her alone.

He spotted Roselie standing just to one side of Josephine, and for a moment, his fears abated. Until he realized Lily was still nowhere in sight.

If something happened to her, how would he tell her family? How would he live with himself? In that moment, Webb realized he would never be able to tear her image from his mind. The gangly little girl might be lost to him forever, but in her place a worldly, intriguing woman was stealing his heart.

Perhaps, he thought, a respectable bride was overrated.

"Monsieur." Roselie rushed over to his side, her fingers closing around his arm. "Why you look as though you've lost something precious."

He smiled as graciously as he could. "I have, Madame. I seem to have misplaced my betrothed. Have you seen Adelaide?"

The lady looked about. "Oh, she was just here. Madame

Bonaparte and I left her in the care of one of these pesky *émigrés*. I didn't think it prudent at the time, for he had the look of a fortune hunter, but dear Josephine insisted." Roselie glanced left and right, her gaze scanning the room until it came to an abrupt halt. Her mouth flapped open as if to say something, then snapped shut as she averted her gaze from the far corner.

"Um, perhaps you should look for her in the hallway, Monsieur," the lady lied feebly, pointing in the opposite direction. "Some of the young people have moved their dancing out there."

"Thank you for your assistance, Madame," he said, his gaze having followed Madame's to the damning evidence. Even now he spotted Lily tucked away with a newfound companion, their heads bent together intimately.

He could see Lily's face clearly, but all he could discern of her companion was his broad back and dark auburn hair.

As he moved closer, he realized her hand sat resting on the man's knee. Then to his shock, her newfound paramour curled his fingers around her chin, a move filled with familiarity and more than just casual acquaintance.

While he'd been nearly out of his mind with worry, she'd been dallying in a corner with some court ne'er-do-well.

A jolt of jealousy rocked Webb out of his earlier fears.

Whoever the hell this amorous cad is, he thought, murderous intent turning his vision red, *has about two seconds to get his hands off my betrothed before he finds himself propelled from the nearest window.*

My betrothed?

He didn't bother to correct himself, at least until he found out whose life, Lily's or her lover's, he was about to cut short.

* * *

"How is it that you are here in Paris and not in London?" Lucien demanded. "And parading about as Adelaide de Chevenoy?"

"Would you lower your voice?" Lily smiled at a couple passing by. Obviously Sophia's note had not reached him. "As I said it's rather hard to explain."

"I don't need any explanation. This has Sophia's doing written all over it!" Lucien leaned back, his arms crossing over his chest. "The next time I see her, I'll throttle her for endangering you so."

"I am perfectly safe. And this wasn't Sophia's doing, I volunteered to come," she lied.

"As if you could do this on your own." He shook his head as if it was an impossible notion. "Sophia may be capable of these types of escapades, but Lily, you know as well as I, you'll end up getting yourself, and who knows how many others, killed."

Lily bristled at her brother's unflattering and cutting conjectures. They had never been close, separated as they were by so many years. He'd been married and long gone barely before she'd gotten out of the nursery. The years of the Revolution had only added to that distance.

Now he presumed to know what was best for her.

"I am perfectly able to make my own decisions about my life, Lucien. For now you have to trust my judgment and leave me be."

Lucien blew out a loud breath. "Leave you be! I hardly think so. The last time you were left to your own devices you ran off with that Copeland lounger." He reached over and patted her cheek. "Don't you see, I have only your best interests at heart."

She looked away from him, not so much to keep him from seeing the tears stinging her eyes, but to hold her tongue in check, biting back the reply burning in her throat.

So what if she'd run off and married the wrong man?

It was her life, she wanted to cry out. A fact no one ever seemed to remember.

Not Lucien, not their parents, not Sophia, and not even Webb.

"You're a foolish, headstrong girl. And I am sure neither Mama nor Papa would approve if they knew what you were up to." He rose, taking her hand in his and pulling her to her feet. "You are coming with me tonight and tomorrow I will see you personally to the coast where you will find yourself on a ship to London." He paused from his speech for a moment. "No, make that Virginia. You'll go back to Mama and Papa where you rightfully belong. Why they ever let you continue to live at the Copeland plantation after that rogue's death, I'll never understand. You should have been brought home right then, where you could be properly supervised."

She did her best to ignore Lucien's more pompous assertions. Go away with him tonight?

Not when she had other plans for the evening.

Foolish, headstrong plans though they were, they were her plans and not her brother's business. But Lily didn't get the chance to tell her brother what she thought of his designs for her.

Webb did it quite nicely.

She didn't see him at first, only the hand catching Lucien at the shoulder. Suddenly her brother spun in a quick circle as if he'd sprouted wings.

"Unhand my betrothed," Webb said, in a low menacing voice.

For a moment, the jealous, raging tone of his voice sent a thrill through her veins.

Jealous? About her? If he wasn't about to make a terrible mess of their mission, she would have danced for joy.

"Leave off, you fool, I'm her—" Lucièn started to say, in a voice too loud for Lily's comfort.

"My newfound protector," she cut in. "Oh, please Monsieur Milne, no violence, not again," she said loud enough for the nearby guests, milling as they were in a curious circle, waiting to catch any note of gossip about the wealthy newcomer, Adelaide de Chevenoy. "The last man who dared look at me is still recovering from your savagery."

She caught several of the women shivering and then saw them give Webb a second, closer look.

"Stop it, both of you," she whispered, elbowing her way between the two posturing men. She turned to Webb, dropping her voice to barely above a whisper. "You fool, you are making a scene over my brother." She flicked her gaze to Lucièn. "There is too much at stake, Lucièn, to risk it over this matter. Look at this man, don't you recognize him? You know who he is." She paused for a second to let her words sink in. "None of this will be decided today. Not now, and not by you."

She laughed out loud and, wrapping her arm around Webb's, sidled up next to him like a contrite mistress caught with another man. "My foolish beloved, Monsieur D'Artiers is a friend of the family. His *chère* mama and mine were girlhood companions. Why, we practically grew up together, isn't that right, Lucièn?"

Her brother looked caught in a quandary. His widening eyes betrayed his recognition of Webb, and the darkening flicker in them told Lily he approved even less of her current course of action or choice of companions. Much to Lily's relief, Lucièn glanced around and more than likely saw the questions on everyone's faces. Slowly he held his hand out to Webb in greeting.

"My apologies," he said, bowing slightly. "Adelaide is like a little sister to me. If I seem overly familiar or protective, it is because of our family connections, and those, Monsieur, are as important to me as *blood*."

Webb inclined his head slightly to acknowledge Lucien's veiled threat.

"Do you remember my father's house?" Lily asked. When Lucien said he did, she invited him to call. "I do so want to hear all about your delightful family."

"I'll be by tomorrow," he said in clipped tones, before he bowed and made his exit. "First thing in the morning."

"Time we followed suit and made our excuses as well," Webb said. "We may have a long night ahead of us."

Pleading fatigue from all her travels, Lily said her farewells to their hostess and then to Roselie, who promised to call the next day.

Lily hoped the only thing Roselie would find at the de Chevenoy household tomorrow afternoon would be a missing heiress.

As they hurried down the long, gilded corridors of the palace, Lily clung to Webb's arm. She sensed an overwhelming tension flowing from him. While she thought at first it was due to their encounter with Lucien, the way he towed her out to the courtyard, led her to believe there was something more on his mind.

Webb halted their frantic pace just outside the main entranceway and waved to their driver, who sat waiting beside the gates.

"That was close," she said, shivering in the damp cold air moving in from the nearby Seine.

The driver clucked to his horses and directed Troussebois's carriage toward where they stood. Steam blew from the animal's breath in great moist clouds.

She looked up at Webb. "Apparently Lucien never received Sophia's note."

"That doesn't bode well for us." He handed her up inside the dark recesses of the carriage.

After he gave the driver directions, she caught him glancing back at the palace and muttering to himself as he climbed in beside her.

"If Lucien didn't get your sister's note, then who did?"

Chapter 12

Webb held back from telling Lily about his foray into the heart of the palace. If they found the journals tonight there would be no reason to worry her about a fate that would never come to pass.

For come the morrow, the de Chevenoy heiress would disappear, a mystery that would leave Napoleon a rich and happy man and Paris society mourning the loss of such a bright flower.

To his relief, she didn't question his earlier disappearance. It was as if she hadn't noticed that he'd been gone for nearly an hour. Instead she sat in moody silence in her corner of the carriage, a thoughtful frown lining her features.

A protective part of him wanted to shelter her from the truth—that if they didn't get out of Paris as soon as possible, in all likelihood their lives, certainly his, would be forfeit.

He'd all but forced her, blackmailed her, into coming on this mission, and now he may well be leading her to her death.

The rational part of him reasoned that Lily seemed to understand the importance of finding the journals and quit-

ting Paris as quickly as possible, without his having to give
an explanation. She'd made no protests about leaving the
Tuileries early but then again her interview with her brother
hadn't looked like it had gone well.

Still, it didn't seem quite right not to tell her.

If Lily were some typical English miss, he realized, she'd
fall into a case of vapors when told of their precarious position. And it was the typical English miss that he'd instructed
his mother to search for in the Marriage Mart. The demure
sort who, once she'd recovered from her faint, would then
give him a firm, but politely worded demand to be taken
home. A woman who would consider the extent of her duty
to her country and husband that of providing an efficiently
managed home, a half score of well-behaved children and
the proper social backdrop to promote his standing within
their carefully chosen social circle.

Lily hardly fit that mold, he thought, as she jumped down
from the carriage without waiting for the coachman, and
made her way, in that direct, no-nonsense manner of hers,
up the front stairs, and opened the door with the key Costard had given her.

No, Lily D'Artiers Copeland, for all her protests of being
unworthy of this assignment, carried her secrets and deceptions like a master spy.

Webb considered that one of her most intriguing qualities.

And for some reason, the idea of unwrapping the lady's
mysteries appealed to him more than the thought of spending the rest of his days wedded to some dewy-eyed miss.

Indeed, Lily was not a woman from whom he could hide
anything. He owed her the truth.

The Costards had left a light burning in the hallway, the
silent house evidence that the couple had long ago sought
the comfort and warmth of their bed.

"Shall we?" Lily whispered, dangling the study key by its green ribbon.

He nodded.

She slid the key into the lock and turned it. The first tumbler fell with a loud thump that seemed to echo through the halls of the quiet house. She frowned at this newest wrinkle.

Before he could offer a suggestion, Lily pulled her shawl from her shoulders and wrapped it around the doorknob, concealing the lock below. As she continued turning the key, the tumblers were silent, their noisy signal muffled by the cashmere.

The knob turned and she slid the door open with the silent, practiced ease of one accomplished in cloak and dagger skullduggery.

He knew he should celebrate her quick, astute handling of each challenge she met, but it seemed each time she succeeded, she left him with more questions about her than answers.

After they entered the study, Webb closed the door behind them. Holding a single taper high, he looked about the familiar chamber. It had changed little with Henri's passing—the same piles of books, scattered papers, and general disorder the man had preferred.

Lily ran her finger through the layer of dust on the shelf. "When I was in here this afternoon with Madame Costard, she apologized for the state of this room. Apparently the study has been off limits since Henri's death."

"This layer of dust is a good sign," he commented. "It means this room has gone undisturbed and we are the first ones to search it."

He set the candle down in a silver holder on the small table next to the chair Henri often sat in to read.

"I'll start with his desk," he told Lily. "Why don't you

start with the bookshelves. Open every book, and make sure the contents agree with the title. Be on the lookout for hidden panels in the shelves or anything else that appears unusual."

She dropped her shawl on a leather-bound chair near the hearth. "Do you have any idea what these journals look like?" she asked, her gaze moving over the floor-to-ceiling bookshelves lining either side of the small fireplace.

Webb shook his head. "I didn't know Henri kept any until my father told me."

Lily sighed and set to work.

For a while they worked in companionable silence, until Lily blurted out, "You wouldn't have believed my brother's audacity tonight!"

Webb waited for her to continue, but then realized she wanted him to prompt her. "What did he do?"

She closed the book in her hand with a decided slam. "He expected me to leave with him. Just like that. He even went so far as to insist that I return immediately to my parents' home in Virginia, as if I were some errant miss run astray. He treats me like . . . like . . ."

"Like older brothers treat their younger siblings." Webb pulled open another drawer and began sorting through the mishmash of papers. "My brothers used to do the same thing to me. When I began working for my father, he thought it best that I apprentice with my eldest brother, James. When James suspected any trouble, he'd ship me off on some useless errand where I wouldn't be in harm's way."

"What did you do?" she asked.

"I outfoxed him, finally. We were in Madrid, and I knew we needed to obtain papers that had been stolen from a naval ship. The information in them was vital to British actions in the Mediterranean. We found out they were being held in the house of a royal aide. When I heard James negotiating with a flash-cove to steal the papers for us, I slipped away and did the job myself. I not only succeeded in half the time, but also saved the Foreign Office a healthy measure in bribes.''

She laughed. ''That's all well and good for you, at least you were able to go with your brother. My family and . . .'' she paused for a moment, ''and others always think of me as 'little Lily.' Always in trouble, always headstrong, as if I'd never aged beyond thirteen.'' She turned away.

Guilt hit him hard. She'd included him in that group, and dammit if it wasn't true. He'd argued against including her for just the reasons she'd stated. In all the years they'd been apart, it had never occurred to him that ''little Lily'' would grow into a woman of deceptive wiles.

One capable of deceiving not only his sense, but also his heart.

Hardly little Lily, he thought, glancing at the curve of her bare shoulders, the soft, sensual glow of her skin, and the very womanly lines from her breasts down to her softly rounded hips.

He should tell her.

Tell her now, before his thoughts wandered any further afield. Webb almost laughed. Nothing like a good discussion about imminent death to kill amorous thoughts!

Yet telling her was akin to trusting her.

Trust Lily? Like she'd trusted him?

Come to think of it, she'd never divulged her reasons for her outright refusal to go to Paris. Or her claimed engagement to the likes of Adam Saint-Jean.

Truly, what could Lily, of all people, be hiding?

But he was fast coming to the realization that their labors were to no avail and he would be compelled to tell her the truth. After Webb had examined every piece of paper in the various drawers, cubbyholes, and nooks, he continued by nearly taking Henri's desk apart piece by piece in an attempt to find the hidden journals.

"Anything in the shelves?" he asked.

She shook her head. "The desk?"

He held out his hand.

She peered into his palm and grinned at the collection of old pen nibs and odd coins. "Some treasure you found there. I'll stick to the de Chevenoy diamonds." She patted the tiara sitting slightly askew on her head, though the stones still blinked and glittered as if they were bedecking a perfectly attired princess.

Lily's once-white dress now held a distinctly grayish hue from the clouds of dust she'd launched with each book plucked from the shelves. Her previously perfect coiffure lay in tired coils down her neck.

Still she worked, tirelessly and without complaint. He could tell she was doing a thorough job, carefully checking each book and studying the text like a lookout scanning the horizon for any sign of enemy ships.

He set to work on the other pieces of furniture in the room, feeling the cushions and upholstery, searching for anything out of the ordinary.

Lily replaced the last of the books. "Any other ideas?"

Webb stood in the middle of the room, eyeing the walls for possible hidden panels. "Let's take down the paintings."

They carefully removed each frame. Webb examined them, but found nothing. In his estimation, they had done just about everything short of chipping away the plaster on the walls, and yet they had not found the journals.

Lily's worried gaze fell on him. "Now what?"

"How do you feel about spending the rest of the night in Henri's bedroom?"

She tipped her head and glanced coyly at him. "I thought you'd never ask."

* * *

Costard stood at the first-floor landing looking down the shadows of the hall toward the closed door of his late master's bedchamber.

"What are they up to?" Mme. Costard asked, startling him with her sudden presence at his side.

"Don't creep up on me like that, wife." He nodded his head toward the telltale shaft of light leaking out from beneath the closed door. "They were searching in the study for the last hour and now they are rifling through the master's chamber."

Mme. Costard shook her head. "They'll be filthy before they're done and probably expecting me to clean their clothes."

Costard frowned. "That's not what should be worrying us."

Madame nodded in agreement. "Perhaps. Still, I hope she had the good sense to change out of that lovely gown before she started nosing around the house. I'd hate to think of such a fine thing being ruined."

He glanced over at his wife.

"Well," she began, "I thought our sweet little girl looked quite lovely in it, and it would be a shame if she couldn't wear it again."

"Madame, you would do well to remember that the woman in there is not our Adelaide."

She nodded. "I know, but it is rather nice to have someone around the house again. And she is a pretty thing, so like our lost girl. And her young man. They are so much in love, I shouldn't wonder that they'll be married in this very house before Christmas."

"Have you gone mad?" An incredulous Costard nearly choked on his words. "In love and married? That pair? They are agents playing roles to infiltrate our home and our lives.

They are no more in love than they are engaged. I think the winter drafts in this house have addled your good sense."

His wife's gaze rolled upwards. "I've seen how she glances at him when she thinks no one is watching. And did you see his face when he saw her tonight?"

"There was plenty to see, I'll agree with you there," he complained. "If she had been our Adelaide, there would have been no going out in that indecent rag. Bah, what they call fashion these days. Mark my words, if there was anything in that man's eyes tonight, it wasn't love."

"Bah, yourself, you foolish old man," she said looking down the hall at the light flickering under the door. "That boy loves her, he does. He just might not know it yet." At this she smiled and wrapped her meaty hand around her husband's arm. "Just like you didn't know 'til I knocked you on the head and told you what for when you finally came to."

Costard remained unconvinced, though experience had taught him that his wife was more often right than wrong in her assessments.

Hadn't she been correct about the butcher and the Widow Henriot last spring? And her with seven children to feed! But just as his wife predicted, the crabbed old bachelor had eloped with the penniless widow.

"Maybe it wouldn't be so bad," he conceded, "to spend the rest of our years serving the two of them, if they do decide to stay." He ignored his wife's knowing smirk. "I never said she's not a nice, polite one, and he seems to have a good head on his shoulders. Sharp too, that one. He'll not let the Corsican shave our necks if there is trouble."

"Well, they aren't going to find anything in there tonight. I'm half tempted to tell them the old master never used that room after the Comtesse died. What with all the trouble they are going through," she said, wrapping her thick wool shawl tighter around her night rail. "Oh, well, it gives them more time to come to their senses. Come along back to bed, husband, so we don't disturb their fool's errand. Let them do their work, so come morning, we can continue to do ours."

"I thought when you invited me up here, you had something a little more interesting in mind than this," Lily said, as she climbed up from the floor where she'd been kneeling in order to peer under Henri's bed. "Now what do we do, Webb? The journals certainly aren't here." She yawned and stretched before plopping down on the canopied bed. Their search of Henri's bedroom had turned up nothing. Her eyes struggled to stay open, sleep pleading with her body to succumb to the comfort of the downy coverlet and soft mattress. "It'll be morning in a few hours," she hinted. "Suppose we continue searching then?"

Webb shook his head. "We can't. We need to find them tonight." He paced from one side of the room to the other, his gaze scanning the room, as if there were something they had missed.

He reached over and shook her. "Lily, you can't fall asleep. When you toured the house, did you see anyplace else where Henri could have hidden his journals? Someplace, anyplace?"

She rose up on one elbow. "What aren't you telling me, Webb Dryden? I won't be sheltered and cosseted from the truth. I get enough of that from my family." She rolled over, until she was sitting upright next to him.

"I suppose you do," he laughed, though it was a hollow sound. "You've proved yourself a powerful partner, Lily. I mean it. Your sister couldn't have done better tonight, what with that business about the convent and running into Lucien." His hand closed down over hers, and they sat there for a moment staring at each other. "You handled things with all the aplomb of a seasoned agent."

She eyed him suspiciously. While she was thrilled to hear his praise, she gathered there was more to his words. Something he wasn't telling her.

His fingers caressed hers. She shivered at the contrast between the cold bedroom and the heat of his touch. Without a word, he took off his coat and covered her shoulders.

Again a charged silence fell between them, like the tension and crackle of a coming thunderstorm.

Lily glanced away, unable to look into Webb's dark blue eyes without thinking of how he'd looked at her earlier in the day when they'd kissed in the salon.

And how much she wanted him to kiss her now.

Somewhere in the house, they heard a door close.

Webb leaned over and snuffed out the candle, plunging them into shadows. In the street below, a lamp glowed, casting a flickering, pale light into the room.

"Shhh," he whispered, his lips just a breath away from her ear, his arms enfolding her into his chest. "Stay still."

As if she would want to go anywhere else. His warmth surrounded her.

For a while they sat there, enclosed in each other's arms, listening to the silence around them. The house creaked once or twice, but besides their own breathing and the hammering of their hearts, it seemed no one else was about.

"Do you think they heard us?" she whispered.

"No," he said. "If they had, they'd have come in to investigate."

His hand stroked her bare arm, leaving a path of gooseflesh along her skin.

"You can't change the subject on me," she persisted. "What are you keeping from me? Our rendezvous with our ship isn't for another fortnight, so why must we find the journals and leave now?"

Her hips bumped against the hardness of his thigh, her legs brushing against the lean length of his. The enticing silk dress, which before had seemed like a good idea, suddenly felt too thin. It allowed the heat of his body to scorch her senses, the intimacy of their touch as if they were almost naked.

Almost. But not really.

And the thought of her body, stripped of its thin silk barrier, pressed against him, their skin sliding over each other, made her breath come in a sudden rush of longing.

A passion so heated, so hard, so long in the waiting that she didn't know how to control it, or whether she wanted to.

This was exactly what she'd planned when she'd chosen this dress and lit her hair and body with the fire of the de Chevenoy diamonds.

She'd wanted to start a bonfire. And now it threatened to overwhelm her senses.

Distract her from the secrets Webb obviously held as tightly as he held his heart.

"What is it, Webb, that you mean to protect me from?"

He turned his head away from her accusation.

"So I am to be protected?" She paused and ran her fingers over the white lawn sleeve of his shirt. "Who protects you, Webb? Who protects you from me?"

His eyes, dark with desire and then anger, gave away his emotions. He rose from the bed so quickly, she nearly fell off at the abrupt loss of his supportive frame. "This isn't a game, Lily. Our lives are at stake."

"So I've gathered." She sighed as she brushed back a stray lock that had fallen over her face. "And when did you plan on telling me this rather noteworthy piece of information? Before we were arrested or on the way to the guillotine?"

To her surprise, Webb laughed. "I think you would have gathered that we were in trouble about the time Fouché and his thugs knocked the front door in."

Not in the mood to be humored, she persisted. "Tell me, Webb. I need to know what we are up against, so I don't make any mistakes."

Mistakes that could kill you, she thought, her brother's dire words echoed back at her.

You'll end up getting yourself, and who knows how many others, killed.

Webb turned his back to her, and in the shadows of the darkened room, Lily felt the weight of his burdens settle over her heart. She rose and went to him, stopping a few inches from his back. She reached out and let her hand fall on his shoulder.

He flinched at her touch, as if it seared through his flesh to his very core.

"Tell me, please," she whispered.

When she'd all but given up that he would ever include her in his worries, he spoke, his words quiet and even.

"Bonaparte has ordered Fouché to find out everything he can about Adelaide de Chevenoy, then publicly discredit you. Hardly a surprise, but it appears our Corsican friend wants control of the de Chevenoy fortune. Fouché, on the other hand, is a more deadly foe. He wants the de Chevenoy secrets. Our secrets." He turned and faced her. "Both men are used to getting what they want. And neither is averse to killing anyone who gets in their way. We haven't any more time, Lily. If Sophia's note is in the wrong hands or you are right about Troussebois, it is a matter of hours, or if we are lucky, days, before they will come for you."

She swallowed. "And what about you? If you heard this much, they must have mentioned Adelaide's betrothed."

"I am to disappear as soon and as conveniently as possible."

Lily didn't have to ask about their mission, it was obvious that if the journals weren't in Henri's study or bedroom they would in all likelihood fail. For the diaries could be in a thousand places, and short of tearing the house apart stone by stone, they would not find them in time.

So their only choice was to continue to search until they were caught.

Lily hadn't come all this way to die, at least not before she'd had a chance to live. And living meant seeing at least one of her dreams come true.

"Then, Webb, if we have only this night left, I suggest we use our time wisely."

She stepped back from him and pushed first his jacket and then the narrow silk bands of her gown off her shoulders. The silk fell in a soft heap at her feet.

Chapter 13

Lily stood naked before him. Not Lily, but a goddess, his goddess. Even in the meager light from the street lamp below, the sight of her fair skin, lush breasts, and graceful limbs stopped his breath.

Stunned by the vision before him, Webb reached out and slowly touched her cheek.

His eyes closed as her fingers slipped under his shirt to run up his chest. This was real, for there was no ignoring the fiery path her fingers traced across his skin.

Tonight she seemed intent on igniting every bit of kindling in her path, until she'd set his senses blazing.

No matter the consequences.

His mind reeled as she pushed his shirt up and over his head. It landed next to her gown.

This isn't right, his reason tried to convince him.

Take her, his body screamed. *Take what she is offering, you fool.*

She tipped up her head and gazed at him. Her soft, green eyes, so full of need, haunted his very soul. "I've always been with you. As you've always been in my heart."

He leaned down to pluck up his jacket and cover her, but she placed her foot over it. "Lily, this is foolhardy. I can't . . ."

"Make any promises? Offer your heart?" She reached up and plucked off her tiara, the diamonds winking at him. She tossed the heirloom onto the bed. Tipping her head, she shook out her hair and let it fall about her head and shoulders in a wild tumble. She smiled, moving closer to him, and stood up on her toes so she could whisper in his ear. "I wouldn't want them if you did. I only want you. Now. Tonight."

The witchery of her sensual offer curled down his spine.

They stood mere inches apart, Lily continuing to torture him with the pure pleasure of her touch. Her fingertips passed over the muscles of his shoulders, along the ragged, raised flesh of his scars—the gunshot during his rescue from the *Abbaye*, a knife fight in a Vienna alley, and his most recent injury when he was winged while slipping out of the Tuileries.

Her fingers traced from his shoulders down through the hair that formed a *V* in the middle of his chest down to the top of his breeches.

She entwined her arms around his neck and brought her body up against his. The silken touch of her breasts nestled against his bare chest. Her hips swayed against him, their sensual cadence awakening a hunger in him he'd only imagined.

Her lips nuzzled at his neck. "Kiss me, Webb."

He nuzzled her hair, inhaling the soft scent of lavender, his arms enfolding her. Then he bent his head so his lips could capture hers.

Lily melted under his tender assault. She'd felt his indecision and his struggle against taking what she offered, and she almost cried out in triumph the moment she sensed the change in him.

He started the kiss playfully, teasing her mouth, encouraging her to open up for him. When she did, his tactics changed, and his lips became hard and hungry, his tongue moving past her lips to challenge her own, gathering up her passion with the thirst of a man lost in a desert.

As if in answer to her long simmering passion, Webb's hands joined his raid on her senses. One hand claimed a breast, reverently exploring with soft light caresses the curves and pebbled surface of her hardening nipple.

She arched toward his fingers, not wanting to miss a single moment of his touch.

All the while, he continued kissing her, until she could barely breathe. When she thought she'd have to gasp for air, he pulled back.

His dark eyes narrowed as he gazed down at her.

"Is this what you want, Lily. Do you really want me?"

She could only nod.

"No more of this nonsense about marrying that Saint-Jean fool, no more false fiancés, no more lies between us."

For a moment she paused. If everything went according to her plans, there would be no more lies between them. At least she hoped there wouldn't be any need for them.

She nodded again.

"Say it," he said, his hands on her shoulders. "I want to hear your vow."

A vow. The words struck her hard. A mistress didn't make a vow, not that she knew of. And if she wasn't his mistress, then what was he asking? Did this mean more to Webb than just one night of passion?

Did it?

She might not live long enough to find out, but she knew

she would at least see the light of dawn—from the warmth of Webb's embrace. She'd promise anything for that.

"I do," she said, leaning up toward his mouth, searching for the heated passion of his kiss.

"What do you promise?" he demanded, holding back his kiss, his touch.

I hope I never have to tell you another lie, she thought. Looking into the dark blue depths of his eyes, looking all the way to his soul, she made her vow. "No more lies," she whispered, hoping to hell that she could stay true to her words.

When he nodded and bent his head to seal their bargain, she felt as if she had just sold her soul.

What if she couldn't keep her word? Not that she worried about tonight, but what about tomorrow, and the next, and if and when they returned to London?

For as his mouth took possession of hers, it was as if he never meant to let her go.

But he would when he found out the truth. Found out that she'd betrayed everything he was, everything he worked for. Betrayed his king, his country, him.

"Webb, I . . ." She tried to tell him, she wanted to tell him, yet the words of betrayal hung in her throat as if there were a noose tied around her neck.

He misunderstood her awkward pause completely.

"I know, hoyden. I feel it as well," he murmured into her ear. "Now it's my turn to give an order. Be quiet, and let this happen."

With that he kissed her again, his mouth swooping down over hers and cutting off her weak protests.

Webb tried to tell himself to stop. But his hunger for the woman in his arms would no more listen to his feeble arguments than he could tell the ebb and flow of the oceans to cease.

This is Lily, his reason screamed. *Remember troublesome, bothersome, Lily?*

More like delectable, passionate, persuasive Lily, he thought, as her hips again rose to brush against his manhood.

She seemed to know just how to tease him, just where to touch him, just when to press her body against him.

Lily was no more the errant child. Instead, she was a woman to contend with.

A woman who, with her courtesan wiles and innocent requests, shattered all his illusions, reawakened his every fantasy.

"Touch me again, Webb," she whispered in his ear. "Please."

He complied most willingly. It was enough to undo a man.

This time though, he let his lips taste where before only his fingers had ventured. He dipped his head down and began suckling at her nipple.

She arched like a cat, a half-sigh, half-purr issuing from deep within her.

His arm wrapped tightly around her back, while his other hand stroked first her belly, then moved lower, parting the heated flesh at the juncture of her thighs.

"Ah, that feels so good," she gasped.

"I think it would feel better if we were lying down." Not wanting to wait another moment to be with her, Webb scooped her up in his arms and carried her the half-score or so steps across the room. He laid her down on a red velvet chaise. She reached for him, but he stepped back, stood towering over her, just wanting, for the moment, to look at her.

God, she was beautiful. He stepped back farther, his gaze devouring the sight of her.

Her blonde hair, loose and falling down past her shoulders, the silken strands shimmering in the pale light. She shifted, raising her arms over her head, giving him a full view of her body, as if she sensed his need just to look.

Her breasts rose, as did her hips, undulating in a slow, sensual wave, as if calling out for his touch.

His arms ached to wrap her in his embrace. His legs tingled with the thought of being entwined with hers. And he ached to fill her, to feel her envelop him.

"What are you waiting for?"

Webb needed no further enticements. He yanked off his boots and with all due haste added his breeches to their pile of forgotten clothes. The cool air hit his skin, but did nothing to cool the fire she'd ignited.

Lily watched Webb stalk back to the settee like a great cat, naked and so masculine. She'd seen a man unclothed before, but seeing Webb like this, she realized how little she knew of them.

Though Thomas had been a handsome, well-formed man, she hadn't realized a man could be so . . . so heart stopping. Webb's life of discipline and constant vigilance showed in the perfection of his body.

Glorious was the word that came to mind as he walked toward her, his muscles moving in taut unison.

How she wanted to touch him, to let her hands and body explore every inch of his muscled flesh.

Lily knew to her dying day, she'd never forget the look in Webb's eyes as he joined her on the chaise. His unfathomable need seemed to devour her senses.

He wanted her as badly as she wanted him. As if he'd been waiting as long as she had.

For a moment he lay over her, just looking into her eyes. With one hand he traced the outline of her face, gently caressing her cheeks, her mouth, her brows.

His touch, whispering now over her shoulder and down to her breasts, left her writhing with pleasure.

No longer satisfied just to be touched, she knew she had to touch him, feel all of him as well.

She ran her hands over his shoulders, marveling at the hard muscles beneath her fingers, at the hot current of need passing from his skin to hers.

His lips captured hers again, and they began another one of those breathless kisses she knew she would never have enough of—yet this time it wasn't enough, she wanted more, to feel more, to give him more.

Instinctively, she reached down and slid her hand over his manhood. The length and hardness gave her both a moment of pause and a moment of sheer anticipation. As her fingers wrapped around him, Webb groaned, the deep, throaty sound thrilling her senses. His body flexed toward her and she continued to stroke him, the pad of her thumb rolling over the silken head and then down the length.

Webb's hand caressed her hip and then moved over to the hot, fevered spot between her legs. Unfolding the soft folds with his fingertips, he traced slow, teasing circles over the bud hidden within.

She'd never felt anything like the coiling tension winding through her body, spreading from Webb's expert touch. She never wanted him to stop touching her, but she knew there was more. She craved to be filled, to have him inside her.

This was what had been missing from her previous experiences—this anticipation, this driving need for more.

"I can't . . . can't wait anymore," she said, in ragged gasps.

"Neither can I."

"Please, Webb, I need you so badly."

Without any further urging, he lowered himself, her legs opening wider.

His raging desire made him want nothing more than to drive himself into her, but she'd driven him to this place with her ceaseless, deliberate touch and now he wanted to inflict the same madness.

Slowly he entered her. First with only a teasing foray, brushing himself into her and then pulling himself out. Beneath him, she twisted and arched toward him, her greedy need trying to catch him and pull him into her.

"Oh, Webb, don't tease me."

He ignored the order, and continued to enter her slowly, back and forth, only going a little further with each stroke, and then pulling himself out nearly to the tip.

He listened to her quick panting, to her sighs, to her gasps, as his guides. Her hips quickly caught his rhythm and swayed insistently against him until finally he filled her.

What he hadn't anticipated was how he felt so complete and lost at the same time, once he found himself sheathed in her welcoming warmth.

Kissing her deeply, while he continued to move inside her, he found himself guided by her thrusting hips and soft cries.

Lily knew she'd been missing something before, but now she knew how much she'd been cheated. Webb's hardness immersed her in sweet torture. She couldn't get enough of his languid strokes. She wanted more, she wanted it faster and she wanted to feel every inch of him as he slid in and out of her.

Each fevered moment called to her, enticed her to take more of him. She felt herself climbing, riding him, wanting him until it seemed her very core, so swollen and close to bursting with need, would explode.

And then it did—in a bright fiery burst, shattering through her in a staggering blast. Webb's deep hard strokes matched each pulse in her body. Her eyes fluttered open and she stared into the triumph of his gaze and then the selfsame torment as he found his release.

She tried to catch her breath, clinging to him, lost in the incredible pleasure that washed away her fevered senses in a succession of soothing waves, leaving her breathless and still but for her pounding heart.

For a moment the stillness of the night surrounded them, broken only by a few stolen kisses and the soft sighs Lily couldn't seem to stop.

"Webb, I—" she murmured sleepily.

"Shhh, hoyden. Go to sleep."

"But I need to tell you—"

He kissed her to still the words. When he pulled away from her, he told her, "We'll talk tomorrow. You can tell me everything then. Sleep, Lily." Webb cradled her in his arms, nuzzling her hair and kissing her lightly on the forehead.

He didn't want to talk, for he was too afraid of the feelings welling up inside him. His arms wrapped tighter around her.

She'd stolen his heart, and it would take a lifetime of chasing her, he decided, to reclaim any measure of it.

They'd find those damn journals, nothing would stop him now.

In his arms Lily mumbled something again, but he couldn't discern the words. Her lashes fluttered, as if she wanted to stay awake, but the more she tried, the faster she drifted into sleep.

Webb watched the woman in his arms. How like Lily to fight sleep, even when it was what she needed most. He brushed back a stray lock of hair that had fallen over her brow. Cradling her tightly in his arms, he wondered at the overwhelming sense of security surrounding them, when he should be fearing for their lives.

What had he been thinking, making love to Lily? It was an

impossible notion, and yet holding her here in his arms, he couldn't imagine any other choice.

Outside, the first rays of dawn were tinting the skyline with faint hints of red and purple. Sighing, he realized their night was coming to an end.

Their night. The first of a lifetime.

Shocked by his own conclusion, the very idea stopped him. *A lifetime with Lily?* First he had to secure their lives, then he could consider such an impractical, foolish, wonderful notion.

He carefully rose from the settee, so as not to disturb her, and gathered his clothing, pulling on his shirt and then his breeches.

He glanced back at her sleeping form. Her hair fell in disarray past her shoulders, covering her breasts. She'd curled up in a ball, her long legs tucked up. He wanted her, wanted her so badly that for one crazy moment he thought of stealing her away from Paris, of leaving his duties and obligations so they could be together.

Forever.

He shook his head at the fantastic notion. This wild, heedless abandonment was not what he wanted. He wanted a gently reared English miss. One who'd run his household with only the most impeccable decorum and sensibility. One whose respectability would be inherent in everything she did.

Decorum, sensibility, and respectability were hardly words he'd use to describe Lily, he thought, as he struggled to pull on his boots.

No, more like conniving, unpredictable, and uncontrollable.

And passionate, and wild, and extraordinary.

Well, he thought, as he picked up his sleeping vision and cradled her in his arms, a man can hardly live on passion.

Why not? The question begged to be answered.

And for the life of him, he couldn't think of an answer.

She stirred a bit, her head still resting on his shoulder. "Where are we going?"

"You are going to bed," he told her as he made his way down the hall to Adelaide's bedroom.

"And you too?" A sly, catlike grin stole over her features. She wrapped her arms around his neck and nibbled at his ear.

He pulled his head back from her witchery. "No."

"Why not?"

"Because I have a bed elsewhere. I don't think Madame Costard would enjoy finding me in your bed. I'd like to keep my limbs attached to my body."

"So would I. I like your limbs exactly as they are." Lily laughed softly before her eyes fluttered shut.

Webb pushed open the door to Adelaide's room with his foot and stalked over to the pink and white ruffled bed. He deposited his sleepy baggage into the satin recesses and pulled the counterpane over her.

She made a few soft noises of contentment and then rolled over, sound asleep.

After standing beside her for a moment, he leaned down and placed a kiss on her brow. "Sleep well, hoyden."

As he rose and turned to leave the room, he spied Celeste standing in the doorway of the adjoining chamber. She wore a red wrapper, her dark hair tied up in a colorful kerchief. From the disapproving set of her frown, Webb gathered she'd seen enough to guess what had happened.

Used to the unconcerned manners of English servants, the West Indies slave caught him by surprise with her direct question.

"Where are that child's clothes?"

Webb felt like a fifteen-year-old caught in the hayloft with a scullery maid. "In Henri's room."

She crossed her arms over her chest. "Are you going to fetch them or do you expect me to?"

"I can," he answered, only too happy to leave the room now.

She made a rude noise in the back of her throat. "Don't bother, you'll probably miss something." Brushing past him, she headed toward the hall. "Though from the looks of it, you did a pretty good job of it, I think."

At that point the first ray of light slipped into the room, blinding Webb. In that brilliant moment, he could have sworn the usually taciturn Celeste was grinning.

Chapter 14

"Wake up, mistress," Celeste said, nudging Lily with a hearty push.

Lily ignored her maid and rolled over. The room was too cold to get up, and when she peeked out from beneath the blanket, the frost on the windows was enough to make her pull the coverlet back over her head.

"Your brother is here."

"I don't have a brother," Lily told her. "I'm an only child."

"Then your friend Lily's brother is here, and he is demanding to see you."

Lily pulled the pillow over her head and groaned. Damn Lucien's hide.

"Mister Webb is with him," Celeste said, her singsong voice holding a hint of laughter.

"Webb?" Lily shot up. "Oh, no." Lucien's stern face when he'd seen her traveling companion hadn't gone unnoticed. Lucien had never approved of their sister's association with the British Foreign Office, and he certainly wouldn't approve of Lily's newfound profession either.

Lucien remained in his heart, despite all the troubles, a loyal Frenchman.

Lily shrugged on the gown Celeste held and tied up her hair as best she could. For a moment she paused and looked at herself in the mirror.

Did she look different? She seemed different.

Webb. She sighed, feeling both the overwhelming love she'd worn on her sleeve as a fifteen-year-old and the content knowledge of a grown woman having found her true heart.

They would find the journals, and then they would . . . they would what?

The realization hit her hard. What future did they really have? She'd thought about it in passing, but had never considered the bond she would forge with this man.

"What is it?" Celeste asked, leaning over her shoulder and staring at their reflection in the mirror.

"I love him, Celeste."

"Well, of course you do. And that is how it is meant to be."

She shook her head. "No, it is wrong. What will I do? How will I tell him about . . . well, you know?"

"When the time comes, he will understand. Of all the men in the world, I think Mister Webb would understand."

It seemed logical that a man of Webb's experience would understand her choice to help her adopted country. Wouldn't he?

She went down to the small dining room expecting to find fireworks, but discovered Lucien and Webb sharing a companionable breakfast. "This is a pleasant surprise," she commented, taking her place at the head of the table. She glanced furtively at Webb, but he was busy chatting with her brother, and when he did look in her direction, his features gave no evidence as to what had transpired between them just hours before.

"Lucien and I met on the front steps some time ago," Webb told her. "We decided a ride this morning would give you some time to catch up on your sleep."

Costard entered the room, bearing a plate of food for Lily.

"I'm sorry for the added company," she told the man. "Is Madame rather vexed with me?"

"She is thrilled to have so many people here to wait on," Costard told her. The man turned to Lucien. "Our former mistress, the Comtesse, always spoke kindly of your dear mother. I hope, Monsieur, she is still well?"

"Yes, Costard," Lucien told him. "My mother and father are very well indeed."

"And how do you find our girl?" Costard said, beaming with pride at Lily.

"I find her an exception to every rule," her brother said. "Did you know that my youngest sister Lily and Adelaide went to school together at the convent. It is on Lily's behalf that I am here."

"How kind of you," Costard said before he left.

After the door closed, Lucien leaned forward and lowered his voice. "Listen well, Lily. I have Webb's promise that no harm will come to you. I understand why you've chosen to do this, if only to repair the damage our sister has caused in her poor choice of allying herself with the English." He paused for a moment and turned to Webb. "No offense, sir."

"None taken," Webb said.

"He has sworn, as a gentleman, that he will see you back to London by the end of the week. No matter the mission, no matter the price to our family, I will not have you in Paris one day longer. Do I make myself clear?"

Lily dabbed her napkin to her lips. "Perfectly. But I have

no intention of following anything you order. You listen to me, Lucien. *I* made my own decision to come here. And *I* will make the decision when *I* leave. If you don't like that, then I suggest you leave."

Lucien's face turned a mottled shade of red. "You stubborn little fool. I could . . . I could . . ."

"You could what? Turn me in? Watch me go to the guillotine? Don't you see that I am doing this for our family, for you and your wife and your sons? For Mama and Papa, so they can return and live out their lives in the country of their birth. So you can reclaim what you want." She leaned across the table and took his hand. "Your life is here, Lucien. Mine is not. My home is elsewhere and it always will be. I've never belonged to any of this, and I never will. I'm like Sophia in that way. We never belonged here, and we know it. So please, can't you fight for the life I want to live, as much as I am willing to fight for the one you want?"

Lucien squeezed her fingers. She knew he'd never say the words, but his meaning was clear.

"I think it is time I bid you both adieu," he said.

They all rose, and after Lucien shook Webb's hand, he turned to Lily.

She didn't know what he was going to do, but all of a sudden, he folded her in his arms and held her tight. "When did you become so wise?"

"When you started listening to me," she told him, looking up at her brother through a sheen of tears.

Lily walked with Lucien to the front door. Suddenly she wasn't so anxious for him to leave, rather, an uneasiness claimed her heart at the idea of being alone with Webb. She was almost relieved to find Troussebois coming up the front steps.

Lily could tell from the worried frown on the solicitor's face his news was not good.

"*Uh, hum,*" he began, "I am glad you are up so early. We have much to discuss."

Lily inwardly groaned, but smiled and invited the man in. She asked Costard to bring a breakfast plate in for M. Troussebois and guided the solicitor into the dining room. Webb nodded at the man, with nary a glance in her direction.

She was starting to believe their late night tryst had been nothing more than a dream.

Troussebois, having finished the coffee and buttery rolls Costard had set out, cleared his throat with an authoritative cough and began. "I have been visited this morning by a secretary from the Minister of Justice's office. The First Consul wants to see your inheritance settled as soon as possible, so he's ordered a citizenship hearing for tomorrow."

"A citizenship hearing? Whatever for?" she asked, feeling Bonaparte's swift hand clamping down on them.

"It is nothing to worry about, just a mere formality. What with all the *émigrés* returning to Paris and making claims for lost properties and incomes, these hearings are a necessity to ensure that only the *true* sons and daughters of France are returned their due."

Lily didn't like the sound of that. "But tomorrow?" she asked. "So soon?"

"Yes, it is rather unusual," he admitted. "Consider yourself lucky that the First Consul has taken such an interest in your case. Once this matter is settled, you'll be able to visit your father's country house near *Malmaison*. Otherwise, your estate could have languished for months, and you would have had little resources with which to live, relegated to only this house, while the country house remained under strict seal."

"The country house is under seal?" she asked, trying to sound confused as well as innocent. "Whatever for?"

Troussebois shifted in his chair. "It was thought best to leave it undisturbed, since that is where . . ."

"Where what?" she persisted. If the journals weren't here in Paris, they would have to search the country house.

"Where your father died."

She shook her head. "No, Monsieur, you must be mistaken. For I distinctly remember in your letter to the Mother Superior you stated that my father died here, in Paris."

Troussebois shook his head. "No, your father died in his country house. And there is talk of taxes and such, which is usual, from what I gather, in large inheritances. In the end you may well have to forfeit that house in order to keep the bulk of your father's estate." The man shrugged his shoulders. "I will do my best, but it is the way of things."

The salon door swung open and Roselie Paville came sailing in.

"Oh, *chérie,* you are up and about. How wonderful. Your mother was always an early riser, so I just knew you would be as well." Roselie frowned at Webb and flicked her glance over Troussebois only momentarily. "I met your maid in the hall. She is a find, a rare find. I would caution you to hide her from Josephine, for she has a fondness for slaves from the West Indies, and she will steal her away. In the meantime, you must have her teach me how to tie one of those wonderful kerchiefs. I've seen Josephine wear them, and I want to as well. It is quite the style, but there is such a knack to getting them just right."

While Roselie continued her nonsensical tidings, Lily glanced over at Webb to see if Troussebois's revelation told him what she had quickly concluded.

If Henri had died in the country, the journals must be there.

They had to get into that house.

"*Tante* Roselie," she said, interrupting the lady's chatter. "Monsieur Troussebois is my solicitor and we are conducting business right now."

"Oh, I can wait," the lady announced, reaching over to the tray and selecting a roll.

Realizing the lady meant to stay, Lily couldn't afford to let their conversation with Troussebois go off course, so she changed her tack. "Perhaps Celeste could show you how to tie her kerchiefs while we conclude our business. It will be so dull for you otherwise."

"Oh, how kind you are, my dear girl. Just like your mother. So thoughtful."

Lily rang for Costard and asked him to find Celeste. Roselie remained seated while they waited for the maid, and Lily realized the woman may be of some use.

"Monsieur," she said to Troussebois, "my father didn't die of some contagion. He died of a heart ailment. Why ever is his house under seal, and why as his daughter, am I forbidden to visit the house where my dear father spent his last hours?" She ended this speech by choking out a few sobs and dabbing at her eyes. She only hoped she could squeeze out a few tears for the effect.

Webb rushed to her side and handed her his handkerchief. "Careful," he whispered in her ear.

Lily responded by choking out a deafening sob. "I just want to be near my dear papa." She turned to Roselie, who was now also dabbing her eyes with a lacy bit of cloth.

"Oh, and you shall, Adelaide," she said, coming to Lily's aid, just as she suspected the lady would. "Monsieur Troussebois, tell this distraught child she will have her country house."

"As her solicitor I will do no such thing," he said. "The house is under seal by order of the First Consul. He wants no one to disturb it until the estate is settled."

That seemed to be enough to quiet Roselie. Luckily for Lily, Celeste arrived and took the meddling woman off for a lesson in West Indies fashions.

Lily continued her sniffling, though in a more controlled manner. "It is kind of the First Consul to go to such measures to protect my interests. But why would he care so much about the country house and not this one?"

Troussebois made a great show of shuffling through his papers and ignored her question.

"Monsieur," she persisted, "why would the First Consul be so concerned about my father or take such extraordinary steps to see my hearing held so quickly?"

"I have no idea," the little man said. For a moment all his blinking and nervous movements stilled. He looked her directly in the eyes. "Do you?"

Lily felt her gambling blood rise. She ignored Webb's fingers as they tightened around her hand. "Perhaps it is because of my father's work."

Troussebois didn't bat an eye. "And what work would that be?"

"You don't know about my father's work? Why I thought you were his solicitor, surely you know about his work?"

Webb's grip started to verge on painful.

The little man shook his head. "With my wealth of clients, it is often difficult to remember so many occupations. Your father was a man of many talents. Which one do you speak of?"

Lily heard the lie and had her answer. Wealth of clients, hah! Gauging from the cheap and out of fashion cut of his jacket, his shabby little carriage, and the way he all but wolfed down every bit of food Costard placed in front of him, Troussebois had perhaps a handful of paying clients, if that. The little man probably knew each one's secrets better than they did.

So if Troussebois felt compelled to play this game of cat and mouse, he must know the truth about Henri de Chevenoy.

But to which side was the solicitor loyal? His client or his country? And did he truly know the Adelaide de Chevenoy before him was an imposter?

Lily had no intention of staying in Paris long enough to find out.

"Why his scientific studies, of course," she said. "What else could it be?"

Troussebois nodded and smiled, looking more than relieved.

Webb let go of her aching hand and spoke. "I have heard that the First Consul is considered a man of letters and a serious student of the arts. Perhaps he wants to protect your father's work from those who might take advantage of your grief."

"Yes, I am sure that is it," the man agreed. "Now let me go over the finer points of your hearing so you can be prepared."

Lily wasn't about to let Troussebois off the hook. Not yet. "Yes, I want to get this out of the way so I can start my life's work."

The solicitor smiled indulgently. "And what is that?"

"Publishing my father's journals."

Webb choked on his coffee.

"Oh dear, this is a surprise to my fiancé," she told Troussebois, as she pounded Webb on the back and then handed him a napkin from the serving tray. "I want to see my father's work given the full credit it deserves and the only way to do that is to see that his journals are published. Do you know where he kept them, Monsieur Troussebois?"

The man turned a deep shade of red. "Well, there is plenty

of time for those matters, but first we must discuss the hearing."

"Oh, bother the hearing," Roselie said, as she reentered the room, her head now gaily decorated with one of Celeste's more colorful kerchiefs. She stood beaming from ear to ear and fidgeting with excitement, her hands flitting from patting the cloth tied around her hair, to smoothing her skirts. "Monsieur Troussebois, I doubt this hearing is as important as seeing my dear Adelaide take her rightful place in society." Now that the woman's ecstatic chatter started, Lily doubted if even the First Consul could stop it by formal edict.

"My dear, oh my dear," Roselie exclaimed. "You have caused quite a stir. Yes indeed, a stir. I've had notes and calls about you practically since sunrise. We have such an interminable amount of things to do before your party this evening."

"My party?" Lily asked.

"Well, of course," Roselie said, as if there were any question of it. "A party in your honor. Madame Benoit insisted and was adamant that she host the first party to welcome you home. How convenient for her that she'd been planning a Christmas party for the last three weeks, ever since the First Consul declared holiday celebrations would be legal this year. Now she can add you as the guest of honor and the party will be called an unqualified success. Oh, I had to endure an hour of her weeping in my salon this morning all because she missed seeing your return last night." A triumphant look crossed Roselie's face as she leaned forward in her confidential, not-so-soft attempt at a whisper. "Madame Benoit has yet to be invited to the Tuileries, so she is just green with envy that she missed out. Just green. Though she claims she was held for nearly a year at the *Abbaye*, I truly doubt she ever had the honor of being arrested. Really, the

Abbaye! Hardly fashionable, that old ruin. No one of consequence was held there. The truly fashionable, like myself and dear Josephine, resided at the Carmelite prison.''

Lily tried to ignore the woman's unbelievable snobbery, which even went as far as a pecking order for the prisons of the Terror. "Yes, well, after my solicitor has given me the particulars of this hearing we can discuss whether or not I want a party in my honor.''

"Oh, we have no time for any of this legal nonsense," Roselie said. "You have an appointment with the modiste in half an hour. Really, my dear, you must find some more demure gowns. The First Consul has made it quite clear that modest is the order of the day from here on out. Then, after the dressmaker's, I promised Madame Benoit we would drop in.''

Lily held up her hand to stave off the rush. "Madame, that all sounds lovely, but Monsieur Milne and I have already made other plans for this afternoon.'' She looked over at Webb and smiled at him, hoping he would jump in and save her from this disaster.

But Webb only shook his head. "My dear, I think you are mistaken. We made plans for tomorrow afternoon, not today.'' He smiled at Roselie, who now beamed with delight. "Why it sounds like a wonderful day for you, especially with all the festivities to prepare for. I am sure Monsieur Troussebois can brief you quickly, but in the meantime I hear my carriage.''

Lily's hands knotted into tight fists in her lap. Why was he leaving her to this woman's clutches when they had so little time?

But Lily had no time to find out, for Webb made his bow to Roselie and nodded to Troussebois before heading toward the door. She followed him and whispered, "Where are you going?"

"Out to the country. You stay here in town, and I will find you later. Just continue, you're doing rather well," he said, his eyes glittering with amusement as he glanced over her shoulder toward where Roselie sat. Out loud he said, "This will be a lovely reward for you. A day with Madame Paville. I can't think of a more fitting way to treat yourself after your hard work this morning."

With that he bid his final farewells and made for the front door. She followed him and caught him by the elbow. "You had this planned all along! Leaving me here while you go out to the country house."

"I'm going to see if I can get past the guards."

She didn't like the careless, devil-may-care twist of his grin. He'd get shot or, worse, killed. Then what would she do?

He kissed her quickly on the forehead, snatched his great-coat from the coatrack, and dashed down the steps to the awaiting hackney. It was a plain carriage, but in good condition—a rarity in Paris.

As he ducked into the carriage, Lily's mouth fell open.

There was another occupant in the carriage. A woman.

Roselie joined her on the steps.

Desperately Lily tried to get a better look, but Roselie caught her by the arm. "*Chérie,* don't be so forward. You really need to be more restrained when it comes to your fiancé. Despite the fact that he is an American, I think even they have some regard for subtlety."

With that Roselie anchored her hand around Lily's wrist. Not that she thought for a minute she could shake the woman free, and even then Lily could hardly leap down the steps and demand to know what Webb was up to now.

Ask him if their night together had meant anything?

Insist he take her along to break into Henri's country house.

Still, she thought, they were partners. She thought he needed her help.

But as the driver slapped the reins and sent the horses moving, she felt as if her heart were being trampled beneath their hooves.

Who was this mystery woman? Webb's mistress?

How could he make love to her and then take his mistress along on the most dangerous part of their mission?

Perhaps this was better, she tried to tell herself as she took one more glance at the departing carriage before Roselie dragged her back into the house.

"Oh, don't look so forlorn," Roselie said, patting Lily's shoulder. "You'll see your young man this evening. I know what it is to be young and in love."

"In love?" she said weakly.

"Why yes, my dear. It is written all over your face."

Lily looked out the window, hoping Roselie couldn't see what else was in her breaking heart.

Perhaps, she realized, she wasn't a very good spy after all. She couldn't even keep her own secrets.

Chapter 15

Joseph Fouché followed Bonaparte's Mameluke bodyguard, Roustam, into the First Consul's private office. Napoleon had brought the captured soldier back from Egypt, knowing the imported guards the Sultan employed were known for their fierce loyalty.

A loyalty now owed to Bonaparte.

"The Minister of Police," Roustam announced.

Bonaparte didn't look up; rather he waved his hand at Fouché to take a seat as he sorted through his afternoon dispatches, muttering to himself, Fouché completely forgotten in the man's tireless desire to rule every aspect of France.

Finally, Joseph coughed ever so slightly to remind the First Consul of his presence.

Not one to linger over formalities, Bonaparte began a series of rapid-fire questions. "Ah, yes, Fouché. What have you found out about this de Chevenoy matter? Can you remove the heiress's claim to her father's money? Have you unearthed anything on this unwanted American? Well, man, what have you to say for your efforts?"

Joseph knew that beneath every question was the one

Bonaparte didn't ask—when could he take control of her money.

"I have had every available man on this matter," Fouché said.

"And?"

"I have some interesting news to impart." He paused allowing the anticipation to grow.

Bonaparte's dark brows rose. "Joseph, you are an excellent minister, but you try my patience. The hearing for her citizenship and estate is tomorrow. You promised me you would uncover enough damaging information to get me what I want. Tell me what you found."

Joseph knew that beyond the man's grasping Corsican relatives, his harlot wife, and her bastard children few dared to push the First Consul to this point.

But Joseph did. Just to remind the man who he was. The Minister of Police with connections in every corner of France. He was Bonaparte's eyes and ears, and he didn't want the man to ever forget it.

"I have a witness who may shed some interesting light on this situation."

At this, Bonaparte's sharp greedy gaze narrowed. "A witness, you say? A good one?"

Joseph nodded.

Leaning across his desk, Bonaparte could hardly contain his excitement, greed lighting his blue-gray eyes. "What?"

"It pains me to say this, but our little heiress is an imposter. Adelaide de Chevenoy died at sea eight years ago."

With Roselie leading the way, Lily reluctantly entered *Frascati,* the luxurious hall where the fashionable Parisians flocked for public dancing.

Their earlier visit to M. Leroy's boutique on the *Rue de Richelieu* had taken longer than Roselie had planned, so Lily had yet to meet their hostess, the illustrious Mme. Benoit. Roselie had insisted that she purchase a thousand little gew-gaws and other "necessities," though Lily had been able to convince her that she did not need a pug puppy, though a much-aggrieved Roselie told her they were all the rage.

As they paused to allow a group of young men to pass by, Lily wondered how any more people could fit into the rooms as she took a deep breath to give the rowdy bunch the extra space they needed to squeeze past her and Roselie. She was starting to doubt the owner's assurances that there was a table waiting for them anywhere in the crowded room.

Lily's feet were already killing her from all their shopping, without adding dancing to the misery.

"Why is Madame Benoit's party being held here?" she asked, surveying a crowd that ran the gamut of every level of French society. Brightly painted *merveilleuses* with their hair cropped into short curls, a style known mockingly as *à la guillotine* and only complete with a thin red ribbon tied around their bared necks. Bejeweled matrons parading with their pampered little dogs trailing behind them on green ties. And everywhere, military officers abounded, in their brightly colored uniforms, gilded epaulets, and shining medals.

"Because everyone holds their parties here," Roselie said. She lowered her head. "No one will admit it, but hardly a soul in Paris has any furniture left, let alone the house to throw a decent party in. Most of the best homes are in ruins." She shrugged the shocking truth off with a quick toss of her shoulders. "These public rooms are all the rage and one can entertain without the embarrassment of obvi-ous poverty. And with everyone celebrating Christmas this year, there isn't a soul in Paris who doesn't want to join in. Besides, the dancing is better here because there is more room. You do adore dancing, don't you?" Roselie hardly paused to catch her breath as she gossiped her way across the room.

A blowsy woman, her face so painted with rouge, Lily thought her taken with a fever, approached them. This, Lily could only assume, was Mme. Benoit.

"Oh, my dear Adelaide. I may call you Adelaide, mayn't I?" she exclaimed, entwining her arm in Lily's and pulling her away from Roselie's patronage. The over-whelming stench of perfume assailed Lily and her eyes watered.

"Your mother was the dearest woman alive," Mme. Benoit continued. "And while I never had the chance to meet her, I am sure we would have been fabulous friends."

She glanced over at Roselie, whose gaze rolled skyward, her expression pained. Lily could almost hear the woman's droll voice extol the sentiment so clearly displayed on her face.

Vraiment. The people you have to associate with these days.

"Oh, I must call you Adelaide, but only if you call me Thérèse."

"By all means," Lily said to the woman whose fame and notoriety, she had learned through Roselie, were a result of Thérèse's careful selection of lovers, having slept her way through most of the Directory and was now cutting a swath through Bonaparte's generals.

Rumor had it before the Revolution she'd been a scullery maid. From the bawdy jest and bit of laughter she shared with a passerby who'd taken a moment to pause and pinch Mme. Benoit in her rounded behind, Lily thought *maid* was probably the kinder description of the woman's former oc-cupation.

"Where is that handsome American everyone is talking

about?" Mme. Benoit asked, looking over their shoulders to the press of people still surging into the rooms.

"My betrothed?" Lily asked. "Why, I have no idea."

Let him spend an evening wondering where I am for a change, she thought, though in her heart she was actually quite worried. When Roselie had dropped her by the de Chevenoy house, Costard reported there had been no sign of M. Milne all day. Celeste had only clucked her tongue at Lily's indignant report about another woman and told her young mistress that she had to be mistaken.

"You are bound to that man," Celeste said, "and he to you. He is not with another woman. This foolish thinking will only bring you trouble."

Celeste's firm convictions didn't alleviate Lily's immediate concerns. Where was he? What if something had happened to him? All she could do for now was continue to play Adelaide and wait for him to return.

"So he isn't here tonight? Oh, that is perfect," their hostess was telling Roselie. "I was so worried there would be a scene."

"A scene?" Roselie's eyes brightened with a delighted glint. "Why ever would there be a scene about our Adelaide?"

The woman put her hands over her brightly rouged lips. "Oh, I wasn't supposed to tell and now I've ruined everything."

Lily, fast becoming bored with the entire situation, started scanning the crowd as Roselie tried to pry the secret from their now-reluctant hostess. She found herself searching for . . . She cursed herself for even considering it—she was looking for Webb.

What if he did arrive, what would she say to him?

She'd never before taken a lover so what did one say? If

she hadn't been stuck in her role as innocent Adelaide, she had a feeling Mme. Benoit could have given her a wide range of advice on the subject.

Around her she suddenly heard excited murmurings, the flutter of fans, and a rising sense of anticipation. When she looked up, she saw what all the fuss was about.

She'd never seen a more handsome man in her life. He appeared to be a familiar sight to the *Frascati* crowd, that or his striking features and height garnered him the open admiration of every woman in the room.

He must have been at least half a head taller than Webb, if that was possible, she thought. Dressed to the height of fashion, his high collar and tightly cut jacket accented the broad muscles in his shoulders. His jet-black hair fell over his brow in a wild, wind-torn type of style. Every feature seemed carved of stone, from the deep cleft in his chin to his hawklike nose and chiseled jaw. His eyes, a magnetic blue, stared only at her, as if there wasn't another woman in the room.

Lily felt herself transported, as if in some romantic novel, like those she and her sister used to read as girls. The only things missing were the white stallion beneath the man, and, at his side, a great broadsword glistening with deadly intent.

All around her the voices, the laughter, and sniping chatter stilled, until the vast chambers of the *Frascati* echoed only with the footsteps of this incredible man as he strolled indolently through the adoring crowd.

He stopped directly in front of her and flashed a blinding smile of perfect white teeth. "Adelaide de Chevenoy?" he asked.

She could only nod and hold out her hand.

He took her fingers in his warm hand and brought them

ever so gently to his sensual lips. The heat of his kiss burned through her glove.

"It is a pleasure, Mademoiselle, to finally meet you."

Lily managed, though reluctantly, to retrieve her hand from the stranger's overly familiar grasp. "And you are?"

"Armand Latour, your rightful betrothed."

Webb entered the *Frascati* ready to kill Lily. He'd arrived at the de Chevenoy house only to find her off to this public arena with Roselie. Shopping was one thing. Public spectacles were another.

He could only imagine the thousand-and-one types of trouble she might find amongst these miscreants and thieves.

As he made his way through the throng of people, he felt the weight of any number of stares on him. The knots of revelers stopped their conversations as he passed and then renewed their whispered gossip in earnest.

He caught vague snatches of it here and there.

"Who will the heiress choose?"

"That Armand is a handsome devil. Can you imagine him in your bed?"

"Bah, the American, now he looks like he can keep a woman happy."

Choose? Armand? Webb tried to avoid the curious gazes and searched the room for his errant betrothed.

What the devil had Lily gotten herself into now?

As he passed the dance floor, he didn't even give it a second glance—if Lily was there, the entire room would be stampeding for the door, but then he saw the awestruck demeanors of the women around him, and the envious, coy glances out to where the dancers whirled and twirled about.

And then he saw her. Lily. Dancing like an angel, she seemed to float and flit across the floor as if her feet had grown wings and she weighed no more than a feather.

Her pale, golden hair sparkled in the candlelight, and her eyes glowed with excitement. Her lithe movements and gracious bearing gave even the fastidious Parisians pause.

"Enchanting," an old woman beside him said, giving him a nudge with her bony elbow. "Why I've never seen anything like it, have you?"

"No, I haven't," Webb said quite truthfully. For a moment he couldn't tear his eyes away from her, caught as he was between her graceful movements and the idea that she had deceived him into thinking that she couldn't dance.

How many more tricks did she have hidden away?

When Webb looked again, this time with a more discerning eye, he gauged her partner. From the swooning gestures of all the women around him, he had to assume this stranger holding Lily too close was the Armand whose name was rife on everyone's tongue.

Webb didn't see what all the fuss was about, the giant buffoon looked like a dressed ape, in his *Incroyables* fashions and his wild mane of hair. He towered over Lily, no small feat given her unfashionable height, and he provided a dark contrast to her fairness.

"Ah," the old woman sighed. "That Armand Latour is a devilish man. If only I were ten years younger. Why I'd steal him away from that young heiress. Oh, I daresay I would."

Webb glanced over at her wrinkled features and thought the woman would be better to make that forty years. But then again there was no accounting for fashion, he thought, as Armand and Lily passed close by, and he heard another round of sighs from the press of women gathered by the side of the dance floor.

The music swelled with a romantic surge and Webb watched Armand turn and pull Lily close, holding her tightly against him.

When Webb thought he'd had enough of watching this

display, he watched Armand dip down and whisper something into Lily's ear.

Her laughter, sweet and clear, echoed through the room. Her lashes fluttered and her cheeks glowed with a quaint rosy hue.

Webb had had quite enough. First this Armand was holding Lily, *his Lily,* too close. And now she was actually flirting with this waltzing baboon!

He resisted the wild urge to march out onto the dance floor and knock Lily's smarmy behemoth on his fancy ass before hauling her out of here and explaining to her just what a proper fiancée does and doesn't do.

Only she wasn't his intended. Not really. A situation he should perhaps remedy.

Marry Lily? He stopped in his tracks. Why it was ridiculous! She was everything he didn't want in a wife.

And now, seeing her like this with another man, and far too happy to be believed, just after they'd, they'd, well they'd reached an agreement.

He frowned. In truth, they hadn't even reached that. He'd told her in so many words how he felt, hadn't he? Obviously it hadn't been enough.

She should trust me, he thought. *She should know how I feel.* His conscience pricked at him.

How? How would she know, when all you've done all her life is try your best to avoid her?

Finally the music ended, and the spectators broke into spontaneous applause as Armand bowed elegantly to his partner, then brought Lily's hand up to his lips in a lingering kiss. His flashing smile to the crowd brought even more cheers and suggestions.

Webb didn't know what bothered him more—the fact that Lily actually looked like she enjoyed the fawning attentions of her inflated beau or the fact that she could actually dance.

Either way, she'd outmaneuvered him once again and he had no intention of letting her get away with it, not now, not ever again.

If Lily had found Armand Latour breathtaking at first glance, their brief acquaintance quickly dashed her romantic fantasies.

Armand turned out to be a pompous boor.

Poor Adelaide, she thought. A death on the high seas seemed merciful compared to a life as this grinning idiot's wife.

"We will dance every night after we are married," he told her. "Such a striking pair we make, we will be all the vogue."

She only smiled. His conversation seemed stuck on two subjects, his fine looks and his social standing. Lily wondered if there really had been a betrothal agreement between Henri de Chevenoy and Armand Latour's father, as he boasted.

Not even Henri de Chevenoy would have been so cruel as to marry his daughter off to this shallow fool.

To his credit, though, Lily found he did have one redeeming quality—he could dance, and with his mastery of the subject, he made it appear like she could dance as well.

Even so, he'd held her far too close for decency's sake and she found his fawning attentions suffocating. About halfway through their dance, she'd been about to send him packing when she'd spied Webb standing nearby.

It didn't take a master spy to deduce his thoughts, for his usually well masked features fairly glowered.

If she didn't know better she'd say he was jealous.

So finally he discovers the other side of love, she thought with amusement.

Then it hit her. Why would he be jealous if he didn't care about her? And if Webb was jealous of her being with Armand, could it mean that he didn't have a mistress?

And certainly if he cared for her, he wouldn't be having an affair with another woman.

Would he?

She couldn't be sure, but she did know one thing, if Webb found Armand's presence in her life unpleasant, then Armand was about to become Lily's favorite new friend.

She entwined her arm around Armand's beefy one and smiled up at the man as if he were the only person in the room. She walked along like this until she nearly collided with Webb.

"Oh dear." She clung to Armand to steady herself. "Monsieur Milne, what are you doing here?"

"I came to find you."

"And so you have," she said. She glanced into his eyes, hoping to see confirmation of what she suspected, that Webb was jealous, but she spied only the professional mask of indifference he wore so well.

Beside her, Armand coughed. "*Chérie*, who is this?"

"I was about to ask the same thing," Webb said, straightening his shoulders and eyeing Armand with a dispassionate glance.

"This is most embarrassing," she said. "Monsieur Milne, I would like you to meet Armand Latour. It seems he and I were betrothed at an early age by our parents. Armand only discovered the agreement after his father's death last summer. By the time he reached Paris to discuss matters with my father, well . . ." she sniffed and turned her head, as if to hide the tears that should be falling at such a moment. "We all know what tragedy he found when he reached

Paris." She paused, as if in reverent silence for her father's passing. "Oh, what a tangle I find myself in. Two betrothals and no father to guide me."

Around them the curious gathered, leaning in to catch every word. She meant to put on a performance that would leave the entire city talking.

"Oh, *ma petite chérie*," Latour said, patting her hand with grave concern. "Your solicitor will agree that our betrothal is the legal one. This other . . ." the man waved his hand as if he thought that would make Webb disappear, ". . . encumbrance is regrettable, *oui*, but as a man of honor, I am sure Monsieur Milne will understand that he has but one choice: to step aside and leave you, so we may live the life our families intended for us."

Lily watched Webb from beneath her downcast lashes and finally, to her delight, saw his legendary control break.

"You are coming with me." He caught her by the arm and dragged her away from Armand.

Lily squeaked out a word of protest, but the look Webb shot her closed her mouth before she dared say anything more.

Besides, she found she liked Webb fighting for her attentions.

"Unhand her," Armand announced, his deep baritone booming through the room. "That woman is mine."

"Like hell," Webb told him, pushing Lily behind him, and swaggering back to face his opponent.

Armand had at least six inches in height and a good stone in weight and muscles over Webb. The last thing Lily wanted was to have the brute pummel Webb into the floor.

She had to find a way to extract him from Armand's challenge, and quickly.

Glancing around the crowd all she saw was the blood lust

in the spectators' eyes. They wanted the fight more than the two posturing men did.

She threw her hand up to her forehead. "I feel faint. Please, someone help me." She held out her hand to Webb, who'd turned and looked as if he meant to catch her.

But Lily miscalculated the distance between them and how quickly Webb could cross it. The only thing that caught her was the floor as she fell hard and hit her head against the wooden planks.

Stars burst before her eyes, and she tried to get up but an overwhelming black void overtook her.

The last thing she remembered was seeing Webb's look of alarm as he towered over her, and then seeing him turn back to Armand, who took advantage of the situation by punching Webb in the chin with an explosive blow.

As Webb reeled back and landed beside her, she smiled.

At least she wouldn't be alone in hell.

"What the devil were you thinking?" Webb asked, removing the cold compress on his bruised chin. He lay on the sofa in the de Chevenoy salon, his feet sticking out over one end and his head cushioned with a generous amount of pillows on the other. He gingerly worked his jaw left and right, and then repositioned the cloth. "Your betrothed just about killed me."

"I was trying to save you," she protested.

Webb let out a loud groan. "Save me? I could have handled the situation if you hadn't thrown me off balance with your fake fainting."

She and Webb had been hauled back to the de Chevenoy house in Roselie's carriage, a contrite Armand in tow. Lily had been placed on the rose-colored settee, but it seemed the Costards and the traitorous Celeste were more solicitous of his injuries than of hers. They'd rushed around Webb and seen to his black eye and swollen lip as if his injuries were life threatening.

Roselie, seeing that there would be no more excitement for the evening, wrapped her arm around Armand's and announced that she would see the poor, distraught boy home. Now that they were alone and the salon door closed, Webb wasted no time in venting his anger at her.

"I did faint," she protested. *After I hit my head on the ground.*

"Well, no more saving me from the likes of Armand Latour. I can take care of myself, thank you very much." He rolled so his back was to her.

"I didn't mean for you to get hit," she said. *I only wanted you to notice me.*

"*Humph,*" came his muffled reply. After a few moments of tense silence, Webb spoke. "Whatever were you doing clinging to that grinning ape? He has trouble written all over him."

"Armand?" Lily hadn't missed the annoyance in Webb's tone. "Why I found him quite charming. If I were the real Adelaide, I think I would be quite in love right now."

"In love?" Webb rolled over and sat up. "With that fortune-hunting charlatan?"

Lily leaned back on the settee and stared dreamily at the ceiling. "I found him quite sincere. Why, you wouldn't believe the compliments he lavished on me. My hair, my eyes, my dress."

"I think all these betrothals have gone to your head."

Lily chose to ignore him. "At least Armand doesn't have a mistress!"

"A mistress? What has that got to do with anything?" Webb asked, readjusting the cloth on his eye.

Lily sat up, ignoring the throbbing in the back of her head. "I saw you this morning, I saw you leave."

"And I saw you," came the weary reply.

"I saw you leave with *her*."

Webb tipped the cloth up and stared at her, his one eye wide open, the other so swollen shut, it was barely able to peek at her. With a shake of his head, he dropped the cloth and said, "You must have been mistaken."

"Webb Dryden, I saw you with another woman. Who is she? Your mistress?"

"Lily, would you please calm down. My head aches enough without these shrill tones. For once and for all, I do not have a mistress."

Lily felt more than a little foolish. Still she couldn't help asking. "Truly?"

"Yes, truly. There is no one in my life."

She waited for him to say, "except you," and when that didn't happen, she considered making his black eye a matching set.

"Now, why don't you ask me what I did find today, other than trouble at your hands."

Lolling back on the settee she ignored him.

"Since you want to know," he said anyway, "I couldn't get into the country house. We'll have to go through with the hearing tomorrow so as to get the house unsealed. The moment the court declares you the heiress, we can tear the place apart until we find the journals."

She turned and stared at him. "You want me to go to this hearing? But it's a trap, it must be."

"I suppose it is," he said. "But not to worry. I think you'll be pleasantly surprised when you see what I have in store for the court."

"Would you care to enlighten me about this surprise now?" she asked.

He shook his head. "Consider the suspense penance for your dalliance with that dancing baboon."

Lily sniffed. "At least Armand isn't afraid to tell me how he feels. Why he said—"

"Oh let me guess. 'Adelaide, *ma petite,*'" he said, affecting Armand's deep voice and overdone Gallic charm, "'I love your dancing, your jewels, your big,'" he paused and waggled his eyebrows, "'dowry.'"

Lily couldn't help herself, she giggled. "He's harmless, Webb. Besides, it's not like I am going to run off and marry him. He's hardly my type."

"And I'm to believe Adam is?"

"You know I'm not going to marry Adam." Lily retrieved Webb's compress and applied it tenderly to the growing lump on the back of her head.

"So I guess that just leaves me in your litany of betrotheds."

Lily stilled. What was Webb trying to say—that he wanted to marry her? As much as she dreamt of such a possibility, and despite Celeste's unholy predictions, Lily knew that that would never be possible. Not after they returned to London.

When Webb found out the truth, the truth behind her deceptions, he'd never forgive her. His wrath would know no boundaries.

He'd hurt her deeply as a child, but that would be nothing in comparison to the anguish she'd feel at having to endure his hatred.

For hate her he would—it was inevitable.

"You don't want me," she said, forcing a light tone to her words. "Remember, you said quite specifically you wanted a wife who could dance. And you've seen my dancing."

Webb grinned. "So I said, but what I witnessed today looked suspiciously like dancing. Though I can't say I admire your choice of partners, you looked like an expert. You told me you couldn't dance—or was that another of your half-truths?"

"I can't," she sighed. "But with Armand, it was quite easy. He practically carried me through the steps. Why I felt lighter than air, like—"

Webb held up his hand. "Enough. I don't think I can stomach anymore of Armand Latour. The moment the court declares you the de Chevenoy heiress, we will ride to Henri's country house, find the journals, and be gone before anyone misses you. Then you can forget you ever heard the name Armand Latour, let alone consider seeing him again." Webb slumped back into the thick cushions, his eyes closing.

"What if your plan doesn't work, and I end up going to prison?"

"That won't happen," he said, not bothering to open his eyes. "But in the unlikely event that it does, I'm sure your beloved Armand will visit you regularly."

Chapter 16

Lily threw open the doors to the small dressing room off Adelaide's bed chamber. She pulled down the smallest of her valises, tossing it on the floor behind her before sorting through the clothes hanging around her.

Pitching into a pile next to the upside-down valise only what was necessary, a fresh chemise, stockings, and a sturdy pair of shoes, she plucked down her traveling dress and cloak as well.

"What is going on in here?"

She turned and found Celeste standing in the doorway, her hands on her narrow hips.

"By all that's holy, Celeste, you nearly scared me out of my wits," Lily said, trying to catch her breath. She turned back to the shelf and pulled down another valise. "Here, take this. Pack up whatever you need—but only what you can carry."

Celeste stared down at the valise in Lily's hands. "And why would I need this?"

"Because we're leaving." Lily tossed the bag next to hers, shouldering her way past Celeste and into the bedroom.

"Since when did Mister Webb say we were going to leave?"

Lily looked over to make sure the door was closed. "Mister Webb didn't say anything. Other than 'don't worry.' This is my decision."

Webb had promised the night before he'd be by first thing in the morning to explain everything, but here it was already one o'clock and he was nowhere in sight.

And the hearing was set for two.

Not to worry. Her imagination ran away with horrid scenarios of what had happened to him.

Imprisonment. Torture. Maybe even death.

Now it was closing in on her turn, and all the master spy had given her to prepare for her imminent death were the comforting words, *not to worry.*

Not worry! Lily wasn't going to worry because she wasn't going to be anywhere near that hearing.

"I'm not about to sit around and let them haul me off to prison. I'll not die because he didn't, he wouldn't, . . . well, he just can have Paris." She ignored Celeste's dark, penetrating gaze and concentrated on stuffing her belongings into the valise.

"Hmm." Celeste walked past the pile of clothes and stood by the door, as if to block her path.

"Celeste, start packing. Troussebois will be here to take me to the hearing any minute and I have no intention of being anywhere within the city gates." She slid the second bag over toward Celeste's feet.

Celeste kicked it right back to her. "You are not going anywhere until Mister Webb says so. He knows what is best and if he says not to worry, then you must listen."

"If you haven't noticed, our trusted leader is nowhere to be found. I've been up since dawn waiting for him to get here. I even sent word to his lodgings, but there was no reply. He's not coming for us."

Before Lily could stop her, Celeste walked over, plucked the valise from her hands, and dumped the contents out onto the floor.

"What do you think you are doing? Haven't you heard a word I've said?" She scrambled over the floor, scooping up her belongings until they were a rumpled mess in her arms.

"Oh, I heard," Celeste said. "I heard the ravings of a selfish girl who's too proud to admit the man she loves may not return her feelings."

This stopped Lily cold. "I haven't the slightest idea what you are talking about." She picked at a loose thread on her cloak. "I don't feel anything for that man."

"No, mistress," her friend and maid said, "you feel everything for him. And that is why you hurt."

Lily glanced away, afraid to show the tears in her eyes. The tears she'd held in check for too long. But they fell anyway, rolling down her hot cheeks and splashing down on her dress.

Before she knew it, she'd dropped her armload of possessions back onto the floor and flopped down beside them. Celeste sat down beside her, while Lily sobbed her heart out.

"I thought, well, after the other night, I just thought after . . ." she said, embarrassed now to admit her wanton behavior, even to Celeste.

"That after you made love to the man everything would be different?"

Lily swallowed and looked up. "You knew?"

The maid's voice shook with laughter. "You weren't exactly quiet. I think half the block heard."

Lily's mouth fell open in a wide *O*.

Celeste laughed again. "I'm teasing you. No one knows but me."

"How did you find out?"

"I saw Mister Webb bring you in, and I made sure all your clothes found their way back to their rightful place."

"Oh." It was all Lily could say.

"I also saw him kiss you before he left, and that was not the kiss of a man who wanted to leave. If Mister Webb doesn't talk, he has a good reason."

Lily felt a flicker of hope kindle in her heart. "You think so?"

"Oh yes, I think so." Celeste nodded sagely. "Let me see your hand and I will show you again how that man is your fate."

Lily's fingers curled into a tight fist in her lap. "No, thank you. You know I don't believe in palm reading."

"What is there to believe?" Celeste shrugged. "I look at your hand and I tell you the future. It is all there for any fool to see."

Lily shook her head. "I think it is better if I don't know."
Better if I don't know that Webb doesn't love me, she thought.

Downstairs the front door bell rang.

"Troussebois!" Lily sprang from the bed and started gathering her clothes and her valise. "We must hurry, Celeste. We'll use the back stairs and hide in the cellar until the coast is clear."

"I'm not going into that cellar. It is too dark and too closed in for me." She sat unmoving on the bed. "I still think you should wait for Mister Webb.

Just then, Mme. Costard poked her head in the room. The woman only gave a passing glance at the discarded clothing and valise, instead sending a glowering look toward Lily. "Adelaide," she scolded, "you aren't dressed! And here is your young man downstairs, ready to take you to the hearing."

Lily let out a sigh of relief, but the woman's next words stopped her in her tracks.

"He's with Monsieur Troussebois. Everyone is assembled and ready to leave but you. What is taking you so long?"

She ignored the last question, focusing on the woman's other statement. "Everyone? Who else is going to the hearing?" From what Troussebois had explained yesterday, it would only be a quick formality to verify her identity as Adelaide de Chevenoy, the daughter and only heir of Henri de Chevenoy. He had her birth and baptismal records, to which she had added the forged school records Lord Dryden had procured.

"Yes, that lazy husband of mine and I are to testify on your behalf. Most *émigrés* are required to produce at least thirty witnesses, but you have touched the First Consul's heart with your sad return and loss, so he has made an exception."

Lily did a mental tally of the possible witnesses. The Costards, Monsieur Troussebois, and her. "Who else?"

"That horrible Madame Paville. Your mother, bless her soul, loathed the woman, but she was never one to shun acquaintances, no matter how vulgar their manners might be, no matter their unlikely attachments."

She had to agree with Mme. Costard's description of the woman. She was utterly loathsome in her toady and grasping ways and it was no wonder the Comtesse de Chevenoy had disliked the woman. But if she was willing to testify on her behalf, and it would open for her and Webb the doors to Henri's country estate, then she could tolerate the woman for another afternoon.

Just the same, with that crowd around, how would she ever get a word in private with Webb?

Maybe it didn't matter, she thought, clinging to Celeste's

assertion that Webb cared for her. What he needed from her now was the performance of a lifetime.

Their lives depended on it.

"Get on with you, *ma petite poulet*," Mme. Costard said. "Get dressed and ready or I'll send Madame Paville up to help you select a dress."

That was all the encouragement Lily needed to rush back into her closet and select a simple, understated gown.

Webb suspected that this afternoon's hearing was a trap.

It had to be.

He knew for a fact that Fouché's spies had been working overtime trying to verify who he was, and so far, at least as far as he knew, they had only been able to determine that he was the man he claimed to be—Henry Milne, an American shipowner.

Now as they pulled up in front of the old hotel that served the local area as an administrative center and stepped from the carriage, he felt the gaze of unknown eyes watching his every movement.

Lily squeezed his arm. "Are we all right?"

How could he tell her he didn't know? The last thing he wanted was for her to panic. "Yes, fine," he lied.

It was bad enough the journals were still missing, but he also wondered how his father's information could have been so bad? Henri had died in the country, not in Paris. Had one of their contacts deliberately given them bad information to send them hunting in the wrong direction?

No wonder the Paris house had turned up empty. It only seemed reasonable that Henri would have his journals close at hand when he died, so they must be somewhere in his rambling country estate.

Now all that stood between them and completing their mission was this hearing.

Climbing the steps into the building, Webb surveyed the surrounding boulevard and neighboring buildings, gauging routes of escape in case of trouble.

He wouldn't have been so nervous if it had been only him, but he now had Lily to consider.

Lily.

He'd avoided her like the plague since they'd made love, hoping his tangled feelings for her would straighten themselves out on their own.

Not that it had worked.

With the nagging feeling that someone was watching him, he felt it best to keep those eyes away from Lily. He'd kept his distance to keep her safe.

At least that was what he told himself. Keep her safe, hah, he thought, more like keep his heart safe.

So instead of spending his time with her, Webb had spent most of yesterday trying to break into Henri's country house. The rambling country manor proved to be as difficult a puzzle as his feelings for Lily. Rotating shifts of men surrounded the place. By their general appearance and professionalism, he suspected Fouché's hand.

Even when he'd slipped past the hired louts, the doors and windows were so efficiently boarded up that it would have brought half the locals running if he'd tried to pry them open or break through the security measures.

No, he reasoned, this hearing was the only way. Once the court declared Lily to be Henri's legal heir, the house would be hers to claim and theirs to ransack.

If Fouché hadn't beaten them to it.

All the way to the courtroom, Webb watched the halls, the lounging guards, and the doorways, weighing and discarding routes for a hasty escape.

He hadn't been so edgy since his first mission.

Troussebois approached Lily. "My dear, this really is a formality and nothing to worry about."

Then why, Webb wanted to ask the fidgety solicitor, *do you look like a rabbit being chased by a pack of hounds?*

Beside him, Lily nodded to the solicitor. She appeared cool and collected, as if she were truly the daughter of Henri de Chevenoy and this was nothing more than an inconvenience interrupting her daily round of visits and shopping.

Still, he had one point to tell her before the hearing began. Something to assure her that everything would be just fine, if only she played along. All he needed were a few seconds to explain the matter to Lily.

Troussebois fluttered about them, his papers under his arm and his black coat flapping about him like the nervous wings of a blackbird. "The judge would like everyone to take their seats," he directed, pointing the Costards and Mme. Paville toward their seats near the front. "I'm afraid, Monsieur Milne that the court has directed this hearing closed. Since you are not a French citizen, you will not be able to attend because you have been disqualified from testifying."

The clicking jaws of the steel trap snapped closed around them. Webb sent Lily's stricken features an assuring nod, even while he noticed the number of guards in the hallway had now doubled.

Before Troussebois could lead Lily away, Webb caught her by the elbow and pulled her close.

"Your bonnet is crooked, my dear," he said, adjusting the green ribbons and smoothing out the white feathers. He leaned close to her ear. "Go along with whatever happens in there. I'll be out here. If there is trouble, and I can't get to you, escape by whatever means you can and get to the Tivoli Gardens. I'll meet you by the ice shop near the corner. Wait for me there. If I don't arrive in two hours, take Celeste and get out of Paris."

Lily smiled up at him, her outward appearance that of a young woman in love, but Webb saw the worried light in her eyes.

"Not without you."

Before he could protest, she turned and made her entrance into the court. The sullen guard slammed the door in Webb's face, and Webb found he had no choice but to wait.

Lily sat through the hearing tensed and waiting for the prosecutor to jump up from his table and denounce her to the judge as an imposter.

But all in all the hearing went as Troussebois said it would, though he hadn't mentioned how long-winded he could be. The only thing keeping her awake was the severe nature of Webb's warning.

On the stand Mme. Costard looked down at her and smiled.

"Your honor, to have our dear girl back in the house has given my husband and me a reason to live, for she is like a daughter to us." The large lady sniffled and wiped her nose and teary cheeks with her sleeve.

"Yes, that may be so, Citizeness Costard," the prosecutor said, still using the Revolutionary form of address so out of favor with Napoleon and his followers. "But is this woman before the court the rightful and legal daughter of Citizen de Chevenoy, formerly known as the Comte de Chevenoy?"

Mme. Costard looked outraged, her mottled face turning bright purple. "Are you saying my sweet Adelaide is anything but legitimate? How dare you! I was there when my mistress, the Comtesse de Chevenoy brought her dear child into the world. My mistress was the most honorable of women, why she would no more—"

The prosecutor held up his hand. "Citizeness, I do not

mean to impugn the memory of your former employer, I just want you to point out the woman in this courtroom and swear to the judge that this woman is Adelaide de Chevenoy."

"Why didn't you say so?" Mme. Costard huffed. She pointed a thick finger at Lily. "The lovely girl there is the daughter of Henri de Chevenoy. I would wager my life on it."

While the prosecutor thanked Mme. Costard and excused her from the witness stand, Lily watched the woman as she looked toward her husband.

The pair exchanged a glance that went beyond these proceedings.

She had seen that selfsame look on the faces of those wagering beyond their means—a fateful resignation that the next turn of the cards would mean either life or death.

So why would the Costards consider this hearing life and death unless . . .

The prosecutor called Mme. Paville to the stand.

Following Mme. Costard's lead, Mme. Paville was in tears before she even reached the simple wooden witness chair beside the judge's bench.

I would wager my life on it. Lily couldn't get the emphatic statement out of her mind.

Had Mme. Costard done just that? Wagered all of their lives with her testimony?

The answer hit her hard.

The Costards know I'm not Adelaide, Lily realized.

It wasn't anything specific, but all the little things that suddenly added up.

And she suspected they'd known since the first day. So why had they welcomed her with open arms and just testified in court that she was indeed Adelaide de Chevenoy?

Then she caught Troussebois glancing over at the Costards

while everyone was distracted by Mme. Paville's great tearful rendition of the loss of her lifetime friend, the Comtesse de Chevenoy.

"I wanted to raise Adelaide as my own dearest child," the woman wailed to the judge. "The Comte cruelly sent her away I suspect, because she served as a daily reminder of the loss of his beloved wife. Look at her. I tell you it is like being reunited with my dear Marie all over."

While Lily nodded politely to the judge, since Mme. Paville had now directed everyone's attention squarely to her, she caught only the briefest exchange between the Costards and Troussebois.

They were in league in this conspiracy. But why?

Troussebois rose and began another summation. In his own words he answered Lily's questions.

"Your honor, I understand these questions are necessary due to the large amount of money Mademoiselle de Chevenoy stands to inherit, but . . ."

Lily didn't need to hear any more.

. . . *the large amount of money* . . .

The threesome were working together to ensure that the de Chevenoy fortune wasn't usurped by Napoleon and his money-hungry ministers.

But for what reason? She looked back at the closed door behind her and wondered how she could get to Webb with this revelation, get his reaction and his thoughts.

Get him to believe her intuition on this.

Even as she looked again at the door, it burst open. An officer hurried in and approached the prosecutor. The man glanced back at the door and then around at Lily.

"What is the meaning of this interruption, Citizen?" the judge asked the prosecutor.

Her heart pounded as the prosecutor approached the bench and whispered over the bench.

"This is highly irregular," the judge muttered. "Citizen Troussebois, approach the bench. It appears there is another witness who says she has important information about your client."

Lily frantically gauged the distance to the door, the distance to the nearest window, to the door beside the judge's bench. She wasn't the only one feeling the alarm, for the Costards looked stunned by this announcement.

But no more so than Lily as she watched an ashen-faced Troussebois leave the judge's bench and shakily take his seat.

"Who is it?" she asked.

Troussebois opened his mouth, but the words that had come so easily to him all morning failed to issue forth from his moving lips.

The prosecutor answered her question.

"The Republic of France would like to call a witness on this matter," he announced. "Marie-Theresa Jeanne Pontavice of the island of Martinique, the Abbess and Mother Superior of the convent school, *Les Dames du Providence*."

Chapter 17

Lily's gaze swung from the prosecutor to the back of the room, but all she could see was the tall, ruddy-faced guard leading in the new witness.

The Mother Superior of Adelaide's convent? Lily saw her future in one bleak second—her hearing would conclude with her arrest and then her execution in the morning.

Perhaps the dear nun would be kind enough to say a prayer for her doomed soul.

As the lady approached the witness stand, Lily could discern little of her face and features, as they were well hidden beneath the veil of her black and white habit.

The lady raised her hand before the judge and in a quiet voice stated her name and place of residence. The judge bade her to take a seat.

Afraid to look the witness in the face, Lily glanced back at the door where Mother Marie-Theresa's escort lounged, an indolent expression on his face.

No escape there.

"Citizeness," the judge said, still unwilling to leave behind the informal address. "You claim to have knowledge about this case."

"Yes, I do, my son."

Lily dreaded looking directly at the lady, knowing full well she would immediately be denounced, but something in her voice caught Lily's attention.

Maybe it was the slight accent, or perhaps the calm, gentle tones, or maybe it was something familiar.

Her curiosity overruling her fears, Lily looked up.

To her complete shock, her fears about her impending arrest immediately abated. In exchange she felt the white-hot sting of betrayal.

Now she knew why Webb hadn't sought out her company last night and whom he'd been with yesterday.

His former mistress.

For gazing serenely out from beneath the black-veiled headdress were the unmistakable Wedgwood-blue eyes of Amelia, Lady Marston.

After the informant delivered his message to the plain black hackney waiting across the street from the courthouse, the occupant of the carriage signaled his driver to move on.

"Tell me again why I am letting this woman steal the de Chevenoy fortune?" Napoleon asked, leaning back in his seat, his arms crossed over his bandy chest, his face a glower.

Joseph Fouché smiled at his employer. "Because she will lead us to Henri de Chevenoy's treachery."

"How can you be so certain?"

"I've long suspected Henri de Chevenoy worked as an agent for another country—though who his employer was, I could never find out. Now I will." His hand patted the note one of his men had intercepted from a British agent.

"So you say, but I dislike the idea of allowing an imposter access to so much money."

"And I say she is not interested in the money. She is after whatever secrets that bastard de Chevenoy didn't take with him. By tonight I'll have all that information, along with her and her accomplices. And then all the de Chevenoy assets will be subject to seizure on grounds of treason, without any questions. We've lulled all his accomplices into the open and now when we arrest them, it will make it all so much more legal, for everyone in that courtroom will be prosecutable for perjury."

Napoleon frowned. "What if you are wrong?"

Joseph maintained his tight smile while inside he seethed. It was becoming more and more difficult to deal with Bonaparte. He could sense the man's faith in him was slipping and he needed this coup to ensure his position in France's latest regime.

"Then sadly," he said, "if she refuses to cooperate, our little heiress will have a rather unfortunate accident, and her estate will fall under your jurisdiction without any questions from her father's friends."

"You have this all figured out." Napoleon nodded. He reached up and opened the blind covering the window. For a moment he studied the passing scenery. "It had better work, Fouché. I intend to see that money put to good use."

Put the de Chevenoy money to good use. Fouché wanted to laugh. That fortune in ill-gotten money would end up frittered away by the man's whore of a wife or absconded with by his grasping clutch of relatives.

Though stung by Napoleon's censure and distrust, Fouché held his tongue. He had survived, just like his long-time adversary Henri de Chevenoy, by knowing when and where to place his alliances.

But then again, Fouché thought with malice, perhaps he wouldn't be serving Napoleon for as long as the rude little Corsican thought. If there was a slight miscalculation tonight, it would be a rather unfortunate accident, but not for Fouché. And with Bonaparte gone, Fouché intended to serve the next regime, or perhaps step into the void himself.

In a few more hours he'd take Henri's gold coins and buy a good bottle of wine to toast the Comte de Chevenoy and the future of a new France, perhaps one without Bonaparte.

Lily's outrage with Webb grew with each passing moment.

After Amelia's reverent testimony as to her former pupil, the court had little choice but to reinstate the citizenship of Adelaide de Chevenoy and declare her the rightful heir to her father's estate.

A now jubilant Troussebois, whose color returned once Amelia pointed out Lily as her former student, declared himself a brilliant solicitor.

Lily struggled to continue her courtroom charade. With the judge watching, she even managed to hug the good Mother and welcome her to France, her face awash with a spate of pretty tears.

The tears had been real enough—Amelia's return meant Webb had lied to her the night before when he had denied having a mistress.

He'd out-and-out lied.

As they moved out into the hallway, Lily watched from beneath her hooded glances while Webb greeted his mistress with a professional demeanor, taking her hand and thanking her for such a kindness to her former student.

Lily didn't miss the dancing lights in Amelia's eyes or the smug flicker of acknowledgment from Webb.

How could she have been so foolish as to have allowed him into her heart a second time?

While the court's decision left them free and clear to search the country house, the only joy it gave Lily was knowing that now they would be able to uncover the journals and return to London.

Then Webb Dryden would be out of her life. For good. And she would finish her work in England and return home to Virginia.

So deep was she in her own misery and anger that she almost missed the quiet exchange between Webb and Amelia.

"Would you be so kind, Monsieur," Amelia was saying, "to escort me to my lodgings?"

Lily didn't even bother to wait for Webb's answer, turning on one heel and heading down the corridor. She needed air, she needed to breathe, she needed to be as far away from them as she could be.

"Adelaide," Roselie called after her. "Oh, do wait, my *chérie*. We must settle on our arrangements for tonight."

Lily didn't stop until she reached the street. Webb caught up with her first, grabbing her by the elbow before she rushed headlong into the street and into a fast-moving cart.

"What is wrong with you?" he asked, spinning her around.

She yanked her arm free. "Don't you ever touch me again. Do you hear me? Never!"

Before he could make any more inquiries, Roselie joined them. "Oh, my dear," she said, looking from Lily to Webb, then back to Lily. "What a terribly trying afternoon you've had, *chérie*. And with the Christmas celebrations tonight and our invitations to the opera, how thoughtless of us not to realize that you must be simply exhausted. Perhaps you would prefer to just go back to your house and lie down for a few hours before I come by to pick you up for the opera?"

Lily could think of nothing she wanted more than to be away from Webb, away from Paris. She readily agreed to Roselie's suggestion. "That would be most kind, Roselie."

Webb stepped in front of her, cutting off her escape as she moved to follow Roselie toward the woman's carriage. But at least he had the good sense not to touch her. "Where are you going?"

"Home."

He nodded. "Good. I'm going to escort Mother Marie-Theresa back to her lodgings, and then I will join you in an hour or so." He leaned closer and whispered in her ear. "Have Celeste pack whatever you'll need for traveling and be ready to slip out." He smiled at her, the one that usually melted her heart, but this time only left her feeling bereft and empty. "You did an excellent job in there. Amelia says you never even batted an eye when she arrived. I'm so proud of you."

"Thank you," she finally managed to say.

He stepped closer. "Don't worry, hoyden. If we've made it this far, I doubt Fouché will catch us now. You've done such a convincing job, no one would ever think you weren't the de Chevenoy heiress. You've bought us enough time to complete this mission."

He kissed her lightly on the forehead and turned to leave.

It wasn't until he'd fallen in step with Amelia and the pair were strolling off in the opposite direction that she remembered her stunning realization in the courtroom.

It was on her lips to call him back, to tell him that he was wrong, she hadn't fooled anyone.

Least of all herself. For while she'd beaten Webb to the truth for the moment, the tears streaming down her face mockingly told her she'd lost the war.

"Your betrothed looked anything but happy to see me," Amelia said, as she bundled up her costume and handed it to her maid. She nodded at the girl, who bobbed her head and left the room.

"Why would Lily care if you were there to testify on her behalf?" Webb asked.

"Oh, no reason." Amelia smiled, having seen full well the murderous intent behind Lily's careful mask. "It was probably the veil obscuring my vision, or I am just out of practice." Amelia had to hand it to the girl, for her first mission, she'd handled the situation with all the aplomb of a seasoned professional. "I seem to remember you thought her akin to a stray mongrel—do you still see her that way?"

"Amelia, you are at it again."

"And what would that be?" she said, flitting about her hotel room, picking up the rosary beads and other stray articles from her appearance before the judge. Then she settled down on the green-backed sofa, leaving a space for Webb to sit beside her. She shot him a dazzling smile and patted the cushion next to her.

"Trying to pair me off with that girl," he told her. "That, or incite me into some compromising position. If you are mad at that lover of yours, don't use me to get back at him. I want to keep all of my body parts attached."

She laughed. Samir did have a terrible habit of dismembering his enemies.

Webb poured himself a glass of whisky from the decanter on the sideboard and held up a bottle of Madeira for her. She nodded her acceptance and he poured her a small glass. "He won't be angry about your coming out of retirement?"

"Samir?" She shook her head. "When I told him I needed to travel ahead to Paris to help a friend, I was most persuasive, and he was, shall we say, most accommodating."

"As only you can be," he said, tipping his glass in acknowledgment of her influential skills. "You look happy, Amelia, happier than I ever thought you could be. He is treating you well, isn't he?"

Amelia knew that few of her English friends or relatives

understood her choice to return to Cairo and to the arms of her lover, an Ottoman pasha. After almost a year of looking for another husband, her thoughts had always drifted back to the one man who'd truly captured her heart. And though she knew he would never marry her, or at least not in the traditional English sense of the word, especially since he already had three wives and a passel of children, she knew she held the primary spot in his heart and affections, as he did in hers.

Theirs was a relationship few could fathom.

But Webb understood, at least she thought he did. For his tone held heartfelt concern for her welfare more than censure for her turning her back on her friends and family in England.

"I was worried about you when the news of Napoleon's landing in Egypt came through. I hoped you would be safe."

"Me?" She laughed and waved her hand at him. "I'm fine. Especially now that Samir has moved his court to Europe. The Sultan," she said, referring to her lover's overlord, the Sultan of the Ottoman Empire, "was very kind to give Samir this posting as his European diplomat. After the horrible losses in Alexandria and Cairo, I expected we'd all be thrown on some burning pyre or pitched into the sea with rocks tied around our necks. But instead Samir was able to convince him that he would be of better use here. I think the Sultan understands that after Samir and the others lost so much to Bonaparte's army, who better to watch the man, than the ones who were defeated at his hands."

Webb nodded in understanding and sat down smiling at her.

"Being here in Europe allows me to circulate once again through all the courts and palaces I love, and my contacts serve Samir's interests . . ." She paused for a moment, taking a small sip from her glass. "And when the opportunity arises, those of England."

They raised their glasses in a silent toast to their island home and to their king, and they drank, each quiet with their own thoughts of home.

"You never answered my question," she finally said. "What do you think of your partner now that she's outgrown all those awkward limbs and puppy ways?"

"You never were one to let go of a subject," he said. "What if I told you I hadn't really noticed?"

"I'd say you were lying or blind or mad." She studied him for a moment. "Perhaps a little of all three."

"I would agree with you on the last point. I must have been mad to agree to this mission. The way my father made it sound we would walk in, gain entry to the house, and then slip out the back door with Henri's journals."

Amelia smiled at this. "Your father always made his assignments sound like an evening at the Bath Assembly Room. A trifling dull, not even a hint of lukewarm intrigue, and home before the stroke of midnight."

"If this were only that simple—I've got not only Fouché breathing down our necks, but now Lily takes it into her head to play heiress. Did you see those petulant theatrics outside the courthouse? What was she thinking?"

Holding her tongue, Amelia would have wagered that Lily had put together Amelia's presence with Webb's recent disappearances and come up with her own version of events.

The poor girl. She obviously still loved Webb.

"I'll straighten her out tonight," he was saying. "We need to complete this mission and get home. After all her protests about not wanting to come, now she acts like we have all the time in the world to gad about Paris."

"Can you blame her? Paris during the holidays. And the first time they've celebrated since the Revolution," she said, carefully swirling the liquid in her glass. "And with dancing back in fashion, the city is much more bearable."

"You haven't seen Lily dance." He leaned back on the couch, his hands folded behind his neck. "She'll set society back about five hundred years with her clomping about."

"Really?"

"She can send an entire room scrambling for safety. If you ever need to clear a room, send Lily out on the dance floor."

"As bad as all that," she said. "I don't see how you tolerate the chit for a moment." She let the condescending air of her statement settle down on Webb and then gauged his response.

He knew exactly what she meant. "Am I that transparent?"

"Yes. You've fallen in love with the girl, haven't you?"

Webb glanced away and then back at her. "I suppose I have."

"Good. Finally an honest answer to my question." Amelia got up and brought the decanter of Madeira back to the couch. Pouring another drink for both of them, she raised her glass. "I am so glad I can say that I've seen the impossible and impervious Webb Dryden eat his own words and be toppled by the one woman he claimed should be locked away."

Webb laughed and joined in. "I'm still not unconvinced about the locking away part. She was furious after the hearing today, and I can't understand why."

Amelia held her tongue. Webb Dryden had always gotten whatever he wanted with a few charming words and a flash of his boyish grin. Lily would be that much more valuable to him if he had to work for her affections.

"So if you can win her, what then?"

Webb downed the last of his drink and put the glass on the table beside him. "If? Why wouldn't I?"

She didn't miss the note of trepidation in his voice. There was more to what was going on between this pair than what Webb was letting on.

He leaned forward. "What if I told you I was madly, passionately in love with Lily and that I plan to take her back to England, marry her, and live a quiet respectable life with the bothersome little hoyden? Would that make you happy?"

Amelia grinned. "I'd say we are getting closer to the truth. That is, if she ever forgives you for betraying her with me."

Chapter 18

"Monsieur and Madame Costard," Lily said, as they returned from the hearing and entered the house, "may I see you both in the salon?"

Lily knew she was taking a risk, but she wasn't about to remain in Paris for another day.

Not if it meant staying in the same city as Webb and his mistress.

The journals were not likely to be found within the four walls of the little house on the *Rue du Renard* and she was of no mind to wait any longer for the opportunity to search Henri's country house, so it seemed logical to Lily that if they existed, the Costards would know where to find them.

Besides, they had just testified that she was indeed the daughter and legal heir of Henri de Chevenoy. That had placed them in direct opposition to the First Consul. When the truth came out, as surely it would, Lily knew nothing would spare the kindly Costards from Napoleon's wrath.

It was time the truth was settled amongst them.

The pair stood beside the sofa, looking anything but comfortable.

"Please be seated," she said.

Both looked down at the sofa and then back at her. "On the good sofa?" Costard asked.

"Yes."

They sat, and Lily took a big breath. She was either on her way to prison or home. Without Webb in her life, those options seemed like one and the same, but at least she might be able to spare the Costards' lives.

"I realized something today while we were in court," she began. "You both know I'm not the real Adelaide."

The Costards exchanged a meaningful glance, and then Costard nodded.

Lily paced several steps before continuing. "How long have you known?"

Mme. Costard smiled. "Since the moment you walked in the door. We knew Adelaide died on the voyage to Martinique, though the old master wouldn't hear of it. He refused to believe he'd sent his little girl to her death." She folded her hands in her lap. "You do favor her, though, and for that we are thankful."

"Thankful?"

Mme. Costard looked over at her husband and then shrugged. "It made our job of convincing the world that you really are the master's daughter that much easier."

Lily couldn't quite believe she was hearing this. "You *wanted* an imposter?"

Costard patted his wife's hand. "Yes. For as long as a de Chevenoy lives in this house, even an imposter de Chevenoy, we have our jobs and the same roof over our heads that has sheltered us for the last forty years."

Overwhelmed by the weight of this admission, Lily plopped down on a chair.

"I'm afraid you've entrusted the wrong woman," she told them. "I was sent for one reason and one reason only." She paused, almost unwilling to give away the confidential information she'd been entrusted with, but there was no other way around it—either she asked the Costards, or their lives were surely forfeit. "I was sent to retrieve your master's journals."

At first the Costards looked at each other, the confusion obvious on their faces. Then Costard's face brightened.

He smiled and then broke down in laughter. "The British sent you, didn't they?"

"Why yes," she answered.

"There you are, Madame," he told his wife. "You owe me a roast chicken dinner and my favorite bottle of wine."

"Bah, I should have known the British would be so thorough," Mme. Costard complained. "The Dutch would never have taken the time to prepare you so well." The lady sighed. "But you must admit, she has an American quality to her."

Lily looked from one to the other. "Why would the Americans or the Dutch care about Henri's journals?"

"They wouldn't care in the least about the journals, for Henri never told them that story. He had other ways to keep his employers paying him for his information."

"Employers?" Lily wasn't sure she'd heard correctly. "Henri was an agent for more than just the British?"

Costard blushed. "Our master spied for anyone with gold."

Lily was glad she was sitting down, though she felt as if she were perched on a powder keg. "For how long?"

The man shrugged. "Off and on for as long as I've served him. And that's been forty years."

"Oh my," she whispered.

Mme. Costard leaned forward. "It has made our lives interesting, what with the last few years and all. Why I remember a few times—"

Costard nudged his wife, putting an abrupt halt to her reminiscing. "We had thought, or hoped," he said, "that you and Monsieur Milne intended to step in and continue the master's work. We figured we'd let you get started, see how you worked out and for whom you worked before we told you about the extent of his ventures. A trial period so to say."

Lily shook her head. "You want me to stay?"

"Oh, yes," they both said.

Lily slumped back in her chair. What had happened to her life in just these few months? She'd gone from being a plain widow to an international spy.

"Mademoiselle, there is nothing to worry about," Costard assured her. "No one could beat our master, a real smart one he was, and he kept his business matters well hidden— where no one would find them. For truly they died with him. He carried all his secrets in his head."

"But that's not true," Lily said. "He kept journals. Extensive journals of his activities."

Again Costard laughed. "Our master was too smart to ever keep something so damaging. Journals? They would have been his death, and ours, if such a thing had ever been found in the house. No, the master never kept any journals. He only told the British he did because they were so slow in paying. One reminder about them and *voilà*, the gold would arrive. The Dutch were never so difficult. They always paid quite promptly."

She couldn't quite believe it. No journals? And yet it made sense. Why would someone of Henri's obvious intelligence and cunning ever do something so foolish as to keep journals?

"If you need proof, I have a letter that I was supposed to send to the British. He wrote it in the event he was captured or died. He didn't want anyone to come fetch the journals and get caught as well, but I never sent it."

He rose and went to the newly hung portrait of the Comtesse de Chevenoy and retrieved it from its nail. Sliding his fingers under the silk backing, he retrieved a letter and placed it in Lily's hands. She looked down at the sealed missive, the wax bearing the de Chevenoy crest.

"I had hoped," he said, smiling slightly at his wife, "well, we hoped that someone would come and take Adelaide's place. To come and live here, so we could continue to live here as well."

She smiled at the kindly couple.

Encouraged, Costard continued. "We can help you start anew with his work and then life will go on as it has for all these years."

"I wasn't sent here to be Adelaide de Chevenoy for the rest of my life. I'm not even a real spy."

Costard looked crestfallen. "Then who are you?"

She owed the couple some measure of truth since they had been so honest with her. "My name is Lily. My mother, who was English, like the Comtesse, was a friend of hers. Since I favor Adelaide, the British recruited me."

She glanced over at Mme. Costard. "And I have lived in America for the better part of the last eight years, so I don't think you owe the bottle of wine, just the roast chicken."

They all laughed and then fell into an uneasy silence.

Lily didn't know what to say. The entire mission as much a sorry tale of fiction as the de Chevenoy journals themselves.

Now she had the unfortunate duty to tell this elderly couple, the mythical life they had tried to create around Henri's lies was about to come to an end.

As chance would have it, she didn't have to break that news to them right away because the salon door swung open. Lily expected to turn and find Celeste in the open doorway, or perhaps even Webb, but instead, there stood a grinning Armand Latour.

If that wasn't bad enough, in his hand he brandished a large pistol.

"Do you mind if I continue to call you Adelaide, *ma chérie*? I think having a wife with two names would be so confusing." With a flourishing wave of his hand, he snatched the precious letter out of her hands.

Webb left Amelia's apartment intent on going straight to the de Chevenoy house to straighten out his errant partner. If Amelia was right and Lily did believe the two of them had renewed their affair, she would be more than just angry, she'd be dangerous to the mission.

There was no telling what she would do if she was as furious as Amelia suggested.

But halfway there he ran into an old friend, Dr. Alexander McTaggart. Though born in France where his parents had fled after the Jacobean Revolt, the man looked as though he had just stepped off the curb in Edinburgh and not the *Rue Saint Honoré*.

"My friend," McTaggart said, setting aside his black medical box and clapping Webb heartily on the back. "I didn't know you were in Paris. How have you been?" He grabbed Webb's hand and pumped it energetically.

"Better before I bumped into you," he said, shaking his throbbing fingers.

McTaggart caught Webb's chin and turned his head to one side then the other. "That is quite a black eye. What does the other fellow look like?"

"Unfortunately, he is unscratched."

The amiable Scot laughed. "You must tell me everything. I'm on my way to join a few friends for a Christmas feast, but before I settle in to stuff myself with goose, let me buy you a drink. I know a place not far that carries a decent Highland whisky, one I know you will like."

Webb knew McTaggart meant a place where they could talk in private and not have to continue this conversation on one of the busiest streets in Paris.

The man may have lived his entire life in France, but he was a Scot first and foremost. He'd served Webb and countless other British operatives over the years, performing minor and sometimes major surgeries on their wounds, and opening his home to them as a place to hide and recuperate if they were unable to get to the coast and across the Channel with their injuries.

Webb knew the man did this not only out of the kindness of his heart, but because he also wanted the McTaggart name cleared so he could reclaim his family lands.

His father's support of Bonnie Prince Charlie had left the family destitute, branded as outlaws and stripped of their property.

"I'd love to, Alex, but I haven't the time. I've got business to attend to with a lady," he said with a wink.

"Would that lady happen to be a certain heiress all of Paris is agog over?"

Webb eyed his friend. "You've heard of her?"

"Aye, and if you have business with her, I am sure you have a few moments to listen to what I've heard. That is, if you're of a mind to keep your head on your shoulders."

Webb nodded, and they walked to a nearby café where McTaggart greeted the owner by name. The bustling man wiped his hands on his greasy apron and showed the pair to a back room, far from the street and far from eavesdroppers.

Once they were settled in the comfortable chairs, a bottle of whisky between them, McTaggart eyed Webb with a sharp, measured glance.

"That shoulder and leg healing up? I noticed you still have a bit of a limp."

"I probably wouldn't if I had gone to a real doctor."

McTaggart laughed at the insult. "I'll remember you said that, my friend, the next time I'm stitching up your miserable hide."

Webb declined McTaggart's offer of a drink.

The man shrugged and poured himself a double measure.

"So what have you heard about this heiress?" Webb asked.

"This is Adelaide de Chevenoy we're talking about it, isn't it?" the doctor asked. When Webb nodded, he continued. "I thought as much. Since I know Henri was a friend of yours, I assume you are here to pay your respects to the lady."

Webb made no comment and allowed the man to come to his own conclusions.

"Just as I suspected," McTaggart said. "Well, stay clear of her. I can fix your broken bones and a hole here or there, but I cannot reattach your head if that Corsican decides to separate it."

"And why would anyone care if I pay my respects to this chit?"

"She's under suspicion for treason."

"I know," Webb told him. "I brought her here."

This brought McTaggart's thick eyebrows up in a sharp arch. "That explains why she is in so much trouble."

Webb grinned.

"I've heard tell she's betrothed to two men," the doctor said, studying the amber liquid in his tumbler. "You wouldn't happen to be one of the lucky gentlemen?"

"Unfortunately, yes. Though after today I'm about ready to let her other beau have the little minx. She's a handful and a half—and she'll put her Armand Latour in an early grave for sure."

McTaggart's eyes narrowed. "Did you say Latour?"

"Yes. Armand Latour."

The man scratched his chin. "Any relation to the Comte Latour?"

"Yes, his only son. Why do you ask?"

"Because I treated Armand Latour once. I can tell you this without breaking any patient confidentiality, because a month or two after I treated Armand Latour in the *Abbaye*, he was guillotined."

Guillotined? Then that meant Lily's Armand was . . . an imposter, and more than likely, Fouché's agent.

It would have been a very funny situation, a fake heiress and her bogus betrothed, if it didn't mean that Lily was in danger.

He rose abruptly from his chair. As long as Lily still considered Armand harmless, Fouché's agent had unlimited access to her. And now that the court had given Lily complete control of the de Chevenoy estates, Fouché would be only that much more anxious to find a way to steal the de Chevenoy fortune.

"I must go, sir," Webb said. "This is very grave news."

As he turned to leave, McTaggart caught him by the arm. "You may well lose your heiress, you realize that?"

Webb shook his head. "Not if I have any say in the matter."

"Then you had best hear the rest of what I have to say."

Taking a deep breath, Webb nodded for him to continue.

"I was visiting a patient this morning, a rather significant patient, who claimed he would soon be living at the de Chevenoy address. He'd been promised it, since it seems the little heiress will no longer need a house."

"Did he say when he was going to take up this new residence?"

Again McTaggart's cool, assessing gaze looked him up and down. "This heiress, she's important to you?"

"She's my life."

"Then I would see to her safety, my friend. My patient asked if I knew a reliable man with wagons to help his servants start packing and moving. To hear him, he'd be in the de Chevenoy house tomorrow if everyone wasn't taking a holiday for Christmas."

Amelia knew it had been rude of her not to offer Webb the use of her carriage to see him back to the *Rue de Renard*, but she wanted him to take the time walking to give some thought to what she had told him.

To tell Lily the truth about his feelings.

And in the meantime, Webb's lingering pace gave her the time to get there before him and finish her work in Paris.

She settled back in the leather seat of her carriage and thought about how to deal with the interview to come. She knew Webb would never approve of her interfering in his relationship with Lily, but this time she had to intervene.

The last time she'd seen Lily D'Artiers, before the court hearing this afternoon, was at Byrnewood Manor over five years ago. She and Webb were leaving for their mission, and for some reason she'd looked back at the ivy-covered walls of Byrnewood as they'd left the house.

This in itself was a strange occurrence, as Amelia prided herself on never looking back, neither for a fine view nor to face regrets.

Life, she felt, should only be faced head-on.

But this once, she'd looked back and she'd regretted it ever since—for there in the second-story window of Byrnewood stood a skinny, forlorn creature.

Lily.

Amelia knew the girl was crying, for she saw the young

woman mopping her eyes and cheeks with her sleeves. And she knew why the girl was crying. Because her heart was broken.

Hadn't she done the same at fifteen when her own father had told her of her impending marriage to Lord Marston?

The sight of Lily that day had been a feeling too close to her own personal sorrows, so she'd looked away and sworn to purge the forlorn image from her mind.

But it hadn't been so simple. She was the source of Lily's pain and heartbreak. She'd done her best to encourage Webb in his horrible treatment of Lily. She'd all but flaunted their relationship in front of the love-struck adolescent. And she'd done the worst thing of all.

As she'd looked up and seen Lily standing in the window, she'd chosen that moment to laugh. Heartily and thoroughly, as if she were laughing at Lily.

It was not a day she was proud of, but now was the time to redeem herself and perhaps even give Lily what Amelia suspected she still wanted: Webb Dryden.

The carriage bounced off the main street onto the *Rue du Renard.* Amelia took a deep breath as the horses stopped before the quaint little house at Number 8.

"Wait for me, Hamid," she said to her Mameluke driver. "I don't know how long I will be."

If Lily D'Artiers slammed the de Chevenoy door in her face, Amelia wouldn't blame her. But perhaps, *her superior skills of persuasion,* as Webb liked to call them, would at least get her past the threshold.

"You seem surprised to see me, *ma chérie,*" Armand said to Lily. "Didn't you think that after your stellar victory this afternoon in court, your betrothed would want to be at your side to celebrate?"

Unsure of how much Armand had heard but willing to bet

it was enough, given that he still held a pistol in his hand, she decided to try and brazen out the situation.

"Armand, of course you are welcome here," she said, rising from her seat. "But why the gun? You are frightening my servants."

"Really, Adelaide, or shall I say Lily, how stupid do you think I am?"

Staring at the muzzle of the pistol, Lily decided not to tell Armand the truth. "I haven't the vaguest notion what you are talking about," she said instead.

He waved the gun at the Costards, who had also risen from their seats. "Sit down," he ordered, "both of you."

They both sat as quickly as possible, the poor couch groaning under them.

He turned to Lily. "So, now, what to do with you, my cunning little betrothed? I should kill you outright for the traitor you are, but it seems a waste to have all the de Chevenoy money revert to the Republic, don't you think?"

Lily looked about the room, trying to find something, anything, that she could use to distract and disarm Armand, but there was nothing. Instead she chose to lull him out of his defensive stance. "Please, Armand, put away the gun. There is no reason for the two of us to be at odds. We have the same end in mind—the money. And there is more than enough for both of us."

"Enough money? I doubt it. I've lived in stinking poverty all my life, and I'm of no mind to go back, ever."

Poverty all his life? That didn't make sense. The Latours had once been one of the richest families in France. But Lily didn't have time to decipher his odd ramblings, only to try to find a way to disarm him.

Then out of the corner of her eye she saw someone she'd never thought she'd be happy to see—Lady Marston. While she still didn't like the woman, Lily could appreciate the lady's bravery. For the demurely feminine Lady Marston stood not far from Armand wielding the stout wooden club Costard kept hanging in the front hall coatrack.

And by the way Amelia held the weapon, Lily had the sneaking suspicion the lady was as good with it as she was at seducing men.

Chapter 19

"What do you propose?" Lily asked, moving a little to her right so Armand's gaze would follow her and distract him from seeing Lady Marston's approach.

Blessings on both the Costards, she thought, for they hadn't even batted an eye at the arrival of their potential savior.

"I propose nothing," Armand said. "I am telling you what you will do. Your lawyer is on his way over here with Fouché. Yes, your trustworthy little solicitor, Troussebois. He may have been loyal to his good client de Chevenoy, but it seems he was looking for more business, and our proposal was obviously better than yours. We offered to let him keep his head." Armand's chest puffed out.

Lily could well imagine the rabbity Troussebois's response—the twitchy little man dashed for the nearest safe hole.

"There is a new will for the de Chevenoy estate, one where you bequeath all your holdings to your lawful husband. You will sign the will and then we'll wed."

Lily shook her head. "I won't marry you. Not now, not ever."

"Don't worry, *ma chérie,* our marriage won't be too much of an encumbrance on you. I fear you won't live to see our honeymoon."

As he made his boast, Lady Marston's gaze rolled toward the ceiling, as if she couldn't take another minute of the man's overblown speech. Glancing one last time at Lily, she slipped behind Armand.

When he started to make his next swaggering statement, Lady Marston raised the club and hit him on the back of the head.

He slumped to the ground in a heap.

"What a vulgar man," she commented, handing the club to Costard, who'd rushed to her side. She smiled at him and said, "Please ask my driver and footman to come in, I think we will need their assistance."

Her regal bearing obviously spoke to Costard's servant heart, for the man fairly rushed out of the room to do her bidding.

She stepped over the prostrate Armand, as if avoiding a child's forgotten toy and settled down on the settee next to an open-mouthed Mme. Costard. "I had hoped to have a private audience with you, my dear," she said to Lily, casting a significant glance at the housekeeper. "If this is an inconvenient time, I can leave." She smoothed her skirts and made no attempts at anything that looked like she was leaving.

Lily shook her head at Mme. Costard not to leave and then nudged Armand in the side with the toe of her shoe. "Is he dead?"

"One can only hope," Lady Marston said.

"I didn't want you to kill him." She reached down and put her hand on his neck. Beneath her fingers she felt a steady, pulsing beat, while his chest continued to rise and fall with his breathing. "Oh, thank goodness. He's still alive."

Lady Marston pursed her lips, as if to say she found nothing to be thankful for in Lily's news.

"What are you doing here?" Lily asked. Realizing how badly that sounded, she continued. "I mean, your arrival turned out to be rather fortuitous. Thank you for saving us."

"Yes, well, think nothing of that," the lady said, patting a stray lock of hair back up into her quaint little bonnet.

Lily looked down at Armand and spied the corner of the letter still caught in the clutch of his hand. She knelt down beside him and retrieved the letter destined for Lord Dryden. "What am I going to do about this?" she muttered to herself.

"I would suggest removing him," Lady Marston said, with a distasteful nod toward Armand. "Especially if he was telling the truth and that ill-mannered Fouché is due to arrive."

"I suppose so," Lily said, rising from Armand's side, still a little unnerved by it all. She looked down at him. "We could lock him in the wine cellar."

Lady Marston frowned. "He'd probably drink every decent bottle down there when he came to." She leaned over, studying the fellow's back. "Is he as handsome as I've heard tell?"

Lily leaned down beside him, and with the help of a still speechless Mme. Costard, rolled Armand over. "See for yourself. If you like dark coloring and chiseled features, you might call him handsome."

Lady Marston rose from the settee and gazed down at Armand with a professional, assessing air. "What color are his eyes?"

"Blue," Lily said. "A rather startling blue."

"Hmmm," she said, as one might when considering a knickknack or piece of sculpture. "Yes, I believe you are right. He is quite handsome. Why he is a magnificent specimen." The lady tapped her chin with her forefinger and then snapped her fingers. "I have it. I know the perfect way to get rid of this beast, permanently."

Lily glanced up at Lady Marston and spied a twinkle of laughter in her gaze. "I don't want him killed." As much as she disliked Armand and his treachery, she didn't want to see the man dead. He was no more than an overreaching pawn in Fouché's game.

"And waste such a beautiful creature? Why I'd never." The lady turned toward the door and said, "Hamid and Alim, would you be so kind as to tie this man up and put him in my carriage."

Lady Marston's driver and footman entered the room, and despite herself, Lily took an involuntary step back. From the looks of the fierce pair, Lily wouldn't have been surprised if Lady Marston told her she fed them women and children three times a day. They hadn't even blinked at their mistress's strange request, as if it was a common everyday occurrence for Lady Marston to kidnap unconscious strangers.

"Mamelukes," Lady Marston said. "The best bodyguards you'll ever find and extremely loyal. They were a gift from my dear Samir. They travel everywhere with me. I'd simply be lost without them."

Gathering up all her courage, Lily stepped in front of the two moving mountains. "I can't let you take Armand until I know what you intend to do with him."

"Oh, I suppose you can't." Lady Marston's hands went to her hips. "Well, if you must know, I thought to send him to the Sultan, as a gift. The Sultan loves to have handsome men as . . ." She glanced over at Hamid and Alim and then back to Lily. "As servants, shall we say. Given Armand's . . ." her gaze swept to the clearly identifiable bulge in the man's tight breeches, "uh, extraordinary assets, he'll spend the remainder of his days as a pampered guest of the Sultan. Truly it is the best way. He'll be out of Paris this very afternoon, and never have a chance to reveal what he overheard." As if she saw Lily's hesitation, the lady added, "It will be best for everyone. No one associated with Henri de Chevenoy will ever have to worry about this man returning to Paris and betraying them."

Lily didn't quite trust Lady Marston's assertion about Armand's pampered status, especially given the odd look her servants shared as the lady explained her plans. Lily had a feeling Lady Marston was leaving out something very important, but if it was true, and the Sultan did like handsome servants and it would keep the Costards safe, then the fate that awaited Armand in the East was better than killing him.

She stepped aside and allowed Lady Marston's servants to do their work. Very quickly they had Armand efficiently bound and gagged.

Costard returned to the room and surveyed their handiwork. He nodded with approval as the beefy Hamid hoisted Armand onto one shoulder as if he were picking up a small child.

"Hey there," Costard told the burly servant, "you can't cart him out the front door, the neighbors will see." He sighed before muttering under his breath, "Foreigners." Puffing up his narrow chest, he bullied his way in between the two Mamelukes. "Take him back to the kitchen and leave him near the garbage pail," he instructed Hamid. He turned to Alim and jerked his thumb toward the door. "You bring that fancy carriage of yours around—as close as you can to the door in the alley. We should be able to toss him in without attracting any notice."

Before Lily knew it, Armand was bundled off for his new life in Constantinople.

Costard returned. "Is there anything else, mistress?"

"Yes, Costard," Lily said. "Please tell Celeste to pack our belongings. Then you and Madame Costard will need to pack as well."

Costard frowned. "Madame won't take that very kindly."

"There is no other choice," Lily told him. "If what Armand said was true, Fouché will be along very soon. Anyone he finds here will be, at the very least, suspect, if not arrested on sight. I think it is best if both of you go to the country house until I can send word to Webb. Is there some place out of the way where we could hide?"

"Yes, a small hunting cottage on the far side of the property. It hasn't been used for years."

"Good," she nodded. "We'll meet there. Call for a hackney and follow Lady Marston's carriage out of Paris. There will be less suspicion then, for it will look as if she is leaving the city with her servants. Once I get word to Webb, I'll join you there and we'll leave for England before Fouché has an opportunity to ensnare us."

Henri's valet looked around the room, his gaze suddenly weary and his face lined with care. "If we must. England, you say? What will Madame and I do over there?"

"You can continue to serve me, if you like. Or I will arrange for positions in my sister's household." Lily crossed the room and patted him on the arm. "It is the only way."

Costard nodded. "I'll go tell Madame. It shouldn't take us long to gather our things." He bowed to them both and left to carry out his duties.

Lily turned to Lady Marston. "As you can see, Lady Marston, I have little time left here, and I think it would be best if you were to leave." She paused before she added, "For your own safety."

"My safety? How droll you are," Lady Marston said, brushing her hands over her skirt before settling back down into the settee as if this were nothing more than the usual afternoon call. "Now, where was I before all this unfortunate business began?"

Not knowing what else to do, Lily perched herself on the edge of a chair. "I'm not sure."

"Ah, yes, Webb. I want to discuss Webb."

Lily shook her head. Thankful as she was for the woman's timely arrival, Webb Dryden was not a subject she wanted to discuss with Lady Marston.

"Before you dismiss me," the lady said, "Hear me out. I've come to see that you don't make the same mistake I nearly made. I want to see you spend the rest of your life with the man you love."

"How very kind of you," Lily said, getting up and hoping Lady Marston would take a hint and leave. "But I don't think this is the best time to discuss this matter."

"Indeed?" Lady Marston looked ready to argue the point, but instead she rose from the settee. "Lily, I have no doubt you think Webb and I have resumed our former acquaintance here in Paris. But I can tell you, nothing is further from the truth."

Lily turned her back to the woman, unwilling to hear her lies.

But when the lady made her next statement, Lily found herself compelled to turn around and listen.

"I love someone else," Amelia said with so much honesty, so much feeling, that Lily's gaze shot up. "Yes, I can see the skepticism in your eyes, but it is true. Webb is delightful, but he is not the man for me. He never was. Nor am I the woman for him."

"Who is this other man?" Lily needed to know, needed confirmation.

"His name is Samir. Until a year ago, he held the title of Pasha and we lived in Cairo. I left the Foreign Office to be with him, and I shall always be with him."

"Then why are you here?"

"I suppose this all looks terribly suspicious, but I'm here at the request of Lord Dryden. Samir and I have been living in Vienna for the last year." She paused for a moment, studying Lily. "No, I really came to help you. I owed you that. I owe you so much more."

"I can hardly think why. Why would you want to help me, especially after . . ." Lily tried to express her bitterness, but she couldn't open herself to the very woman who'd been partly responsible for her grief.

But there was no need. Amelia readily admitted her fault.

"After the way I treated you, yes that is a good question." Amelia looked away and when she looked back, there were tears misting in her eyes. "I owed you my assistance to repay the debt between us."

"You repaid that by testifying this afternoon and by getting rid of Armand. Consider yourself absolved," Lily told her.

"No, that doesn't even began to clear the debt between us. After I left Byrnewood that summer, I realized how hollow my life was. You had such a grand passion for Webb, for life, and I had nothing but my work. You made me feel so empty and lost, much as I am sure you felt as you watched Webb and me leave Byrnewood."

Lily's lips pursed shut. She closed her eyes and tried to block out the long-held pain from that day.

Amelia stepped closer and placed her hand on Lily's shoulder.

"I saw you that day," Amelia said. "You didn't think anyone would, but I did. I couldn't get the image of you out of my mind. You made me see how petty and hateful I'd become. I never made love to Webb again."

Lily's lashes fluttered open.

"Truly," Amelia told her. "I couldn't. So I went in search of my grand passion, and I have you to thank for helping me find him."

"And is that why you came here?"

"Yes. To thank you for helping me find my heart again. And to set yours free. I know what it is like to live for years besieged by bitterness. When I was fifteen, my father married me off to Lord Marston. Sold me, would be a better description." The woman laughed bitterly. "I was in love with someone else, and marrying a rank old lecher such as Marston was the worst fate possible. By the time Marston died, my true love had married elsewhere. Happily so, as it turned out. And there was no room in his life for me. So I drifted into the service."

"And that's how you met Webb."

"Exactly." She sighed. "When I saw your face at the hearing this afternoon, I realized you must have come to the wrong conclusion about us."

"So you and Webb haven't . . ."

Amelia shook her head. "No. Even if he didn't love you, I don't think he'd risk it. Samir would have him disemboweled."

Even if he didn't love you . . .

Lily clung to those words. "He loves me?"

"Yes. I can say quite truthfully, Webb Dryden is around the bend about you. You won't be rid of him for quite some time."

Tears sprang to Lily's eyes. "Oh, that's terrible. Now what am I going to do?" The mist of tears turned into a deluge. "I can't have Webb in love with me."

Lady Amelia pulled out a handkerchief, handed it to Lily,

and escorted her to the settee. "How can this be such a Haymarket tragedy?"

"I've been less than honest with Webb."

Amelia laughed. "Haven't we all been that way with a man? Though I have a feeling this goes beyond how much you spent on your latest gown."

Lily nodded her head. "I wish it were so simple."

Just then, Costard entered the study. "Those foreign devils have Armand ready to go and they are awaiting her ladyship's orders."

"Tell them I will be right there, Monsieur Costard," Lady Marston said.

Lily held out her hand to Amelia. "Thank you, my lady, for your assistance."

"Lily, whatever you think you've done to betray Webb, it can't be all that bad. You have to trust him," Amelia told her, ignoring Lily's outstretched hand and taking her into her arms in a sisterly embrace. When she let go of Lily, she said, "Promise me you will confide in him. Trust his love for you that he will do the right thing." Lady Marston smiled and left.

As they went to the foyer, Lily found Celeste and the Costards packed. She ordered them to get into the hackney that had arrived. Lady Marston had told her that Webb was on his way to the house, so the two of them would shortly follow behind everyone else. Costard offered to stay with her until Webb arrived, but she declined.

Once she saw her servants safely on their way, she took one last walk through Adelaide's home. As she entered the hall, her fingers trailed along the edge of a framed picture of a long-past de Chevenoy relative.

It saddened her to think of all of Henri's beautiful possessions ending up in the hands of Fouché and eventually Napoleon, but without any real heirs, how could it be helped?

She heard the sharp sound of hooves and the crunch of carriage wheels, and thinking Webb had finally arrived, she hurried to the front door, catching up her pelisse and bonnet.

Halfway down the steps, she glanced up at the passenger exiting the carriage. For a moment she smiled, thinking her gaze was about to fall on Webb, but in an instant her mouth opened in dismay.

For stepping down from the carriage was Joseph Fouché, followed by a contrite looking Troussebois.

"Mademoiselle," Fouché said. "Where could you be off to?"

"To finish some holiday shopping," she quipped, casually smiling at the men as if they were unexpected guests.

"So late in the day? Why most of the shops are closed." Fouché straightened his coat, his appraising gaze looking her up and down. "And I do believe you forgot to close your front door."

For a moment she thought of trying to run, but the leering and able-bodied footmen posted at the rear of the carriage appeared only too eager for her to take such a gamble.

Lily suspected they'd relish the opportunity to manhandle her. Still, she had nothing to lose.

"If you don't mind," she said, "I really must be on my way." She made as if to brush past him, but she came up short, his tight, authoritative grip on her elbow.

"Not so fast, my dear," he said, nodding to his grinning henchmen, who came down from the carriage and took her by either arm. "We have some business matters to discuss."

Without further ado, the footman hauled her up the steps and into the house.

All too quickly, Lily found herself in Henri's study.

"Get out the documents," Fouché snapped at Troussebois.

"Tell me, Mademoiselle, have you seen your betrothed this afternoon?"

While the nervous little solicitor opened his leather folder and began sorting through his papers, Lily scratched her forehead. "Which one?"

He nodded to one of the henchmen and the brute caught Lily's hand in a powerful grip, his fingers like hot iron tongs closing over her. With another nod from Fouché, the man twisted her arm up behind her back.

She gasped in pain, then cried out as the man lifted her arm even higher until she stood on her tiptoes.

Fouché leaned forward until he was inches from her face. "Tell me where Armand is."

"I . . . I . . . don't know," she stammered, trying to catch her breath against the white-hot pain stabbing through her arm.

Fouché nodded again and the man yarded her arm even higher, until Lily thought he would pull it from the socket.

"He was here," she cried out. The man relaxed his hold, but only slightly. "But he's gone now. He left before you arrived."

"That seems highly unlikely," Fouché commented, "given that the man thinks he is to be rewarded tonight. You," he said, pointing a long, elegant finger at the closest of his two nefarious assistants. "Search the house and find that worthless actor. He said he would meet us here, and considering his expensive taste in clothes and lodgings, he'll not be far. Check the wine cellar and the attic in case he spoke out of turn and has found himself being detained."

Armand an actor? His odd statement earlier about poverty suddenly made sense.

"I have everything in order," Troussebois said, his words trilling with a nervous stutter.

"Good," Fouché said. "Now, Mademoiselle, I had hoped

to catch you and all your accomplices, but it appears you have already moved your associates. I commend your quick thinking. But I shan't worry about that now, for they cannot have gone far. In the meantime, I think it is time for you to get married and turn the de Chevenoy fortune over to a husband who can appreciate your bounty."

"I won't marry Armand or any man to help you," Lily told him.

"Oh yes, you will. I have it all here. The marriage license and your new will. You will sign these documents, and you will sign them now. Then once we have found your dear betrothed, you will be wed. Imagine Troussebois's good fortune today. He gained you the de Chevenoy fortune and has been appointed a commissioner this afternoon. He has the power to perform your marriage. And then I will control your estate and the de Chevenoy fortune."

Lily knew that no matter what she did, they would force her to sign the documents, and given the painful demonstration of what Fouché's handyman was capable of, Lily was in no humor for false bravado.

She took the pen offered by Troussebois and signed the documents.

Fouché added his signature as a witness, as did the henchman, who placed a flourished X on the line Troussebois pointed out for him.

"How will you control it if I am married? How can you trust Armand to give you what you want?" she asked.

Fouché looked up from the papers, which Troussebois was carefully sanding and adding the correct seals to ensure their authenticity.

"I have no doubt he will be quite cooperative. Unfortunately, like you, he will be quite dead, and then I will control the de Chevenoy fortune, rather than have it squandered by our illustrious leader."

"Don't you think someone will notice if you murder the de Chevenoy heiress and then claim her properties for your own? The de Chevenoys are held in quite high regard. There will be an inquest at the very least."

"Oh yes, there will be an inquest, but it will be to find the Royalist perpetrators who killed you and attempted to kill the First Consul."

"Kill Bonaparte?" she whispered.

"Yes, the First Consul. Quite ingenuous. I'll be hailed a hero when I expose France's enemies."

Out of the corner of her eye, Lily saw the henchman raise his fist. Before she could move or even flinch, he brought it down on her head. An explosion of stars burst before her eyes and then the frightening blackness of oblivion closed around her.

Chapter 20

Damn this mission, damn his father, and damn Henri's journals, Webb thought as he hastened his way through the rain-splattered streets of Paris toward the *Rue de Renard*.

As far as he was concerned, Lily was leaving Paris within the hour. The fact remained, despite her obvious triumphs, she was an untried and untested agent, and the stakes now had grown considerably higher.

He'd not listen to any of her protests or her arguments. As he turned the corner, he spied a black hackney pulling away from Number 8, a single lamp rocking from the front of the conveyance.

About to cross the street, he noticed the front door of the house stood wide open. A single candle burned in the window of Henri's study.

Where was Costard? Where were the rest of the lights?

Webb drew a deep breath, looking down the street where the hackney had now disappeared from sight. He glanced back at the open door before him.

Go into the house or after the hackney?

As much as he feared losing the hackney, he continued on

past the house, and at the first opportunity found a space between the houses and cut back into the alley.

The back door was also wide open, the kitchen cast in shadows and darkness.

He pulled out the small pistol he always carried and cautiously entered the house.

Lily, he wanted to scream out. *Lily, where are you?*

But he held his tongue and silently crept through the still room. Drawers and cupboards had been left open, their contents scattered on the drainboard. Further inside, it appeared a hasty retreat or search had been made, evidenced by the general disarray, which stood in stark contrast to Mme. Costard's usual starched and waxed order.

As he entered the main foyer, the single candle in Henri's study still cast its weak light. From inside the room, he heard a shuffling of papers, a muttering voice, and the hasty opening and closing of drawers—the only sounds in the otherwise still house.

Moving silently to the door, he found the puzzling sight of Troussebois rifling through Henri's study.

"Troussebois," Webb said.

The little man jumped, nearly overturning the table and candle. *"Sacré!* You frightened me, Monsieur. I didn't hear you come in." The solicitor blinked furiously.

"My apologies," Webb said, "I hardly meant to frighten you."

Caution. None of this looks right, he told himself. *But the way to snare a rabbit and keep him alive is with gentle coaxing and carrots.*

"I called once or twice from the door, but no one answered." Webb moved into the room a step or two and turned slightly. He still didn't know if Troussebois was alone in the house so he didn't want his back completely to the door. "So busy in your work that you didn't hear me, eh?"

"Yes, something like that." Troussebois fidgeted, his fingers picking at the hem of his jacket.

"Working on Christmas Eve, and so late in the evening? You are a dedicated man, Monsieur Troussebois. My hat is off to you for your devotion to your employer's concerns."

The man gulped. "Yes, well, I think it is time for me to take my leave." He gathered a collection of papers, clutching them to his narrow chest, and tried to scurry past.

Webb caught the little man by the arm, startling him and sending his papers flying about the room in a snowstorm of parchment.

"Unhand me," Troussebois squeaked.

Rabbits always squeal when caught, Webb thought. Dragging the solicitor over to Henri's leather chair, he shoved him onto the hard seat.

When the man made a half-hearted attempt to rise, Webb brought his pistol to rest atop the man's twitching nose. "Move one hair, and I'll send you to hell with the rest of your breed."

Satisfied that the man wouldn't try anything, Webb turned and picked up the candle, holding it over the haphazard litter of legal documents Troussebois had dropped.

"What is this," Webb mused aloud. He gathered up the document that had caught his eye. It wasn't the title that sent his pulse pounding. The *Last Will and Testament of Adelaide de Chevenoy* only became of interest to him when he spied the signatures on the bottom. Notably the companionable scrawls of Bernard Troussebois and Joseph Fouché.

"Is it often that your client's wills are witnessed by the Minister of Police?" Webb asked, holding the damning evidence up for Troussebois.

The man's lips fluttered as if he wanted to answer, but no sound came out.

Webb cursed himself for not following the carriage, for now he feared Lily had been inside it. His anger turned toward the one man who could answer his questions.

As his gaze flicked from the paper in his hand and back to Troussebois, something else caught his eye.

A civil document from the local Prefect for the City of Paris. He thought at first it was the official nature of the document that drew his attention, for the red seals set it apart from the other bland clutter in Henri's office. But as Webb looked further it was the title of the document that stopped him cold.

A *Registry for Marriage*, dated today.

With the name of Adelaide de Chevenoy written in as the bride, complete with her signature at the bottom.

The groom's name had been left blank.

A marriage certificate and a will.

Fouché's plan became only too clear.

"Where has he taken her?" he said, grabbing Troussebois by his flimsy cravat and hauling the man to his feet. "Tell me now, or you will be the one in need of a will." He shoved the pistol up under Troussebois's nose and pulled back the trigger.

"To the Tuileries," the man whispered. "He took her to the palace."

"The Tuileries?" Webb prodded him again with the pistol. "Do you think I am a fool? He means to kill her. Now tell me where they've gone."

Troussebois began to cry. "Please don't shoot me. I'm telling you the truth."

"Then where is the mademoiselle?"

"In a carriage. Just outside the Tuileries. There is a planned assassination attempt tonight against the First Consul. A bomb. It will kill the heiress."

Damn and hell, why hadn't he chosen the carriage over the house!

Webb hauled a now-pleading Troussebois out of the study and back toward the kitchen.

"Please don't kill me, Monsieur," the man begged. "My clients would be lost without me."

"It seems your concern for your clients comes a little too late, Troussebois." Webb opened the door to the wine cellar. "Where is this bomb?"

Troussebois shook his head in an unprecedented show of bravery.

Webb repeated his question, this time with the pistol pointed at the narrow space between Troussebois's closely set eyes.

Troussebois swallowed. "I'll only tell if you promise not to kill me."

Taking a deep breath, Webb nodded.

As if weighing the choice between instant death and life as a traitor, Troussebois, true to form, opened his mouth. "The *Rue Saint-Nicaise*. The bomb is hidden in an overturned cart not far from where the *Rue Saint-Nicaise* joins the *Rue Saint-Honoré*."

Webb replied by shoving the man into the wine cellar and slamming the door in his face.

Inside he heard the man's scrambling footsteps on the wooden steps and his bleating protests.

"Monsieur, you promised. You promised you would let me live."

"And so I have," Webb told him.

"But you must let me out. You promised you wouldn't kill me. Fouché will not be so kind if he finds me."

"That, Troussebois, is where you erred. I promised not to kill you, but I never promised to let you go. I won't kill you, not tonight. But I made no promise for your good friend,

Fouché. I fear you will have to make your own black-hearted deal with him."

Webb fled from the kitchen, racing through the house toward the front door, his footsteps echoing to the frantic beating on the cellar door.

As he got to the study, he paused. If Lily was still alive, there was a chance he could yet outwit Fouché and give the man the comeuppance he deserved.

Webb snatched up the will and marriage registration, stuffing them into his jacket.

If . . . no, when, he corrected himself, he found her, Lily would never again be far from his side. And never again in this type of danger.

Dashing down the front steps, Webb looked left then right.

The *Rue Saint-Nicaise* was not close enough to reach on foot, in time to stop Fouché's bomb. His head swung at the *clip-clop* sound of hooves at the corner. There he spied a man riding past on the intersecting avenue.

Webb grinned. That solved his first problem.

He raced down the street, careful to keep his footfalls quiet, and sticking as close to the shadows of the tree-lined boulevard as possible.

As he approached the man, he realized this was no ordinary citizen but an officer in the Hussars, Napoleon's light cavalry.

He had hoped to find a country yokel who could be talked out of his nag with the aid of a few gold coins.

But luck was on his side, for as he drew closer to the officer plodding along aboard his fine horse at a casual amble, Webb heard the slurred refrain of a Christmas carol coming from his target.

"*Noël nouvelet, Noël chantons ici*," the man sang. Christmas comes anew, O let us sing Noel.

How had he forgotten? It was Christmas Eve.

He made his own wish for the holiday, a silent one offered up on this holy night.

The man swayed in his saddle and started the next line of his song. *"Devotés gens—"*

"Excusez-moi, Monsieur," Webb called out. "I am lost. Could you possibly give me directions to the *Rue Saint-Nicaise?"*

As the man turned in his saddle, Webb caught him by the front of his elaborately decorated dolman jacket and pitched him out of his seat. The man fell to the street in a heap.

"I've had too much to drink," the man declared, staring up at Webb, his expression bleary-eyed and stunned. "Be a good fellow and help me to remember the next line." He scratched his head and then began to sing, *"Chantons Noël pour le Roi nouvelet, Noël."*

Webb hated to do it, but he had no other choice. He slammed his fist into the unwary man's jaw, knocking him unconscious. Grabbing the reins of the now nervous horse, he spoke to it softly.

"Easy, my friend. Easy there."

The horse side-stepped and pranced amongst the puddles, its wild gaze going from its fallen master to the stranger holding its reins.

Webb mounted the animal in one fluid movement, quickly gaining control of the nervous beast. Taking one last look at the fallen officer, Webb felt a pang of guilt.

Stealing a man's horse on Christmas Eve, he should be ashamed of himself. Quickly he cut the officer's leather *sabretache* from where it hung on the saddle, so at least when he awoke he would still have his personal effects. As one last gesture of goodwill, Webb plucked a small pouch from his jacket and tossed it down so it landed beside the man's elbow.

Enough to cover a new horse and another round of Christmas cheer.

With that, he reined the horse around and rode hell-bent for the *Rue Saint Nicaise*. He raced past holiday revelers, all but deaf to their drunken cries of well wishes.

It was the first time in years Parisians were openly celebrating the holiday, and they were making the most of it— drinking in the local taverns and making rounds of visits to friends and family.

As he galloped down the *Rue Saint-Honoré*, he offered his prayer up one more time.

Please, let Lily live.

But as he turned onto the *Rue Saint-Nicaise*, he saw a carriage he recognized as the First Consul's hurtling toward him. The driver was whipping his horses, and as Webb reined his horse to a stop, the fast moving carriage and the accompanying guards careened wildly past an overturned cart laying haphazardly in the middle of the road.

The overturned cart. The bomb.

For a moment Webb rejoiced that he'd made it in time to stop Fouché.

But in that instant, a second carriage, this one a black hackney, turned out of an alley and whipped toward him at the same breakneck speed.

As it sped toward the cart, he watched in horror as the driver jumped from his perch, rolling to safety.

The horses continued pulling the hackney toward the cart, their movements erratic without the firm control of their driver.

"Lily!" he screamed, spurring his horse to follow the hackney.

And in that instant the cart exploded, sending flaming debris and wreckage through the clogged street—wreckage from a black hackney now destroyed and smoking amidst the carnage.

Chapter 21

The first explosion threw Webb from his horse and the second blast covered him with debris.

As he struggled through jagged pieces of carriage and shattered glass from the adjacent shop windows, he tried desperately to see through the smoke and flames toward the hackney.

The scene he witnessed wrenched through his gut. Mangled bodies, the sweet smell of blood, the crackle of fire, and the acrid stench of burnt flesh. His ears rang with the cries of the wounded and those struggling to find the loved ones who just moments before had been walking down the promenade beside them.

Webb stumbled to his feet, his head pounding in protest, his vision swimming at the quick movement. He put his fingers to the sharp pain in his forehead and came in contact with the warm, sticky feeling of blood.

Wavering on his feet, he cried out, "Lily! Lily, where are you?"

Somehow the horse he'd stolen had survived the blast and was only a few feet away, standing dumfounded and stunned amongst the broken pieces of siding and lumber. He caught the animal's reins and tied them to a twisted lamppost.

Staggering, he continued past the wounded, toward the wreckage of the hackney. He stumbled once and looked down to see Fouché's henchman, the driver who'd thought to save his own life by leaping from the racing carriage.

The blast had thrown a piece of metal into his chest, and now it protruded from his blood-soaked jacket. His lifeless eyes stared up at the night sky.

Webb pulled aside a tangled wheel, the springs from the leather seats. He fought his way like a blind madman, for his vision was now clouded in the red of his own blood. But there was only one thing that could stop his mad pursuit.

Lily.

He had led her to this. Insisted that she come against her wishes. Blackmailed her into it. Her secrets, the past that she refused to share, they mattered not at this moment.

If only she lived, so he could tell her. Tell her he loved her.

The remaining shell of the carriage was upside down. One horse, still caught in the traces, screamed and struggled to break free. The other horse lay silent, its legs jutting out at odd angles.

Webb pulled at the carriage, trying to find a way to right the smoking pile.

For Lily, he knew, was somewhere underneath all this.

From out of nowhere a man approached him.

"You are hurt, Monsieur, you must get help," the kindly stranger said, gently pulling at Webb's sleeve.

"No!" Webb roared. "Get your hands off of me. I won't leave her."

The elderly man's eyes went wide with fright, but he did not back away.

Struggling to regain his composure, Webb reached for the man. "Help me, please. I must find her."

"Of course you must, my son. I am Father Michel." The man bowed his head slightly and then called out to another man who knelt beside the body of the driver. "Father Joseph, we need your assistance and your good back."

The three of them put their shoulders to the wreckage and righted what remained of the carriage.

Webb stepped back and, to his horror, saw a pair of white arms sticking out of the wreckage, the wrists bound in rope.

On one finger winked the strange little bumblebee ring Lily always wore.

"No," he sobbed, dropping to his knees, pulling away at the scraps of wood and metal, and desperately trying to free her. She was wrapped, almost shroudlike in a thick horse blanket that Father Michel quickly cut away with a knife he pulled from his robes.

The priests continued cutting and pulling away the heavy wool covering until they had completely uncovered her.

"It seems we have discovered an angel," Father Joseph said, making a sign of the cross over Lily's head.

Webb reached for her, his fingers caressing her warm skin.

Please let her be alive. Please, I'll never doubt her again, if you only let her live, he silently prayed.

He looked up and saw a single star peering through a break in the clouds. It twinkled once, as if in response.

And then beneath his fingertips, he felt it.

Lily's pulse. Steady and true.

He looked up and saw that palace officials and guards had begun arriving. Fouché hadn't killed her, at least not yet, and Webb wasn't going to give him a second chance.

Father Joseph's gaze followed his. "I suspect you need to get her out of here."

Webb nodded, lifting Lily from the street and into his arms. Her weight combined with his own loss of blood left him swooning, and he would have fallen if Father Michel hadn't stepped forward and caught him by the elbow.

"You need a doctor, my son. You both do." The priest steadied Webb with a firm, solid grip.

Father Joseph got on the other side of Webb, offering his support as well. "We've just returned to Paris. I'm afraid I don't know where we can find one for you."

They guided Webb out of the street.

"There is a surgeon not far from here," he managed to say. "Dr. McTaggart. He will help us." He nodded toward his horse. "Bring him. I should be able to ride."

Father Joseph laughed. "You can barely walk, my son, let alone ride double with an unconscious woman." The priest untied the reins and led the horse after them.

"Where is this doctor?" Father Michel asked.

The pain in his head was starting to become more than he could tolerate, and he knew the two priests were right. He'd never make it to McTaggart's alone.

"He lives above the Flaming Thistle, a tavern run by a Scot. Do you know of it?"

Father Joseph laughed. "I'm a Dubliner by birth, my son. I know where to find the nearest thing to Irish whisky there is in this God-forsaken city. I'm only too familiar with the Flaming Thistle."

Fading in and out of consciousness, Webb found himself hoisted up on his horse and Lily laid across his lap. Father Michel and Father Joseph walked on either side of the horse, steadying him and his precious bundle.

Try as he might, he couldn't stay awake, and he collapsed over Lily's still form.

"What do you think we have here, Father Michel?" Father Joseph stepped closer to the horse and caught hold of the man and woman before they tumbled into the street.

"I'm not sure, Father Joseph." The older man guided the

horse over the old *Pont Royal*, now known as the *Pont de la Reunion* and into the Left Bank neighborhood of the Flaming Thistle. "In Paris, it is better not to ask and trust that we won't be led astray."

Alex McTaggart had just settled in for his own version of holiday cheer. He'd shared an early dinner downstairs with a collection of fellow Scottish expatriates and stumbled upstairs to find his new mistress had left him an unexpected Christmas gift—herself, wrapped only in a lacy peignoir that must have cost him a small fortune.

No matter, the little baggage had been teasing him for a month, and now he was about to reap the rewards of a conquest well spent.

"Ah, my dear Giselle, what are you doing here?"

She giggled. "An examination, Monsieur Doctor. I feel a great pain here," she said, her hand resting over her right breast.

He stepped closer. Gently he took her fingers and moved them to the left. "I think you mean here, over your heart, my little flower."

Giselle giggled again, her pert breasts nearly jiggling out of the silk confines that barely concealed their bounty. "Oh, yes, my heart, it grieves me so."

You little tart, I doubt you have one, he thought, as he pulled her closer and started his examination by thoroughly kissing her.

The bell that announced his patients jangled loudly.

He let it ring and continued his examination by fondling her rounded buttocks and pulling her closer to him.

The bell clattered again, this time with a greater sense of urgency.

"Damn," he cursed, wrenching himself away from his Christmas present.

"Can't you tell them to go away?" Giselle pouted.

"If it's not a matter of life and death, lass, they'll be gone before you catch a chill," he said, crossing the room and yanking open the window. He stuck out his head and looked down at the street below.

Two cloaked figures stood on either side of a horse. Astride the animal was a man holding a young woman.

"Monsieur, this man asked us to bring him here," one of the men said before he tossed back his hood.

McTaggart saw the collar of a cleric and cursed.

He wasn't an overly religious man, but he still held a holy if not fearful respect for priests. How could he explain to the good father that he wasn't open for business because he was of a mind to commit enough sins to keep him in confession for a month?

He glanced wistfully back at Giselle. The wanton girl sat straddled on the arm of the sofa, her plump thighs spread wide and inviting, her finger curled in invitation.

If only he could be that sofa, he thought.

"Can you open the door, Monsieur Doctor?" the priest called out. "Before he passed out this man intimated he was in some sort of trouble."

Trouble? Alex nodded to the priest. "Pull him under the lamp and let me get a look at him."

The priest sighed loudly, as if asking for a little patience from on high, and then slowly guided the horse under the light. He tipped the man's head up and gave Alex a look at his patient.

"Damn it to bloody hell," he cursed, looking down at the bloodstained face of his foolhardy friend. The woman, he could only guess, must be the de Chevenoy heiress.

Trouble was hardly the word to describe the situation.

"I'll be right there." He slammed the window shut and turned to Giselle. "Sorry my sweet, but I've got patients."

Her full red lips curved into an unhappy moue. "I could help," she said, twirling the strings of her peignoir.

"Not unless you relish the sight of blood."

She shuddered and traipsed to the bedroom, slamming the door behind her.

Alex took the stairs to the street two at a time. He threw back the bolts and flung open the door. One of the priests had the girl in his arms and the other was carefully pulling Webb down from the horse.

"I'm fine," Webb muttered, much to Alex's relief.

"So you are alive," he said, grabbing Webb's arm and throwing it around his shoulder. With his hand around the man's waist, he helped him toward the door. "I was afraid I wouldn't get paid for this one. Dead patients can be so difficult about their bills."

"A true Scot you are, Alex. More worried about your bill than about the patient," Webb said, his words slurred.

Alex turned to the priest by the horse. "Take that beast around back and rouse the stable lad. Tell him McTaggart said to see that it's well fed and cared for. Then once he's done that, to take the saddle and anything else with a crest on it and see it tossed in the river."

He watched the two priests exchange a look, as if to say, I told you there was something wrong about all this.

"I thank you both for your help, and if you'll leave the name and address of your parish, I will see a contribution sent there in appreciation of your assistance," Alex told the man carrying the girl up the stairs.

The priest huffed and puffed his way to the top and then laid his burden carefully on the sofa.

"I have some experience with healing. I could be of assistance," the priest said, his tone more that of an order than of a question. Especially when he proceeded to remove his cloak and jacket.

No arguing with a cleric, Alex thought. Besides, with two patients, he might just need the help. He opened the cabinet where he kept his medical supplies and pulled out bandages for Webb's head wound, then he caught up a pitcher of water and a bowl he kept handy. Kneeling beside Webb, he started to sponge away the blood on the man's head so he could find the source of the bleeding.

Webb shook him off. "I'm fine, you horse doctor. Take care of Lily first," he said, pointing his finger at the girl.

Alex handed the bloody rag to the priest. "If you're of a mind to help, clean up his face, so I can stand the sight of him."

The priest grinned. "Scots. I never get used to your blunt manners or brusque ways."

Alex eyed the man. "Is that a brogue I hear to your speech, Father? An Irish one, if I'm not mistaken." He relaxed as the man nodded.

"Father Joseph O'Brien, late of Dublin and traveling through Paris on our way to Rome."

If not French, his loyalty wouldn't be in question, Alex thought. And if he was as he said, just passing through, he wouldn't be in the city long enough to tell anyone what he'd seen. "Well then, do a good job there, Father Joseph, and I'll dig out a bottle of my finest Highland whisky. Good whisky, mind you. Not that poor watery stuff you Irish drink."

"From the sound of your voice, you've already been into it," Webb commented.

"Mind your manners, lad," Alex told him.

It took every ounce of Webb's patience to sit still while the good Father Joseph cleaned up his head wound.

He stared across the room, guilt and fear twisting his gut.

If he hadn't stopped for a drink with Alex . . . If he hadn't insisted to his father that she should come along.

If . . . If . . . If . . . his head throbbed with recriminations.

Webb watched each movement Alex made, hopeful that his patient would open her eyes and let into him with the tongue-lashing he probably deserved for not reaching the de Chevenoy house in time.

"Webb?" she whispered, her voice dry and cracked. "Where are you?"

"Lily, I'm right here." He crossed the room in two quick strides, and then dropped beside the small settee on which she lay. Despite the dizziness washing over him, he tried to focus his eyes on her face.

Her image blurred and swayed in front of him and he caught up her hand, the one uninjured from the blast, and held on to her. The other hand had minor burns, which the doctor had cleaned and covered with an ill-smelling salve and clean linen.

It seemed the thick horse blanket that Fouché's henchmen had wrapped her in had protected her from the worst of the explosion.

He looked at Alex for the answer to the question he was too much of a coward to ask.

How is she?

Alex shook his head. "I don't know what's wrong. But this happens with head injuries. She's got a hell of a blow here," he said, pointing to the ugly beginnings of a bruise by her temple. "And enough bruises over the rest of her body to have internal injuries, but I can't tell just yet. It would be better if she woke up. I won't lie to you, lad. The longer she's out like this, the worse it will be."

"Webb?" Lily's fingers tightened around his palm.

"Lily, you're going to be all right, but you have to wake up."

She tossed and pushed his hand away. Her face twisted in pain as she moved.

Webb leaned closer. "Wake up, little Lily. Wake up. I won't leave Paris without you. I won't ever leave you. Not for anything. Just wake up and live your life with me."

Her breathing became frantic, as if she'd just tried outrunning a thoroughbred. "Go," she told him. "Please, go." For a moment her lashes fluttered as if she were going to open them, but then her body relaxed and her breathing evened out.

The clock on the mantel struck eleven and Alex put his hand on Webb's shoulder. "You should get some rest. I'll sit up with her."

"No. I'm not going anywhere." Webb shot an angry glance over his shoulder. He turned back to Lily and took her hand in his. "Do you hear that, hoyden? I'm not going anywhere."

Lily opened her eyes and found herself in a shadowy room. She heard the solid ticking of a clock, the soft sounds of a banked fire. An odd, pungent smell pervaded the room, the likes of which she couldn't place. She blinked her lashes and tried to discern where she might be, but nothing was familiar.

Nothing save the man at her side.

Webb's head lay against her, his hand holding hers. She sighed.

Webb was safe.

But then she looked again and saw the linen cloth wrapped around his head, his tousled brown hair matted in places with dried blood.

As she tried to reach out to him, to offer him comfort, she

stopped as a sharp pain throbbed through her arm all the way down to her fingertips. She looked at her hand, which was covered by a bandage similar to Webb's.

"So you are going to rejoin us, my lady," said a voice she didn't recognize. "That will make our friend very happy."

She turned her head toward the speaker and saw a man wrapped in a thick wool plaid sitting up in a straight-backed chair. While his black hair was peppered with gray, his unlined face belied any specific age. He could be thirty or twice that for all she could tell. "Do I know you?"

The man grinned. "I'm your doctor."

She closed her eyes for a moment. "So why do I feel so awful?"

The doctor laughed, a low friendly chuckle. "Oh, I couldn't have picked better myself."

"Picked what?"

"A wife for that stubborn fool at your side."

She struggled to sit up. "I'm not his wife."

At her abrupt movement, Webb roused. His expression was first confused, and then instantly his eyes grew wide and his mouth split into a lopsided smile.

"Hoyden! You're back!" He leaned over and kissed her, his mouth tenderly caressing her lips, though beneath his caring burned a passion barely held in check.

She let him kiss her once, well, maybe twice, and then pulled away. "I told you not to call me that," she said. "There was an explosion. How did you find me? How did I escape? Are you badly injured? You look terrible. Where are we?"

Webb glanced up at the stranger. "A complete recovery, Alex. She's as ornery and full of questions as ever."

The doctor coughed politely, his eyebrows arched in dubious lines. "Let me be the judge of that." Alex knelt beside her and placed his hand on her brow.

"How is he?" she asked, her gaze moving from Webb's injuries back to the doctor.

"He'll make a complete recovery, as will you, if you'll let me do my job. Our friend's untrained assessment notwithstanding, how do you feel, my lady?"

Webb was going to be fine. She couldn't think of a better diagnosis.

As for herself, for the most part she felt as if she'd swallowed a handful of loose wool. Fuzzy and scratchy all at once. She closed her eyes for a moment and did a mental tally of the general aches and pains. She searched her memory for what had happened, and for a moment, all she could see were flames, but then out of the fires, came images and words.

An explosion.

Fouché's threats. The meeting in Henri's study.

The blow from the henchman.

The moment she'd come to in the carriage, sputtering as a drink was forced down her throat.

And then nothing but a hodgepodge of noise and smoke and voices.

"My head hurts, but that could be whatever it was they made me drink."

The doctor cocked his head. "Do you know what it was?"

She shook her head. "No, it was something to make me sleep so I wouldn't draw attention to the carriage. It tasted sweet."

"Probably laudanum. No wonder you have a headache. And no wonder you were out for so long." He tipped his head and studied her. "Anywhere else?"

"Just my hand," she told him, holding up her injured limb.

The man smiled at Webb. "It sounds like your bride-to-be is going to live long enough to make the nuptials. I'll send you my bill along with a little something for the wedding." The man crossed his arms over his barrel of a chest. "It appears once again I have been exceedingly brilliant."

At this, Lily noticed two shadowy figures rising from pallets beside the fire.

"Is she coming around?" a kindly voice inquired.

"Aye, Father," Alex told the man, who had gotten up and now stood behind Webb. "It looks as if you and Father Michel saved both their lives by getting them away from the blast so quickly."

"A priest?" Lily asked. "Did you think I was going to die?"

Webb grinned. "No. They came to my aid when I was trying to pull you from the wreckage. Without their help we would never had made it here to Alex's, to safety."

Safety. She knew what that meant. Alex knew all about Webb's duties and had obviously helped him from time to time, given the easy familiarity between the two men.

"Alex was kind enough to offer them a place by the fire for the night," Webb said. "Besides, I did want them nearby for when you woke up."

Her gaze narrowed suspiciously. "Whatever for?"

"Why to marry us, hoyden. Before the sun rises, I intend to make you my wife."

Chapter 22

"Marry you?" Lily sat straight up. "I can't. I won't."

Webb smiled indulgently. "Lily, don't be ridiculous. Of course we're going to get married." He took her hand in his. "I love you. I don't know how it happened or when, but it did. You matter more to me than anything. I think I've always loved you, hoyden. Doesn't that count for something?"

It counted more than she cared to admit. Where had everything gone so wrong? Webb loved her. She should be dancing in his arms. But instead she felt like crawling into the nearest gutter.

Webb loved her. She held back the tears threatening to fall.

"No, Webb, I can't marry you. Not ever." She looked down at the floor. "Do we have to discuss it now?" she whispered, peeking up at the embarrassed expressions of the strangers around them.

He turned to the others. "Can you give us a moment of privacy?"

The three retreated to a room that Lily guessed was the

doctor's office. Once they were alone Webb's steady gaze returned to her. "You're right that we shouldn't be discussing this in front of strangers. But the fact remains, we have to get married." He reached inside his jacket and pulled out several pieces of paper and handed them to her.

She glanced down at the familiar documents. "Where did you get these?"

"From the study. I arrived just after you left and found Troussebois finishing Fouché's handiwork."

Lily took a deep breath. "Troussebois betrayed us. You could have been killed."

"Yes, I assumed so with all the signatures. I left him bleating and crying in the wine cellar."

"He has no room to complain," she said, before she could stop herself, "he could have shared Armand's fate."

Webb cocked his head. "Armand?"

Lily glanced away.

"What have you done?" His voice rose with alarm.

"I didn't kill him, if that's what you mean. He's quite well, as far as I know. Besides, it wasn't completely my idea. Amelia helped," she said in a rush. "She promised he'd be well cared for."

"Amelia? What has she to do with this?"

"She arrived in time to stop Armand from revealing what he'd overheard."

"Which was?"

"He overheard me telling the Costards that I wasn't Adelaide de Chevenoy," she said quietly.

"What?" Even Webb's swollen eye managed to open, though only a little. "I know I got tapped pretty hard on the head, but I could have sworn I just heard you say you told the Costards you weren't Adelaide."

She cringed and nodded her head.

Webb sat back on his heels, his jaw falling slack.

"I didn't want to stay in Paris any longer, and I thought—" she stopped herself from telling the truth.

I thought you and Amelia were lovers and I couldn't live with it.

Instead she rushed on. "I just thought it was time to find the journals and be done with our mission. And then when Armand heard me, he said he was going to kill me and he'd probably have killed the Costards or at least turned them over to the guards, so I agreed with Amelia that he couldn't stay in Paris."

Webb crossed his arms over his chest. "So what did you and Amelia decide to do with Armand?"

"Amelia suggested giving him as a gift to the Ottoman Sultan," she told him.

Webb stared at her as if she'd gone mad.

"Truly, it was Amelia's idea. After she hit him on the head and knocked him out, she suggested giving him to the Sultan. According to Amelia, the Sultan likes good-looking men for servants. She promised he'd be well cared for and more than likely live out his days being quite pampered."

His mouth opened in a wide *O* and then snapped shut.

"I thought it sounded unusual, but Amelia thought it quite amusing."

"She would." Webb laughed.

"So you aren't angry with me?" Lily asked. The time would come soon enough for Webb to despise her. She wanted to live a little longer in the fantasy that he loved her.

"Not as much as I should be. I'd forgive you anything, hoyden. You know that. At least you should." He held up the papers. "Look here, Troussebois said the groom's name was left blank because Armand hadn't arrived on time. So I filled in my name. So in a sense, we are already legally married. I just thought you would prefer having the ceremony blessed, so I asked Father Joseph to formalize what the law already considers binding."

"How can that be a real marriage? I signed under duress and it isn't even my real name."

He pointed to the first line. "Is that your signature?"

"But I—"

"—is it?"

Her brows furrowed. "Yes, but—"

"—and is this a marriage license?"

"We are not married. I do not consider that legal or binding."

"It is to me, Lily. No matter the names on this certificate, French law considers us married, which means we are married." His tone brooked no resistance. "Besides, now that we are married, Adelaide's will designates all her worldly goods to her lawful husband. Since Troussebois also left this blank, I'll fill in my name. The de Chevenoy properties are secure now until I can return and claim them."

"Fouché will never let you get away with it."

"How can he argue against it? Look, his signature is here as a witness. Mark my words, that weasel will find a way to worm his way out of this and back into Napoleon's good graces."

"There is only one problem—I'm still alive."

Webb grinned. "Not for long."

"I don't like the sound of that."

"Unfortunately, according to Dr. Alex McTaggart, Adelaide de Chevenoy died of injuries sustained in last night's tragic explosion. Lily D'Artiers Copeland Dryden is thought to be on the road to recovery."

"Poor Adelaide," Lily said. "But what will you do for a body?"

"No need. Alex completed your death certificate, the good fathers signed as witnesses, and your coffin is already sealed. Adelaide will be buried before Fouché has time to know what we've done."

"Well, that's a relief. I thought for a minute you were going to send me to the Sultan as well."

Webb shook his head and looked down into Lily's innocent gaze. "I doubt you are the Sultan's type." He didn't want to have to explain to her what fate she'd cast Armand into for fear his well-meaning partner would ask him to go after Amelia and stop her.

Leave it to Amelia to give a cad like Armand, or whomever he really was, his comeuppance. However, Webb suspected the wily Armand would probably take the Sultan's court by storm and live out his days, much as Lily said, in the lap of luxury.

He smiled down at her. "Now that Adelaide's dead, you can't stay here any longer, so I'm taking you back to London. Since we haven't been able to find the journals, I doubt Fouché will either, short of tearing down the houses brick by brick. Which, given the state of the inheritance, not even he could justify. In a few months I can come back and quietly find the journals."

She shook her head. "You don't have to come back."

Lily was worried about him. That, he felt, was a good sign. Whatever her reluctance to get married, he was going to find a way around it. "I know you're concerned, but I'll be fine and you'll be safe in my house in London."

She closed her eyes, her mouth set in a purposeful line. "Just let me finish what I am trying to say." Her lashes fluttered open and she sighed. "You don't have to come back to Paris. There are no journals. Costard told me."

"Costard?"

"Yes, when I asked him this afternoon, he told me Henri never kept any journals."

"You did what?" he said. If his head pounded before, now it felt ready to explode.

"I told you before, when we were discussing Armand. He

was there when I told Costard who I was. But I don't think he heard me ask Costard where Henri kept his journals."

"Why would you do that?"

"In the courtroom, it was apparent the Costards knew I wasn't Adelaide, and it was also obvious Troussebois knew, so I realized our time here was limited. My instincts told me the Costards were in it for different reasons than Troussebois." She twitched her nose in imitation of the man. "I'd never trusted him. But I trusted the Costards. So I asked them."

A few days in the field and suddenly she's an expert on instincts! "Why of all the unorthodox, idiotic, foolish . . ."

When he paused, Lily jumped in. "Yes, go ahead and say it, I'm the worst agent in the world."

He didn't. Instead he asked, "How do you know the Costards are telling the truth?"

She turned away from him a little and then reached inside her dress and pulled a small, folded letter out from her bodice. She handed it to him. "I haven't opened it, but Costard told me that this is from Henri de Chevenoy. It was to be delivered to your father in the event of Henri's death." She shrugged. "I suppose it explains it all. You could say, Henri's last laugh at your father's expense."

He turned the missive back and forth in his hand. The handwriting was certainly Henri's, as was the seal. Sliding his thumb under the wax he popped it open.

Ignoring her protests that the letter was for his father and his father only, Webb scanned the lines. Lily had, in fact, discovered the truth.

There were no journals. Henri confessed to using them as a ruse to keep his payments current. He apologized and then urged Lord Dryden not to send anyone to France as a replacement, but only to see what he could do for the welfare of the Costards given their long years of loyalty.

Webb rose and walked over to the fire, where he fed the last piece of damning evidence against de Chevenoy into the fire. He stared into the flames for moment before he asked, "Why didn't you tell me about your plan to confront the Costards?"

"You were occupied at the time."

Amelia. He returned to her bedside. "If you think that Amelia and I were . . ."

She put her finger to his lips, stilling his flow of words. "I know you weren't. She told me."

Webb could imagine how that conversation had gone. Catching up her hand, he kissed the finger that just moments before had brushed against his lips. "Then why didn't you tell me about your suspicions, that you were going to confront the Costards."

"Because you would have told me not to."

She was right there. But telling the Costards? It was a tremendous risk, even by his reckless standards.

"Webb, you may argue with my means, but I got to the truth of the matter rather quickly. According to Costard, Henri wasn't so foolish as to keep anything in a journal, in fact he—" Her words came to an abrupt halt.

"He what?"

"He . . . he was . . . quite brilliant at remembering it all," she said, struggling over each word, as if she'd forgotten her lines in some play. "Yes, and according to Costard, he never kept any records that might incriminate him."

He suspected Lily wasn't telling him the entire truth, but now wasn't the time to search it out. If what she said was true, then their mission was over.

"I can see the disappointment in your eyes," she said, softly. "We came here for nothing."

Nothing? He could hardly call it that. The British agents on the Continent could now rest easy knowing that a record of their activities wasn't about to be handed over to Bonaparte, Henri's estate was now safe from the grasping upstart; and they could see to Henri's last wish, the safety of the Costards.

But even beyond all these things, he'd unearthed something far more valuable than Henri's journals.

He'd found his direction, he'd found his life.

He'd found Lily.

Now he'd have to find a way to make her believe in this same impossible notion. Only before he could get to that, he had a few more unanswered questions. Like, where were the Costards now? And where was Celeste?

As Lily outlined the rest of the evening's events, until Fouché's abduction, he felt a growing pride at how she'd handled the situations.

Now there was nothing left to do but gather together the Costards and Celeste and make a hasty retreat to the coast where they would meet their ship.

"That leaves only one unanswered question, Lily," he said, kneeling before her. "Why won't you marry me tonight?"

She looked up at him, her green eyes clear and round. For a moment he thought he spied tears there, but it may have been only a play of light.

"Webb, it was wrong for us to make love, it was wrong for me to come here. And it would be an even bigger mistake if I were to marry you." She paused and took a deep breath. "My life is back in Virginia and yours is working for your father. I'm not suited for this life, as you can well attest. Please, just forget about our time here. Forget about us. It was a mistake."

He caught her by the shoulders. "I don't believe that and neither do you. Tell me, Lily, why you won't marry me."

Her face set in determined lines and her shoulders straightened. "Because I don't love you. I wanted to get even with you for the way you treated me all those years ago, and I suppose now I've succeeded."

Chapter 23

England
New Year's Eve, 1800

Though back in London, Lily's emphatic statement that she didn't love him, still left Webb reeling. Looking across the carriage toward her, he took only a quick glance at her quiet features.

Had she truly deceived him? His pride was too stung to ask her further.

Before they left Paris, Lily had asked Webb to send a note to Lucien. She prayed her brother needed her advice and returned immediately to his family in Virginia.

Paris was no longer safe for any of them.

With Lucien warned, they'd left Alex's and raced to Henri's country estate where they'd skirted Fouché's hired thugs, found the secluded hunting lodge, and gathered up Celeste and the Costards. They'd traveled nearly without pause toward the coast, stopping only to change the horses and grab quick meals. In the crowded carriage there had been little privacy, and when they did stop, Lily avoided him as best she could, staying close to Mme. Costard and Celeste.

Thusly, they arrived back in London a little past midnight,

an astounding six days after the fateful explosion on the *Rue du Nicaise*.

He'd dropped her off at her aunt's house well past midnight, and he'd told her he'd be by early the next morning to escort her to his father's office for their report. Then Webb had left the report he'd drafted during their crossing on his father's desk at the Foreign Office, knowing full well his father would find it bright and early in the morning, before their interview.

Eventually he'd sought his own bed and drifted in and out of a restless sleep.

Much to his surprise, the next morning when he called at Lady Dearsley's house at quarter past nine, he found Lily waiting for him. He'd half expected her to have fled the city.

And him.

Now as they rode along in Webb's carriage, Lily still avoided his glance and said almost nothing in response to his questions and inquiries.

"The Foreign Office is coming up," he offered, hoping to extract some response from her.

She only nodded.

The carriage slowed in front of the expansive building near the Thames, the smell of the river filling the carriage with its rank odor. When it stopped, Webb got out and then helped Lily and Celeste down.

Lily had insisted that Celeste accompany them. For modesty's sake, she'd claimed. But he had a feeling that it was because she didn't want to be alone with him.

"I don't know about you, but I find that smell offensive," he commented. "I can't wait until we are finished reporting to my father, and then we'll be off on our honeymoon and out of this wretched city."

"We aren't married, Webb."

He looked directly into her green eyes. What emotion was

there, she quickly hid, glancing away and refusing to look him in the eye. "Perhaps not. I suppose I should thank you for not acknowledging our marriage. Then I'll be able to find a bride who isn't so obstinate and prone to telling lies."

Celeste made a rude noise in the back of her throat, and Lily shot her maid an angry glance.

Webb didn't have time to comment further, as his father's secretary, Cecil, awaited them at the front entrance and ushered them through the warren of busy offices.

Calling Lily a liar had brought out the desired result. Her face now shone a rosy pink.

With Celeste settled on a bench outside the door to his father's spacious den, Webb and Lily were announced.

"I have just finished reading your report, Webb," Lord Dryden said, rising from his desk and inclining his head toward Lily. He waved his hand toward a chair for her.

Once she was seated, Webb and his father followed suit, taking their respective chairs.

His father, never one for formalities, launched into a series of questions he had regarding their work and observations. Webb answered most of the questions, but occasionally his father would direct an inquiry toward Lily, and she would give him a straightforward answer, sparing no more words than necessary.

Finally, their interview began to draw to a close. His father sat back in his chair, removed his glasses, and rubbed the bridge of his nose between his fingers.

It struck Webb for the first time that his father was aging. The lines around his eyes seemed more pronounced and he had a tired air about him that was unusual for his always alert sire.

"I must apologize, Lily," Lord Dryden said. "For sending you on this fool's errand. I can only tell you that it was quite necessary to validate our information and assure everyone that Henri de Chevenoy did not keep a record of his activities." He paused and glanced back down at the report before him. "Why if they had existed and any of that got into the hands of the French, or even the Dutch or those pesky upstarts across the Atlantic, begging your pardon, why, I can't think of how long it would take to repair the damage."

Lily sat primly in her seat, her hands folded in her lap. "I am only glad that I was able to assist you in your time of need. You have been quite generous to my family, and I am pleased that I could, in my own small way, repay some of that debt."

"Nonsense, my dear," Lord Dryden said with a wave of his hand. "Your family's service to this country has been a tremendous help to British interests and welfare. It is I who should be thanking you from the bottom of my heart and on behalf of the King."

"Is that all?" she said, rising from her seat. "If it is all the same to you, I would like to return to my aunt's house so I can make my arrangements to rejoin Sophia before her happy event."

Lord Dryden nodded. "Yes, yes. Your sister and her delicate condition. I can understand your haste, but if you have just one moment further, I thought you might like to be here for a bit of news I have to impart to my son."

Lily sat, this time on the edge of her seat, as if she were ready to leap for the door the moment she was released from this meeting.

"My dear boy," his father began, "it is with great pride that I share with you this happy news. In light of your years of service to your King and country, His Majesty has decided to reward you with the title of Viscount Weston, along with all the lands and grants that this title holds."

"But Weston Hall is . . ."

"Just south of Dryden Manor. Yes, I know. The old Viscount died last year without an heir and it reverted back to the Crown. In light of your service, His Majesty decided to bestow it upon you, since your brother James will inherit my titles."

"And it is all decided?" Webb wasn't too sure he wanted the honor. He had thought to retire simply as Mr. Dryden, and fade from the limelight of society.

"Yes, it was decided just after you left. You are now Lord Weston. Congratulations." He reached across the desk to shake Webb's hand. "Now all you need is a Lady Weston to help you fill that nursery." His father laughed, and then shot a pointed glance toward Lily.

Webb did his best to ignore him.

"What say you, Lily. My boy a viscount with a large house and ample lands. You'll have to come see it for yourself."

She smiled, though her lips barely moved. "I doubt that will be possible." She turned to Webb. "Congratulations, my lord. I am sure you will fill the title quite admirably." She rose again. "Now I really must be going. I promised my aunt I would breakfast with her, and she should be arising within the hour."

"Not so fast, Lily," his father said. "There is one more bit of news I wish to ask your opinion on."

Webb watched her stop, her shoulders rising and falling as she took a deep breath.

"It is about Mr. Saint-Jean." His father shuffled through the mountain of papers on his desk until he found a stack tied with a black ribbon. He sorted through these papers, setting aside several and then retying the stack.

"Adam?" she asked. "I planned on calling on him and his mother this afternoon before I leave for Bath. Is there something you wish for me to ask him?"

"I hate to be the one to tell you this, my dear," Lord Dryden said, folding his hands. "Especially considering your *tendre* for him. But I doubt you will be calling on him this afternoon. Or any other afternoon for that matter."

For the first time in days, Webb saw Lily finally react to something. She paled slightly, but for the most part held her composure.

A small part of him felt a pang of jealousy. She had said her engagement to Adam Saint-Jean was false, but was that another of her lies?

"Is Mr. Saint-Jean ill?" she asked, an almost frantic note to her voice.

"I don't know how to say this or prepare you for it, but I suppose the truth is best just blurted out," Lord Dryden said. "Mr. Saint-Jean was arrested for spying. Your man of business, and shall we say, former betrothed, is an American agent. Apparently he's the head of a ring of spies that have infiltrated the Customs and Shipping Office. There are even rumors of contact within the Admiralty." Lord Dryden shook his head at the sorry business.

"There must be some mistake," she whispered.

"I am sincerely sorry, Lily, but Mr. Saint-Jean has been tried and convicted of treason. The man will be executed on the morrow."

Lily sat perfectly still as she listened to Lord Dryden's dire edict.

Adam arrested? Executed for treason? She struggled to think of something more to say, of how to respond.

"I find it amazing how truly devious Mr. Saint-Jean was in his deception. He quite fooled all of us, including his mother," Lord Dryden was saying.

"Mrs. Saint-Jean?"

"Yes." Lord Dryden shuddered. "Though I respect in some part your loyalty to the Saint-Jeans, that woman is the worst sort of harridan. We finally placed her under house arrest, for her own well being, you understand."

"They aren't going to execute her?" Lily realized she had practically knotted the strings of her reticule. She smoothed them out and tried to settle her jangled nerves.

"Oh, heavens no," Lord Dryden said. "It was obvious from the start we had our man when we caught Mr. Saint-Jean. His mother will merely be sent back to the Colonies as a warning that England will not tolerate such high-handed tactics."

She could hardly tell Lord Dryden he'd captured the wrong man. That the man they sought was actually a woman.

The very woman seated before him.

Leave it to Adam to try to finish her work. Always the gallant, trying to protect her from the world.

Lily pulled her handkerchief out of her reticule and dabbed the lacy bit of linen at her tearless eyes.

She needed to come up with a plan. "Can I see him? Surely there is some mistake. Perhaps if I were to speak to him and . . ."

Lord Dryden shook his head emphatically. "I can't see that there is anything you can do at this point, my dear."

Mercy and Mary, how had this ever happened? Lily thought. Well, with Adam anything was possible, she had to realize.

"You didn't know about any of this, did you, Lily?" Webb asked.

She'd almost forgotten he was in the room—almost, that is. The suspicious tone in his voice carried a line of tension encircling her in its power.

All she could do was shake her head. He was so close to the truth, so close to discovering who she truly was.

Now you see why I can't marry you? she wanted to shout. *I'm an American spy. A traitor to your country.*

A traitor to your heart. And mine.

Webb asked her another question, but she was so lost in her own scattered thoughts that she could only ask, "What did you say?"

Webb leaned forward. "Are you sure you didn't know about Mr. Saint-Jean's involvement with the American government?"

She shook her head. "Adam isn't the head of any spy ring. I know this is all a mistake," she said quite truthfully.

Why had she let Adam talk her into allowing him to travel with her? Though she'd needed a man to handle the transfers of gold and holdings in London, since it would have been frowned upon or outright forbidden for a woman to do it, she could have used one of the more experienced agents already stationed in London.

And now she'd let him talk himself right into a date with the hangman.

"Are you sure you never noticed anything unusual in Mr. Saint-Jean's business or the people with whom he associated."

Just me, she thought to herself. Feeling the weight of their critical gazes on her, she tried hard to force a few tears from her eyes by stabbing her fingernails into the palms of her hands.

Giving up, she finally resorted to quiet sobbing.

"This is all so distressing," she told them, biting her lip and bringing the handkerchief back up to her eyes.

"Yes, well, it is a sad bit of business. Not suitable for the gentle ears of our society. My apologies for bringing it up, my lady," Lord Dryden said, reverting back to his usual gruff, formal manners. "But considering your former association with the man in question, I thought it best to inform you straight away."

"Thank you, my lord," Lily said. "I fear this news has left me quite fatigued."

"Yes, it must have come as quite a shock," Webb said. "Father, if you have nothing of immediate importance to discuss, I think I should escort Lily back to her aunt's house. She appears quite distraught by all of this."

He caught her by the elbow, not in the comforting touch of a concerned friend, but with the viselike grip of a man holding his anger barely in check.

While he all but dragged her from his father's office, Lily's mind whirled with explanations, denials, bluffs.

"What is this big hurry?" Celeste complained as she followed in their wake through the hallways of the Foreign Office.

"Adam was—" she started to say, but Webb gave her a rough shake.

"We will *not* discuss it here."

She glanced back at Celeste, whose eyes were wide with alarm.

He knows? the question behind the woman's upraised black eyebrows seemed to say.

Lily shook her head only slightly. *Not yet.*

She heard Celeste's breathy sigh and hoped the woman, for once, would not start telling their fortunes or predicting the dire consequences of the situation.

Lily could see the future quite clearly in the angry set of Webb's mouth and the determined length of his stride.

And it didn't look very promising.

They literally flew down the stairs to Webb's awaiting carriage. He all but tossed her in, though he was a little more gracious with Celeste.

She heard him give the driver curt instructions to take

them to Lady Dearsley's town house, and before she could think of a way to escape, Webb bounded in and took the seat opposite her. The door was shut with a definite shudder, and the carriage was off and away.

"What is going on?" Celeste demanded, her arms crossed over her chest. "What has happened?"

"Adam was—" Lily started, until Webb cut her off.

"—Your mistress has been playing me for a fool."

"Oh, that," Celeste said, immediately looking bored with the entire theatrics.

"That, as you so blithely point out," Webb said, "is treason."

"Webb, as I told your father, Adam is not responsible for this. They've arrested the wrong man."

Celeste laughed. "That Mr. Saint-Jean? You think that man is a spy. Oh, more the fool you are."

Lily shot Celeste a cautioning look.

The woman only shrugged and continued. "He is no spy, Mister Webb, not that one. I've seen his palm and I can tell you, very truly, Adam Saint-Jean is no spy."

"I am afraid, Celeste, the British courts do not hold palmistry as proof positive of one's innocence."

"Then they are fools, too," she said, sounding more than a little miffed at the very notion. "Anyone who looks at Mr. Saint-Jean can tell he is no spy."

"I agree, Celeste, I don't think Mr. Saint-Jean is a spy at all. But I do wonder who could have been directing him."

Much to Lily's relief, Celeste had the good sense to close her lips and keep her overdrawn divinations to herself.

Webb glanced from Celeste to Lily. "What? No speculations? No predictions? From either of you?"

"Please, Webb, you have to do something," Lily pleaded. "Adam is no spy. These charges are false. You have to do something to save him."

He sat back in his seat. "I'm sure if I had the name of the true leader of this spy ring, the mastermind behind these incredible feats, I could convince my father to get a stay in Adam's execution, but I wouldn't know where to start to find this fellow. Would you?"

"How would I know?" Lily snapped. "This is all a mistake."

"You damn well know, and I'm not about to let you go until you tell me everything." Webb stared at her, the heat of his gaze so searing, she felt forced to glance away or be revealed by its penetrating light.

This time Lily didn't have to struggle to force her tears, they came in a torrential burst of pent-up emotion and the struggle to continue her lies. But even that didn't stop her from lying again.

"I don't know." She turned her tear-stained face to Celeste's shoulder. "Oh, such a nightmare. Poor Adam," she sobbed, as Celeste, joining in the charade, wrapped Lily in a motherly embrace. Lily continued unabashedly, now that she had the tears to back her up. "It's all my fault."

"How's that?" Webb asked, leaning forward.

"Because I didn't want the Copeland matters to be mishandled. I should never have had him come to England with me. He's so naive and foolish. It's obvious he's been set up. Can't you see that?"

Lily peeked out from beneath her tear-soaked lashes and gauged the effect of her performance.

The tears were working, to some degree, for Webb's features were now a mixture of concern and suspicion.

She went to work on the concern. "How will a man like Adam survive in prison? Where do you think they have him? If it is some horrid dark cell, I won't be able to live with myself."

Webb shook his head. "More than likely they have him

locked away in the Foreign Office cellar. It's damp, but hardly a stay in Newgate."

Lily couldn't believe her good fortune. The Foreign Office! That would surely be easier to break into than a real prison.

She sniffed a few times for good measure. "It sounds horrible. This is all my fault."

"Yes, you can sure say that," Celeste muttered.

"Are you positive you knew nothing of this, Lily? Nothing whatsoever?"

Lily sat up, wiped her tears away, and looked Webb square in the eye. "I can say quite honestly that I knew of nothing that would indicate Adam could ever be the head of a spy ring. It is unfathomable, it is completely a shock, why it's—"

Celeste gave her a small nudge in the ribs with her elbow, as if to say enough was enough.

She sputtered to a stop and went back to dabbing her eyes.

If only Webb looked more convinced.

Never one to shy back, Lily knew she had to satisfy his doubts utterly and completely if she was going to do what had to be done.

Find a way to free Adam and his mother and get them out of England.

She couldn't ask Webb to help her or trust her now. There were too many lies between them. All of them from her.

"Webb, you believe me, don't you? I know Adam is innocent. He had nothing to do with any of this. I know it in my heart."

Webb studied her, and then much to her relief, his stance relaxed.

"Yes, Lily, I believe you."

Just then the carriage stopped in front of Lady Dearsley's town house. Lily didn't waste any time, she bounded out of the carriage with hardly a glance back. Then she stopped and turned.

"Webb, I'm sorry about how things turned out. About the mission," she paused. *About us.* Afraid she would say what was so close to her heart, she turned and fled up the stairs into her aunt's house.

Celeste watched her mistress's hurried flight and turned her most disgusted expression on Webb. The man was busy watching the empty space left in Lily's wake. Gathering herself up, Celeste started to get out of the carriage, but she paused at the doorway.

Reaching over and catching Webb's hand, she turned it palm up and glanced over the deep strong lines that marked his destiny.

And Lily's.

She could see they would end up together, but she couldn't help but push the stubborn pair along.

"What do you see, Celeste?" he asked, a bemused expression on his face.

"Harrumph." Celeste dropped his hand back into his lap. "I see a foolish man."

His brows arched. "How so?"

"For now, of all times, you have chosen to believe her lies."

Chapter 24

Webb arrived at the Dearsley house after dusk, nodding to one of the men he'd assigned to watch the place. He doubted Lily would make her move until she had the cover of night. In the meantime, he'd heard all the reports from the Bow Street Runners he'd hired to track anyone who'd come and gone during the course of the day.

She'd make her attempt to rescue Adam then, and he'd be right here waiting for her.

As he watched a maid lighting the rooms of Lady Dearsley's town house across the street, he recalled Celeste's words, words that had struck deep in his heart.

And to think, he'd been about to believe Lily.

Not that he didn't think she wasn't involved, but because if he chose to think of Lily as innocent of those crimes, he could move on with his life and forget about the enticing hoyden who'd stolen his heart.

But as his carriage rolled away from her aunt's house, away from Lily, he saw his new life stretched out before him in one long, boring line.

Viscount Weston. The necessary trip through the Marriage Mart. A respectable English bride. Seasons in London, summers and holidays at Weston Hall. Eventually, a brood of well-behaved children.

Exactly what he'd always planned.

But now, that life would be missing something he'd never planned on—Lily. A life without her crazy, scheming ways. Without those long, storm-tossed nights of passion.

He turned up the collar of his coat and shivered against the cold.

So as he'd allowed himself to get further and further from her and the traitorous plans he was positive she was hatching, he'd mused over his choices.

Turn her in to his father.

Haul her off to Weston Hall and lock her in the cellar until the entire Adam mess blew over.

Or help her.

If he helped her, he would be turning his back on everything he'd worked for and believed in up to now. His King, his country, his father. To help Lily would mean having to walk away from all of it.

It was hardly a decision to take lightly. And one he'd spent a number of agonizing hours going over before he'd finally made up his mind.

He looked down at his palm and wondered for the hundredth time what it was that Celeste saw when she looked there earlier in the day.

For once, the woman had unnerved him with her West Indies hocus-pocus. He'd felt as if she'd parted his soul and peered into places deep in his heart, places not even he liked to know existed.

For in that moment, when Celeste had told him nothing about his future, she'd told him exactly what he had to do.

★ ★ ★

Lily slipped into the dark mews of her aunt's house and moved toward the shadows alongside the street. She blew into her hands to warm them against the bitter winter chill, hoping she wouldn't have to wait long for her contact to pick her up. She would remain well hidden until the carriage arrived, concealed as she was by the dark breeches and jacket Celeste had stolen from one of the footmen's rooms.

While Aunt Dearsley had fussed and cooed over her unexpected arrival, she'd been able to convince her elderly aunt that all she truly wanted was to stay at home for the evening.

By the relieved expression on the woman's face, Lily would have bet her aunt was thankful that her presence was not required.

If there was one thing Aunt Dearsley didn't do well, it was stay at home.

While her aunt had been out most of the afternoon making her round of calls, Lily had been receiving visitors of her own—contacts who had determined where Adam was being held and how best to get her friend out of the Foreign Office cells.

Lily hadn't any choice but to get him out and to do it herself—for she wouldn't have anyone else risk their lives for what was her responsibility. She'd brooked no arguments from her fellow agents and explained that all she needed was a hackney to carry her to the Foreign Office, to Mrs. Saint-Jean's residence, and then on to the docks where she would personally see the Saint-Jeans placed on the first boat out of the London pool.

Much to her relief, that boat turned out to be the *Charity,* the ship on which her youngest brother, Julien, served as first mate.

Julien D'Artiers, unlike his elder brother Lucien, cared little for the trappings of titles and his lost French heritage. Instead, the youngest D'Artiers had followed his heart and taken to the sea at the age of twelve, barely a year after their family had escaped the Terror in France.

Since Julien had always wanted to be a pirate, he was more than happy to assist Lily in this illegal venture, assuring her that his captain would welcome the two extra passengers.

Especially, he explained, when it meant thwarting the British—who on the *Charity*'s recent crossing had taken eight sailors off their ship, claiming the Americans were deserters from the Royal Navy.

The men, Julien cursed, had been born and raised in Boston and had never once set foot in England.

Seeing the Saint-Jeans slip out from a British noose would be a fair exchange, in Julien's estimation. So he had promised to be at the dock all night with a crew and rowboat ready to take her "shipment" at a moment's notice.

Pleased that she had an escape route for her friends, Lily turned to the more difficult part of her plan.

Getting Adam out of the Foreign Office seemed almost easy when she considered she'd also have to get the verbose Mrs. Saint-Jean out of London without the lady waking half the constabulary and Bow Street with her complaints.

Patting her pocket, she reminded herself that she had her own measure of insurance for keeping the woman in line.

Down the street, a hackney turned the corner, the horse plodding a steady course straight for her.

Just as she was about to step out and make herself known, a hand clamped down over her mouth and she found herself being hauled back into the shadowy mews.

She fought, swinging her arms and trying to hit her assailant, but his arm swept around her, pinning her to his chest, trapping her in his hold.

She brought her foot up, thinking she could give the bounder a sharp taste of the heel of her boot, but the cold, hard voice in her ear stopped her midstomp.

"Going somewhere, hoyden?"

Lily brought her heel down and caught him on the shin and the top of his foot.

He cursed in surprise and she took off running for the hackney now directly in front of her. She grabbed the door and jumped in, yelling at the driver, "Quickly, I am being chased by thieves."

The young man atop the hackney picked up his reins and gave them a sharp snap, sending the horses plunging forward.

Thrown off balance, Lily landed awkwardly in the seat, her cloak covering her face. As she whipped it off, she found a breathless and angry Webb Dryden climbing into the moving vehicle.

"Get out," she ordered, pointing at the door. "You have no right to—"

Before she could continue her tirade, Webb's hand snaked out and caught her by the wrist. With a quick, determined motion, he hauled her across the interior of the coach and settled her onto his lap.

She opened her mouth in surprise and found her lips promptly covered with his.

Whatever protest she wanted to utter, the words were quickly swept aside.

Once again in Webb's arms, his mouth devouring hers and arousing her senses, Lily couldn't think or breathe. How long had it been since they'd kissed? Since they'd made love?

By the intensity of the passion coursing between them, Lily felt like it had been forever. And she wanted this moment to continue for just about that long.

His hands cupped her cheeks, and she tasted once again the searing desire in his kiss.

"This is how it is supposed to be," he whispered into her

ear as they both gasped for breath. "We are meant to be together."

Together. It seemed so perfect.

Perfectly impossible, she realized, as the carriage hit a hole in the road and jolted them apart.

Webb caught her and pulled her close, but she couldn't risk being carried away by his powers of persuasion—most notably his kiss.

"Get out," she ordered again, this time considering using the pistol in her pocket to get the meaning of her words across.

But she discarded the idea immediately. She would never be able to shoot Webb and he'd just take the pistol away from her.

"Get out of this carriage right now," she repeated instead.

"Are we going over that again?" He reached out and toyed with a stray tendril of her hair.

Lily didn't like him touching her, any part of her, for it was too distracting. She needed to concentrate and to do that she needed Webb out of the carriage and her life. "I'll scream. The driver will not be as forgiving as I am."

"I rather doubt that," he said, rapping on the trap door to the roof.

The hatch opened and the young man looked down.

"Stop this carriage and get this ruffian out of here," she told him.

The driver shook his head. "Oh aye, m'lord. She's a right live one, jest like you said. Have you a change to our plans or should I do as the lady asks?"

"Continue on, Ned."

Much to Lily's horror the trap door slammed shut and she found herself face-to-face with a rather smug Webb Dryden. She scrambled out of his lap and took the seat opposite him.

"Ned?"

"Yes, Ned. My driver. Didn't you make his acquaintance this morning?"

Her hands balled into fists. "This is kidnapping. I'll have you brought up on charges, I'll have—"

"And how exactly will you explain to the court what you were doing skulking around your aunt's mews dressed like a footpad?" he said smugly. "Where did you get that outfit? It looks like you stole it from a climbing boy."

Damn, Lily hated it when he had her like this. But she wasn't going to let him off just yet. "I was on my way to a masquerade if you must know. My aunt is expecting me to meet her there and she'll be quite worried if I am late. So please let me out."

"A masquerade? How quaint. Tell me where and I'll drop you off." He paused, scratching his chin. "No, come to think of it, that would hardly be the gentlemanly thing, now would it. As a viscount I have to think of my reputation and the reputation of my wife."

"I am not your wife."

"I beg to differ. And if you refuse to acknowledge the French court's view on the subject, then I intend to rectify the situation tonight, so that not even an English court could argue that we are not legally wed. You'll be my wife, whether you like it or not."

Not sure how to argue this, Lily glanced out the window. She smelled it before she caught a glimpse of it—the foul stench of the Thames. They were near the river. "Where are you taking me?"

"The Foreign Office. That is where you were headed, isn't it?"

Her mouth opened and then closed.

"Come now, even in this meager light, I can see it in your eyes. You were going to free Adam. What I can't figure out

340 Elizabeth Boyle

is why? Because you love him?" He paused. "Now that I doubt, given the strength of your passion a few moments ago, so I have to find another reason. Guilt perhaps?"

She looked away.

"I thought so. You weren't lying today when you told my father that he had the wrong man, were you?"

Looking into his blue eyes, Lily sought to find something there to guide her—cynicism, concern, compassion.

Nothing but the dark blue depths of his unfathomable soul.

"Tell me, Lily. For once, tell me the truth. Who is Adam being sacrificed for?"

She shook her head. Even now, she couldn't do it. "You don't want to know. Please, can't you just let me go? Let me do what I have to do tonight. If anything happened to you, I'd be . . ." Lily tried to finish her sentence, but found the words lodged next to the ache in her heart. Amelia had told her to trust Webb, but how could she? Especially now?

"You'd be?" he prompted. "What would you be?"

Lost. But wasn't she already?

Webb leaned forward and placed his hands on her knees, turning her so she looked at him. Gently, he cupped her face, his fingers smoothing back a stray strand, touching her cheek. Lily closed her eyes, unable to look at the depth of emotion in his eyes.

Concern. Admiration. And love.

Webb loved her still.

Mercy and Mary, why couldn't they have gone on as it was before? Hating each other. It had been so easy, so clear, so familiar.

"Why? Why won't you tell me?" he asked. "Because you think I'll stop loving you? I doubt it. I wish I could. But I don't think there will ever be a day that I don't love you, even if you drive me to distraction most of the time." He leaned forward and caught her hands in his. "I'll love you no matter what. You could tell me that *you* are the head of this American spy ring and I would still love you," he said with a little laugh, as if the idea were preposterous.

Lily blinked, her vision blurring with tears. "But I am."

Chapter 25

Webb felt as if the floor of the carriage had given way. He couldn't have heard Lily right. "You're what?"

"The head of the American spy ring your father thinks he's routed out."

He laughed, though to his ears the notes sounded slightly unbalanced. "Lily, this isn't a time for jests."

"I'm not jesting." Something in the weary droop of her shoulders told him she'd just let go of a horrendous burden—the secret she'd been hiding from him since she'd arrived at Byrnewood. "I was recruited by Vice President Jefferson to represent American interests while I was here in England. There's more, but I'd prefer not to discuss it."

Numbly, he nodded in agreement. The treason of her words stunned him, but she was right not to say more. The less he knew, the safer it was for both of them.

When Celeste had told him not to believe Lily, he thought she'd meant Lily's promise not to rescue Adam, but not her denial of knowing about Adam's involvement.

No wonder she'd turned so pale at his father's announcement about Adam.

Right man, hah! His father had missed it by a mile and had had the correct answer sitting practically under his nose.

"Say something," she whispered.

"I'm trying to think what one says when one finds out his betrothed is a spy. A real one."

"Well, it never bothered me," she snapped. Lily glanced up at him ever so slightly, her feathered lashes concealing most of the sparkling emeralds beneath. "Do you mean it? Betrothed? After what I just said, you would still want to marry me?"

Webb took a deep breath. Marry a traitor? Not in a thousand years had he ever thought that possible. The road before him suddenly turned more bleak than it had moments earlier. He'd thought he'd be spending the coming months honeymooning with Lily somewhere far from England, once he'd helped her break Adam out of jail.

His father would not be happy when he found out, but Webb had left him a long note explaining all, in the hope that one day his father would understand. How, he'd written to his father, could saving Adam Saint-Jean from the hangman's noose be treason when they both knew his father had the wrong man?

Lily, the leader of the American spy ring. The person who should rightly swing in Adam's place.

But he couldn't let Lily die. He couldn't betray her and live. So was there any course other than the one he'd originally plotted?

Treason. He took a deep breath. Now he was committing treason.

But was he truly giving up the life he loved? More like trading it for another type of trouble. Marriage to Lily would be wild, tempestuous, and foolhardy. Just the way he liked to live.

So if he'd already made up his mind before, why should her revelation make any difference?

If anything, it finally answered all his questions. Her reluctance to go to Paris, her wild schemes and uncanny skills at subterfuge—everything now made sense.

Glancing out the window, he gauged that they were drawing near the Foreign Office.

"Lily, I—"

"—I'll understand," Lily interrupted, "if you feel obliged to turn me in to your father."

"Well, Lily, I—"

"No, don't explain." Her words fell out in a terrible rush. "If this means Adam can go free—"

Webb reached over and clamped his hand over her mouth. "Hoyden, if you say one more word, I will clap you in irons. At least until *we* get your former betrothed out of jail."

Her green eyes lit with uncertainty.

"I love you, Lily. My life is with you, wherever that takes us."

The doubt faded away to be replaced by a fire of excitement. He pulled his hand away from her mouth to replace it with his lips, sealing his promise and their future.

This time, as she opened herself to his kiss, he knew there would never again be any secrets between them. And while he was losing everything he'd ever worked for, he knew he held in his arms a love he'd never thought possible.

The carriage stopped in an alleyway not far from the solid row of government buildings. Reluctantly they parted and alighted from the carriage. He took her hand and led her to the end of the alley before he turned to her and said, "Promise me one thing."

"Anything," she whispered.

"No more fiancés. I don't think I can take getting rid of anymore of them."

She laughed softly. "I can do that just fine on my own, thank you."

"Cecil! Cecil!" Lord Dryden bellowed.

His harried secretary hustled into Lord Dryden's office, his wig askew and his spectacles practically falling off his nose.

"M'lord? I didn't think you were coming back tonight," Cecil sputtered as he caught his breath.

"I wasn't planning on it, but I decided to drop by before I joined my wife at Sir Wentworth's New Year's party."

"Is there something I can help you with, m'lord?"

"You can start by telling me who's been in my office." Lord Dryden pointed to the folded letter on his desk. "I want to know who brought this letter into my office this evening."

Cecil's narrow shoulders rose in a shrug. "I haven't the vaguest notion, m'lord. I only went out for some supper and just returned as you arrived."

"Supper, eh? When did you start taking supper?" Lord Dryden only asked because Cecil was legendary in the Foreign Office. It was said he hadn't left the building in over forty years, but then again Lord Dryden knew that was impossible, though there was rarely a moment in his long days and often nights that Cecil wasn't at his familiar post just outside his office. "Well, never mind. I don't like the idea of just anyone coming and going about my office."

He picked up the letter and examined the seal. Though familiar, it was one he didn't recognize offhand.

"Whose is that?" he asked, handing the letter to Cecil.

"Lord Weston, m'lord. Your son."

Lord Dryden brightened, but at the same time felt suddenly sad. He wasn't as sharp as he used to be. His job, always demanding, loomed heavily over him of late. And now he'd gone and made an ass of himself in front of Cecil, not recognizing Webb's new seal.

He was getting too old. And so was Cecil.

Taking supper, indeed.

"Well, yes," he said. "Just testing you, my good man. I'll take that." Retrieving his letter, he ripped it open as Cecil withdrew.

He lit another taper on his desk and tipped the letter into the illumination to read Webb's scrawling words. At first the letter made little sense, littered as it was with words like "resignation," "hard choices," and "woman that I love," but as he got to the end, the entire message spelled out the shocking truth.

"Why the stupid, headstrong idiot."

"Yes, m'lord?" Cecil asked from the doorway.

"Summon the guards," Lord Dryden bellowed.

"The guards, m'lord?"

"Yes, you gaping jackanape, the guards. Assemble all the guards outside my office. All of them, immediately!"

Cecil scurried from the office and fled down the hall, repeating Lord Dryden's order in his own high-pitched squeak.

Lord Dryden pulled his spectacles off and began polishing the lenses.

"Damn fool," he muttered. "Damned reckless, fool."

"Where are we going?" Lily asked, as they turned away from the Foreign Office and continued on toward the river.

"To break Adam out of jail."

Lily glanced over her shoulder. "Isn't the Foreign Office over there?" she asked, jerking her thumb in the direction opposite the one they were traveling.

"Yes, but you weren't planning on just marching in the front door and demanding his release, were you?"

Lily shrugged, embarrassed to admit that was exactly what she had planned on doing.

"Americans," he muttered. "No wonder we let you go."

"The Americans won their independence, I'll have you know."

"Yes, but they didn't do it by barging into Parliament and demanding it."

He walked over to the embankment and took a narrow, broken set of stairs down to the water's edge. He tore a large splinter of wood from the stairs and tossed it into the water. For a moment it swirled around in the eddies and flow of the river, but then slowly began to move upriver.

"Devil take it," he cursed.

"What?"

"The tide is coming in," he said.

Not wanting to know why this was a bad piece of information or how that had anything to do with Adam, Lily held her tongue. She stayed where she was, perched at the top of the stairs, doubtful the rickety wooden frame would hold both of them. Down below, Webb held up the small lantern he'd brought from the carriage, and with his other hand, felt along the embankment. Around his ankles, the wretched water and refuse swirled with the moving tide.

"What are you doing?" she asked, afraid he was about to ask her to follow suit and dip her feet into the murky swill.

"Getting us into the Foreign Office," he said as he pushed on a portion of the embankment and a small doorway opened up. "Come on."

She gamely followed, with Webb guiding each step. She grimaced as she got to the end and the cold water of the Thames rushed into her short boots. Before she could complain, Webb stepped into the doorway and pulled her along with him. The door swung shut behind them, the hinges pulling it closed and plunging them into almost complete darkness. He turned up the lantern and her eyes slowly adjusted to their surroundings.

They were standing in a narrow passageway. She couldn't see more than a few feet ahead of them. The walls dripped incessantly, and the stench enclosing them brought tears to her eyes. As she tried to walk, she discovered her feet were encased in a thick mud that sucked and pulled at her boots with each step.

"What is this place?" she asked, as Webb held the lamp high in one hand and pulled her forward into the darkness with the other.

"A secret way into the basement of the Foreign Office. It isn't often used, in fact I don't think there are many people left who know of its existence. My brother showed it to me years ago when I was just a child and he was a new agent. He left me down here in the dark and told me to find my own way out."

"That's terrible," she whispered.

"Yes, especially when you consider that when the tide comes in, it nearly fills to the top with water."

Lily came to an abrupt halt. "But you said the tide was coming in."

"Yes, I did." He leaned over and kissed her quickly on the brow before continuing their steady march through the shadows and mud. "That means we'll have to do this quickly."

After what seemed like hours, but was probably no more than a few minutes, the pathway forked. Lily followed Webb to the right, and a few yards later, they came to a ladder.

He held his finger up to his lips and then leaned close enough to whisper in her ear.

"Now for the moment of truth" he said. "Be very quiet, because just above us is one of the junior offices. Hopefully our government official isn't the dedicated type."

He held up the light and was about to blow it out, when Lily caught his arm.

The narrow space frightened her, and she couldn't stand the thought of being without the light, of being caught in this darkness where the water, even now, was starting to flow in around them.

He pulled her close, his lips claiming hers in a long, sweet kiss. When he pulled back from her, his fingers brushed over the wayward strands of her hair. "We can't have the lamp on."

She nodded, and then immediately regretted it, as they were cast in complete darkness. Her heart hammered so loudly she thought the noise alone would bring the entire guard down on their heads.

But before she could start to breathe again, Webb was up the ladder and easing open the floorboards that made up the hatch.

The rising water now sloshed around her knees, its bitter cold sending chilblains of panic up her limbs. How had Webb done this for so many years?

If we get through this, she prayed, I'll never wish for adventure again. Never.

Suddenly a light filled the passageway from above, and Webb was leaning down the hatch, offering her his hand.

"All clear," he whispered.

Webb had stripped off his muddy boots and bade her do the same. "They'll leave too many tracks. Dry your feet off on that bit of carpet over there."

She did as she was told, marveling at his daring skill.

And she'd thought herself an agent. Clearly she was in the presence of a master.

They left the small office and continued through the bowels of the government building. Webb cautioned her to wait for him, and she stayed put as he rounded a corner.

"Hold up there," a voice called out.

Lily heard Webb skid to a stop.

"Now, what's this? A river rat," the man said. "The boss said to be on the lookout for the likes of you, and now I'll be a hero."

Lily peeked around the corner and found Webb slowly moving in a circle. Then she surveyed the guard holding him hostage and nearly died.

The man appeared to be a giant. He towered over Webb, his thick limbs and knotty complexion resembling an oak tree sprung to life. "Hold still there," the man ordered.

She glanced again and realized they were not yards from a cell. Adam stood behind the bars, staring open-mouthed at Webb.

By continuing to circle, Webb had successfully repositioned the guard so that the man's back was to her.

And then he nodded ever so slightly to her.

She took a deep breath and reached into her pocket to retrieve her pistol. She'd never figured out how to load it, so if it came to a fight, she'd only have her bravado and a good bluff to aid her.

Looking back at Webb's captor, she knew she needed more. Then out of nowhere, she recalled Amelia's stance and movements as she'd stolen up behind Armand.

Taking another breath, she grasped the barrel with both hands and crept up behind the man. In one swift motion, she cast a prayer heavenward that once would be enough, and she clouted the mighty guard on the back of his large head as hard as she could.

And like a mighty oak, the man teetered and wavered before he finally gave up his post, falling with a heavy thud between them.

She stared down at her victim open-mouthed. She'd done it. Just like she'd seen Amelia do it.

"Really, Lily," Adam said, his voice full of amusement, "that was hardly sporting."

Lord Dryden and Cecil sat in a carriage outside the Foreign Office. A veritable army of guards surrounded the building. Cecil smiled to himself as an alarm sounded among the men.

"He's escaped. The prisoner is gone." The men began swarming into the building to begin their search.

Lord Dryden leaned out the window and turned toward his ancient driver.

"Bertram," he said, "take us closer to the river, down there where it bends slightly."

The driver nodded, and the carriage rolled away from the Foreign Office.

"Are you quite sure about this, m'lord?" Cecil asked.

"Are you?"

For the first time in the history of his employment, Cecil grinned. "Always thought it would be a pip to be a field agent. Just once that is."

"Well here's your chance, my boy. Our last day together."

Lord Dryden tapped on the roof and the carriage slowed to a stop. He climbed down and Cecil joined him. The pair looked out at the city and river, as if they were doing nothing more than enjoying the nighttime vista.

Below them a doorway splashed open. Startled, Cecil peered down as three people emerged waist deep in water. But then again, he shouldn't have been surprised. It was exactly as Lord Dryden had said things would come about.

After his lordship had summoned all the guards, they'd been dispersed around the perimeter of the building, leaving the interior unguarded.

Then after this unusual order, Lord Dryden had called Cecil into his office and closed the door. Shoving a drink into his hands, his lordship had told Cecil what they were about to do.

And Cecil had listened, stunned by what he heard.

"Cecil, quit wool-gathering over there," Lord Dryden said, shaking his secretary out of his reverie. "Guide our guests into the carriage, while I give the directions to Bertram. I don't want anything to go wrong. Not now, the eve of our retirement."

Retirement. Cecil didn't know what to make of it. But if his lordship thought it time for them to hand the leadership of the Foreign Office to his eldest son, James, then Cecil wasn't about to argue.

"Aye, m'lord," Cecil said. "I've a mind to see a bit of the world after this." He caught ahold of Lord Dryden's future daughter-in-law and helped her up the embankment, followed by the Viscount Weston and the notorious American spy.

It was, in Cecil's estimation, a real slap-up night and a fine finish to their careers.

"Father," Webb Dryden said, the awe and admiration in his voice overwhelming.

"Don't say a word, my boy," Lord Dryden warned. "I'm not speaking to you. Not until you truly marry this woman and produce a passel of grandchildren. And don't try and foist off that phony civil registration from Paris as a license to make this woman your bride. I want banns posted, I want a real ceremony."

"I'm afraid that won't be easy since I was planning on leaving the country for a while."

Lord Dryden looked away, and Cecil gauged the old man didn't like the idea of his son being exiled. He knew the man had never thought twice about sending his sons on dangerous missions, but this was different. Webb Dryden might never be able to come home after this.

"Well then, have the captain marry you. Just make sure the next time I see you I have grandchildren. Then, maybe I'll forgive you." The man clapped his son hard on the back and hustled him off to the carriage.

Cecil turned away, for fear the others would see the sudden rush of tears in his eyes.

"But what about my mother?" the dangerous American was asking.

"We're off to fetch her next," Lord Dryden told him. "Now into the carriage, all of you, before one of those idiots over at the office notices us."

Cecil followed his employer and the others into the carriage.

"I don't know if Mother will agree to this, a ship voyage in the middle of the night, leaving all her things," Mr. Saint-Jean said. "She'll put up a regular fuss."

Beside him, Mrs. Copeland, soon to be the Viscountess Weston, reached into her pocket and pulled out a small tincture. "Adam, this will keep your mother most agreeable."

"What is it?" he asked.

"Laudanum." The audacious woman grinned.

"You intend to drug my mother?" he asked.

"Most assuredly," she told him.

Cecil decided right there and then what he was going to do with his retirement. Lord Dryden may want to spend his remaining days living the life of a quiet country gentlemen, but Cecil had other plans.

He'd find himself a wife as brazen as Webb Dryden's bride-to-be.

That, he determined, looking over at the beautiful woman—her face aglow as she gazed at her future husband as if they were always meant to be together—would be much more exciting than a field assignment.

Decidedly so.

Epilogue

"Are you glad to be home, hoyden?" Webb Dryden, the Viscount Weston asked his wife of five years as she snuggled up next to him in the huge carved bed that took up a large portion of the master bedroom in Weston Hall.

"Deliriously so," Lily told him. "Anywhere I am with you makes me happy." She laid her head on his chest, his fingers gently toying with the silken strands of her hair.

He laughed at this. "Don't let Mrs. Miles hear you say that. I think you scandalized the housekeeper by taking half the clothes presses in here for your own gowns and telling her to make up the previous Viscountess's room for guests."

"Then I'd better not let her see those breeches I've got packed away."

Webb grinned. Even with three children, his lady wife had yet to give up her hoyden ways. He'd caught her more than once pulling on the breeches she'd stolen that long ago night and wearing them for an early morning ride. He had a feeling the neighboring country gentry would be as scandalized as Mrs. Miles, but in the end they would discover that beneath her wild heart was a woman of deep generosity and unquestionable loyalty.

"No, truly, Webb, I'm glad to be back in England," she said, rolling over and looking at him with those green eyes that still held so many secrets. "I think you were right to accept James's offer to come back to the Foreign Office. With the peace gone, no country is safe from Bonaparte's grasp. He must be stopped."

"We'll do it. And we'll do it together," he said. He almost laughed out loud as he thought of the bride he'd once asked his mother to find for him. He doubted the gentle English miss he'd described then would ever have so completely enraptured him like the woman in his arms.

He pulled her closer, his hands roaming over her naked breasts, marveling that even after all this time, the feel of her skin and the scent of her perfume still sent him reeling with need.

"What say we see if this bed is as comfortable as the one we had in Virginia?" he whispered into her ear.

She laughed. "The last time we did that we ended up with a daughter."

"A hoyden just like her mother," he said, trying to keep a straight face.

"Adelaide is a Dryden through and through," she countered. "I caught her demanding that Mr. Reed show her all the secret passageways in the house. I thought the poor butler was going to fall over."

"And did he?"

Lily nodded. "Your daughter charmed him into showing her the priest's hole and stairwell in the south wing. We'll never get her to use the front stairs again."

Webb leaned back on the pillows, a foolish grin of fatherly pride spreading across his face. "That's my angel."

Lily groaned. "Your encouragement doesn't help."

"Addie will be fine. She'll be just like her mother and drive all the men to distraction."

Lily sat up, shaking out the loose strands of her hair, her hands over head, knowing only too well how her naked form tantalized him. "Do I still distract you?"

He nodded and reached for her.

Lily thrilled as his mouth covered hers in a heart-stopping kiss. Five years . . . five years of passion-filled nights, of this insatiable claiming that brought them together every night. She didn't know how she would live without him in the coming months as he worked in London, but right now . . . well right now, she was the one distracted.

His hands caressed her as if he were discovering her body anew. His touch seemed both reverent and hungry.

A hunger she shared avidly.

With both hands on his shoulders, she pushed him down onto his back. Like he had done to her, she took a moment to marvel at his perfect form. How she loved the muscled planes, the tangle of tawny curls that led her down his chest to the one place she loved most about his body.

Straddling him, she smiled as she claimed his manhood with her hands and guided it into her.

His eyes closed as a lazy smile spread across his face. She, too, felt contentment and satisfaction as he filled her. With slow easy movements, she slid up and down on him, guiding his passion and taking hers.

He seemed to know just when she was about to find her release, because he caught a hold of her hand and gave it a gentle squeeze, even as she began to softly cry out his name.

I love you, hoyden, his touch said to her. As it had since the first time he'd made love to her those many years ago and every time since.

Webb caught her hips and she continued to ride through

her waves of passion, tightening around him until he was carried along with her.

She collapsed over him, his arms winding around her, pulling her close, their fevered bodies still joined.

They whispered timeless words to each other, soft, quiet confessions for their ears only.

Lily opened her eyes and looked around the shadowy room. This was her new home, one that many a woman would envy. But she knew the real treasure of Weston Hall was the man who held her in his arms.

She couldn't remember a time when she'd felt any other way than she did at this very moment or how she could have felt any other way.

Webb Dryden, I'll love you 'til the day I die.

Author's Note

While the Christmas Eve assassination attempt on the life of the First Consul of France, Napoleon Bonaparte, is a historical fact, there is no evidence that Joseph Fouché knew about the incident beforehand. Despite Napoleon's nearly bloodless takeover of the country in 1799, France at the time of *Brazen Heiress* was still rife with dissent, including Royalist factions and pockets of those still clinging to the extreme views of the Jacobins. Bonaparte was loathe to give up any of the power he held, and it has been suggested by historians that the Secret Police, headed by Fouché, created plots against Bonaparte to strengthen their position and authority under the First Consul. The Christmas Eve bomb gave Fouché the excuse he'd been looking for to mount a witch-hunt of Napoleon's enemies, executing both Jacobins and Royalists for the crime. Like our own modern-day speculations on twentieth-century assassinations, isn't it easy to suppose that Fouché, as I have suggested in my story, knew all along that a bomb awaited the First Consul on the *Rue Saint-Nicaise*?

If you're looking for romance, adventure, excitement and suspense be sure to read these outstanding romances from Dell.

❋

Jill Gregory
- ☐ **CHERISHED**   20620-0 $5.99
- ☐ **DAISIES IN THE WIND**   21618-4 $5.99
- ☐ **FOREVER AFTER**   21512-9 $5.99
- ☐ **WHEN THE HEART BECKONS**   21857-8 $5.99
- ☐ **ALWAYS YOU**   22183-8 $5.99
- ☐ **JUST THIS ONCE**   22235-4 $5.99

Katherine Kingsley
- ☐ **CALL DOWN THE MOON**   22386-5 $5.99
- ☐ **ONCE UPON A DREAM**   22076-9 $5.99
- ☐ **IN THE WAKE OF THE WIND** 22075-0 $5.99

Joan Johnston
- ☐ **THE BODYGUARD**   22377-6 $6.50
- ☐ **AFTER THE KISS**   22201-X $5.99
- ☐ **CAPTIVE**   22200-1 $5.99
- ☐ **THE INHERITANCE**   21759-8 $5.99
- ☐ **MAVERICK HEART**   21762-8 $5.99
- ☐ **OUTLAW'S BRIDE**   21278-2 $5.99
- ☐ **KID CALHOUN**   21280-4 $5.99
- ☐ **THE BAREFOOT BRIDE**   21129-8 $5.99
- ☐ **SWEETWATER SEDUCTION**   20561-1 $4.50

Connie Brockway
- ☐ **ALL THROUGH THE NIGHT**   22372-5 $5.99
- ☐ **AS YOU DESIRE**   22199-4 $5.99
- ☐ **A DANGEROUS MAN**   22198-6 $5.99